THE AIR B
THE BUIL

Jeremy shut _____n
spell, couched as always in the form of advertising
copy. He shut his eyes and completed preparations
for his spell.

With the spell in motion, he saw his companions
standing in positions of watchfulness and
anticipation, as the old mage cried out the last
of his own spells. Beyond the mage, a zone of
death had sprung up and vegetation wilted as
though blasted by heat.

The old mage brought his staff down, directing
the force of his spell. Jeremy felt a breathless
rush of power pouring out, almost saw it leap
toward the darkness, where . . .

Nothing happened.

His power drained. The mage gasped, "Now the
young man from Earth must try. . . ."

Jeremy felt his muscles freeze. Something *had*
happened, after all. Cutting through the grass,
making directly for them, was a twenty-yard-wide
swathe of death. Part of the force of darkness
had broken off and was coming straight for them!

WORLDS OF IMAGINATION

WIZARD'S MOLE

A Fantasy Novel By

Brad Strickland

A ROC BOOK

ROC
Published by the Penguin Group
Penguin Books USA Inc., 375 Hudson Street,
New York, New York 10014, U.S.A.
Penguin Books Ltd, 27 Wrights Lane,
London W8 5TZ, England
Penguin Books Australia Ltd, Ringwood,
Victoria, Australia
Penguin Books Canada Ltd, 2801 John Street,
Markham, Ontario, Canada L3R 1B4
Penguin Books (N.Z.) Ltd, 182–190 Wairau Road,
Auckland 10, New Zealand

Penguin Books Ltd, Registered Offices:
Harmondsworth, Middlesex, England

First published by Roc, an imprint of New American Library, a division of
Penguin Books USA Inc.

First Printing, January, 1991
10 9 8 7 6 5 4 3 2 1

 ROC is a trademark of New American Library, a division of
Penguin Books USA Inc.

This is for Klon,
who loves all things fantastical,
and for Tom,
who knows how to create them.

Map by Thomas F. Deitz

1

Something happened.

Jeremy Moon started awake from a deep sleep, his heart pounding in his chest. For a confused moment he thought himself back on Earth, back in Atlanta, caught in the nightmares of the bad old days. Then he heard the regular breathing of his wife, Kelada, in bed beside him, became aware of the strange large moon, nearly full, peeking in the west-facing window, and knew that he was— still—in the magical universe of Thaumia. In fact, Jeremy realized, he had been awakened by some fundamental and very great upheaval in the subtle web of magical energy which permeated everything and everyone in Thaumia.

It was a disquieting realization, for by now he recognized such disturbances as the Thaumian equivalent of a volcanic eruption, or of the explosion of hundreds of nuclear weapons; and yet the night drowsed on, even as the sweat of sudden fear cooled on Jeremy's bare chest.

He swung out of bed, felt the warm prickle of carpeting beneath his bare feet. By the blue-white light of the swollen moon he hastily pulled on trousers and shirt, and by feel he retrieved his shoes from beneath the bed and slipped them on. His first stop was the small adjoining room, where Emily, not yet a year old, slept in her own little bed. She lay in peaceful sleep, a thumb thrust securely in her mouth, her blond curls pale in the moonlight. Reassured that his daughter was well, Jeremy went through the sitting room of the tower apartment, descended the stair, and walked down an echoing arched corridor of slate-gray stone.

He judged that it was close to dawn—in Earth terms, four o'clock or close to it. Whitehorn Keep seemed wrapped in slumber, though Jeremy knew that Tremien, the magician who was master of the castle, had alert guards posted even on such a peaceful summer night as this. Tremien was a cautious old fox, and as long as the Great Dark One—as the evil master of the southern lands was called—still lived, Tremien would not be taken by surprise. Jeremy was on his way now to Tremien's apartment, for if anyone could explain the surge in the magical potential of Thaumia that had awakened Jeremy, the old wizard surely could.

Jeremy met Barach, his extravagantly bearded teacher, on the way. "Were you summoned?" Barach asked, rightly divining Jeremy's destination.

"Not exactly," Jeremy said. "I felt something. You?"

Barach shrugged, his broad face ruddy in the diminished wizard-light of the hall. "Being bereft of magic, I cannot say that I sensed anything specific. But certainly I woke from sleep with a deep foreboding." Barach had thrown on a threadbare maroon robe; he belted it with a sash as he fell in beside Jeremy. They rounded the last corner of the hall, and Barach grunted. "Tremien is awake," he said. "See the light under his door?"

Jeremy knocked once and the heavy, dark door opened of its own accord. "Come in," said a deep voice from the inner chamber. Jeremy and Barach passed through an austere room, dominated by a table and several scattered chairs, into Tremien's more homelike bedroom. A servant, a young and distant cousin of the mage, was just helping Tremien into his white robe. "Thank you," the old wizard said, carefully smoothing his shining white beard. "You may leave now." The boy withdrew without a word. "So," Tremien said, his bright eye turning to his visitors. "You felt it as well, did you?"

"Something," Jeremy said. "What was it?"

Barach cleared his throat. "For my part, Mage Tremien, I felt no warning; but somehow I sensed your distress."

Tremien nodded. "I thought of you, old friend. Though you have lost your magic, I believe our old association still attunes you to my needs—and fears. Let us go to the library."

They passed in by a back route that Jeremy had never taken. At a word from Tremien, a light sprang up in the huge book-lined room. The man-tall fireplace was dark, for summer was upon them, and the high windows were open, letting in the cool mountaintop air. Tremien paused beside his desk, looking at a huge parchment-colored globe of Thaumia. "Here," he said at last, touching a forefinger to the globe, low on the southeastern portion of the continent of Cronbrach-en-hof.

Barach bent over, his bushy gray eyebrows contracted. "The peninsula of Dubruliond," he said. "Far to the south. What of it, Mage Tremien?"

The old wizard sank into the chair behind his desk. "Evil, I think. Something, at least, that does not belong in our northern lands. We must investigate as soon as possible. A moment, please." Tremien bent his head and murmured a cantrip. "Gareth," he said softly, speaking to no one in the room.

The soldier's sleepy voice answered out of thin air: "Mage Tremien. What is wrong?"

"Much, I fear. But exactly what, remains to be seen. You will recruit a small reconnaissance force—no more than a dozen should suffice—and report to me in the library as soon as you're armed and ready."

"It will be done."

Jeremy, coming as he did from a world where telephones were a fact of life, still had a bit of trouble getting used to the communication spell, the magical equivalent of reaching out to touch someone. "Tremien," he said, "I know you have focused your awareness to sense any threat to Cronbrach. But what, exactly, did you feel?"

The old wizard shook his head. "I cannot tell *exactly*, Jeremy. But it was as if some great magic was worked there, some magic half-cloaked from me; and heretofore the only wizards to attempt to hide from me have been servants of the Great Dark One. The magic was, I think, baleful. I mislike the feel of it. It has all the seeming of a move by our ancient enemy."

Barach sank into a chair. "So he is stirring again."

"We knew he would," Tremien said. "Oh, he lost a good deal of his power when Jeremy destroyed his magic mirrors, but he has had over two years to recoup. What disturbs me is not so much that he is moving once again as that he seems to have touched directly on Cronbrach—something that he has not dared to do in many a long year, not since the Wizards' War."

"It could be a trick," Jeremy suggested.

Tremien nodded. "Yes, it could possibly be a trick; most of his doings are tricky, as well you know. Still, we cannot afford to neglect any suggestion of his presence. He is a great danger." Tremien rubbed his eyelids, and Jeremy noticed how thin the old hand was, how fragile the bones beneath the saddle-colored skin. "I am weary. Weary of watching, weary of fighting. I wish—"

A tap at the door broke off Tremien's wish. Jeremy turned as the mage granted entrance. The handsome soldier Gareth, now a *denamat*—a major, as Jeremy considered rank—came in alone. Jeremy smiled and nodded at the tall, dark-haired man and once again envied him his impressively muscled shoulders. Gareth had only recently come back to Whitehorn from Arendolas, the erstwhile haunt of the Hidden Hag. With the help of the lovely sorceress Melodia, the soldier had held the valley while Tremien's beneficent magic healed the damage done to its land and people by the malevolent Hag. "The detachment is arming," Gareth said. "We shall be ready to go within the ona."

"Very good," Tremien said.

"Mage," Barach put in, "it occurs to me that you will need eyes and ears there as well as soldiers. I will volunteer to accompany the party."

Jeremy sighed. "I don't want to have anything more to do with the Great Dark One," he admitted. "Speaking to him is like foreseeing your own death. Still, someone has to go. Count me in."

"I will not compel you to go," Tremien said.

Barach chuckled and put a large hand on Jeremy's shoulder. "Come, Tremien, cannot you see through this young rascal's subterfuge? He's grown tired of writing plays for those rascally mummers you shelter. This is his way of escaping from Winyard and his players for some short time."

Despite himself, Jeremy smiled, for it was true enough that the old ham was giving him trouble—specifically, insisting that the elder Capulet was the *real* hero of the Thaumian version of *Romeo and Juliet* that Jeremy had recently finished. Accordingly, in Winyard's view, the part had to be rewritten completely. "There's something in what Barach says," Jeremy admitted. "Although I'd face a whole theater full of Winyards before I'd willingly exchange another word with the Great Dark One. But I'll go."

"At any rate," Barach said, "we shall be honored to do this small task for you, Mage Tremien."

"Thank you both. I would not ask you if there were others I trusted as much. We have friends in that part of the world: the wise Jondan, for one, and the Sea Mage Idoradas; then there is Celissa of Saboy Forest. I will speak to them all of your coming, and they will offer what help they can. You had better prepare; return here as soon as you are ready."

In the corridor, Jeremy asked Barach, "What is Dubruliond like?"

"You have neglected your study of geography," Barach said.

"I have not. I know what it is—a low flat peninsula about eleven hundred leagues to the south of us—but not what it's like."

Barach pursed his lips, bunching his heavy gray mustache. "A warm country. Sandy soil. The farmers grow fruits and vegetables, mostly, but almost no livestock. The farms are in the coastward river valleys of the peninsula. There are only two major towns, both seaports: Shoringal on the eastern coast and Savoyan Delar, near the southern tip. The interior of Dubruliond is mostly jungle. Many pestering insects, few dangerous animals. The climate is very hot and humid."

"Florida," Jeremy said, "without the condos."

"I beg your pardon?"

"Forget it. What are we likely to need?"

Barach shrugged. "I should think it wise to equip yourself for a full day's stay, no more. Tremien will want a report before sundown. Dress for warm weather; don't worry about rations, for the soldiers will provide the food."

"Weapons?"

They had reached Barach's apartment. The heavyset mage paused in the doorway, his eyes serious beneath the projecting gray tufts of his bird's-nest eyebrows. "Oh, dear, yes. I should think so."

Jeremy had some difficulty in preventing Kelada from accompanying them, but in the end she agreed to stay home

just this once. He downplayed the importance of the trip;
but her eyes darkened when he took up the crossbow and
quiver of bolts that Captain Fallon had given him. Over a
short-sleeved tunic of homespun linen he donned his mail
shirt—if it had been of any Earthly metal it would have
weighed an oppressive twenty-five pounds or more, but
Jeremy had gotten it from Bial, Tremien's quarrelsome quar-
termaster. The mail shirt was magical, and being an enchanted thing, it was no heavier than a good woolen jacket.
He buckled a heavy leather belt around his waist, feeling
the reassuring weight of the rapierlike sword that he had
caused to be forged for himself some months earlier; then,
having replaced his shoes with heavy walking boots, he was
ready.

Gareth and the other soldiers had assembled in the library
by the time Jeremy got back there. The room was large
enough to make even a company of thirteen seem small,
and the soldiers were uncharacteristically quiet, as though
abashed by their surroundings or their mission. Barach joined
them a moment later, wearing a shirt and trousers and
looking very much out of place. Tremien wished them god-
speed and pronounced the travel cantrip for them, and a
second later they were on their way, lost in the swirling
no-color of transportation. Even during the transmit time no
one seemed disposed to speak, not even Barach, who, wonder of wonders, found no stories to tell.

When they popped into Thaumian existence again, Jeremy had a moment of pain, for they had come from an
elevation of six thousand feet to sea level, and the air
pressure squeezed his eardrums. He swallowed hastily,
blinked, and took a deep lungful of sea-scented air. For a
moment he felt suffocated; but then he realized that the
problem was a sharp change in humidity and temperature,
for Whitehorn had enjoyed the cool, dry air proper to its
altitude, while Dubruliond sweltered in muggy heat.

It seemed darker, too, as Jeremy tried to get his bearings.
The sound of surf came from not far ahead. A damp wind
stirred his short brown beard and whipped his hair seaward.
It was still dark, though a red glow to his left promised
dawn soon. Jeremy could see the flat horizon line of a
night-black ocean straight ahead—and out on it, some dis-

tance to the right, a fiery beacon. "What's that?" he asked Gareth, pointing out to sea.

"It shouldn't be there, whatever it is," Gareth answered.

"It's a ship," Barach said, peering into the darkness. "And it's on fire. Jeremy, this calls for magic."

Jeremy grunted and after a moment spoke in English: "To the fiery ship bring cooling rain, to quench its flames and make it safe again." It wasn't even decent doggerel, and it certainly wasn't much of a spell. Only the fact that it was spoken in the alien tongue of English gave it any force at all; but within seconds a low cloud had formed over the ship, its sagging belly illuminated from beneath by the red fire. Another few seconds passed, and the flames began to die down.

"We need to search the craft," Gareth said.

"I could use the travel spell—"

"No!" Barach's shout made Jeremy start. "You know that the spell is uncertain over salt water."

The light in the east was growing steadily, a ruddy glare now, touching the wave-tops with bronze. Jeremy could see Barach's stern features in the dawn-glow, and they were surprisingly serious. "But I can *see* the ship," he protested to the old mage.

Barach shook his head. "It makes no difference. You can safely travel over seawater if you have previously been to your destination and if you have anchored yourself there with a suitable spell—but even so, the destination must be solid ground, not a drifting vessel, and you must first have visited the place by mundane means to pronounce the anchoring spell. If you tried to move us to the ship out there, we could end up on the deck—or a hundred leagues at sea."

Jeremy shrugged. "Well, if we can't go to the ship, I suppose the ship will have to come to us. Let me think." After a moment he came up with another simple English spell: "Wind, blow from the sea; bring this ship close to me." A rushing sound and a commotion in the water told him that this spell, too, had worked. In Presolatan, the common tongue of Cronbrach, he explained to the others what he had done.

The sun peeked above the eastern horizon a few minutes later. In its light they could see the silvery shafts of rain pouring from the small black cloud, the smoldering decks of a dismasted ship, and the white-flecked disturbance in the water around it as a wizard's wind, contrary to the prevailing airs, chopped the sea, pushing the hulk nearer and nearer the shore.

"I know where we are now," Gareth said. Jeremy was hardly surprised, for the soldier seemed to have visited every part of Cronbrach at least once. "We're on one of the sand islands at the tip of Dubruliond. Thelara, I should think. Behind us is a narrow channel, and beyond that would be Savoyan Delar."

"That sounds about right," Barach said. His nostrils twitched. "I can smell the smoke now."

The uncanny wind had brought the smoke to them, and following the smoke was the ship itself. Its coming seemed to take forever. Jeremy had time to look about him as the smoking hulk slowly lumbered back and forth in the light surf a half-mile from shore, and he thought to himself that his comparison of Dubruliond to Florida was not far off: the trees inland from the dunes were not really palms, though they had a similar form, but the beach on which he stood was packed white sand, littered with shells, and the flat landscape behind him was thick with prickly-looking low scrub growth. Add an amusement park or two, a few hotels, and pave the landscape with asphalt and you'd have a reasonable facsimile of Fort Lauderdale, Jeremy mused.

The ship, its fire now completely extinguished, ground to a halt a hundred yards or so from shore. "We'd better wade out," Gareth said.

The sun was barely up, but it was hot already. Jeremy, sweating, removed his boots and followed the soldiers, wading into water of almost blood heat. Jeremy's conjured rainstorm, its job done, was dissipating now, leaving the wooden ship glistening, its sound sides streaked with black soot, a few plumes of white steam and gray smoke still drifting from fallen, charred masts and yards. The hulk had run aground and rolled to starboard at a twenty-degree list. An outgoing tide had stranded it, but it still wallowed just a bit with the slap of the waves.

Jeremy approached the starboard side and found himself chest-deep in salty water, the deck a good ten feet overhead. "I don't see any way up," he told Gareth. "Shall I try some magic?" A breaking wave came up to his forehead and staggered him. He coughed and spluttered, wiping the stinging water from his eyes.

Gareth, taller and heavier than Jeremy, had stood his ground. "Don't waste your magic," the soldier said. He shouted an order to three young men, and they disappeared around the prow of the ship. "They'll be able to climb the far side."

Barach, even his beard sodden, put a hand on the side of the ship. "A southern craft," he said.

"Yes," Gareth agreed, his voice surprisingly grim. "A ship from Hadoriben, I judge. And we know whom they serve in far Hadoriben."

Despite the heat of the water, Jeremy shivered a little.

A few more waves rolled in, though the tide was rapidly ebbing and they were less troublesome; then a rope ladder banged against the hull of the ship a few feet away from Jeremy. "I'll go up first," Gareth said. "Then the longsword men, I think; then you, Jeremy, and you, Mage Barach. The rest stand by here."

Jeremy watched the four soldiers scramble up the ladder. When they cried out no warning, he followed them, and behind him the heavy Barach wheezed his way up.

The deck was a shambles, piled with blackened masts, broken yards, burned rope, the sooty remains of sails. And—Jeremy sniffed—yes, there was the ominous smell of burned meat in the air as well. Turning, Jeremy offered a hand to Barach and hefted the older man aboard. "Careful," he warned. "It's steep."

The soldiers had clustered over something halfway to the stern; walking toward them was like descending the pitch of a reasonably steep roof. The stench grew as Jeremy neared them, and he took only one sick glance at the charred things on the deck.

"The crew," Gareth said in an unsteady voice. "What's left of them, anyhow. Cover them." He turned away as his men spread a partially burned canvas over the heap. "The hatches are open. Let's take a look."

Glad to be away from the grisly remains, Jeremy accompanied him. "What happened to them?" he asked.

Gareth shrugged. "There was a small boat tied to the deck, from the looks of it. I'd say they tried to unlash it—but somehow the fire took them in a group before they could escape. It has the look of magic. What have we here?"

What they had was a dark square hole into the bowels of the ship. Jeremy conjured up enough wizard-light to show them what lay within: a few casks, a few sacks, and a flooring of smooth, wet black rock. "Ballast," Jeremy said.

Gareth grunted his agreement. The forward hatch was just the same: whatever cargoes the ship had once carried, it had none aboard now.

Barach waited for them at the stern of the ship. "The cabins will be belowdecks here," he said. "Perhaps we should take a look."

Gareth ordered two of his men to inspect the crew quarters in the forecastle; he himself and two of his swordsmen took the lead down the companionway to the stern cabins.

There were five of them altogether, cramped and small; and the first four were empty. The hatch of the last one, the large stern cabin, was sealed. Gareth pressed his ear to the wood. "I hear nothing," he said. "Conjure it open."

Jeremy spoke a simple unlocking spell in English and reached to turn the metal handle—

"Ouch!" he cried, jerking his hand back. "Damn! Why didn't you tell me it was hot?" He shook his hand, then held it up to examine the blisters already forming on the first joints of his fingers.

"It wasn't hot when I tried it," Gareth said.

"Wizardry," Barach said quietly from behind them. "Jeremy's spell reacted with a counterspell, a lock spell. Someone does not want the doorway opened."

"Break it," Gareth said to his men. Jeremy and the major stood back while the two brawny soldiers, barely able to stand side by side in the narrow passageway, kicked the door panel. On their third try the lock gave way with a splintering crash. Light from the stern ports burst on them as the hatch opened inwardly.

But neither of the men seemed eager to look inside. Gareth pushed past them, and Jeremy came close behind. After the dimness of the corridor, he blinked in the bright cabin: the morning sun streaked in the ports, showing a compact but well-appointed compartment, equipped with a small table, built-in chests and cabinets, and a bed. A human figure, muffled with a dark brown blanket, stirred feebly on the cot. Gareth whipped the blanket back, revealing a man, bald, slightly built, dressed in a dark blue robe, lying facedown—and tied hand and foot.

"He's alive," the soldier said, turning the man onto his back. "He's been gagged—"

"*No!*" Jeremy cried, striking away Gareth's hand before he could loosen the gag.

Above the band of dark cloth a pair of deep-set eyes glared madly at them. The old man made choking, gurgling sounds, attempting to speak—or perhaps to formulate a spell. Jeremy shivered again. From behind him, Barach asked, "What have you found?"

The face was the same that Jeremy recalled: the high, domed, bald forehead, the prominent cheeks, the thin, pinched nose hooked over a thin-lipped mouth. Jeremy had seen it before, had known those baleful eyes only too well. "Not what," Jeremy said, his throat constricted. "Who." He took a deep breath. "It's him," he said. "It's the Great Dark One himself."

2

The party's return to Whitehorn cast Tremien into an even darker mood than before. For a few moments he stood listening to their story and glaring down at the prisoner; then he called a healer to attend to the bound-and-gagged old man.

She was Tintaniel, a sorceress who was somehow obscurely one of Tremien's cousins, and she had great skill at her art. For a brief time she knelt beside the patient, who had been placed on a sofa that had been brought into the library. Tintaniel spoke some charms, too softly for Jeremy to hear, and then stood. She gestured Tremien aside. Jeremy was just close enough to hear her say softly, "There is no hope for him. He has little life left inside; he will die within moments."

"We must question him," Tremien said.

"You may. At least he has no great pain. He is simply wearing out from great age, I fear."

Tremien stepped forward again. Tintaniel hovered behind him, dejection showing in her expression. On the sofa the patient grunted and mouthed muffled syllables as he struggled feebly and ineffectively against the cords that tied him hand and foot.

After a moment of thought, Tremien, standing before the darkened fireplace, murmured a spell of some kind; Jeremy felt the hair of his arms prickle from the electric feel of powerful magic at work. "There," Tremien said. "I have cast a spell of silence on all magical pronouncements in this room. We may safely hear what he has to say now."

Barach looked worried. "Mage, I am not sure you are right. After all, he is a very powerful wizard."

Tremien's smile was grim. "Not, I hope, more powerful than I in my own place. But you are right to urge caution; let us test the spell. Jeremy, try a simple act of magic: levitation, say."

"All right." Jeremy concentrated on raising the globe beside the desk a few feet; he visualized it floating; he began to formulate the necessary spell—and broke off in confusion. The third necessary stage of magic, actualizing the spell by speaking it aloud, was totally beyond him. "I can't do it," he said, surprised. "I can't even think of the words."

"Nor will you be able to do so in this room; not until my spell's virtue is exhausted in a day's time. Gareth, set the man free."

With apprehension in his eyes, the soldier removed the Great Dark One's gag, but the cloth might as well have remained in place for all the intelligible sounds the ancient man pronounced. His voice, a thin screech, mumbled meaningless syllables, while his eyes glared madly, darting from face to face with implacable hatred flashing from them. Even Tintaniel shivered before that hateful gaze.

"He is trying to spell us," Barach said. "But this is no language I have ever heard."

Tremien stood at the head of the sofa and stared down intently at the wizened figure before him. "It's is no language at all. Save, perhaps, the tongue of madness. Untie his hands and his feet as well, Gareth; he is no danger to us."

Gareth did as he was bidden, but the old, old man on the sofa proved unable even to rise. He tried twice or three times to start up from where he lay, only to sink back with a groan. "Listen to me," Tremien said, bending closer and speaking very distinctly. "Death stands ready to take you. Your time is short. Why have you come to trouble us?"

"Kill you," the scarecrow figure on the sofa snarled. "Kill you all." He coughed and broke into gasping sobs; and then a strange look, half-mad and half-crafty, came into the sunken eyes. "But wait. Let us live. Yes, let us live. We can offer riches, yes—"

"You can offer nothing which we would take," Tremien said. "Why were you aboard the ship?"

"Left us," the old man panted. "Left us, flew away, left

us to die." The bony hands plucked at the loose robe over the Great Dark One's thin, heaving chest. "Left us to die," he blubbered again, shaking with sobs. "Save us." The eyes flared. "You can do it; you, Tremien, old spider—"

Tremien shook his head. "I can do nothing for you. But you can tell us—"

"Curse you all!" The ancient mummy of a man jerked halfway up. "They come," he said with terrible intensity. "Awakened from long sleep, from the dust of death, yes! They will take your power, steal it, make him more terrible than ever! And he shall see you die, curse him, curse you—"

Barach stepped forward; the Great Dark One had gone stiff and trembling, eyes glaring, froth standing on the stretched dry lips. His breath rattled harshly in his throat, and after a moment he fell back with no breath at all. Tintaniel alone seemed free of the fascination that had fallen on the room. Stepping forward and kneeling beside the sofa, she felt the old man's throat and shook her head. "Dead," she murmured.

"This vessel is," Tremien said.

Jeremy shivered. He knew well the special talent of the Great Dark One: the ability to pass his essence, his soul, from body to body, possessing each new mind in turn and corrupting it as he absorbed his host's personality—and powers. "You think he's taken a new form?"

"Almost certainly. This wretch is merely the husk of what he was. The spirit of the Great Dark One has found another home."

"Then he might be someone in Cronbrach," Jeremy said.

"I fear he must be," Tremien answered. "Though, from what I know of his possession-spell, the victim may not be completely changed yet; it seems to take some days for the Great Dark One's consciousness to grow to full power in its host."

Barach closed the glaring eyes of the corpse. "I do not like what he said about awakening someone from the sleep of death. He has had fell servants in the past, if his history be only half-true; who knows what he may have stirred into being?"

Tremien shook his head. "It is a riddle we must solve, and as soon as we may. I have felt nothing for many years like the foreboding that is now on me."

Jeremy, studying the shrunken, shriveled features of the dead man, shivered. "I feel it too," he said in a voice little louder than a whisper. "As if—I don't know—as if the sun were veiled, or as if the air had gone stale."

"There is great magic at work," Tremien said. "It seeks to hide itself from me, and it is in some wise successful in concealment. Yet I know its presence, and its evil intent."

"Evil?" Tintaniel stood up with a sigh. "He was pitiable. So afraid of death."

"He has always been afraid," Jeremy said. "I think fear made him what he was."

"What he still is," corrected Tremien. "Gareth, see that this body is burned, and gather the ashes carefully. I think they must be magically sealed and taken far from here, for I cannot trust my ancient adversary even in death. Barach, Jeremy, I believe I must call a meeting of the Great Council."

Barach raised his bushy eyebrows. "Have we time for that? Preparations for a full meeting will take a day or more."

Tremien scowled. "I know the need for haste as well as anyone. Yet clearly this is a matter for the Council and not for me alone. I wish there were some better way, some quicker way, to deal with our problem, but none comes to me."

None came to Jeremy either. At midday he witnessed the cremation of the body, on a rocky ledge a few hundred yards below the castle's outer walls. Gareth and an armed guard kept careful watch over the pyre, anxious that nothing, no bird, no insect, should even fly through the smoke. From where he watched on the north-facing wall walk, Jeremy saw the flames leap high and the white smoke roil, dispersing harmlessly into the clear mountain air. The flames completely hid the body from him—for which Jeremy was inwardly grateful.

"Good that he burn."

Jeremy jumped at the sound of the voice, a throaty, harsh mutter; then he laughed. "Hello, Nul," he said to the pika as the chest-high creature craned to stare down at the pyre. "You startled me."

Nul grunted and turned his great round beach ball of a head to give Jeremy a surprised glance from his orange eyes. "Didn't mean scare you. Should've wakened me last night. Would have gone with you."

"You would have drowned in the surf," Jeremy said.

"Pikas swim when have to," Nul returned. He glanced back at the burning body on the ledge below. "Like to have helped capture that. Was he gave me this." The pika rubbed a three-fingered hand over his right leg, noticeably crooked from injuries he had received in the Hag's Uprising. "Was hard to catch?"

"He was caught already," Jeremy said. "All we did was bring him back." He told the story of the burning ship in a few words, Nul nodding to himself as he listened.

"Don't like," Nul said when Jeremy had finished the tale. "Dark One full of tricks. Always before Dark One crafty; never yet do such a thing as this. Before, when he come, he come with soldiers, with army; now he here alone. He mean us evil."

"Tremien agrees with you," Jeremy said. "He's summoning all Council members here for a meeting right now. And Barach has dived into his books to try to find what the Great Dark One meant when he said he'd awakened someone from death."

Nul began, "Hope he find—"

"Jeremy, my lad! Jeremy, my soul!" came a booming voice from the courtyard below.

Jeremy groaned. Winyard, the actor, had found him. He turned and shouted back, "Yes?"

The mummer, flamboyantly dressed in baggy yellow trousers and a bloused red shirt, waved up at him. "I have had more thoughts on the noble tragedy of Capulet," he called in his fruity bass. "We must discuss this matter at once, while it is fresh in my invention!"

Nul grinned at Jeremy, showing a startling semicircle of pointed white teeth, like a new crescent moon against the dark gray of his facial fur. "You talk," he said. "I go play with Emily."

"Yah, you animated teddy bear," Jeremy grunted. "That's right, desert me." With a sigh he took one last look at the cremation fire, feeling heat on his face even at a distance; then he took his heavy heart down to the courtyard to confer with the overeager actor. It took him the rest of the day, several bottles of wine, and all his eloquence to persuade Winyard that, perhaps, the play was barely acceptable as Shakespeare had written it—though of course Winyard considered the Thaumian translation to be entirely Jeremy's work and therefore open to revision.

But after long consideration Winyard finally agreed to a trade-off: he would allow the play to stand as a showcase for the younger actors in his troupe, for Juliet, Romeo, Mercutio, Tybalt, and the like, *if* Jeremy would consent in return to pen a play suitable for a man of Winyard's bearing and age.

Jeremy agreed, inwardly more determined than ever to stick Winyard with a part that would stretch the mummer's histrionic talents—admittedly, very good ones—to the limit. Let the bastard take a crack at Lear, he thought. At long last, late into the night, they drank a final cup together, sealing the agreement, and Jeremy reeled away, drunk with wine and fatigue. He had no trouble falling asleep, nor were his dreams visited by any night fears or any thoughts of the Great Dark One.

"Wake up, Jeremy." Kelada's voice was soft, but even so it rolled through Jeremy's head like a bowling ball over a ten-foot washboard.

"What?" He groaned, opening one eye, only to close it in agony as a spear of morning flashed in from the window. "Arggh," he commented.

"I've warned you about trying to match the players drink for drink. You have no head for wine," Kelada said.

"I have no head, period," he said. "Just a size-seven-and-a-quarter package of aches. Damn that Winyard, anyway."

Kelada sat on the edge of the bed. "You don't mean that. He's made my husband a famous man."

Jeremy experimented with opening his eyes again and managed to crack them enough to see Kelada's blurry figure. "Too bad there's no money in it," he muttered.

"There would be, if you cared to charge," Kelada said. "Other play-makers are paid by other acting companies."

"Other play-makers don't steal their stuff from Shakespeare and company," Jeremy returned. With a great effort he rose to a sitting position. From the floor Emily cooed at him. She crawled to the bed, grasped the cover, and pulled herself up to her feet.

Jeremy, his hangover not exactly forgotten but at least ignored for the moment, lifted the toddler up onto the bed. "Hiya, daughter," he said in English.

"Don't talk magic to my baby," Kelada said, reaching to smooth Emily's curly hair away from her forehead.

"Huh. You insisted we give her an English name."

"She should have something from her father. After all, she has her mother's good looks." Kelada's teasing tone became more serious as her elfin face took on a thoughtful expression. "I hope she has some of your magic too."

"You have your share of magic," Jeremy said.

"I can do nothing," Kelada said. "Only borrowed magic works for me: travel-spells and such. No spell that I have ever made up has even once succeeded."

"Yes, but you have that handy little talent of never being lost. That's worth something, isn't it?"

"To a thief, perhaps. But not to a mother."

"Come here." Kelada leaned close and Jeremy kissed her. Emily gurgled and laughed.

"That's enough," Kelada said, pushing away. "Time for you to get up. You're lucky that Barach is busy with the guests—if he were attending your training, you would have been roused before sunup, aching head or no."

The thought of the Council meeting brought back the chill feeling around Jeremy's heart. He rose and dressed, picked at his breakfast, and then went glumly down to the main chambers of the castle.

The chaos there made his head thump even harder. Cronbrach was a confederation of different city-states and districts, each one more or less independent in local affairs, but all working together in matters of defense and in certain matters of trade. Each political unit was ruled by a person or group—queens and kings, mayors or town masters, councils or parliaments, according to whether the locals felt more secure under monarchy or democracy—but each one also depended on a local magician of some standing, and in matters beyond the purely immediate, these wielded the real power.

The magicians, nearly five hundred of them, made up the Great Council. Each wizard or sorceress specialized in some branch of magical study, and each one was responsible to the city or district that hired him or her. From their numbers the magicians elected a smaller group, the Council Mages—usually the most talented and powerful sorcerers—and these made up the Inner Council, the equivalent of a senate. In turn, the Inner Council of two dozen or more appointed the High Council, which served as a sort of supreme court and adjudicated questions of magic or of crimes that went beyond local jurisdiction.

The High Council's Chief Mage (Tremien for many years now) was, to all intents and purposes, the president of the confederation. It was he who assumed the heavy responsibility of detecting any untoward events in all of Cronbrach's Five Countries, the five main geographical divisions of the continent.

To Jeremy it seemed that every magician of Cronbrach was in the Great Hall now, chattering and gesturing, arguing and laughing, making life sorrowful for those with aching heads. He found Barach in the turmoil, engaged in deep conversation with a middle-aged woman clothed in silver and black. Barach nodded a greeting as Jeremy approached, then paused in his talking to perform an introduction: "Lady Alena, this unworthy rascal is my pupil, Jeremy Moon of Earth; Jeremy, bow before Lady Alena of Karken's Hold, a woman graced with beauty and a most magical way with growing things."

Lady Alena smiled at Jeremy. "I have heard of you," she said. "And I know enough of Barach to tell how fond he is of you."

"And I of him," Jeremy said.

Barach looked pleased. "We begin to mend the young scamp's manners," he said. "A wonder beyond any I have yet seen. I am reminded of the apprentice Hustin and his master Delamor—"

Jeremy listened to the inevitable story and laughed politely at its conclusion. "How long until the meeting?" he asked.

Barach glanced around the crowded room. "Not long now. Tremien can be most persuasive when he must be—and he seems to have managed to persuade practically everyone to drop present business to consider the problem at hand. Look, there's Walther."

Jeremy turned. A portly man, somewhat under middle height, with gray-streaked black hair and beard, had popped into existence on a stair landing. "Melodia's father," Jeremy said, grinning. "Well, Tremien must have been exceptionally persuasive if he got the old hermit here."

Barach nodded. "I have often thought it odd that Walther, the celebrated creator of Walther's Travel Spell and then of Walther's Fast Travel, journeys so little himself."

"Too busy counting his money, I suppose. I heard that after he introduced the Fast Travel spell a couple of years ago he doubled his fortune within three months." Jeremy sighed. "Now, if he'd had advertising to help him along, just think how rich he could be."

The crowd had become even thicker with new arrivals. Tremien's deep voice, seemingly coming from the ceiling above, suddenly boomed over the assembly: "Council members, greetings! Our number is complete; for your attendance, my thanks. We must lose no time in useless words, for a dark foreboding is on me. Let us commence as soon as we may."

But it took some time, some scurrying in of chairs, some sorting and greeting and questioning among the members, before at last the room was set for the meeting. The High Council sat at a long table on a dais at the head of the huge room; the rest sat in rows of chairs facing the table. Jeremy, an honorary mage, had the lowest seat at the Inner Council table, off to the left. Barach abandoned his usual place beside Tremien to sit beside him.

Tremien, at the center of the table, called the meeting to order. This morning he wore rimless spectacles that made him look owlish, oddly professorial. At his request, Barach rose to recount their discovery of the Great Dark One and to tell of the sorcerer's end. Jeremy sat and listened and wished he had an aspirin.

When Barach's story was over, Tremien said, "There is more. Three of our number were close at hand when the Great Dark One's magic was wrought on our northern shores. I wish them to speak. First Jondan."

Jondan, a thin and austere mage of the High Council, rose from his place. "I was in the port city of Relenda Chai a night ago," he said in his flat voice. "The people there had summoned me because of bad weather—a curious storm that had swept in from the south and that seemed to hang off the shore, driving the ships to shelter. My best weather magic failed to disperse it; and not until midnight did it disperse of its own, with a feeling of great magic at work."

The mage sat down again. Tremien nodded and turned to the audience. "Idoradas, the Sea Mage," he said.

Idoradas sat at the other end of the table from Jeremy. The youngest member of the Inner Council, he had been elected not more than a year ago. He was a reddish-blond young man with mild eyes the color of a calm ocean. Appearing a bit abashed at having to speak before so many, he cleared his throat. "As most of you know," he said with evident hesitation, "my special province is the protection of sailing vessels. My home is in Webberley, though for some time I have been working in Savoyan Delar, the trading port at the southern tip of Dubruliond. The storm that Mage Jondan speaks of passed there two nights ago, and then, as he said, paused at sea—to the east of Savoyan, to the south of Relenda. I have little power over weather, but I also tried my spells and found them wanting. Like Jondan, I felt the great magic; it was strong, dark, and very close by."

For a moment it seemed that Idoradas would add something to his tale, but he did not. When he had sat down again, Tremien called, "And last, Celissa."

Celissa, as it proved, was a raven-haired woman of thirty or so, pretty but not strikingly beautiful. She stood midway back in the Council. "And I actually encountered the black storm," she said in a clear and sweet soprano. "I had taken ship with Captain Tharnow Eblands from Relenda to the island of Catthertian, for he wished my protection against the pirates of those waters; our voyage was over and we were returning to port when the black clouds swept up from the south, traveling on their own winds. I cast a spell to reveal its nature—"

"And it failed," sighed someone on the front row.

"No. It succeeded."

The audience, murmuring, turned toward her with new interest. "The Great Dark One was in the midst of the storm, all right; but there was something else. There was—I cannot express it well—there was a void. Something that swallowed my magic; something that took it and gave nothing back. Anyway, in an instant the Great Dark One was aware of my spell, and he lashed at me in anger. I turned aside his attack; then we were caught in an evil wind and driven far south again to sea. The spell holding the storm snapped late that night."

"And yet," Tremien said, "Celissa was unable to communicate with anyone to tell us of these happenings."

"Why didn't she use the communication spell?" someone asked.

Celissa bowed her head. "I had not the power. My magic was weakened by my contact with the Great Dark One; it is not yet fully recovered. I had to wait until we reached port in Shoringal before I was strong enough to call Mage Tremien; and that was at dawn today."

Tremien nodded. "And now tell the rest," he said.

Celissa took a deep breath. "We made for Shoringal, the trading and fishing city on the eastern coast of the Dubruliond Peninsula, midway between Relenda and Savoyan; we had suffered some damage, and the winds were most favorable for that port. We arrived at first light—and in Shoringal we heard that a path of the sea is dead."

"Dead?" Jondan asked sharply.

Celissa nodded. "It was along the track of the storm. Those waters were rich in fish, but for a space a thousand-pace broad and many thousands long, no fish were left alive. The sea is healing now, the tainted waters mixing with the whole, but in Shoringal the sailors tell a tale of ruin. Ships that crossed the track found that magic would hardly work there; and they sailed through shoals of dead and rotting fish."

Barach stood, holding up a hand to silence the uproar that broke out. "This has happened before," he said.

"When, Loremaster?" cried a voice from the rear of the hall.

"In Relas," Barach said.

Jeremy felt cold. He well recalled his short visit to the blasted landscape of Relas: a desert country, dry and lifeless as an ancient skull.

"I fear," Tremien said, "that Mage Barach is correct. Whatever forces the Great Dark One used ages ago to drain the life from Relas have been reawakened. They now threaten us. They are in Cronbrach now; they are on the move; and as you must by now have guessed, their dark master is with them."

After a stunned moment of silence, the Council erupted into a pandemonium of shouted questions, recriminations, and curses.

"Do you agree?" Tremien asked, his voice hoarse.

Jeremy and Barach were closeted alone with Tremien in the library; the tall leaded windows looked out on a soft summer night. Barach, to whom the question had been addressed, sank into a deep chair. "I must," he said. "Yet I would be unwilling to make such a charge."

Jeremy had recovered from his hangover but was weary of a long day of fruitless debate, which had settled nothing but had delegated the authority to act to the High Council. Suddenly aware that he had dozed and had missed the import of what Tremien had been saying, Jeremy spoke: "Wait a minute. Do I understand you correctly? You think the Great Dark One has possessed a Council member?"

"I'm almost certain of it," Tremien said. "Almost. And if he has, I think it must be one of three: Jondan, Idoradas, or Celissa."

"They are surely the most likely. But which?" Barach asked. "I could see no alteration in any of them."

Tremien, slumped in his chair behind the great desk, shrugged. "Nor could I, even with the aid of the spectacles. The evil one covers his traces very thoroughly. I cannot tell."

"Then how do you know it happened?" Jeremy asked reasonably.

"Because were I the Great Dark One, that is what I should have done. He has obviously developed some way of concealing the full operation of his magic; the fear of exposure was the only thing that formerly kept him from some such move."

"But why the three of them?"

Tremien tented his fingers. "They were closest; each worked some magic, thereby alerting the Great Dark One to their presence; and any one of them has sufficient potential magic to be an attractive host."

"Wait, wait," Jeremy said, sitting up straighter in his chair.

"I thought the possession spell required personal contact."

Barach, who specialized in the study of the history and theory of magic, nodded. "It does," he said. "But the three magicians were only a few leagues apart, it seems. Each was, ah, within range of the Great Dark One; he could have visited any one of them. Further, if his magical powers were cloaked, it is unlikely that any one of them would have recognized the old man as the Great Dark One."

"But what about the others? Maybe one of them—"

"None was close enough," Tremien said. "Do not forget, Jeremy, I make it my business to keep track of the magicians in our lands."

"And it's unlikely that he would bother to possess anyone of lesser standing than a magician," Barach said. "Remember, to some extent the Great Dark One takes on the characteristics of his host. He would need a host with considerable magical talents to be able to work his own thaumaturgy to full effect."

"And his powers have grown strong again. I am quite sure he has some cloaking magic about him," Tremien added. He stretched out a thin hand and grasped at air. "Transmute and ensorcel it, I feel it yet—a sense of magic at work, yet no sense of the nature or source of the magic itself."

Barach said, "Perhaps I once would have agreed, Mage Tremien, but the loss of my magic also dulled my sense of its workings, I fear. At any rate, Jeremy is at least partially correct: the possession spell needs to be worked out in the vicinity of the next host; that would take some little time, perhaps two or three hona. But then the actual moment of consummation—the time when the sorcerer and host need actually be in physical contact—is over in an instant."

"Then we have to find which one of the sorcerers is now the Great Dark One," Jeremy said.

Barach coughed. "As Hrunstan once remarked to a fire elemental who complained of the heat, you have a remarkable grasp of the obvious, Jeremy. But that is precisely the problem."

"We could," Tremien said, "destroy them all."

"What?" Jeremy blinked unbelievingly at the old mage. "But that would mean killing two innocent persons—"

"Perhaps three," Tremien said, his voice bitter and weary. "For I may be mistaken. It is very unlikely, but the

Great Dark One may be housed in some lowly apprentice's body hundreds of leagues from here, for aught I know."

Jeremy pushed himself up from his chair. Tremein regarded him with a cool level gaze as he began to pace. "Mage Tremien," the younger man said, "I don't believe you would do this."

"It is an evil," Tremien acknowledged. "But to allow the Great Dark One to work his will unchallenged—that is a greater evil still."

"But—damn it, suppose for the sake of argument that the Great Dark One *has* taken over Jondan, or Idoradas, or even Celissa. There must be some trick you could play, or maybe some truth-revealing spell you could use—"

Barach held up a hand, silencing Jeremy. "I have studied what we know of his ways and his spells," he said. "I am certain a truth spell would have no effect, for two reasons. First, the transference is very subtle; in a sense, the Great Dark One has ceased to exist, and so he cannot be said to inhabit anyone's body. But the drive is there, the will to evil; and over the next few days it will grow and consume, awakening the spirit of the Great Dark One in its new host. Still, if Idoradas, say, were now host to the Great Dark One, he is not the less Idoradas. It is simply that Idoradas would be in the process of melting into the Great Dark One, of becoming the new incarnation."

"I'm not sure I follow that," Jeremy said. "But what's the second reason?"

Barach joined his hands across his ample stomach. "The second is that the Great Dark One has deep magic of his own. He is very old, Jeremy, perhaps ten times as old as Tremien. In all the two thousand years of his existence he has had more than enough time to perfect dark enchantments. I believe he would be immune to any ordinary spell of truth."

Jeremy shook his head. "I'm sorry. Even so, he's sure to give himself away, sooner or later. No actor is perfect. If he's walking around in someone else's skin, he's bound to make some mistake, do something uncharacteristic. I suppose you tested the three of them as much as you could?"

Tremien nodded. "Yes, of course. And they passed every test, magical and mundane." He clenched his hands, then relaxed them. "And yet I know, I sense, I feel in my very bones, that one of the three is host to the dark spirit."

"You can't condemn three people to death because of a feeling," Jeremy said.

"You are very nearly right," Tremien said, his voice very soft. "I would find it difficult. If I do so, I will no longer be Tremien; if he betrays me into suspicion of my friends, into the murder of two of them, the Great Dark One has to some extent captured my spirit as well. And yet, for my soul I can see no other clear way."

"Let me talk to them," Jeremy said. "I spent some time with the Great Dark One; maybe I can learn whether he's taken over one of them."

Barach spoke up: "That is not a wise idea, Mage Tremien. From what Jeremy has told us of his encounter, we know that the Great Dark One coveted his Earthly magic. It might be all too easy for him to take Jeremy too, if we throw them together."

"I agree," Tremien said.

"But we have to do something," Barach continued, frowning. "Unfortunately, Jeremy is right: only someone who knows the Great Dark One well would have much of a chance of detecting his presence in another's body. And at that, Jeremy does not know him *well*; he had one audience with him, and that was two years ago."

"No one knows the Great Dark One well," Tremien agreed. "He has an unpleasant habit of murdering his minions. Perhaps the Hidden Hag could have seen through his disguise, but she is dead; and there is no one else in our northern lands who has had any sort of dealings with him."

"Sebastian," Jeremy said.

Barach turned. "I beg your pardon?"

"Sebastian Magister," Jeremy repeated. "My Thaumian double. The one who made the mirrors. The one who took my place on Earth. He worked with the Great Dark One—damn near lost his soul to him, from what you've said."

Barach and Tremien exchanged a glance. The older magician said, "True enough, Jeremy. But Sebastian can be of no help, for he is inaccessible to us."

Jeremy leaned on the desk. "Perhaps not. You worked a spell to send me back to Earth, Tremien. Couldn't you—?"

The old magician shook his head. "You have no idea how much power that spell took," he murmured. With a tired smile he added, "Once, perhaps, when I was younger, it might have held more virtue and might have worked twice; but I am far too old for such wonders. I could not bring Sebastian back, nor even communicate with him. The window I briefly opened to Earth is closed forever."

"Mage Tremien, if youth is called for, perhaps someone else could succeed. I could try—"

Barach coughed. In a voice of mild rebuke he said, "You overreach yourself, Jeremy. Of all the masters of magic I have known, Tremien is by far the greatest; and even at that, Mage Tremien's spell took a month or more to formulate. More, it was a spell of such force that it took ten sorcerers lending their power in concert to activate the magic. We cannot spare that kind of power now, when the Dark One is moving; and, too, we lack the luxury of time. Even if you had sufficient control of the spell to realize it, to reformulate it would take many weeks."

Tremien stroked his white beard. "What Barach says is true enough. And yet it occurs to me," he said, "that there may be a way."

Barach looked skeptical. "A way to move between worlds? I intend no flattery, Tremien, but without your skills I hardly think that all of the magicians of Cronbrach acting together would have the power and the control that such a feat would require."

"But there is a Gate," Tremien said.

Barach slowly rose to his feet. "That is true," he said. "I had almost forgotten about that. However, no one has used it for a century, and no one has ever been able to constrain and channel its power. Do you suppose—?"

"What is the Gate?" Jeremy asked.

Tremien did not even acknowledge the question. "Jeremy's magic is—very strange. Of all the wizards I know, Jeremy alone just might manage it."

"It means a journey," Barach said.

"Yes. I think you'd better begin at once."

"Wait a minute," Jeremy objected. "What is the Gate? Begin what?"

"Begin something pretty desperate," Barach said. "Yet it could work."

"Of course," Tremien said, "there would be the imbalance of forces to reckon with; we could not keep Sebastian in our world for long, not while Jeremy is also here."

Barach sounded excited: "But if Sebastian could give us a clue, then even a temporary visit to Whitehorn might—"

"Damn it!" Jeremy shouted. "You just convinced me that it's impossible to bring him here; now you're arguing about his accommodations! What are you talking about?"

Barach blinked at him. "Oh. Sorry. There is an island to the south—not many leagues south and west of where we were in Dubruliond, in fact—which has, ah, pockets of primeval magic scattered about on it. A tricky, odd place; not one that many people care to visit. It is almost uninhabited, in fact. But there is one—"

"One somewhat like yourself," Tremien picked up. "A woman, a most strange sorceress, with decidedly odd powers. She is the Keeper of the Gate; but despite her title, even she has no ready means of using the Gate."

"What," Jeremy asked in plaintive tones, "is the Gate?"

Barach took a deep breath. "It is a fracture in the universe," he said. "A concentration of the strongest old magic of Thaumia. It is a way to other worlds and other times; but it is utterly uncontrolled. The Keeper cannot use it herself, but she sees to it that nothing dangerous comes into Thaumia by means of it—and that nothing from Thaumia strays into other worlds by passing through it."

"There is the problem of directing the power, you see," Tremien added. "The Gate is like, oh, a window looking into a billion worlds at once; but it may linger on one for a moment only, then pass to another. It might return to the first, or it might jump to a third; it might remain fixed on one for a week, or skip from world to world with ten times the speed of a heartbeat."

Barach nodded. "The problem, simply put," he said, "is that unless you could find some means of controlling the focus, of concentrating the magic, why, you might find yourself in some world totally alien to Earth or to Thaumia. And you might be stranded there forever."

"All right, I think I understood most of that," Jeremy said. "Now, what was the part about an imbalance of forces?"

Barach cleared his throat and settled into his lecturer's stance. "The universe is complete of itself," he said. "It has a fixed measure of magical energy and of mass, and anything alien that intrudes into it throws it out of balance. Normally nothing can intrude. However, by means of such portals as the Gate or Sebastian's mirrors, to a limited extent it is possible for things from other realities to—well, to leak through, as it were, to Thaumia. Small imbalances normally have no very great impact. An animal here or there, or a person perhaps, can be assimilated into Thaumia, made part of it, with no terrible results. Unfortunately, with Sebastian the imbalance is serious; you see, the problem is complicated because in your case you have an exact double."

"Sebastian," Jeremy said.

"Yes, Sebastian. He belongs to this universe; you, even though you are essentially the same person, do not. What is worse, both of you are formidable sorcerers, with great resources of magical potential about you, although from what you have told us, I gather that Sebastian's usable *mana* is thoroughly depleted. Well, you have exchanged universes with Sebastian. Fortunately, through the law of correspondences, you are close enough to Sebastian to be able to take his place in our universe—and he can replace you in yours. Thus the balance is maintained. But if both of you are together in one universe, it's a violation of natural law. It's—it's one person being in two places at the same time. Since that is an impossibility, the magical potential of the entire universe is disrupted."

"I take it that's bad."

"There would tend to be a gathering of forces which, theoretically at least, would eject one of you—perhaps to your own universe, or perhaps into the void."

Jeremy swallowed. "You mean the Between?" He had no desire to return to that realm of dreams and nightmares.

"I mean," Barach said firmly, "the void."

"It sounds chancy."

"It is very dangerous," Tremien said.

"And time would be short," Barach added. "If the Great Dark One's forces are at work, we would have no more than a week or so to act."

Jeremy stood leaning on the mantel, looking into the huge dark fireplace. "And the alternative is to destroy Jondan, Idoradas, and Celissa."

Tremien settled back in his chair and kept his voice level: "It is one alternative."

Jeremy looked at him. The old wizard's face showed

concern and kindness. "One question. How do you know the Gate thing can even make contact with Earth?"

Tremien said softly, "We know it for a very simple reason. The Keeper of the Gate herself came through it many years ago."

"You mean she—"

"She is from Earth," Barach said. "The same as you."

Jeremy's heart pounded a little faster. "Well," he said. "Let's go."

3

"**N**ow, this," Jeremy said with a broad smile, "is more like it."

"What *it*?" Nul asked from his position in the bow of the *Arrow*, a trim little yellow-painted sloop.

Jeremy spread his arms, taking in by implication the sparkling blue sea, the sapphire sky, the taut white canvas. "Sea voyage, Nul," he said, laughing. "Warm weather, a calm ocean, a fast ship—not like the trip north to Twilight Valley, eh?"

Nul wrinkled his furry gray face. "Nah, nah, not like stormy ocean and cold sleet. This a good calm warm ocean. Like crew more, too. Five happy young men, not bunch of cursing old sailors like on *Gull*. Think the *Arrow* a better ship. Not much better, though. Still have fish to eat."

Barach, who had been having a few words with Faskon Kilclaven, the young owner and captain of the *Arrow*, made his way forward. "We're making good time," he said. "It is not yet noon, and before sundown we should be within sight of Gateway Cay." He yawned, clapping a hand over his mouth—which was normally invisible behind his heavy gray beard anyway. "If this craft were large enough to afford a comfortable bed, I'd be in it now. I'm too old to subsist on three hona's sleep."

"I've always heard that you need less sleep as you grow older," Jeremy said.

"Wait and see," Barach growled.

"Anything to eat besides fish?" Nul asked, swinging down from the forward railing.

"If you don't care for the provender, why did you come?" Barach asked.

39

Jeremy grinned. "He likes the company."

"Nah, nah. Just—don't know, itchy. Tired of staying in one place."

"Why, you returned only last week from the Bone Mountains," Barach said. "It occurs to me, Nul, that for a titular king you spend little time with your subjects."

"Nah, nah. Brother Tol king of Zarad-zellikol now, not me. I just—what was word, Jeremy?"

"Ambassador. Nul and I have been teaching each other pikish and English. That's an English word, and we decided that he's the permanent ambassador between humankind and pikas."

"Ya, ya, good word," Nul said. He had taken up his pack, which lay with the others at the foot of the mast, and was rummaging in it. "Pikas need humans, humans need pikas. Hard to make them both see that, but true. Ahh." He had taken something rather like a spongy and gray catcher's mitt from the pack. Breaking off a corner of the mass, he popped it into his mouth. "Good. Want some?"

"What in the world is it?" Barach asked.

"Grayskin mushroom. *Pwikstaga*, we call it. Good pika-food. Brought back from Bone Mountain caverns. Is good. Full of juicy little worms, see?" Nul held up the mushroom, exposing the broken part; in the white flesh of the mushroom a host of frantic threadlike red tails wriggled furiously.

Jeremy's buoyant mood became leaden, sinking as his gorge rose. "Ulp," he said.

Even Barach turned a pale shade of green. He waved away the proffered morsel. "We, ah, wouldn't care for any, thank you."

Nul shrugged. "Is good." Mercifully, he turned away to nibble on his snack while scanning the clear horizon ahead.

Barach swallowed hard. "How he can eat that—"

Jeremy hastened to interrupt: "Uh, Barach, you said last night—this morning, that is—that you'd tell me a little more about this woman."

"So I did. Yet there is little to tell, for few know the Keeper of the Gate at all, and no one knows her well. But you are right; you should know what is before us, for forethought is as good as prescience, they say." Barach leaned on the bow rail for a moment; then, as Jeremy tried hard to concentrate on his words and not on Nul's happy munching sounds, the old wizard began to speak of Gateway Cay and its aloof Keeper.

Gateway Cay, as Barach explained, had always been an uncanny sort of place, and very few people ever lived there. It was farther south and west than the real cays, a string of half a dozen low-lying sandy islands, and it was different from them in nature, being volcanic and rocky. The waters around it were fish-poor, treacherous shoals; the soil was not particularly fertile; and worst of all, there were pockets of magic scattered about the island, magic that the mages believed to be left over from the creation of the world. Unlike human magic, the variety found on the Cay did not require a spell to activate it.

Most of it was harmless; it might temporarily make a person forget where he was, or it might cause his hair to grow at an ungodly rate, or it might alter his perception of time so that a heartbeat would seem like a day, or vice versa. Most of the magic seemed to have a freakish, prankish quality to it, though it operated within very narrow geographical bounds. Some was more serious and more dangerous. But the worst problem of all was a cavern on the side of Storm Mountain, a gaping opening that somehow had trapped the most potent magic of all: it was, indeed, the Gate that eventually gave the island its name.

For as long as human memory could trace, the Gate had been the source of trouble. Anyone standing before it and looking inside would as often as not see merely a luminous whirl of many colors, shapeless and ever-changing. But sometimes, at unpredictable intervals, the colors would shimmer, steady, and for a few moments resolve themselves into alien landscapes, some most beautiful and some most terrible. At such times an onlooker could step through the Gate and emerge not into a normal cavern but into another world.

Or things from other worlds could leak through into Thaumia.

The problem was, of course, that the magic was never still. As Tremien had observed, a Gate to an alien world might hold for a day or more; or it might shimmer to nothing within moments. And if that happened after someone or something had passed through, the visitor would be stranded, for the Gate never seemed to visit the same world twice.

As it happened, not many people from Thaumia ever passed through; the nature of the Gate became known early, and after a few abortive attempts to control the magic had been made by Thaumian wizards, the mages at length contented themselves with guarding the area to make sure that no one slipped into other realities accidentally, and that nothing alien came through to threaten this world.

For the most part, such caution was hardly necessary. Many of the beasts that slipped through the Gate into Thaumia died immediately, asphyxiated by the strange air—which led one to wonder about the fate of those Thaumians who had unwisely stepped into the cavern to other, perhaps suffocating, worlds.

But once in a while, rarely, some animal came through that could live in Thaumia's air: odd birdlike creatures, creeping things, tough insects. And very, very rarely, something rather human would slip through.

That had last happened just about a hundred years ago, with the coming of the Keeper. She had been a young woman then, about twenty years old. At that time there was a tiny colony on Gateway Cay, scratching out a living from cultivating small farms and from doing some hunting.

In fact, a hunter found the girl one morning in a clearing near the Gate. The young woman had been strangely clad and was completely bewildered. She spoke no language that anyone on the island could understand, and since no one there knew enough magic to work a language spell—for in those years the wizard charged with overseeing the Gate lived on the mainland, a day's sail away—she had to learn how to speak Presolatan very slowly.

The hunter and his wife took her in, for they had kind hearts, and their son, who was about the same age as the girl, gradually came to love her. The two were married a year or so later. By then Adelaide (for such was the girl's outlandish name) had learned the language fairly well, and she knew that her chances of returning to Earth were vanishingly small.

For a few years the two of them had an uneventful life: Adelaide bore her husband three children and continued to learn more and more about Thaumia. Finally the wizard who was nominally the guardian of the Gate passed away, and a new one took his place, a man of somewhat more curiosity than his predecessor had been. The new wizard came to the island to examine the Gate, and only when he met Adelaide did her life change; for he sensed in her the potential for great magic.

The islanders thought at the time that it would be rather a good thing to have their own wizard or sorceress. There were fewer than a hundred people there, and life for them was precarious; a magician could help them in many small ways and in some very important ones. Adelaide's husband had no objection, and the new guardian stayed behind on the island to tutor Adelaide, though he had inherited his predecessor's home on the mainland and eventually intended to return there.

Under his instruction, Adelaide learned rapidly. And when some strange creature broke through the Gate, something the size of a horse but with terribly sharp teeth and claws, something that tore apart two men who tried to kill it, she—not her master—captured the beast and tamed it with her magic. The sorcerer announced to the islanders that Adelaide had proved herself worthy of a title, and he gave it to her. From then on she was the Keeper of the Gate; that seemed to be her destiny and her nature, her tutor pronounced, and she was happy enough to assume the responsibility after he returned to his home on Cronbrach.

Years passed. Adelaide, sustained by the life-extending elixir of the eternity plant, a potion that Barach and Tremien also used, saw children grow up, move away, and old folk die. Gradually over the years the colony dwindled to nothing, until at last she was a recluse on the island. She lived there still, attended always by a daughter or a granddaughter or a great-granddaughter; she tutored them in magic, as she herself had been tutored, but none of them ever volunteered to take her place. And so she still kept the Gate herself, protecting Thaumia from anything that might come through it and keeping Thaumians from slipping into other worlds.

There was more to her story: as she had aged, Adelaide had become, well, not evil exactly, but difficult and eccentric. She valued the strange beasts of Thaumia more than most humans did; she saw that over the past generations the number of men had steadily increased and that, concurrently, the number of wild creatures had diminished. Using her magic, the Keeper had called to Gateway Cay many of the unusual beasts of Thaumia; and there they lived under her protection, even the more unpleasant ones. She had become so devoted to her creatures that she tended to resent any human intrusion.

At any rate (Barach concluded), there she was and there the *Arrow* was bound. After a century or more of life on Thaumia, Adelaide regarded the island and the Gate as her special care, almost as her property; and though as an outsider she had never cared to throw in her lot with Tremien and the Council, still she had always been at least cordial toward them. "We may hope," the old mage concluded, "that she will also feel kindly toward you, Jeremy, for you and she come from the same world."

Jeremy nodded. "But we come from different times," he said. "Where, exactly, did she come from? What country, I mean?"

"Alas, that I do not know. She spoke but little of her former life, and little of what she did say has been written in the books of lore."

"Adelaide," Jeremy mused. "It's an English name, anyway. But she's incredibly old by Earth standards; in my world she'd be dead by now. I don't know how well I can communicate with someone from the nineteenth century."

Nul, who had long since finished his snack, said, "You do all right, Jeremy. Then you spell Gate, grab Sebastian, make everything fine again."

"I wish I had your confidence. If no one else has been able to put a spell on the Gate, I don't see how I'm going to do it."

Barach stroked his beard thoughtfully. "As to that, I think it is possible. Your magic is alien, after all, even as the magic of the Gate is. Then, too, there should still be some lingering ties of sympathetic magic which will ease your way to opening a path to Earth."

"Then why didn't Adelaide try to use the Gate to go home? She's from Earth too."

"Ah," Barach said, and possibly he was smiling behind his vast mustache, "she came to love Thaumia, you see. By the time she had gained mastery over her own magic, she was one of us heart and soul. Having no desire to return to Earth, she never made the experiment."

Nul had swung up onto the rail again. "That it?" he asked suddenly.

Jeremy and Barach peered forward. For a few moments Jeremy could see nothing; then he finally made out a dim purple shape on the horizon, an unmoving pinprick against the blue sky. "Looks small," he said.

"It is, rather," Barach said, shading his eyes as he looked to the south and east. "Yes, I see it. That must be Gateway Cay; nothing else in these waters for scores of leagues." He cocked an eye at the sun. "We made very good time indeed. Better than I had hoped."

"I didn't expect it would be so tiny," Jeremy said.

Barach clapped him on the back. "Well, never mind that, my boy. After all, it is said that the bee-catcher, the humblest and smallest of birds, thinks the whole universe lies within the shell of its egg."

"How you know what bird think?" Nul demanded.

"It's a saying," Barach explained. "The bee-catcher lays only one egg a year. If it fails to hatch—"

"Birds don't talk," Nul said. "Not bee-catchers, anyway. Too small—even too small to eat. How know what bird thinks?"

Barach counted to ten. "Never mind about the bee-catcher. But the island, now—it's larger than it seems," he said. "It holds mountains, valleys, and rivers; forests and seashores. And there is the Gate, remember. That means the small island holds worlds within it."

"But bee-catcher egg just hold little bird," Nul said.

"Jeremy," Barach murmured, "did you *have* to tell him he could come along?"

A bloated red sun was almost resting on the western rim of the ocean when the *Arrow*, having threaded its careful way through a maze of tawny sandbars, hove to and dropped anchor a few hundred yards north of a half-moon cove. Jeremy looked shoreward and could make out a low range of dunes, and past them ragged stands of piney trees, their branches tortured into grotesque shapes by the island's winds, their needles blue-green in the dying light of day. Past the trees the land began to rise, first in round-topped hills and then in three conical mountains, the dead volcanoes that had formed the island in ages gone by.

Kilclaven lowered a small boat for his passengers, and

Jeremy, Nul, and Barach descended into it. A grinning, sun-reddened southern boy wielded the oars, shooting them in with the breaking waves. "Holt on, now," he said. "Have t' watch our chance." He raised the dripping oars and the boat bobbed alarmingly on the backs of a couple of waves before he dropped the oars again and took a few hearty pulls.

The little craft shot forward. Its prow scrunched sand; a wave frothed to cream around the stern, rocked them, and withdrew; and the three passengers scrambled out into calf-deep water. Jeremy bent to push the boat away. The boy at the oars nodded his thanks, pulled hard again, and shouted, "Our next call can be in ten days. Be headin' back south then, could stop here and pick you up then if you want. We'll stop, anyhow; maybe Herself'll want summat of the goods we're pickin' up northwards. Farewell, now!"

Jeremy waved good-bye, then waded to shore, where his companions waited for him. "Now what?"

"Now we find the path that Kilclaven says leads up to the cottage," Barach said. "And we'd best hurry; it's a good walk, and we've not much light left."

Indeed, the sun was just disappearing from view. Jeremy watched the last bright bit of it vanish, leaving the west afire with red afterglow, and then he shouldered his pack and followed Barach over the dunes.

A small stream meandered inland from the head of the cove, its banks lined with the pinelike trees. The path Barach sought paralleled the stream for a hundred yards before veering away to the left, through yet more trees. Strident insects chirred and buzzed in them, a chaotic symphony of jungle music. The scents were strange too, exotic airs perfumed with the balsam of unknown leaves, spicy-sweet or sharply pungent. By the time they had left the roaring of the waves behind them, the sky had deepened to violet. Sometime later, when they had climbed a rolling hill and had come to a clearing, a few stars winked overhead.

"A little light, if you please, Jeremy," Barach said. "But not a great deal."

Jeremy thought, modified his personal cantrip for wizardlight, and spoke a spell that produced a soft glow, more like a slightly more intense moonlight than like the beam from a flashlight, that traveled with them, and illuminated their way.

Their path led over the crest of the hill, down into a shallow valley, and up another hillside. Gradually the twisted piney trees gave way to other kinds, taller and straighter, and the sandy path became lined on either side with waist-high scrub growth, thick-leaved succulents and bayonet-bristling plants resembling palmettos. "How much farther?" Nul huffed as they toiled up still another hillside.

"A good way," Barach said. "I have never visited the Keeper myself, but the maps are reliable ones. There should be a hardwood forest next, then a clearing, then more woods, and in the next clearing we'll find the cottage."

"In middle of night," Nul grumbled.

"Come on. Mend your pace and it won't seem so long," Barach said.

They passed through what felt like a barrier of clinging cobwebs, and Jeremy caught his breath at a sudden fall in temperature. "That was magic," he said.

"Mm, yes," Barach agreed. "The island's become something of a wildlife preserve, you know; the Keeper adjusts portions of it to suit different kinds of animals. Notice the trees."

"Hardwoods," Jeremy said, squinting up at the leaves reflecting the dim wizard-light. "Looks more like a northern forest."

"And it was meant to. Come along, though—no time for sightseeing."

The path descended again. The moon, past full but still large, had risen in the east, though they caught only intermittent glimpses of it through the trees. But then the trees fell away and they stepped into a round bowl-like valley, blue with moonlight. Round boulders had shouldered through the grass here, and they shone like silver; and in the center of the valley, almost perfectly round, was a shimmering pool.

Nul, behind Jeremy, hissed. "*Kirana!*" he whispered.

Barach stopped so suddenly that Jeremy blundered into him. "Where?" Barach whispered back, ignoring the impact.

"Pool. One, two, three—many of them. Nine or ten. See, past three big rocks?"

Jeremy strained his eyes. He could see three house-size boulders all right, and the pond beyond them with more boulders scattered in its shallow water, but that was all. Of course, his eyes, unlike Nul's, were not accustomed to the dimness of underground life—but that could be remedied. He whispered an amendment to his earlier spell, and the wizard-light brightened.

"No," Barach warned, but too late.

Jeremy gasped. "Unicorns," he said, utterly enchanted.

The animals, which Jeremy had mistaken in the dark for stones in the water, turned their heads and pricked their ears toward the intruders. They were like horned horses—but only to the degree that a gazelle is like a water buffalo. In the sudden light they shone like mother-of-pearl, achingly beautiful; their dainty heads and large liquid eyes, their pointed ears, their impossibly delicate legs, all made them unearthly. But their horns, easily a foot and a half long, spiraled, white—their horns seemed luminous of themselves, shedding light like snowflakes as they tossed their heads and—

Charged!

"Quick!" Barach yelled, dragging Jeremy back.

Jeremy stumbled after him. Behind him he heard snorts of rage and a pounding of hoofbeats. Ahead of him he saw Nul reach a tree, go straight up the trunk, and swing out onto a low branch. "Hurry!" Nul yelled at them.

Barach, for all his girth, reached the tree ahead of Jeremy. With a leap he just managed to grasp the base of the branch that Nul occupied, and the pika gave him a hand up. Jeremy jumped and missed.

The unicorns had closed in. One of them lunged at Jeremy, and he barely evaded the horn, which scored a deep gash in the bark of the tree. The unicorn's teeth champed at him, and Jeremy yelped as they closed on the flesh of his right forearm. With this encourgement, Jeremy managed on the second try to leap high enough to grasp the branch and pull himself up—and not a second too soon, for another unicorn embedded its horn in the tree not a foot beneath him.

"Higher!" Barach said from overhead. "And no magic! That's important—no magic, do you hear?"

Jeremy hugged the trunk and pulled himself up two more branches. Here, where the tree divided, he found Nul and Barach, each seated on one of the main branches. Jeremy had to stand on a lower limb, his arms thrown over the crotch of the tree. Below him the unicorns snarled, but they couldn't even come close to his feet. "Damn," Jeremy panted. "My arm's bleeding."

"Stay still," Barach ordered. He bent close to take a look—the wizard-light had followed the three into the tree, it seemed—and grunted. "Well, you've lost a finger-wide chunk of flesh," he said, "but it isn't too bad. I can't get to the medicines in my pack, so I'd suggest a little spell to stanch the blood."

"But you said no magic."

Barach teetered back upright. "It is a very small spell, and a helpful one. I do not think it would disturb the Keeper."

Perched precariously in a tree as he was, Jeremy found the three-stage process of magic more difficult than usual, but at last he managed to formulate, visualize, and realize a sort of healing spell. It lessened the pain, at any rate, and stopped the warm trickle of blood down his forearm.

"Wish I had bow," Nul grunted. "Or spear."

"Why did they attack us?" Jeremy asked.

"*Kirana* always do that," Nul said. "Dangerous things. Eat grass when they have to; eat meat when they can spear it. Pika meat, human meat, makes no difference."

"Go away!" Jeremy bawled, but the unicorns showed no interest in leaving. The nine of them, a larger one that Jeremy guessed was the stallion, five smaller mares, and three young ones, circled the tree, snuffling and snarling. One of them reared and scraped its tiny, sharp, cloven front hooves on the tree trunk, shaving two curled parings of bark right off. "Why can't I use magic on them?" Jeremy asked Barach.

"Because they're protected by the Keeper," Barach explained. "She's surrounded this whole area with a protective spell; no telling what the clash of forces might do."

"We can't stay up here all night."

"Watch me," Barach said.

The unicorns settled down around the tree trunk below, except for two, which endlessly circled them. Jeremy, looking down, was reminded more of a pride of lions than a herd of horses. "These things are carnivorous?" he asked Barach.

"Oh, yes. They used to be very numerous in Arkhedden Forest; they preyed on the smaller animals there. But when the foresters came, the unicorns had no fear of them and attacked them. So of course they were hunted out. They still live in small groups in the more northerly woods along the Old Forest Road from Jalot down to Forest Town, but they are much fewer in number than in the old days."

Jeremy rubbed his arm, which had stopped bleeding completely but which had begun to ache with a dull pang that magic could not fully ease. The beast had taken a semicircle of flesh from his right forearm three inches below the elbow. It was a shallow bite, taking mostly skin. Clearly, though, had the animal's aim been a little better, Jeremy would have been badly damaged by the wicked teeth.

The moon climbed higher, dappling them with light shining through the canopy of leaves. Jeremy's legs began to ache, then to tremble. "I can't take this," he grunted.

Barach was more or less reclining on his branch, his hands clasped over his considerable belly. "Perhaps Nul could go a little higher up his limb," he said. "Then you could at least climb up into the divide and take the weight off your legs."

"Nul try," said the pika. Cautiously he began to edge upward, hugging the huge branch. Now that the excitement of the attack had worn off, Nul was very slow in his movements, for pikas are not by nature climbers of trees. But his spidery limbs stood him in good stead as he found handholds and lodgments for his feet. After a few moments he had crept about ten feet up the branch, coming to another major division, where he was able to lie back fairly securely.

Barach gave Jeremy a hand up. Jeremy scrambled into the crotch of the tree, coming to a rest as though in the world's most uncomfortable saddle, his legs splayed apart by the branches, the rough bark of the tree against his back, his backpack resting uneasily against the rising branch. "Look, couldn't I set some twigs afire and—"

"No," Barach said. "We cannot begin by antagonizing the Keeper, not if we expect any help from her. We'll simply have to wait them out. They'll grow tired of lurking about sooner or later and move on in search of easier prey."

"Meanwhile," Jeremy said miserably, "how do I go to the bathroom?"

The night was long and sleepless, the unicorns uncommonly vigilant. The moon slipped down the sky and paled with the coming of dawn; and by the time the sun was well up, the unicorns were too, browsing on the grass around the tree but showing no disposition to leave.

"This is ridiculous," Jeremy grunted.

Barach, who despite his dishevelment managed to look comfortably at ease, said, "I agree. But, unfortunately, the unicorns have no sense of the absurd."

"Someone coming," gasped Nul, who had begun to complain of dizziness as soon as the day had become bright enough to show him just how high they were in the tree. "From that way."

Jeremy followed his gaze. Through the intervening leaves he could glimpse a grassy hillside a quarter-mile away or more, and through it indeed someone—or something—was moving; but the dense yellow-green grass was five feet high or more, and it was impossible for him to see what was disturbing it in passing.

"The unicorns appear to have noticed too," Barach observed.

Jeremy glanced down. All nine animals were on their feet, heads low, bodies tense, quivering nostrils pointing toward the grassy hillside. Then eight of them bolted, running away from the tree, back down toward the pond, around the edge of the water, and off into the forest. The remaining unicorn, the one Jeremy supposed was the male, growled and shook his horn menacingly.

Glancing up, Jeremy saw a flash of color—someone dressed in blue, he realized—and almost at the same time he heard a clear, high voice, a girl's voice: "Who's there, please?"

"Look out!" Jeremy shouted. "There's a—"

The girl stepped into sight under the tree. Her face, turned upward, was sweet and pretty, with wide blue eyes and full lips. "Look out!" Jeremy yelled again.

The unicorn screamed and charged toward the girl—

"Oh, go 'way," she said, and slapped it resoundingly on the nose.

The beast shrilled out in alarm, whirled with the quickness of a cat, and fled after the vanished herd. Jeremy looked at Barach, who raised one bushy eyebrow at him.

From beneath the tree the girl called up, "Are you all right?"

"Uh—yes," Jeremy said. "Mostly."

"Well, do you want to come down, then?"

Jeremy swung his right leg over the tree branch and found his muscles prickling with pins and needles. "I suppose so," he said. "But it's awfully comfortable up here."

The girl's brow wrinkled. "Is it really?"

The bark abraded Jeremy's cheek as he carefully lowered himself down to the next branch. "Ugh. Oh, yes . . ." he puffed. "I think soon everybody's going to be spending—ugh—the night in trees. Is my foot anywhere near the limb?"

"You're teasing, I can tell. Move your foot toward me. Yes, a little more. There, that's it. Who are you?"

"Visitors," Jeremy said. "We've come—oops!—to see the Keeper of the Gate." He perched on the lowest branch for a moment and then jumped the eight feet to the ground, coming down hard with an ankle-twisting flare of pain. Groaning, he got back to his feet and tottered against the trunk. "Careful," he called up to Barach.

The old mage was already down to the lower limb. He paused a moment, sizing up the drop, and then swung adeptly down, dropping neatly onto his feet. "Nothing to it, my boy. Nul?"

"Coming," said the pika.

"Oh—what is that? What kind of animal?" the girl asked, staring up at Nul.

"A pika," Jeremy said.

"Peek-ah?" the girl asked, getting it nearly right.

"Yes. And he's not an animal. More of a furry person. His name is Nul."

"Oh, I'm sure that Grammy will want to see him. He's so different."

"Help!" wailed Nul from the crotch of the tree, where he had seemingly become stuck.

"Ah, my dear, we have not been introduced," Barach said. "I am Mage Barach, Loremaster; this is my pupil, Mage Jeremy Moon of Earth; and as you heard—"

"Earth? The same place that Grammy came from?" the girl asked, her blue eyes growing round with wonder.

"Yes, child. And as you heard, that is Nul the pika above us; now, if you believe your, ah, Grammy wouldn't mind, perhaps Jeremy could just use a bit of magic to help Nul down."

"Oh, I'm sure it would be all right, as long as it doesn't harm her animals."

"I'll be careful," Jeremy promised. "Nul!" he shouted. "Grab a leaf!"

The pika extended one trembling three-fingered hand and plucked a single leaf from a nearby twig. "Got leaf. Now what?"

"Wait a second." Jeremy quickly formulated and visualized a bit of magic; then he said in English, "Never be stuck in a tree again! Not with Wonder-Leaf, the world's smallest parachute! Wonder-Leaf floats you gently to the ground. It's so much fun you'll get stuck on purpose!"

"Leaf feel funny," Nul complained.

In Presolatan, Jeremy called, "It's supposed to. Hold tight to the leaf and try slipping down the tree."

Nul took an audible deep breath before making the attempt. But once he started down, he began to laugh in his strange urfing chuckle; and after a moment he pushed completely away from the trunk. He floated to the clearing as gently as a descending soap bubble, suspended from the tiny leaf.

The girl clapped her hands, delight dancing in her smile. "Oh, how nice," she said. "Could I try once, please?"

Despite himself, Jeremy grinned at her. She had chestnut hair, cut rather short, and a berry-brown face, and she was so enthusiastic . . . "Well, maybe once," Jeremy said.

Nul gave her the leaf, and she scrambled right up the tree, quick as a monkey, the blue fabric of her blouse and trousers soon disappearing into the leaves. "Here I come!" A moment later she came floating back into view, giggling and swinging her legs.

"Now," Barach said when she had landed again, "I've told you our names. Perhaps you should—"

"Oh, I'm sorry," the girl said. "I'm Regina. This morning Grandmama—well, she's really my great-great-grandmama, but that's rather a lot to say, so I just call her Grandmama—knew you were coming and sent me to find you and bring you home. So if you're ready, we can start. May I keep the leaf?"

"Please," Nul said. "Nul not want to be up tree again soon."

She thanked him and laughed again. Barach insisted on

treating Jeremy's bite, though now it was little more than a black U-shaped mark. Regina watched the mage apply a healing poultice with keen interest; then she led the way back up the grassy hillside. "Regina," Jeremy said as they walked, "how did your grandmother know that we were in the tree?"

"The book told her," Regina said simply.

"Oh," Jeremy said, as mystified as ever.

"Of course the unicorns have been naughty. Grandmama is working on a way to strengthen her spell over them now. The night before last they pushed through their wards, got into the hen yard, and killed two of our chickens."

"You don't seem afraid of them, though."

Regina gave him a coy, blushing look back over her shoulder. " 'Course not, silly. I'm a virgin," she said.

"Oh, uh—sure," Jeremy stammered.

"They never bother virgins. So I guess that means none of you—"

Barach coughed. Jeremy looked back at Nul. Nul grinned and shrugged, his orange eyes suspiciously pale in a pikish blush. "Guess not," Jeremy said. "But anyway, *I'm* married."

Regina giggled. From there on they walked in silence. Before long Jeremy shivered as they passed through another magical barrier and the climate altered itself again, becoming cool and damp, the air rich with the smell of imminent rain, though the sky overhead remained clear.

The cottage was on a green knoll in a little grove of very Earthlike oak trees, a neat and compact two-story house, the top floor half-timbered, the ground floor gray stone, the roof thickly thatched with golden straw. "Looks English," Jeremy said as they crossed the lawn.

"Grandmama's that. English," Regina said. "She's teaching me some of the language. Good for spells, you know. Was that spell you spoke an English one? 'Cause I thought I recognized some words. 'Leaf' and 'tree' and 'ground.' Those are English words, aren't they? Am I saying them right?"

"Yes, just right."

"Grandmama says I never listen well enough. But it's a hard language. Here we are." Regina opened the door—it had no lock, but in a land of magic, few doors did if they belonged to an accomplished magician's house—and the three travelers entered a cool, dim hallway. Jeremy had no sooner stepped over the threshold before he heard a curious dry hissing at his feet. He glanced down and yelped as he leapt backward, colliding with Barach.

"It's only Redfellow," Regina said, stooping to pick up the five-foot snake. It was a brilliant red, sleek and glistening, and it immediately coiled around her arm in comfortable loops. Its bright eyes regarded them coldly, and a blue-black tongue flickered from the lipless mouth. "He's harmless. Grandmama found him injured, didn't she, Reddy?" She kissed the top of the triangular head.

"Remarkable," Barach said. "A red viper. Most deadly."

"Only if they're surprised or frightened." Regina let the reptile slip to the floor again. It slithered under a tall bookcase against the left wall, its tail still protruding a foot or so. "Redfellow is very friendly. He wouldn't dream of biting anyone. Just don't step on him and you'll be fine."

"Ah—perhaps you'd better go first," Jeremy told Barach. The old mage stepped carefully to the other wall of the hallway and edged his way past the bookshelf, with Jeremy and Nul following in his footsteps.

"Grandmama will receive you in the parlor," Regina said. "That's the second door on the left."

Jeremy coughed as Regina opened the door. "Any wildlife in there?"

"I don't know. I suppose there may be. There generally are a few about. Just a moment." Regina stuck her head into the room and whistled.

A fat gray hare hopped out, looked up at her, looked at the visitors, scratched its chin vigorously with its long right hind foot, wriggled its pink-lined ears, and lolloped away past the bookcase, ignoring the snake. Jeremy caught his breath and ducked as something—a small gray bat—fluttered out of the doorway; but it found its way to a ceiling beam, locked its feet into it, and hung there. After one enormous yawn the animal wrapped its leathery wings about its body and, to all appearances, fell asleep.

"Is that all?" Regina asked, surveying the room from the doorway. When nothing else appeared, she said, "I suppose so. Grandmama will be with you shortly. She won't let me stay—I've got to go and milk the cow and keep the unicorns shooed away from the chickens until she finishes her spell. 'Bye."

"What a charming child," Barach said as they entered the parlor.

"Very nice. But . . . are all teenage girls that talkative?" Jeremy asked.

"I don't know," Barach returned. "Wait a dozen years and then see how your Emily is."

Jeremy grimaced. "That's what I was afraid you'd say." He looked carefully about him, but there were no animals in sight.

"Food!" Nul cried in delight.

The room was pleasantly light—three tall, narrow windows looked out onto the grove of trees and a meadow beyond them—and furnished with tall-backed chairs, several small tables, and, near the center, a larger table with breakfast laid out on it. Jeremy's mouth began to water at the sight of the assortment of cheeses, the round loaf of sweet bread, the creamy butter in a round dish, a tall glass pitcher of milk, its sides beaded with condensation, and several pots of jam. "We did miss a meal," he said. "But perhaps we had better wait for—"

A tap at the window made him start. Regina was outside; she gestured for him to raise the sash. He did, letting the fresh morning air into the room. " 'Scuse me," she said. "I forgot to tell you, Grandmama said go ahead and eat. She'll be with you as soon as she works out her spell." She waved, then skipped away toward some outbuildings that Jeremy could just glimpse off to the right.

"Well," he said, turning, "did you hear—"

"Pass cheese," Nul said, his mouth already full.

Their meal was interrupted once, briefly, when a fat green frog came hopping out from under Nul's chair, startling Jeremy for a moment. But the frog paid them no attention, stretched its hind legs elaborately, and then plopped its way out the open door and into the hallway, sounding like a pouch of wet sand continuously dropped along the way.

"Hope snake not hungry," Nul said with a grin.

"I suppose the animals are all under some sort of amity spell," Barach said. "Otherwise they wouldn't be within yards of each other."

"I hope they're friendly toward humans," Jeremy growled.

"Oh, they are." It was an old voice, a woman's voice, but

bright and chipper. Jeremy and Barach rose from their places; Nul, whose short legs could not reach the floor from where he sat, merely reached for another slice of bread.

The woman came in, poking stray tendrils of pure white hair into some sort of order beneath her bonnet. She was withered as a winter apple, but her eyes were startling and bright, a porcelain blue, and her movements were all bustle and energy. Jeremy smiled as she came in, a chubby, tiny woman, unsmiling but obviously friendly. "Those unicorns," she sighed. "Never satisfied with what they have. I suppose you are no different."

"I trust we may prove you mistaken, madam," Barach replied. "We are—"

"Tush, I know you all," the woman said. "You are Barach Loremaster, now of Whitehorn Keep; this is Jeremy Moon, your student in magic; and there is Nul, the king of the pikas who live in the Bone Mountain caverns of Zaradzellikol. You've come to ask me about that beastly Gate, which you need to deal with the Great Dark One—his real name is Jilhukrihain, or used to be—I think self-given titles are dreadfully vulgar—"

Barach gave Jeremy a baffled glance. Jeremy coughed. "Uh, excuse me—you are Adelaide, the Keeper of the Gate?"

"Well, of course, young man. Honestly, I don't know whether it's at all wise for you to meddle with the wretched Gate. Of course, I could ask the book, but then, that's so dreadfully limiting, you know—"

"Ma'am?" Jeremy asked in a small voice. Adelaide reminded him rather uncomfortably of Miss Ada Gold, his third-grade teacher. "If you don't mind, may I ask how you knew about us?"

"The book told me, of course," Adelaide said with a tiny frown. "It also told me you're from Earth. I suppose that's true?"

"Yes, it's true. But I've lived in Thaumia for—"

"Tell me," Adelaide said in English with an impeccable upper-class British accent, "how is the dear old Queen?"

For a moment Jeremy was so startled that he could not reply. Then he said, "The Queen of England? She's quite well, or was the last I heard."

"Oh," Adelaide said in a tone of mild disaappointment. "You are an American."

"Well, yes—"

"Dear me, what am I thinking? Surely Victoria must be dead by now."

"Uh, yes, ma'am. But Elizabeth is on the throne, and—"

The porcelain-blue eyes became sharp. "Pray do not trifle with me, young man. You cannot be from Elizabethan times; why, the red Indians held your country then."

"Not Elizabeth I," Jeremy said. "Elizabeth II. She—"

"Ah, I understand now. And the Empire?" Adelaide asked. "How does it fare?"

Jeremy swallowed and looked at Barach; but Barach, who knew no English, merely shrugged. "Uh, well, things are proceeding as they have, uh, in years gone past." With a sudden inspiration, Jeremy said, "Some years ago there were two wars—world wars. And, uh, the United States and Great Britain were allies in fighting them—"

"Whom were they fighting, young man?"

"Ah, Germany and—"

"Those dreadful people. My father thought it would come to that in the end," Adelaide sniffed. "I suppose we won?"

"Yes, and . . . and Great Britain and the United States have been the best of friends ever since." Jeremy smiled hopefully.

"How nice." But there was no delight in her voice.

In Presolatan, Barach murmured, "I hate to interrupt, madam, but our mission is most urgent. Yet I would like to know more of the book that told you of our coming, for I was once a rather good magician myself, and its lore still interests me."

"Ah," Adelaide said. "The book came from your home, in fact, about two or three years ago. It seems you cast it out—"

"I, madam?"

"No, not you, Barach. Your pupil there. Gave it life of a sort and then"—she sniffed again—"ignored it. So of course it came to Gateway Cay; all living things in trouble seem to have an instinct for this place."

"Oh, my word," Barach said, turning to Jeremy. "Your first spell!"

Jeremy, who had been trying hard to follow the conversation, nodded. He remembered very well that cold evening in his tower room when, new to the study of magic, he had attempted to levitate a heavy book of magic and had, instead, animated it. It had broken through a window and had gone flapping off through the night like some ungainly bird. "I didn't mean to abandon it," he said humbly enough. "It's just that the spell was a poor one."

"I should think so. Well, it has found a home here; I don't suppose you should care to reclaim it now?"

"Oh, no. It, uh, is welcome to stay here. On my part, I mean."

"That's as it should be. It is quite dangerous now, you know."

Barach frowned. "Dangerous?"

"Oh, yes. You shall see it for yourselves. However; the question, I believe, was about the wretched Gate. I shall have to think about that and perhaps even consult the book. Please make yourselves comfortable until I return."

Adelaide turned to go. Before she reached the door, Jeremy said, "If I may ask a question—you came here when? I mean, when in Earth terms?"

Adelaide regarded him with her grave, unsmiling face. "That sounds like impertinence."

"It isn't meant to be."

"Perhaps not. I remember it well; it was in August 1890. One fortnight before my one-and-twentieth birthday. I recall thinking how dreary it was to be an adult."

Jeremy blinked. "Then you were born—"

"In September 1869." For the first time Adelaide smiled, her bright eyes twinkling in impish mirth. "I was correct, young man; your question was impertinent. Never ask a lady her age."

Then she was gone, leaving the door ajar behind her. Almost at once a cat came into the room. More properly, it flew in.

Jeremy cried out in astonishment as the long-haired gray tabby fluttered in from the hallway; on wings beating almost as fast as a hummingbird's, it circled the room twice, a foot below the ceiling, and then it dropped almost noiselessly onto the table. The wings—they were batlike and lightly furred—folded themselves along the cat's back, the animal stretched once, and then it contentedly began to nibble a wedge of cheese.

Even Nul looked surprised. "Enchanted kitty," he said.

Barach tilted his head. "Yes, I should think so. Perhaps the work of Bowenchild of Darkheath; he has always gone in for the more difficult enchantments of living flesh. Here, puss, puss."

The cat stepped delicately around the dishes remaining on the table and submitted to having her chin scratched while she purred in contentment. "Friendly little creature," Barach observed.

"I suppose she keeps the bats under control," Jeremy said. "Why in the name of God would anyone make a flying cat?"

"There is no practical use that I can see," Barach said. "Curiosity, perhaps. The mere urge to learn whether it could be done."

The cat had settled down at the corner of the table to wash herself. She nibbled delicately at the membrane of her right wing, then licked it clean with vigorous attention. "Wonder if there others?" Nul muttered.

"Probably not," Barach said. "I'm almost certain that puss, here, is a product of sorcery. Changing living creatures is the most difficult magic of all—and, as you know, a spell works only once. I should judge that the cat is just an experiment, as it were; perhaps a dry run for a Great Spell designed to produce, oh, a flying horse, or a race of them."

The cat, having finished her washing, leapt lightly to the floor and padded to the window. She jumped up to the sill, looked over her shoulder, and meowed in an expectant tone. "Think it want out," Nul said.

"Should we?" Jeremy asked.

"I don't see why not." Barach opened the sash a little wider, and the cat took to the air, gaining altitude and finally vanishing above the oaks. "I hardly think," the mage said as he turned from the open window, "that a cat of that sort is likely to be a house pet."

They waited for what seemed a long time, undisturbed by frogs, snakes, bats, or cats. At last they heard a step in the hall, and Adelaide herself returned. Under her arm she carried a heavy brown leather-bound book. Jeremy recognized it at once: it was the one he had enchanted.

"You have met Alice," Adelaide observed, looking at the open window.

Barach, who had risen, raised his eyebrows. "Alice?"

"Yes, the unfortunate cat. I named her after the child in the Reverend Dodgson's book—tumbled into Wonderland, you know, through no fault of her own. I think people who enchant things should take responsibility for their work. Don't you, Mr. Moon?"

Jeremy blushed as she gravely laid the book on the table. "If there is anything I could do—"

"Tush, it's enough that you will leave the book with me. It is far too dangerous to be allowed into the world. Unlike poor harmless little Alice, who flew here bedraggled and miserable late one cold winter's night, poor little creature. Honestly, the thoughtlessness of some sorcerers passes human understanding."

"Excuse me," Barach said. "But why is the book so dangerous? It is only a treatise on transmutations."

"Perhaps it used to be that," Adelaide sniffed. "But it has grown into something quite different. Open the book, Mr. Moon. To any page you please."

Puzzled, he did as he was asked, turning to about the middle of the tome. He glanced at the page and blinked.

Hello, Jeremy, it said.

"What in the—"

"No!" Adelaide cried aloud. "For your life, do not ask a question now."

Jeremy's eyes grew wide. A page had turned in the light breeze from the window. Now he read: *Ask no questions of me. Listen to thy hostess; do not question.* And the next words were in red italics: *It could cost thee thy life!*

4

"It can answer any question you put to it," Adelaide said, her delicate boned right hand resting on the brown leather cover of the book, lying closed now on the table. "And it seems happy to do so. But the problem is that any answer you receive becomes irrevocable."

Adelaide had been explaining the book's nature to them, and Barach, listening with fierce attention, seemed very impressed indeed. "Extraordinary," he said. "Then if one should consult the book on some matter of the future—even something trivial, say, such as whether or not one should undertake a journey—then the answer, once read, would become fate?"

"Precisely so," Adelaide replied. "To use your example, a spice merchant might ask the book, 'Shall I journey to Akrador in search of Vaclafan pepper?' To which the book might reply, 'Thou shalt, but thou must die on the journey thither.' Then what the book says will inevitably happen, no matter how the merchant would struggle to avoid such a destiny."

Jeremy asked, "But what if he doesn't struggle at all? I mean, what if the merchant simply decides not to take the trip to Akrador in the first place?"

"Then circumstances will arrange themselves so that he must travel, whether he will or no; perhaps his entire business will seem to depend on the journey, or perhaps he will be kidnapped and taken to Akrador by desert nomads who have no knowledge at all of the prophecy. He simply has no choice in the matter, once the question has been asked. Perhaps you are familiar with the *Oedipus Tyrannus* of Sophocles, young man?"

"I read it in college," Jeremy said.

"Not, I daresay, in the original Greek."

"Well, no. . . ."

"My father never approved of the American approach to education. He saw to it that my brothers and I had a thorough grounding in the classics."

"I have to admit that I read it in translation. Nevertheless, I do know the play. You were referring to its theme: the futility of human endeavor in the face of destiny."

"Yes, though that is a rather vulgar reduction of the dramatist's philosophy. However, the tragedy of Oedipus becomes the tragedy of anyone who questions the book and reads the answer—perhaps doubly tragic, in that the questioner knows his inevitable fate, whereas until the *peripeteia*, Oedipus did not."

Jeremy regarded the book dubiously. "I suppose I'll have to take your word about it. But what if the question had never been asked?"

"In that case, the merchant would still have free will to undertake the journey or not, as he pleased. The future is not fated until it is known."

Barach stroked his beard. "Some learned philosophers of magic would dispute that notion, madam. They say that the great wizard-duel of Cardamon and Stelidos was fought on the question of predestination and freedom of will. If Stelidos was correct—if our apparently free decisions are secretly fated after all—then perhaps the book merely made the merchant's doom known; perhaps the merchant never had the freedom of choice."

Adelaide undid the bow at her chin and carefully removed her dark blue bonnet. Her hair beneath it, parted in the center and done into a neat bun in back, was a pure, snowy white. "Certainly he did. The man who sent the book to me asked that very question of it before he parted with it. The book told the man that the future is unsettled before being foreseen, and so it must be, for the book does not lie. Not that the answer did the poor man any good at all. He is dead now, of course."

"Does every person who ask book question die?" Nul asked, sounding a little uneasy.

"No; but several have. The book has come into the possession of many people in the past year or so; and generally each new owner has been all too happy to part with it. At last someone had the wit to send it here to me, where it would be safe. I have but little interest in knowing anything whatever about the future."

Adelaide took her hand off the volume, and it immediately opened of its own volition. Jeremy could read, upsidedown, what the page said: *I do not seek to do evil. But I am compelled to tell the truth.*

"I understand the book belonged to you originally, Mage Barach," Adelaide said, rather pointedly ignoring the words on the parchment-colored leaf. "Now I must ask you a most serious question; pray consider it carefully. Do you wish to reclaim your property?" Her blue eyes were very direct, very challenging.

"God forbid," Barach said, his manner equally grave. "I fear such uncanny magic as it now has, and, lacking in *mana* as I now am, I should surely be tempted into making use of it. No, let the book rest here on Gateway Cay, for I gladly renounce any claim I might have to it. Tend it well, and may it be safe from prying eyes."

Jeremy leaned across the table and tugged at Barach's sleeve. "We could use it."

"No, we could not." Barach's tone left no room for argument. "If we should ask it how to retrieve Sebastian, for example, then it might answer that we could not do so. Or should we ask it whom the Great Dark One now possesses, it might respond that we could not find out until it is too late to stop him. No, thank you; if our destiny is an evil one at last, I would prefer to strive toward it of my own will and in ignorance."

Chastened, Jeremy said, "Perhaps you had better put the book away, ma'am."

"And so I shall," Adelaide said. "But I brought it because it has something to tell you."

"Me?" Jeremy's mouth was suddenly dry. "Uh . . . maybe I'd better not."

"Nonsense. It feels—well, I do not know whether it feels or not, properly speaking, but at any rate it does seem to be able to think—and it thinks itself indebted to you for the spell which gave it this odd sort of consciousness. The message it wishes to communicate is something given freely and in response to no question; and therefore it is not binding.

But it seems to be advice you need, and so I would have you read it." She turned the book around so that Jeremy saw it right-side-up, and immediately a page turned as of its own volition. "Read," Adelaide said.

Jeremy read: *Be warned: when two who are one share common space, the magical pressures build rapidly. Three stormy days will be the uttermost limit; after that the one must become two.* A page turned of itself, and the next leaf bore heavy black letters: *Great evil has been awakened from long sleep. Magic flows into the Shadow Guards as water into a chalice. Beware their thirst. Beware him who drinks from their cup! Most of all, beware thyself.*

Again, a page turned without Jeremy's touching it. The new page was scribed with letters less imposing: *In thy great need, summon the heroes who shaped thy life. Against true belief, not even the Shadow Guards can stand: lose not thy faith, or thy life and all thou lovest are likewise lost.* As soon as Jeremy read the last word, the book closed with a snap.

"There. It seems to be finished," Adelaide said. "I must say, your book has been troublesome. It flew, literally flew, from its shelf last night and opened itself before me, telling me of your coming and insisting that you must have a look at it when you arrived. It was most adamant that you should receive that message, young man; I hope that you shall profit from it."

Jeremy swallowed. "I'll try," he said.

"See that you do. Now, the other matter: the Gate. Pray tell me, why should you be allowed to meddle with that great and ancient magic, seeing the mischief you have already caused with a mere book?"

Barach stepped in: "Madam, Jeremy did not intend to alter the book in such a manner. The change occurred just as my apprentice was beginning to learn about magic and its dangers. It was an accident of too much magical potential coupled with the recklessness of youth."

"He is not so very young," Adelaide said. "Not so young as I when the Gate's magic brought me here."

Jeremy began, "But—"

"Still, he is an American," Adelaide continued imperturbably. "I suppose one must make allowances. See here, young man, what do you know of my mission?"

Barach gave Jeremy a lowering look that meant *be careful*. Jeremy thought for a moment. "I know that you care for the living things of Thaumia," he said. "That when no one else will protect them, give them shelter, or see to their needs, you will do so."

Adelaide nodded her white head. "And so you should if you took a bit of thought before you acted." She sighed. "My father was the vicar of Banbridge Wells," she said. "That is a small village; you will not have heard of it, but it is quite near Oxford. He was rather a stern man, and I fear he did not understand the heart of a young woman."

"Excuse me," Jeremy said, "but what does that have to do with—"

"A dreamer," Adelaide said. "That is what he called me; and he often warned me that life was an earnest pursuit, that only a serious young woman could hope to deal with it properly.

"I, on the other hand, trusted my fancy more than I did Father's hardheaded realism." She paused and appeared to muse on something for a moment. "I suppose that is what I liked about the Reverend Dodgson. He was not, in many ways, a pleasant sort of person. He stammered most dreadfully, and he once asked Mama if he might pose me for—well, for indecent photographs. But he did tell the most marvelous stories."

"*Alice in Wonderland*," Jeremy said suddenly. "I'd forgotten. Charles Lutwidge Dodgson wrote the book as Lewis Carroll."

"That was his *nom de plume*," Adelaide said. "So you do know of the book?"

"It . . . it's a classic," Jeremy said. "The whole world knows about it. There have been movies and—"

"Movies?" Adelaide frowned. "I do not believe I am familiar with the term."

"Movies are sort of like photographed plays. People go to dark auditoriums to see them projected on a screen, like—ah, like magic lantern slides. But they're brightly colored, and they move and talk—"

"Moving and talking photographs? It sounds perfectly dreadful. I cannot think that an author would care to have his work thrown on a screen in such a manner."

"Well, yes, you have a point—but *my* point is that the

Alice books have become classics, that Dodgson is probably more celebrated today than he was in your time."

For the second time Adelaide smiled, but the expression was perfunctory. "How nice for him. However, as I was saying, I cared very little for the man, aside from his marvelous stores. Stories of gryphons and unicorns and jabberwocks and snarks. The beasts of the mind, do you see? Many a summer's afternoon I sat enthralled as the Reverend Dodgson spoke of such wonderful creatures. And so when I came here, when I found the originals of the beasts he had made me love, why, of course I became their protector."

"I understand," Jeremy said. He glanced at Barach and Nul, who stared at him with polite bafflement. Jeremy realized that he and Adelaide had lapsed into English. With a conscious effort he changed to Presolatan: "And your love of the beasts of Thaumia, your desire to protect them from harm, are the very reasons you should help us reach the Gate."

The smile vanished, replaced by a cool patrician aloofness. "You may explain."

"Well, I have met the Great Dark One. He is a master of death, not of life. He is hostile to everything that breathes; not just men and women, but the animals you treasure. And should he triumph in his struggle with Tremien, then all of Cronbrach will fall under his killing hand."

Barach nodded. "Jeremy speaks truly, madam. You must know of the wasteland the evil one has made of green Relas, across the sea far to the south. And should he succeed in his designs against the forces of the north, inevitably the same fate will befall Gateway Cay."

Nul, too, joined in. "Nul not good talker," he said in his querulous, grumbling voice. "But he know that what Jeremy and Barach say is true. Great Dark One sent soldiers, many years ago, to kill and enslave Nul's people. He hate them not because they many or strong or dangerous; they few, weak, and harmless. He hate them just because they live."

"Well, well," Adelaide said. She rose from her chair with a heavy sigh. "I do not like intrusions of any kind. They are impertinences, and impertinence should never be encouraged. But you have told me that the wretched Jilhukrihain would bring worse still to my island. It seems then that I must choose the lesser evil. Very well. You may try your fortune with the Gate. I do not see how you can make use of it, for its magic is chaotic and wild and has resisted many great magicians in the past. But neither do I see harm in your trying. It lies far up Dragon Valley, in the cliffs—"

"Dragons?" Jeremy asked.

"Yes, green ones. Pay attention, please. You'd best journey there on foot, for travel spells tend to become uncertain in the neighborhood of the old magic. If you set off just after noon, you should arrive there well before sunset. You will probably be there for some time."

"Dragons?" Jeremy asked.

"We have our packs and rations," Barach said, ignoring Jeremy's question. "We can camp there for days, if necessary."

Adelaide nodded. "In addition to your own, ah, supplies, I suppose you had better take a picnic basket along, and I shall ask Regina to accompany you as a guide." She replaced the bonnet with movements slow and formal, tied the bow neatly beneath her chin, and rose from the table, a stately little woman with pride in her bearing. "I believe that concludes our interview, gentlemen. You may remain here until Regina has made preparations for the journey to Dragon Valley."

With the heavy book under her arm, Adelaide left them alone. Jeremy blinked unhappily at Barach. Again, plaintively, he asked, "Dragons?"

Well, yes, dragons. Bright green dragons with pebbled hides, iridescent as emeralds in the tropical light and muggy heat of the early-afternoon sun over Dragon Valley, where Adelaide had cast no climate-altering spell. They were winged dragons, serpentine-necked beasts with bodies the size of draft horses, with long tails adorned with a single row of vertical plates, like those on a stegosaurus. They were ruby-eyed dragons that reared their heads suddenly from the undergrowth and hissed at the travelers like overgrown and miscolored barnyard geese.

They were vegetarian dragons.

"They eat *grass*?" Jeremy demanded. Thirty yards away, four of the creatures were lounging on their bellies beneath the shade of some willowlike trees on the far side of a broad brook that spilled down from the higher shoulders of the mountain. They had all wallowed in cooling mud, and great patches of it now dried into gray crumbly smears on their emerald skin. "*Grass?*"

Regina, striding along the pathway ahead of him, giggled at his ignorance. "Oh, yes, and leaves from the quaking saltberry trees, or sawbrush, or even ginnyflowers. They aren't very particular."

One of the four dragons across the stream ambled into the sunlight, yawned—exposing flat-edged teeth that were all at the front of the mouth, like a cow's—and belched with a deep note like that of a hopal, a Thaumian woodwind of bass register. The dragon's leathery wings, shaped like Chinese fans and colored a lighter shade of green than its body, unfolded from its shoulders and fluttered in a gentle breeze.

"Is it going to fly?" Jeremy asked.

"Fly?" Regina stopped dead in her tracks and gave Jeremy an exasperated look. "Whoever told you that dragons can fly? They can't; not the green ones, anyway. What an idea!"

"But the wings—"

"Dragons are cold-blooded, Jeremy," Barach said. "The wings are really membranes of skin supported by extensions of the vertebrae. They are very rich in small blood vessels; when they are unfolded, they radiate excess heat. If you would consider the great mass of the dragon and the inadequate area of the wings, you'd see very quickly that flight is out of the question."

"Radiators," Jeremy marveled. "I'll be darned." The dragon lowed at them, sounding like a two-ton lamb raised on a diet of rusty barbed wire and steroids. Jeremy sighed. "I don't suppose they breathe fire, either."

"Well, no, not strictly speaking." The whole party had paused—they had been walking for more than two hours by Jeremy's reckoning, and the respite was welcome—and Barach gestured toward the dragon, which had begun to browse among the reeds at the edge of the brook. "You may notice the large pouches at the base of the neck. See, they look something like flattened sausages running beneath the skin down along the dragon's sides? Those are gasbags."

The dragon pulled up a clump of dripping reeds with a sideways tug. It munched them with an absent, bovine expression on its long scaly face, its red eyes blinking incuriously at the humans. "Gasbags," Jeremy said. "Containing—?"

"Gas, of course," Barach said. Nul chuckled, but the wizard ignored him. "In being digested, the dragons' vegetable diet goes through a process of fermentation. Methane gas is a natural by-product of digestion; an organ behind the breastbone filters the gas from the bloodstream. It is collected in those subcutaneous pouches and expelled from time to time in, ah, burps. Mixed with air, it is a highly inflammable vapor. Should the dragon belch it out in the presence of fire, it ignites explosively."

Jeremy nodded. "So if some peasants bearing torches approached a dragon—"

"It would probably belch, yes; dragons do when they're stressed or frightened."

"And the gas would burst into flame, and the peasants would think it had breathed fire on them—I see." Jeremy grinned. "I think I'm beginning to glimpse the source of all kinds of Earthly legends. Some of these critters must have slipped through the Gate back in medieval times and frightened the bejesus out of the populace. Poor old Saint George! He probably never knew he'd killed the reptilian equivalent of a milk cow."

Rested, the group resumed their walk, leaving the ruminating dragon behind. As the path gradually rose, they heard more of the beasts bawling from the forest on either side of them, and more than once they had to step around large green mounds of droppings—dragon patties, Jeremy thought. They looked remarkably like the leavings his grandfather's cows used to scatter throughout their pasture.

Regina told them a little more about the dragons as they walked along, explaining that the reptiles had always been very rare, their range restricted to no more than half a dozen tropical and subtropical islands, of which Gateway Cay was the most northerly.

Lethargic and rather stupid, the dragons had proved easy prey for humans, who killed them even though dragon skin was too inflexible to make decent leather—the thick pebbly surface concealed disconnected horny inclusions—and even though dragon meat was nauseatingly unpalatable. So humans killed the animals just for sport, if you could call puncturing an uncomprehending plant-eater with thin, sharp spears and letting it slowly bleed to death, sport. The beasts on this particular island had dwindled to no more than a few dozen when Adelaide first came to Thaumia; but under her protection their numbers had increased, and now a herd of nearly five hundred browsed in this valley and three others like it.

The watercourse ran parallel to their path, and as they climbed toward the head of the valley, the brook became livelier, chuckling its way over smooth-worn black or gray stone, leaping over small terraces in waterfalls a few feet high, forming occasional deep, clear pools in which silvery fish darted over gray sand. The valley became narrower, too, the trees on either side of the brook more crowded, and dragon-sign less obvious. Finally, as the sun dropped down toward the west, they came to a side path which turned toward a steep gray cliff, visible above the serrated tops of the palmlike trees. "This way," Regina said, turning right.

From there they made just a short walk through the forest to a stony clearing. Jeremy squinted: in the dimness between the tree trunks ahead, he could see what appeared to be very fine cobwebs woven of some luminous pale-blue stuff. "Magical wards," he told Barach.

"Well, of course," Regina said. "Grandmama *is* the Keeper of the Gate, after all. That's how she prevents things like dragons and ripper bats from going into the cavern and getting lost, silly. And the wards keep the things from the Gate on their side, too, and out of Thaumia. But we can pass through Grandmama's spell, all right."

They did, with no more resistance than any magical field would offer: a tingling, prickling sensation on the skin, a feeling of sudden chill, and they were through none the worse for the experience, although Nul's fur did rise on end, giving him the appearance of a badly alarmed tomcat.

"There it is," Regina said, and for the first time her voice was hushed.

She lingered behind as Nul, Barach, and Jeremy crossed the rocky clearing to the cliff face itself. Jeremy felt a stirring of awe at the appearance of the Gate, for that was indubitably what he saw before him: an oval opening in the pitted gray stone of the cliff, framed by meandering growths of some tropically exotic dark-green vine that bore huge

trumpet-shaped golden-red flowers. The opening into oth-
erness stretched at least fifteen feet high and twelve broad.
The Gate, at that moment, showed a bubblelike surface of
swirling, dancing colors, shimmering through all the variations of the rainbow. Looking at it, Jeremy found himself
reminded of the dream-whorls of the Between, those storm-
like disturbances that marked a dreamer's shaping of the
neutral materials of the borderlands into sweet dreams or
nightmares.

"This is near enough for now," Barach said, halting ten
feet away from the Gate.

"Feel strange," Nul complained, hovering behind Barach.

"So do I," Jeremy said. The Gate gave off a definite
emanation: a feeling something like that of any magic, but
unsettling, too, awakening butterflies in the pit of his stomach, making his breath come more rapidly and shallowly in
his lungs. He felt—what? Not fear or dread, exactly, but an
apprehension that was something like fear; and, yes, he felt
a fascination, too, a pull toward those swirling colors, an
urge to explore the spectrum, to step into it, to wear its hues
like gaudy clothing. To lose himself utterly.

"Something happening," Nul said.

And something was. The colors were arranging themselves, taking on outline and shape. The three were suddenly looking on an uncanny landscape: a forest or something
like it, but a forest of leafless plants, pinkish-gray fungi the
size of trees, each one a somewhat irregular cylinder rounded
at the top, like partially melted test tubes. Patches of other
fungi grew on the sides of the "trees," each one shimmering
blue-green. The ground from which the larger plants sprang
was blood-red, the sky over them a deep aquamarine, and
two suns—a huge orange one and a small fierce blue-white
one—cast two colored shadows of each growth. Something
enormous and black, something like a flying manta ray,
rippled across that sky, momentarily obscuring the smaller
sun; then the alien world shivered and dissolved as the
colors of the Gate swirled again to chaos.

"Kazazz," Nul grunted. It was a pika's expression of
wonder.

Jeremy swallowed the lump of fear in his throat. "Must
have been Yuggoth," he muttered. Neither Barach nor Nul
replied.

The Gate cleared again, this time showing a red world of superheated stone and leaping flames, and scuttering among them, insectlike creatures, many-legged carapaced things seemingly as big as Nul. Jeremy squinted into the light. He had no feeling of looking at a surface. The Gate was more like an open doorway to another place, a place of all the dimensions of Thaumia, but with different physical laws. The illusion was so lifelike that he was surprised to feel no heat from those fires; but, he reflected, to do that he had only to walk into the Gate, where he would no doubt be incinerated in a second.

"To work," Barach said. "Our first task is to prepare a binding spell. Then we must couple it with a finding spell, so that the Gate can operate to show us Earth. After that, I fear it's up to you, Jeremy."

Jeremy licked his lips, which had gone dry. "I think we'd better move back under the trees while we formulate the spell," he said. "This is too distracting." With a last brilliant flare the world of flames disappeared, replaced by the formless chaos of color again.

Nul was hungry, a fact which did not surprise Jeremy, since the pika was always hungry, and so was Regina. The two of them dug into the picnic basket as Barach and Jeremy conferred.

Barach, fortunately, had a superb knowledge of the theory and practice of all branches of magic, even though he himself had lost his powers in a confrontation with the Hidden Hag of Illsmere. He knew the requirements of every sort of spell, the tricky loopholes that the spell caster had to close, the guards that had to be part of every well-wrought enchantment. With his theory and Jeremy's gift for formulating verbal magic, complemented by his un-Thaumian origin, the two were confident of their chances.

But simply speaking their desires aloud, even in English, would not produce success. In order to work properly, the spell had to be expressed with some structuring principles. Some mages used song as the organizing force; some used poetry. Barach had favored Neforlan rime, an obscure poetic form, which he whispered for small spells or boomed out in a lusty baritone for great ones. Jeremy, who found that his spells were most effective when spoken in his native tongue, used advertising slogans. It made him feel foolish sometimes; but it worked.

There were other considerations, other pitfalls that Barach had to take into consideration. Verbal formulations triggered magical reactions on Thaumia, but there was a vital catch: each spell could be spoken effectively only once. Thereafter its magical virtue was outworn, and nothing would happen if it was spoken again. Some variant of the spell would have to be formulated before its effects could be duplicated.

So a truly effective spell had to have more qualities than effectiveness. It would do no good at all to focus the Gate on Earth if the focus lasted only a few seconds; the spell, therefore, had to have some permanence. More, the Gate might be a pathway in time as well as in physical and supraphysical dimension, and the spell would consequently have to have the quality of chronological selectivity. And finally, the Gate would have to open on one particular person—Sebastian—to be of use, so targeting was also a matter for concern.

Like elements of a mathematical formula, these principles had to be placed in a proper equation with all the other requirements of thaumaturgy. The problem of duration meant that the formulation had to have some of the qualities of a Great Spell, a magical pronouncement worked out so that it was essentially incomplete. These spells frequently took years to create; they had to include hundreds, thousands, or even in some cases millions of cantrips, words which when spoken would ease the spell toward eventual completion and exhaustion. Walther's travel spells were such: each time a travel spell was used it effected transportation, but each use consumed part of the vast magical energies of the universe and edged the whole along the path of mundane entropy.

Jeremy and Barach lacked the time to create a truly Great Spell. They would have to settle for the minimum of control over the Gate, hoping that would be enough to accomplish their ends.

Barach thought long and hard and, with a pencil and a sheaf of paper, began to diagram lines of force, to enumerate possible dangers, and to delineate the shape of the spell that Jeremy would have to speak. Regina left them long before the incantation was ready, promising to return in the morning. Nul went exploring, probably searching for more food, for nuts, berries, bugs, or something delightfully disgusting.

In the distance the dragons bellowed and belched, making sounds that boomed over the trees and echoed here at the rocky edge of the valley. Shadows grew long and the humid air cooled somewhat. At last, though, Barach was satisfied. "That ought to do," he said, "if anything will. But it's very touchy; if this one fails, we may be here for days trying to formulate an alternative. Be careful in your translation."

Jeremy nodded. He used the pencil and paper himself, not trusting the spell to memory as he normally did. The sun set; he conjured up wizard-light and worked in its cheerful sourceless glow for a long time. He conferred with Barach, made changes and adjustments. Nul came back, chewing on something. Ahead of them, half-hidden by the trees, they caught occasional glimpses of the Gate, glowing with its own inner light as it shuffled through its repertoire of countless strange lands and creatures.

Finally Jeremy looked into Barach's eyes. "Well," he said, "here goes."

The three travelers approached the Gate once more, with Nul still hanging back a bit, anxiety in his very attitude. Jeremy took a deep breath and began to speak in English—not an advertising slogan this time, for that was too limited, but rather something like a whole multimedia ad campaign on behalf of the pan-universal Gate.

Something began to happen almost at once: the radiance of the Gate intensified, the colors became brighter and more saturated. The movement of their restless swirl increased, like a pool of water roiled by stirring, or like the iridescence on the surface of a soap bubble as it weakened and got ready to pop. The electrical feeling of magic grew stronger, prickling Jeremy's hair and beard and making Nul into a fuzzball again.

Jeremy's heart began to beat harder, and he gasped for breath between sentences. Magic was sometimes a confrontation of wills, a wrestling with invisible forces; and that was what he felt now. Power drained from him, physical as well as magical, making his knees tremble and demanding ever more concentration from him. The Gate began to pulse, brighter and then darker, as he sped through the spell, carefully pronouncing each word correctly, making no mistake in order or accent—for the smallest stumble could affect the meaning, and that would render the entire spell ineffective.

"Look," Nul said as the Gate shimmered toward something like solidity, shivering in and out of focus on what might be a group of human figures.

"Hush," Barach said, knitting his gray brows together.

Sweat stung Jeremy's eyes and made the wound on his forearm burn and itch. The Gate was trying to form a pattern, gaining soft-focus definition and then losing it again. The letters of the final lines of his spell blurred in Jeremy's vision; his knees shook, almost giving way beneath him. But he continued, relying on memory and on momentum. He took a deep breath and pronounced the sealing words: "And the Gate can be yours, now!"

With a final seething upheaval the surface of the Gate rippled, shimmered, and fell into form.

Jeremy had closed his eyes. He opened them now to look.

Through the Gate he saw a stage. Three men and one woman sat there, smiles on their faces. The men he did not recognize, but the woman was Cassandra. Cassie. Once his lover, now Sebastian's wife. She was trim, delectable in a pearl-gray dress; her hair was styled differently than he remembered, longer, a soft blond frame for her face. And she was as beautiful as always.

But not even Cassie could hold Jeremy's attention, for at a lectern center-stage stood Sebastian himself.

Jeremy wondered again at the resemblance. Oh, Sebastian was clean-shaven now, not bearded, but aside from that, everything about him, from his brown hair to the dimple in his chin, from his size-eight feet to his good-humored hazel eyes, everything made him an exact duplicate of Jeremy. It was more unsettling than looking into a mirror; it was more like watching a movie of himself doing things that he knew he had never done.

They could not hear his words, but Sebastian was speaking into a bank of microphones, and from the way he paused for what must have been applause or laughter, he was speaking quite effectively. He was dressed in a conservative three-piece suit of brownish gray, and he wore—Jeremy chuckled to himself—a yellow tie with tiny chocolate-colored polka dots.

"That him," Nul said. He had crept slightly closer to the Gate. "Go and get him."

"Not yet," Jeremy said. "We can't just snatch him from in front of a crowd of people. If the spell works decently, all we have to do is wait to catch him alone."

"It seems to be holding properly," Barach said. "Good work, Jeremy."

He shrugged. "It was mostly yours, but thanks. Let's see what's going on here."

But, frustratingly enough, he could not quite tell. There was a banner of some kind behind Sebastain, tacked to a maroon curtain at the rear of the stage, but only its lower fringe showed, and he could see only the bases of the letters, not enough to read. The talk went on for some time before finally Sebastian gave a grinning double wave of his hands and the men behind him stood up, applauding with evident enthusiasm. Sebastian shook hands with one of them, then embraced Cassie, who planted a quick kiss on his cheek.

"What they doing?" Nul asked.

"In technical terms, that was a smooch," Jeremy said. "It denotes affection—"

"Know what kiss is. Not that. All the talk, talk. What that about?"

"I can't read lips, so I don't know. Looks like a meeting of some kind. Like the Council."

Nul sniffed. "Humans have meetings on Earth too?"

"They certainly do."

"Boring place," Nul pronounced.

"You said it, chum."

Sebastian, anyway, was boring enough as spectacle. For a long time he merely sat smiling and nodding as one of the other men stepped to the lectern and gave a spirited harangue. Then he rose, clapping, at the conclusion of the talk. All the men on the platform—and Cassie too—lined up and waved. Then they walked offstage.

Like a movie shot all in one take, the Gate followed them, Sebastian always at the center. A knot of men, some in suits and others in shirtsleeves, clustered around Sebastian, shaking his hand, talking, waving their hands, nodding.

Sebastian kissed Cassie on the mouth and she walked away, out of the picture as it were.

Nul grew very excited when Sebastian and two of the other men went outside—it was dark, and Jeremy could not recognize the street, though he had the feeling that he was seeing some part of downtown Atlanta—and the three climbed into a long black limousine. Jeremy had some trouble explaining to the pika what cars were; but Nul was fascinated with the picture he saw. Sebastian sat in the center of the rear seat and through the window behind him a stream of cars was visible. Nul got so close to the Gate that Jeremy put a hand on his shoulder to hold him back. Nul seemed to be on the verge of saying, "Poop-poop!" and lapsing into motorcar mania, like Mr. Toad.

"Won't he ever settle somewhere alone?" Barach asked.

"We'll see."

The automobile ride ended at last, in the parking garage of some building. Sebastian and two of the men climbed out of the car, rode an elevator up, and came out in a carpeted hallway. They entered an opulently appointed office; they had drinks. Finally Sebastian rose, said something, and left the other two behind. "Get ready," Jeremy said to himself.

Sebastian opened a door and went into a white-tiled room, its walls gleaming beneath fluorescent lights. "What that?" Nul asked as Sebastian approached a chrome-and-white-porcelain fixture hanging on the wall.

"Never mind," Jeremy said. "He's alone now. Wish me luck."

He took a deep breath and stepped into the Gate.

5

"**H**i there," Jeremy said.

Sebastian Magister started violently—not a delicate movement, considering his occupation at the moment—and jerked his chin over his shoulder, his eyes wide with shock. "You! What the hell—?"

"Better finish up."

Sebastian turned his attention back to the business at hand. When he zipped his fly, Jeremy said, "Listen, we have to talk."

"Here?" Sebastian asked. He crossed to the sinks and ran water over his hands. "Good God, how did you manage to get here? Not through the mirror?" He stared at the mirror, reflecting the two of them, one taupe-suited and sober, the other bearded, wild of hair and aspect, clad in a long silvery-gray robe and boots. And yet the two were similar, like brothers, like twins who had gone separate ways in life. "I thought the mirrors were—"

"I didn't use magic mirrors," Jeremy said. "And, yes, they've all been destroyed. I came through—" He broke off, his throat tightening in panic; in the mirror there was no sign of the Gate. But when he looked behind him, there it was, a shimmering oval curtain hanging only one long step away. Through its translucence the forms of Nul and Barach were dimly visible. "Through that," he said, gesturing with relief.

Sebastian had turned. He hit the button of an air dryer with his fist, and as it whined into action, he frowned without comprehension. "Through the *stall*?" he asked.

"No. Through the Gate. Can't you see—" Jeremy broke

off, realizing that Sebastian's puzzled look was genuine. "You can't see it, can you?"

"I can see you," Sebastian returned, dry-washing his hands in the flow of hot air. "Look, why don't you go back to where you came from and leave me alone? I don't have time to deal with you, and you don't know how complicated my life is right now."

Jeremy looked from Sebastian's harried face to the Gate and back again. "Concentrate hard," he said. "Use what you remember of your magical sight. Can't you see anything there behind me? Besides the stall, I mean."

Sebastian's frown deepened. "I think there's a kind of shadow," he said. "But I can't make it out." The dryer clicked off, but for a few seconds he continued to rub his hands together absentmindedly.

"Old buddy, I think you've worn all your magic out," Jeremy said. "Look, we need you. The Great Dark One is loose again, and you're the only one who can help us."

Sebastian glanced back in the mirror and straightened his tie. "Are you crazy? I'm you now, or everybody believes I am. I've built a whole life for myself here in Atlanta; I can't drop anything and disappear off into Thaumia on some damn-fool quest. I have responsibilities, I—"

"I didn't mean to imply that you had a choice. You're coming," Jeremy said, grinning.

"No. No, I'm—look, what do you want me to do?"

Jeremy sketched in the situation in a few words. Sebastian nodded, so much like a mirror image that Jeremy found himself nodding in sympathy. "So," he finished, "Tremien thinks that you might be able to spot the new host. Meanwhile, there's something damn strange happening in the south, and that's tied in to the Great Dark One too."

"A mole," Sebastian said.

"What?"

"A mole, I said. Not the animal. For God's sake, don't you remember spy fiction at all?"

"I always preferred science fiction and fantasy."

Sebastian shook his head. "Escapist drivel. Shows where you went wrong. Anyway, in espionage a mole is a double agent in deep cover—someone who pretends to be on your side but who is really on theirs. He burrows in, you see, and stays hidden until it's time for him to act."

"All right," Jeremy said. "A mole, then. One of the three is the mole, according to Tremien; and we have to have you to learn which of the three it is."

Sebastian looked at his wrist. It sported a wafer-thin gold Rolex, Jeremy noticed. "You came at a terrible time. I suppose you don't plan to let me off the hook on this?"

"Not a chance."

Sebastian bit his lip. "Look, you have to cut me some slack here. I mean, my God, if I just disappear from the men's room, there's going to be an unholy fuss. Jesus, even when you were here you couldn't just vanish without a trace—there'd be too many questions.

"What do you suggest?"

"I don't know. Let me think." While he thought, Sebastian turned to the mirror and combed his hair, still rich and brown and styled expensively—more expensively than Jeremy's had ever been. "Okay, can I assume that your method of getting here is reliable?"

"It's as good as Barach and I could make it."

With a sigh that sounded like relief, Sebastian said, "That's a little better. If Barach Loremaster is helping you, that's a different matter. I never liked the old windbag, but I respect his talents. Okay. Do you know where we are?"

"Not exactly, no."

"Well, we're in the corporate headquarters of . . . Never mind. We're in the offices of an important company, and I have some important people waiting for me. I can't possibly go with you right this minute, and you can't stay with me."

"Why not?"

"Why not? Look at yourself! Hell, you'd be out of place at a sci-fi convention, let alone in a respectable office."

Jeremy had not even considered his costume; but now that Sebastian mentioned it, he understood that a magician's robe, blue homespun trousers, and heavy leather walking boots were probably out of place in a corporate setting. "I guess you have a point."

"Damn right I do."

"Maybe I can borrow an extra suit from you. We used to be the same size."

Sebastian rolled his eyes in obvious exasperation. "I don't have a suit here, idiot."

"Too bad. That looks like a nice one."

"It's new. Glauber and Sons made it for me," Sebastian said, giving the vest a self-conscious tug.

Jeremy shook his head. "Using old man Taplan's tailor, huh? You've come up in the world. But we're getting side-tracked. Tell me your proposal."

"Okay, here's my deal: you go back to Thaumia. Can you keep track of me?"

"Oh, yes."

Sebastian made a sour face. "Yeah, I thought that would be possible. This is the first time I've been alone all day; you waited for that, didn't you?"

"Right."

With a nod, Sebastian said, "I guess I should be grateful for that, anyway. Okay. Look, I've got to get away from these guys, and then I have to go home. This is Friday; I can clear my calendar for tomorrow. Give me"—he looked at his watch again—"give me twelve hours. Just until eleven tomorrow morning. Then I'll be alone again, and you can come through to talk this thing over. I can't guarantee that I'll help—in fact, I'll tell you right now that I probably won't—but at least I'll promise to hear you out."

Jeremy looked into that plausible face, wondering if he had seemed so intense, so earnest, so determined and forth-right, back when he had been a copywriter for Taplan and Taplan Advertising. "You realize," he said, "that if you try to hide in the crowd, I'm coming through anyway. And if necessary I'll drag you back to Thaumia kicking and screaming."

"I get the picture. I won't double-cross you. Come on, think what a problem it would have been for you to disappear without any explanation. Twelve hours, that's all I ask."

"See you tomorrow, then." Jeremy backed away and toward that insubstantial oval that only he could see. He felt something like a mild electric shock; then he was looking at Sebastian from outside the Gate. Sebastian stared toward him without focusing, took a handkerchief from his breast pocket and patted his face, and then left the rest room.

"What did he say?" Barach asked as they watched Sebastian return to the men he had left in the office.

"Well, he's agreed to discuss it," Jeremy said. "But asked for some time to prepare. It's a reasonable enough request. I'll go after him tomorrow morning. For tonight we can get

some sleep—if the bugs will let us." For the insects of
Gateway Cay were both more numerous and more vocifer-
ous than those of Whitehorn, and the night rioted with their
clacking, rasping, whirring, clicking, wheeping songs.

Barach smiled. "I, for one, am weary enough to ignore
the noise. But we must take great care. It will be a good
idea to keep a watch on Sebastian."

"You not trust him," Nul said.

"I do not. Unless he has changed beyond all likelihood,
Sebastian Magister is a very tricky person." In the Gate
they could see Sebastian shaking hands with the two men,
all of them laughing heartily. "Very tricky indeed," Barach
said.

Jeremy's spell held throughout the night. Nul kept the
first watch, and when he awakened Jeremy for his turn, he
reported that Sebastian had gone from the office to a den in
a big building where the woman waited for him. They had
nibbled at each other's face some more, Nul said, and—

"I understand," Jeremy told him. "Get some sleep."

Which was what Sebastian appeared to be doing. The
Gate opened into his darkened bedroom. Jeremy, yawning,
noticed that it was not his old apartment, but a more spa-
cious and more elegantly appointed chamber. A painting
hung over the bed, hard to make out in the dim light, but it
seemed to be a desert landscape. Jeremy remembered the
Pearlstein that Cassie had admired so extravagantly in the
Dunwoody gallery; the one that bore a price amounting to
roughly one-third of his annual salary. Jeremy wondered if
Sebastian had purchased that painting, but it was too dark
in the room to tell for certain.

What was obvious was that the bed was huge, the carpet
thick, the whole elegant. The bedroom matched Sebastian's
suit and watch in good taste and expense.

But then, Sebastian's fortunes had been on the rise for
more than three years. Even as Jeremy had become accli-
mated to the world of magic he had found on Thaumia, so
Sebastian had adapted himself to the mundane world of
business and finance on Earth. Jeremy ruefully reflected
that, judging from appearances, Sebastian had been considerably more successful than he at making himself a part of
his new surroundings; Jeremy's solo efforts at devising Great

Spells had come to little, and he certainly wasn't as far advanced in the profession of wizardry as Sebastian seemed to be in business.

For Jeremy, watching Sebastian was like watching the dullest movie ever filmed to the accompaniment of the cacophonous night insects, the worst film score ever conceived. All Sebastian did was sleep, nestled with Cassie beneath designer sheets on the king-size bed. There was very little light in the room—it had the pale blue hue of moonlight, what there was of it—but there was enough to make out the two people-shaped mounds. It occurred to Jeremy that he could not discern Sebastian's features, though, and he idly wondered if somehow Sebastian had given him the slip. Maybe instead of his quarry there was just a pile of pillows under the sheets, like in the old movies—

No. Sebastian stirred and tossed in his sleep, proving himself animate. And in the 99 & 44/100% mundane surroundings of Earth, how could he affect the focus of the Gate? Jeremy grunted, sat with his arms wrapped around his knees, and vainly tried to find a comfortable spot on the volcanic stone in front of the Gate.

He woke Barach some time later—the Thaumians did not use hours as a measure of time, but Jeremy judged that four had passed since he came on watch himself—and he warned the old magician that nothing exciting was likely to happen. Then Jeremy crept back into his bedroll, cushioned on some crackling palm fronds that seemed only marginally preferable to the bare sand and stone as far as comfort went. But he fell asleep again almost at once, lulled by the boring routine of keeping watch.

He woke a second time with the sun well up. Nul was eating and watching the Gate; Barach had retreated to his own bed and was snoring gently. Jeremy got up, stretching and scratching. "What's happening?" he asked the pika.

"Sebastian with some people," Nul said. "I wonder: what happen if some of them wander through Gate? What we do with them?"

"They won't," Jeremy said. "Barach worked a safeguard into the spell. I can go freely through the Gate, either way; and anyone or anything that I'm actually touching can come back through with me. As we've worked the spell, no one can fall through from Earth into Thaumia on his own.

However, there's nothing to stop you from falling from Thaumia to Earth if you get too close."

Nul, who had been sitting within a yard or so of the opening in the cliff, nervously edged back from the Gate. "Think pika be out of place on Earth." He grinned. "So when you go get Sebastian? He tell you he would be alone at forenoon?"

"Yes. Somewhere around eleven o'clock, his time. Let me see." Sebastian, dressed now in a summer-weight suit of pale blue, was sitting at a table with two women and two men, nodding as one of them read from a pad, accepting papers from another, initialing them with a black ball-point pen, and passing them along to one of the women, who put them in a folder. All had cups and dirty dishes in front of them. "It's early," Jeremy said. "They've just had breakfast."

"Wish Nul had breakfast already. Hungry. Time there same as time here?"

"It seems to be pretty close. I suppose the days coincide exactly, since the year does—that was one reason why Sebastian was able to make contact with me by using the mirrors, you know. He chose a time of exaltation to do it, a time of year when Thaumian magic is especially strong. There are four of them, coinciding with the turning of the seasons back on Earth."

"Well, if time the same, it some way yet to forenoon. Time enough for Nul to have something to eat."

"Sure, go ahead," Jeremy said. "I'll watch Sebastian."

Sebastian, though he looked noticeably more harried than he had the evening before, showed no inclination to get away from the four other people at the table. Jeremy frowned, wondering what they were talking about, wishing that he had set up the spell to allow sounds to pass through from Earth. But since he had not, there was no use speculating. Nor was there any use in wondering what was going on back on the mainland, though of course Jeremy could not help doing that either.

Perhaps it was just as well that Jeremy could not use clairvoyance to see the events taking place back on Cronbrach. They were not calculated to reassure him.

Early that morning, the eleventh day of Hamarth, the month of high summer, a young sorcerer of considerable ability had answered a call from the town master of Narofrod, an important trading settlement at the juncture of the Bronfal and Vaskflod rivers. The sorcerer's name was Sanklar Aveskhan, and since his special province was the protection of traders and trade goods, he supposed that Narofrod was having problems with thievery again; the busy river docks were tempting targets for small bands of hit-and-run robbers, and in past months he had worked a number of spells to secure the goods off-loaded there.

But Sanklar found Chagandis Delavolarn, the middle-aged town master, in a state of strong apprehension. "Something is coming from the south," the man told him without preamble as soon as he arrived.

Sanklar, an angular, tall young fellow in the cream-white robe of an adept, looked down at the portly master of Narofrod. "What is coming?" he asked.

"Feel it," Chagandis snapped. "Feel it for yourself."

They stood at a fifth-story window of the town hall, the fourth-tallest place in the whole settlement; Chagandis had thrown the casement open to the humid morning air. Looking past him, Sanklar saw a vista of rooftops, shops and houses; a scattering of dusty, dark-green jimalia trees in yards; the clustered masts of the small river vessels off to the left; and, stretching away to the south, the broad, brown, placid face of the Bronfal itself, nearly a thousandpace wide this far to the south. It rolled on, seemingly currentless, another three-hundred leagues or so to Relenda Chai, whose name meant "the hundred ways," where it divided and branched again and again, spilling into the southern sea through a formidable barrier of low delta islands.

Sanklar breathed in the muggy air, testing the scents of a riverfront town: the decaying stench of mud and algae, fish, tar, a hundred mingled aromas of foodstuffs and trade goods. "I see," he said.

For something was wrong. A strange coppery haze muddied the blue sky. An oppressive feeling lay heavy on the town, like the feeling that sometimes presaged the great afternoon thunderstorms that swept in from the west, from the grassy plains south of the Arkhedden Forest. Yet the day was clear, except for that puzzling haze: no wind ruffled the face of the Bronfal or swept aside the hundred blue fingers of smoke rising from morning chimneys. "What word from the south?" Sanklar asked.

"None yesterday," Chagandis replied. "And that is strange, too; for a whole midsummer day to pass without at least a few Chai traders making their way upstream, bringing their fish and spices to trade for wool, flax, or glass."

"Strange," Sanklar agreed, rubbing his thumbs across the tips of his fingers. He felt something, some stickiness in the very atmosphere, as if he had coated his fingers with a light brushing of honey. The feeling was wholly unfamiliar to him, a fact which gave Sanklar pause. It was not the sensation that presaged the operation of great magic—his late master Manvenkor, the sorceress of Gravas Khu, had taught him the knack of anticipating by as much as a day the operation of fell enchantments by detecting the alteration in the magic potential caused by a mind working up a Great Spell.

This sticky sensation did not in the least resemble that feeling, a tingling, slippery texture in the air, as unmistakable to the fingers as the taste of peppered oil to the tongue. No, it was not that, but still there was *something* in the air, something that felt evil.

Sanklar bowed his head and considered. He was a reliable sort of magician: not mage level, of course, a long way from that, but he had encountered no trouble in rising rapidly to adept level, and he looked forward to election to the Council soon. Still, Sanklar knew his limitations.

He came to a decision. "Send for the ward captains," he said at last. "Have them organize the warders to empty the town. I think it would be unwise to use the travel spell, for there is some alteration in the magic potential here that I cannot understand. The evacuation must go overland, then. Let those who have boats move upstream, to the north, to Broadpools or beyond; let everyone else withdraw to the west, along the road that follows the course of the Vaskflod, to Galadine—"

"But without magic, that's a week-long journey," Chagandis objected. "And what do the shopkeepers do to protect their stores while they are away from town, or the homeowners to protect their houses?"

"Leave that to me," Sanklar said. "I will work the best

protection spell that I can; I'll lower a dome of magic all about the town, so that nothing evil can happen."

Chagandis scratched the bald spot on the crown of his gray head. "In that case, why should we withdraw at all?"

"Because," Sanklar said, "I may well fail." For some reason the thought made him shiver. He stared away to the south. It seemed to him that the copper-colored haze was somehow denser there, that the southern horizon bore a concentrated spot of metallic brown just to the left of the Bronfal, on the far side of the river; but he could have been mistaken, he supposed.

Chagandis was still argumentative. He began, "You underestimate our people, young master. I tell you—"

Sanklar cut him short: "Listen to me, town master. Death is on the way. I do not fully understand it, but I feel it. It comes even now from the south; and it comes rapidly. And if it plans to cross the river, the Great Bridge of Narofrod is its first opportunity, so it must pass by here. If you would not have it destroy the town, do as I say. Order the ward captains to assemble now. The town should be empty no later than nightfall."

"I cannot do that," Chagandis said, his voice aggrieved and stubborn. "I tell you, my people will not leave their homes. They have a strong loyalty to the city and indeed to me. If something is threatening them, they will want to stand and fight."

"If they remain, they will die," Sanklar said. "No, don't argue with me. I know what I am saying, although it is hard to tell you exactly how I know. I can tell you this: whatever is coming from the south is more powerful than a dozen cities the size of this one. Have you ever seen a fang-cat devour a hare at one gulp? I tell you Narofrod is that hare."

The town master looked at him for a long time. At last the older man blinked and swallowed. "Very well. I will send for the ward captains," he said at last.

Sanklar stared out at nothing. "Leave me alone for a while. This is beyond my understanding, and I, too, must prepare."

Chagandis nodded, started to say something, thought better of it, and walked out, closing the door behind him. Sanklar gazed southward again, frowning. "Who are you?" he asked of the air. "What do you hide?"

He expected no response and received none. He crossed his hands, palms inward, and spoke a cantrip. "Sanklar Aveskhan, adept of the year 1223, requests speech with Tremien of Whitehorn," he said.

From the air ahead of him a quiet, deep voice, elderly but sharp and clear, said, "Tremien here. What do you wish to say, Sanklar?"

"Mage Tremien, I may be wrong, but I believe something dire and evil is moving northward along the Bronfal River, coming from the direction of Relenda Chai. I am in the town of Narofrod, some five hundred leagues to the south of you. Whatever it is, it has not reached here yet; but I feel its approach and it cannot be far away."

"One moment." For a space during which Sanklar might have counted to two hundred, the voice was quiet. When it resumed, it held an edge of worry. "Sanklar. I have used my searching spell to examine your area. I can detect no specific focus of magic to the south of you; yet I agree that something is amiss. There is . . . a disturbance, a blank, a void, as it were, in my perception. What do you propose to do?"

"I have asked to the town master to move the people away, to a place of safety. I shall try to use Flarendal's Dome Spell, or a variant of it, to protect the town—"

"That is a work requiring considerable power. Are you capable of that?"

"I have never tried so great a spell. But, yes, if there is time, I believe I can do it."

"Go ahead, then."

"Then if you will permit me to try, I shall remain in the town to keep the spell active and to observe. I shall report what happens to you."

"Do you need help?"

Sanklar bit his lip. It galled him to make the admission, but he realized that it was necessary: "I believe that I may. My Council master is Jondan. Shall I call him and ask for his assistance?"

Another pause, this one long, hesitant, and distinctly uneasy. "No. I think not. Jondan is engaged in another matter at the moment. Let me send a representative of Whitehorn to you."

"Very well, Mage Tremien." Sanklar hesitated again, but

once he had admitted his need for assistance, there was no sense in holding back his very real gratitude. "Any help will be welcome."

"Will you need some help in persuading the townspeople to leave the city?"

"I may."

"I thought as much. They have always had the reputation of being stubborn. I shall speak to the town master myself. I believe it is still Chagandis, is it not?"

"It is. A man of praiseworthy courage, although at times his bravery springs from ignorance of the foe."

"Then I shall speak to him. Thank you, Sanklar; your vigilance is as worthy of praise as the courage of Chagandis."

"Oh, I have vigilance to spare; I only hope it is misdirected," Sanklar said.

Tremien laughed. "A noble and unselfish wish," he said, "since if it comes to pass, the townspeople will revile you for your actions in forcing them to leave. But enough talk; it is time to act."

From a nearby room came an angry clamor of voices, their words not clear but their emotion strong. Chagandis must have just broken the news of the evacuation to the ward captains; and from the sound of their objections, they did not like it at all. "Time to act," Sanklar agreed, feeling apprehensive, afraid, and strangely elated.

At long last Sebastian shed the other four people, climbed into an automobile—a sporty new black Porsche convertible, Jeremy observed—and drove north, into familiar territory. Jeremy's last visit to Atlanta had been a little more than two years ago, and he saw that the landscape had changed in the interim: buildings reared where he did not even recall scaffolding among the trees. But he had driven the same route every morning for several years, and, sure enough, Sebastian made his way to Taplan and Taplan.

Except now the discreet blue sign read "Taplan, Taplan, and Moon Advertising Agency." It was a shock; but then, to the world in general, Sebastian was Jeremy Moon, a keener, meaner model, and no doubt Sebastian's ferocious ambition had led to his gaining a partnership in record time.

Sebastian let himself in with a magnetic key card. The building seemed deserted except for a blue-uniformed security guard whom Jeremy did not recognize. It was a Saturday back on Earth, he recalled; no one would be at work today.

Jeremy shook his head as Sebastian rode the elevator to the top floor, got out, and opened a door into a suite of offices. He had the office that Taplan Junior had formerly occupied, complete with its well-stocked wet bar, its private bathroom, and its notoriously commodious gray leather sofa. Jeremy wondered why Cassie, who also worked at the agency—or anyway, who used to—had not demanded the removal of that tempting item of furniture.

Sebastian locked the outer door behind him, opened the inner office door, and then locked that. He stood near the immense walnut desk in an attitude of expectation. Jeremy reached down and shook Barach awake. "He's ready," he said as the old magician stretched and yawned. "I'm going after him."

"Where is Nul?" Barach asked.

"He said he was hungry; he's out foraging, I suppose. Hope he doesn't try to eat a dragon."

"He'll be all right." Barach squinted up at the sun. "Nearly noon. Regina should be back soon. Try to make it brief, will you?"

"I'll do my best," Jeremy said. And he stepped through the Gate.

Sebastian closed his eyes. "I was hoping you wouldn't come," he said.

"I told you it was important." Jeremy looked around, noting the new carpeting, the Sony large-screen television and VCR in the corner opposite the desk. "Nice office."

Sebastian ignored the last remark. "Important for you, maybe. Not for me." He ran a hand through his hair. "Care for a drink?"

Jeremy shrugged. "Okay. It's been a long time since I had a Coke."

"A soft drink, you mean?"

"Sure. What else—oh. No, I was never into that."

Sebastian snorted contemptuously. "A Coke. Right. I'll have to go downstairs to the machine for that. Will you trust me out of your sight?"

"I can find you again if you try to run out. I'll entertain myself while you're gone." Jeremy was amused to see that the drifting portal followed Sebastian across the thick carpet and out the door—although, being much larger than the door, the Gate simply floated through the walls.

As soon as Sebastian left, Jeremy wandered over to the TV setup. A videotape marked "J. S. Moon: Samples" lay on top of the VCR. Curious, Jeremy turned the power on, popped the tape in the machine, and pressed "Play."

For a moment he was rewarded with the chaos of snow. Then the tape kicked in and the screen resolved itself into darkness. A homemade title read *Accnt HW1009: Sakato Mfg.* It meant nothing to Jeremy. The screen went black again, and then in the lower-right corner a bright blue logo appeared: Bush Country Farm and Garden Implements. That faded as a melancholy piano played "Für Elise" and the darkness dissolved to reveal a sleeping woman, a beauty in what appeared to be a low-cut white evening gown dozing on a made-up bed. Her red lips pouted, and a mane of rich chestnut hair spilled over a white pillow. The camera examined her in a series of lap dissolves, showing a close-up of her perfect face, a view of her right cheek pillowed on her white-gloved right hand, and a full-figure shot that showed she was sleeping on a pile of furs and overcoats, as if she had slipped away from a late-night party.

Then the screen showed a point-of-view shot: the camera had become the eyes of a man looking down at the woman; Jeremy could see the man's arms and hands, arms clothed in the gleaming white fabric of a silk formal shirt, onyx cufflinks glistening at the wrists. The right hand reached offscreen; the left caressed the woman's hair, lifting it, letting it cascade through the fingers, then grasping it. The right hand came back into the shot, armed with a pair of scissors. They bit through the hair, leaving the left side of the woman's head close-cropped.

Tight shot on the woman's face: her eyes popped open, shockingly blue; one tear slipped from the left one and rolled down over her cheek and to the pillow. Her lips silently mouthed the single word "Why?"

Then a close-up shot of a wastepaper basket. The shorn hair dropped partly inside, bounced up in slow motion, finally came to rest balanced on the rim. The scissors fell point-foremost to the floor, impaled themselves in the oak parquet, and quivered. Fade to black; and once again the blue logo (the shade of the letters exactly matching the woman's eyes, Jeremy realized now): Bush Country Farm and Garden Implements.

What the hell? Jeremy scratched his head, trying and failing to see any connection between product and image. The tape continued with another amateur title: a message scrawled in black Magic Marker on white paper said *Accnt SE1122: Hargraves Electronics*. The name, at least, was familiar. A hustling importer of Japanese-manufactured home computers, Hargraves had been one of Jeremy's accounts in the old days.

This commercial opened with snowy gulls flashing past against a blue sky. The camera began a long reverse tracking shot, pulling back and away, making the gulls recede to flashing white abstract shapes. A murmur of conversation, too low to be understood, and a clatter of china and silverware rose on the soundtrack. The camera retreated through an open window, framing the sky and the gulls. Filmy white translucent curtains blew in the breeze on either side of the window. The camera continued its retreat over a breakfast table.

First in profiled close-up, then in medium shot, and at last in full view, two men and two women sat at the table, sipping coffee, munching English muffins; the men wore polo shirts and jeans and were barefoot, while both women wore only bright red bikini bathing suits. Their conversation remained barely audible murmurs, with nothing clear enough for Jeremy to understand.

The camera continued to pull back—the whole commercial, Moon realized, had been made in one long tracking shot—into a medium-dark room, the brilliant light of the window now dazzling over the breakfast table, the men and women reduced to soft-focus silhouettes. Something black and silver began to obscure the foreground, a horizontal line at first out of focus, then becoming gradually sharp as the camera moved farther back. It was the top of a black leather-and-chrome sofa, Jeremy realized, its back to the window and the table. The camera stopped at that point, and from out of the frame a woman sat up suddenly, facing away from the camera, looking over the back of the sofa at the breakfast table.

Jeremy could see her from slightly below the waist up,

and her back was to him, but she was clearly naked. Her face was not visible, but her hair was long and blond, her skin sleek, her shape alluring. The camera shifted to deep focus without a change of scene, making every face in the room sharp and clear. The foursome at the breakfast table broke off their incomprehensible conversation and turned toward the nude, their eyes wide in astonishment. One of the women at the table said, "Who the hell are you?"

The screen went white, and in stark black letters the message appeared: *We are Kiwi Computers.* A two-beat pause, and then a second line: *Now, who the hell are YOU?*

The office door opened and Sebastian came back in with a can of Coca-Cola. "Watching my work?"

Jeremy switched off the machine before seeing the next commercial, one for a jeans manufacturer, according to the handwritten title. "Is that what you call it? What kind of commercial was that?"

"The oblique sell," Sebastian said. "My baby."

"Oblique sell? You've got to be kidding."

"Try a junior partnership at age twenty-nine. Try sixty K a year. Tell me if that sounds like kidding. Here's your drink." He passed the ice-cold can to Jeremy, then opened the small refrigerator and took out a miniature Perrier bottle for himself. He twisted off the top but did not drink.

"We used to call that yuppie wash," Jeremy said, grinning. He opened the pull tab and took a long sip. "I didn't know how much I'd missed that," he said. "Oblique sell, huh? And those are successful?"

"You'd better believe it. You see the Kiwi Computer one? First time a major TV ad used the word 'hell.' See, the strategy is to understate. You hook the audience with a little bit of drama, a little bit of mystery. You make them mad as hell or you fascinate them—"

"Sounds crazy to me. What about the product?"

"Who gives a damn about the product? We're selling image here, not substance. Sizzle, not steak. And it works, buddy boy. Hell, half the agencies in the country are stealing the approach from me now."

Jeremy raised his eyebrows. "It still sounds nuts. I can't believe you really sell the product with those things."

"Screw the product. It's the message that counts. Hey, if I

valued your company I'd show you the fifteen awards those babies have won."

"No, thanks. Aren't you going to drink that?"

"Cheers," Sebastian muttered, looking anything but cheery, and he took a sip. "Look, let me be honest with you: this isn't going to work. You'll have to find some other way of dealing with your problem; I can't come to Thaumia again, and that's that."

Jeremy settled himself in one of the three comfortable chairs in the office. "You've gained weight," he said. "What do you weigh now, one-ninety?"

"A hundred and seventy-five," Sebastian said. "I work out at the Executive Club every other day."

"Uh-huh."

"You just think I've put on weight because you've gotten skinny," Sebastian said. "You've lost, what, fifteen pounds?"

"I don't know. No scales in Thaumia."

"You look thinner, anyhow." After a moment, Sebastian added grudgingly, "And in better condition."

"I probably am. Barach works me pretty hard."

Sebastian sniffed. "The last time I saw the Loremaster, he was as bloated as a dead whale."

"Good thing he can't hear you. He's watching us right now." Jeremy waved at Barach, visible in the floating Gate a few paces behind Sebastian. Then he tilted the can and drank again. "Why can't you go back with me?" he asked. "It may not take very long."

"There're a hundred reasons," Sebastian said. "I'm a junior partner now—"

"All the better to take off for a couple of days. Relieve executive stress, that sort of thing," Jeremy said. "Come up with your own excuse. Taplan Junior always used to operate pretty much on whim, as I recall."

"Which is exactly why I'm in this office now instead of him," Sebastian said. "But there are other reasons too. I . . . I have other responsibilities—"

"Cassie still working here?"

"I . . . What? No." Sebastian sipped his Perrier. "I . . . we decided that it would be better if she left the art department. She's free-lancing some, but . . . We don't have to discuss my marriage."

"Just curious. Anyway, it's my marriage too, sort of. What name is the license in, after all?"

"It's my marriage," Sebastian said, glaring. "Mine and Cassie's. Period."

"Okay, okay. So what are the other reasons?"

"There are a lot of them—"

"Enough crap," Jeremy said. "Tell me what's bothering you."

Sebastian took a long breath. "Well," he said at last, "you might as well know. I'm running for office."

Jeremy stared at him. "You son of a bitch," he said. "So the business world is too small for you, huh?"

"I don't have to explain myself to you."

"Maybe you do," Jeremy said.

"Shit." Sebastian had been resting with one hip on the desk. He stood and strode to the window. "Wind's kicking up," he said, looking out at the tossing pine trees between the building and the Perimeter highway. "Early for a thunderstorm."

"Thanks for the weather report. At least tell me what office you're running for."

"State senator," Sebastian said to the window.

"Oh, terrific. Let me guess. Conservative platform, right? Boost business and industry. Up the corporations. Protect the rights of—"

"You got it," Sebastian said, still not looking at him. "But you make it sound dirty. It's more sensible than that—"

"Great. You're against everything I ever believed in. I hope you're managing to explain all this to my former friends," Jeremy retorted. "Or do I have any left now?"

"Some," Sebastian said. "A few of them think you've finally come to your senses. Of course, a few others think you've gone quite mad. It evens out, I suppose."

"I suppose." Jeremy finished the last of the soft drink. "Look, Sebastian, I'm not taking you away from Earth forever. And besides, Thaumia needs you—you've dealt with the Great Dark One before. You know what he's like."

Sebastian nodded. Beyond him Jeremy could see clouds rolling in, moving fast, as though on a squall line. "Of course Tremien would tell you that the Great Dark One is thoroughly evil," Sebastian said, his voice dripping with sarcasm. "And of course you'd never think to question the great Tremien."

"I've seen the Great Dark One myself," Jeremy replied. "I can tell what he's like myself. A power-crazed murderer. A homicidal maniac who wants to be a god."

Sebastian turned, silhouetted against the darkening forenoon sky. "And you think Tremien is sweetness and light? Grow up, Jeremy."

Jeremy crumpled the red aluminum can, crushing a coupon and thereby denying himself the privilege of a reduced admission to Six Flags over Georgia. "The Great Dark One wants immortality," he said. "For himself. Period. He's wanted it so long that he doesn't care if the whole world dies because of his desire to live forever. In fact, he seems to seek that."

"Doesn't matter. You're making a mistake in choosing your allies. The Great Dark One is a powerful force," Sebastian said. "A smart man would know how to deal with such a force. How to use it to his own advantage."

"The way you did when you got his help in shaping your magic mirrors," Jeremy said. "But he didn't exactly value your friendship. Once you had completed the mirrors he wanted you to make, you were nothing to him. He certainly didn't rush to your aid when the Great Council banished you to the Between."

Sebastian's smile was cold and perfunctory. "I didn't ask him to. I take responsibility for my own actions, Jeremy. What about you?"

"I try to watch out for myself. And for those I care for."

"So you take Tremien at face value. You think everything the old spider says must be true."

Jeremy shrugged. "He's never done a thing to harm me. He's given me a home and has allowed me to work at developing my magic."

"And you've always done everything he's requested you to do, out of pure loyalty. Good God, Jeremy, can't you see how he's been manipulating you? He wants you to believe in him so he can use you as a pawn in his fight against the Great Dark One. One of these days you really ought to grow up. Use your common sense for a change. What do you suppose would happen if Tremien ever defeated the

Great Dark One? If he managed, somehow, to kill him once and for all?"

Jeremy leaned back in his chair. "If that ever happened, I suppose Thaumia would be a better place."

Sebastian laughed, a short, sharp bark of scorn. "It would be a dictatorship. Under the thumb of wise, benevolent, paternalistic, domineering old Tremien. Two sides of a coin, Jeremy. That's what you see with Tremien and the Great Dark One. Two sides of a coin, that's all."

"You're wrong."

"Am I? Think about it. You don't give your life to a coin, not if you're a wise man. If you get your hands on a coin, you spend it. You use the power it can buy for your own ends. But look at you—you give up everything for some damned crusade that you can't possibly believe in."

"You're still wrong."

"Wrong or right, I'm not coming with you. I can't take time from my own life to help you."

"Not even if the lives of thousands of people depend on it?" Jeremy asked. "Can you live with that?"

Sebastian's voice rose, becoming edged with anger: "They're nothing to me now. I never thought I'd see anyone from Thaumia again. It was something I'd resigned myself to. Yes, I can live with it. And with myself."

Jeremy tossed the crumpled Coke can into the wastebasket. It clattered in. "Two points," he said. He pushed himself up from the chair. Outside the office, thunder grumbled in the distance. "Well. So I'm self-deluded, and so Tremien is no better than the Great Dark One. So you're too busy running for the damned legislature to care about me or my friends. I can't offer you anything to make it worth your while. I guess that's it, then."

"Yeah." Sebastian looked relieved.

"Good thing for you I happen to believe in principles," Jeremy said. "This whole thing started for me when you kidnapped me into Thaumia. Did it ever occur to you to be grateful that not everyone in creation shares your methods?"

Sebastian shrugged. "You've got your own style," he said. "I just like mine better."

"I'll tell them back in Thaumia how much you care for them," Jeremy said. "Thanks for nothing. I hope you lose your election, friend." He stuck out his hand and gave Sebastian a rueful grin.

Sebastian returned the grin. "I've got a fat incumbent trying to make sure of that. I hope you can find some way of dealing with your problem, Jeremy. I mean that sincerely." He clasped Jeremy's hand in farewell.

"I just found it," Jeremy said, tightening his grip. Sebastian tried to pull away, but too late; with one strong tug Jeremy tumbled sideways, into the Gate, and he pulled Sebastian after him.

6

"**G**rab him!" Jeremy shouted as his captive tried with startling alacrity to twist out of his grasp.

Barach and Nul (who had returned from his food-seeking expedition) helped Jeremy drag Sebastian away from the Gate, into the woods, beyond the magical wards. Sure enough, as soon as they released him, Sebastian rushed back toward the clearing, only to meet the nearly invisible web of the magic wards. He tried to push through by sheer strength, but a few seconds of effort made it clear to them all that he would be unable, on his own, to make it through. He turned on them, his chest heaving and his eyes glaring in anger. They focused on Jeremy with a kind of enraged reproach. "I thought you were too moral to stoop to kidnapping," he growled.

"I'm full of surprises," Jeremy returned. "Surprise: you're here and you have no power. So I'd say that if you ever want to return to Earth, you'd better help us out."

Sebastian tugged at his tie, loosening it. Sweat stood on his forehead and cheeks. "You, Barach Loremaster. You used to pay lip service to the cause of good. Is it good to steal me from my own world without my consent?"

"Your world?" Barach said, raising his bushy eyebrows. "Ah, I see. It is like the fable of the worm in the apple. The worm laboriously climbed a tree one day, picked out the reddest apple, and bored his way in. That afternoon a man picked the apple and, not noticing the worm hole, bit into it. The worm thrust his head out and cried, 'My home! You've destroyed my home! And after all the work I put into improving it, too!'"

"Worms not talk," Nul objected.

100

Sebastian paid no attention to either of them. "You realize that you can't force me to help you," he said to Jeremy. "Oh, you can bring me to Thaumia, and you can keep me here; but if I don't want to help, there's no way you can make me."

Jeremy sat on a fallen tree. "I guess that's true enough. On the other hand, the only way you'll ever get back to Earth is to help us. If you don't want to return, you're welcome to stay here. Of course, you made quite a few enemies when you were here before. They'll probably have a few scores to settle with you. Since you're without magic now, it might go hard on you, don't you think?"

Sebastian hissed something between his teeth. There was a sort of flicker in the air, like a quick cool breeze. "Travel spell," Barach said. "It does not work for you anymore, Sebastian. You have indeed exhausted all your magic."

"Worm not even have right kind of mouth to talk," Nul said.

"Think it over," Jeremy told Sebastian. "I've got my own magic now—not as fancy as yours used to be, and sometimes there's a problem with control, but it's enough to give me the edge. It's really simple. You help us and we'll send you back to Earth. Refuse and you're stuck here." Jeremy grinned. "It's what I call the direct sell," he added.

"Damn you," Sebastian returned.

"Same to you again."

Barach raised his hand. "Let me intercede, if I may. Sebastian, you may recall that when you came before the High Council, only Tremien and I spoke for you. If we had our way, you would not have been banished to the Between—and you would not have switched places with Jeremy here. I take it you will recall that Tremien and I both stood for leniency?"

"I remember, Loremaster," Sebastian said.

"Then you will know that I bear you no particular ill will. Let us reason together. Why will you not help us?"

Sebastian took a deep breath and rehearsed his objections once again. Nul had great trouble in grasping the concept of a political campaign, but Jeremy shushed him with, "It's something like an adept trying to be appointed to the Council." Barach heard Sebastian out, occasionally nodding to show that he understood.

At last the old magician stroked his tangled gray beard thoughtfully. "If I may suggest a possible solution," he said. "We are a good day's sail southwest of Savoyan Delar, it is true. That means an unavoidable delay of two days in travel if you remain here—unless we use Jeremy's magic to empower the travel spell."

"Hold on," Jeremy said. "I thought it was dangerous over water."

"It is," Sebastian replied. A wind had begun to rise, ruffling the tops of the palmlike trees. He glanced up at the broken blue sky visible through their fronds. "You've got about a one-in-four chance of misdirection if you use the travel spell over any considerable expanse of ocean."

"You underestimate Jeremy's powers," Barach said. "I propose that he effect a spell like the Anchor of Tchetstitlan; that will make the use of the travel spell feasible."

"Can he do that?"

"He has the power. I'll assist him with the planning."

Sebastian crossed to the fallen tree where Jeremy sat and stood glaring down at him. "All right. You've got the cards this time. But whatever happens, I have to be back Monday morning. Get moving if you want my help."

Barach went aside to consider the difficulties of the spell. Before he had finished, Regina appeared again, lugging a heavy basket filled with more food from Adelaide's table. Nul fell on this with an assortment of happy grunts, and after Jeremy had performed the introductions, he and Sebastian shared the food with Nul and Regina.

"I have heard of the Keeper," Sebastian said, helping himself to a hard-boiled egg. "But I am surprised that she would have anything to do with the outside world."

"Mage Jeremy convinced her," Regina replied. She had been closely examining the two of them, looking from Sebastian to Jeremy with evident wonder. "You are most alike, the two of you. Except that Jeremy has that handsome beard."

"The child has taste," Jeremy murmured.

"There's a reason for that," Sebastian said. "We are doubles; born in two universes at the same time, we are reflections of one another."

Regina had spread a cloth on the ground near the fallen tree and was sitting on it. She rose up on her knees and said, "How wonderful! Does everyone have a double? Do I?"

Sebastian bit into the egg and shook his head. When he had swallowed, he said, "No. It is a rare occurrence. I became aware that Jeremy existed only when I was in the Between and had great need to escape. His existence was just a fortunate piece of luck for me."

With a disappointed sigh, Regina sank back to a sitting position. "I've always wanted a sister," she said. "I thought maybe I'd have one on Earth."

Nul reached into the basket for another huge chunk of brown bread. "Nul have lots of sisters," he said. "They nothing but trouble. Talk, talk, all the time. Not like worms. Worms quiet."

The day had been growing steadily overcast, the wind stronger. It rattled the palm fronds overhead now, threatening to storm. Regina glanced up. "Grandmama's spells usually keep the bad weather out to sea," she said. "I can't think what could be wrong."

"What's wrong is that I'm here," Sebastian told her. "When two doubles are together in the same universe, things are disrupted. Jeremy raised a storm back on Earth when we were together; now it's happening here."

Barach had returned. "What have we here?" he asked, rubbing his hands together. "I hope you have saved me some."

"There's a crust and part of a bottle of wine left, I think," Jeremy said. "Enough to keep life in you."

"Well, well, that's all I ask," Barach said, reaching into the basket to retrieve a full bottle of wine, a handsome wedge of cheese, and a good portion of the bread. "I believe I've solved the theoretical problems, Jeremy. There are several factors to be taken into account: the ocean, of course, but also the proximity of the Gate and its ancient magic and the effect that the two of you will have on any magical field. But there is nothing that cannot be overcome. Have you finished your meal?"

"I suppose so," Jeremy said.

Barach fished inside his shirt and produced a few sheets of paper. "Then withdraw and study these. The spell is there and should work; but it's up to you to find the correct mode and cast it."

"If it's all the same to you," Sebastian said, "I'd rather you cast it, Loremaster. You have a little more experience with magic than Jeremy does."

"Impossible," Barach said, raising the bottle and somehow finding his mouth in the wilderness of beard. "Ah, that is good. Of course you haven't heard, but I lost my magic in a confrontation with your old friend the Hidden Hag of Illsmere. I can't even cast a travel spell now." His brown eyes twinkled. "So I understand how you must feel, since you are now without magic as well. It is painful to trust one's fate to a mere stripling, but there it is. Resign yourself."

"Oh, wonderful," Sebastian said with a sigh. He stretched his hand toward Barach. "Give that bottle to someone who needs it."

No wind stirred the sultry air over the town of Narofrod. Sanklar Aveskhan had climbed to the roof of the tallest building in town, a crane-house over the river docks, to prepare himself for the protection spell. From his vantage he could see the exodus: upstream beyond the Great Bridge a ragged string of riverboats, painted red, yellow, blue, every color but the unlucky shade of orange, was making its way upstream, propelled by dipping oars or, in one or two cases, by local breezes raised by magic.

Each boat was crammed with people. From this height Sanklar could not recognize them individually, but he could see the pink specks that were faces. He supposed many of them were turned toward him, offering bitter curses. Well, let that be. He shaded his eyes and looked far to the north, where the broad brown river disappeared into the distant haze. No boat had yet gotten that far upstream, but they were all on their way.

He turned and looked westward. Through breaks in the buildings and trees he could just make out from here a few glints of silvery light from the Vaskflod, a tributary of the Bronfal that led to the broad sheep-dotted pastures of the High Dales, south of the Arkhedden Forest. A few of the boats would probably turn and make their way up the Vaskflod, which was navigable as far as the Klidden Rapids, a hundred and sixty leagues to the west and north. Some of the citizens of Narofrod had relatives in the town of Galadine, another river port and the center of trade for the wool merchants of the High Dales and the grain farmers of the South Downs.

But few of the riverboats would make for Galadine, for there were ancient and continual disputes about shipping rights and passage fees among the rivermen of the two towns. Most of the boats would go against the lazy flow of the Bronfal, northward to Broadpools, a smaller and weaker settlement than Galadine, but at least one which had the good sense to submit to the sensible regulations imposed by the rivermen of Narofrod. The traffic westbound to Galadine, then, would be mostly along the road, merchants trundling away as much as they could load on carts and wagons, families trudging together in the suffocating southern heat and dust. From here Sanklar could not see the road itself, but he could see the dark-green line of the trees that bordered it, soft-wooded trees like pinelas, redcups, and sedrons, and he thought how welcome the shade would be to the travelers by late afternoon.

Turning once again, Sanklar gave the southern horizon a worried glance, but it was empty as it had been all day. Then he looked at the great stone-and-wood bridge that spanned the Bronfal not far upstream from the crane-house. Five stone arches, each of them tall and broad enough to permit passage of the largest riverboats, strode into the water from each shore; the middle portion of the bridge was timber, trestle-built, and without supporting piles for such a distance that he knew magic must be in the work, possibly even that of the legendary Durelianus, the Bridge-Maker of Hest. No one passed over the bridge, however, for on the far side the main road turned south, following the course of the river down to the sea and to Relenda Chai. Except for ferry points, the bridge offered the first opportunity for crossing the Bronfal, and Sanklar expected that whatever was coming from the south would take advantage of it.

No refugees, however, would flee to the south, nor would any take the long road to Skelmouth on the coast, for the people of Skelmouth were a proud and self-contained lot, and their language sounded strange to the ears of inlanders. No river-dweller from Narofrod would care to cast himself on the mercy of seafaring Skelmouth folk.

The young adept sighed. His task was difficult enough without the distraction of worrying about the comforts, the prejudices, the petty feuds and squabbles of these townfolk. He turned again to look away to the south, where the sky had definitely grown dim. The obscurity was not a haze, not like the summery dimness away in the north; rather it was a seeming absence of light, an alteration in the sky itself. The sticky feeling was stronger now, impossible to ignore.

Tremien's representative still had not come. No matter; something had to begin, and soon. Sanklar took a deep breath and began the recital of poetry that served him as the activating force for spells. This was nearly an epic, for the dome of magic was a difficult thing to manage. If legend spoke truly, it had been used only three times before in the north: at the siege of Caloddan, in the Grimwood Wars, and over Klon's Keep. Every former use had been at least partly successful in repelling opposing magic, and in no case had the protected castle or town fallen to sorcery. Each use of the spell, of course, had to be reformulated from the beginning, or the enchantment would have no hold.

What Sanklar wanted was a grand version of a simple magical ward. Ward spells were in high demand, and magicians worked diligently to master them; Sanklar had busied himself, back during his apprenticeship, with exploring all possible variations of them. He had a ready store available now, worked out but not pronounced, suitable for sealing anything from a money changer's stall to a warehouse; but until today he had never planned a magic strong enough to seal an entire town.

As he chanted the third canto of his spell, Sanklar felt the power streaming out of him. Making magic always left him exhausted in body and spirit, always made his head ache savagely behind the eyes, and this time was no exception. His breath came shallow in his chest, burning as if he had run a thousandpace as fast as he could. Sanklar ignored the pain and concentrated on the words, on the magic the words would unleash.

The fourth canto; the fifth. Sanklar looked up into the sky, the strangely tinted sky, and saw unmistakable flickers of energy there, magic trying to form and shape itself to his demands. It was like watching a pale daytime aurora: the streaming flares of purple had the same urge toward order, the same hint of lines of force behind them.

The sixth and seventh cantos. The eighth. And then the

last, the ninth, the set of lines that would seize the lines of force, that would bind them securely to Narofrod. Sanklar was dizzy now; the river, the town, seemed to spin around the derrick-house, and he seemed precariously balanced on a floor that pitched like the deck of a ship in storm. He sank to his knees and put a hand against the rough, hot wood to steady himself physically, but he took care that his voice did not lose its clarity and force.

Nevertheless, he was losing the battle.

Sanklar felt a hot rush of nausea. The spell was not beyond him, but the required power was. He was simply not ready to conduct such a rushing tide of magical force. He could feel the dome of power shivering, threatening to collapse—

A hand closed on his shoulder. Through the hand, magic flowed into his body, filling him like a vessel. Sanklar gasped, closed his eyes, and roared the last few syllables of the spell. He felt the passage of power from the stranger into him, from himself into the dome of protection. When he opened his eyes again, he could see the orderly lines of the ward, etched ever so faintly against the sky.

"You did well," said a soft voice.

For a moment Sanklar could not even reply. He was drenched with sweat, and his limbs trembled violently. "Thank you for your aid," he said at last.

He looked up. The newcomer wore the unadorned dark brown robes of a teacher of high magic. He was entering middle age for a wizard; he looked fifty, but might have been a hundred and twenty or more, with a clean-shaven face, close-cropped silver hair, and direct blue eyes. "Rest a moment," he said. "You will be better presently."

"Thank you. You come from Tremien?"

The man nodded. "Yes. I am Themogar, one of Tremien's grandnephews. Normally I am a teacher at the High College of Morennon, away in Vanislach, but it seems you have more need of me at present than my students. How are you now?"

Sanklar got to his feet, swaying slightly. "Better." He chanced a look downward into the streets. "Blast them, why won't they leave?"

Themogar stepped to the edge of the flat roof and gazed downward. "You won't be able to persuade them all to leave, you know. No matter how convincing you are, there will always be a few stragglers determined to protect the town—or to loot it."

Below them a few men milled in the cobbled streets, their movements almost aimless, it seemed, less purposeful than those of ants around an anthill. "Looters will have a hard time of it anyway," Sanklar said. "If my spell is as good as I think it is, no thief will prosper in Narofrod this summer."

"It is a good spell," Themogar said. "I've never seen a finer." But his voice was abstracted as he peered off to the south.

"Be careful," Sanklar said. "You are very near the edge."

Themogar shrugged and stepped off into thin air. Sanklar gasped and lunged forward to grab him—but the teacher of magic merely hovered, levitated by some spell of his own. "I take precautions," Themogar said. He drifted back to the roof of the crane-house. "Whatever is coming moves slowly," he said. "Faster than a man afoot, but more slowly than a racing horse. Unless it resorts to a travel spell, I think it will not be here before nightfall. We could travel southward to meet it, I suppose, but somehow that does not strike me as wise. I suggest, young Sanklar, that we busy ourselves among the remaining townspeople. You were right; something dreadful is coming, and the more of them who leave, the more will be alive to see the morning."

The weather worsened overhead as Jeremy declaimed the spell designed to anchor them to the Gate glade. In the distance he could hear the forlorn hoots and bellows of dragons as huge, cold drops of rain began to pelt down, snapping the palm fronds overhead and making quarter-size dark spots on the volcanic stone. At last, though, Jeremy was satisfied that the spell had worked. Their travel spell was now firmly tied to a quadrangle of four large stone blocks.

"Ready to try it," he said. Regina had gone back to the cottage sometime before. The other three clustered under a trio of taller palms, sheltering from the spasmodic but painful raindrops.

They joined Jeremy in the quadrangle, Nul crossing his long spidery arms over his huge head for a little added protection, and Jeremy spoke the travel cantrip. Their surroundings faded away, replaced by a whirl of glowing colors. "So far, so good," Barach murmured, settling down to endure the fifty minutes or so of subjective time that the fast-travel spell inevitably took, whether the traveler journeyed for thousands of leagues or for only a few steps.

"Where are we heading?" Sebastian asked. "Whitehorn?"

"Right," Jeremy told him. "Tremien has the three of them there, detained on the pretext of formulating a strategy to deal with the Great Dark One's coming. We should materialize in the courtyard of Whitehorn."

"If all goes well," Barach said.

Nul's orange eyes grew a bit pale. "What does that mean?"

"Well, Jeremy has tried to anchor the spell, so as to counteract the forces of natural magic and of water. He may have succeeded. If he has, we shall appear in the courtyard of Whitehorn, just as planned; but if he has failed, we may materialize over the ocean, or in the middle of Arkhedden Forest, or we may never materialize at all."

"What?"

Jeremy put his hand on the pika's shoulder. "Relax, Nul. Everything's going smoothly. If something were wrong, I'd feel it."

Nul heaved a great sigh. "Barach had me frightened."

Sebastian sniffed. "He didn't do me any good either."

As it turned out, Jeremy was right. With another painful pop in his ears, he and the others were suddenly standing on the clean gravel of the Whitehorn courtyard, not far inside the great gate. A stony voice from overhead grated out, "Visitors! Mage Barach, Mage Jeremy, Nul the Pika King, and a stranger, within the gates!"

"Oh, shut up, Busby," Jeremy shouted at the rear end of one of the two stone gargoyles that stood watch above the gate.

"It's my job," the gargoyle returned, without looking around. "Even if there's no one to hear it."

Fred, the younger and more careless of the two, said, "I heard it. You almost cracked open that scar along my left shoulder." Fred had been wounded some time before, and he was inordinately proud of having lost a small chip in a confrontation with a broadsword.

"Young marlstone."

"Hmpf. You're not very gneiss."

Jeremy groaned. "Let's go inside."

Kelada met them at the main door, stood staring from Jeremy to Sebastian and back again, and finally embraced and kissed her husband. He hugged her, wincing at a twinge of pain from the place where the unicorn had sunk its teeth into his arm. "What's wrong?" she asked at once.

He rolled up his sleeve. The bite was healing well, but it looked satisfyingly gruesome, a horseshoe-shaped black scab puckering the flesh a few inches down from his elbow. Kelada cried out in concern and hurried him off to care for the wound while Barach and Nul escorted Sebastian to Tremien's chambers.

Jeremy joined them there not long afterward, sporting a clean bandage and feeling happier than he had in days. The dark expression on Tremien's face, however, punctured his mood as soon as he entered the room. "There you are, Jeremy," he said. "I was just beginning to explain to the others that something most odd is happening away to the south. I have heard from some of my friends in Gaffort that a strange plague has affected people, livestock, and even crops at a spot near the coast between there and Relenda; and it seems that all traffic along the Old North Road between Relenda and Narofrod has ceased."

"What is it?" Jeremy asked.

Tremien shook his head. "That I cannot tell."

Jeremy almost laughed. "What? You keep track of everything that happens in Cronbrach!"

Tremien tented his fingers. "Normally, that is true. But when I turn my perception to the south, I find nothing truly amiss; just a . . . a lapse in my vision, as it were. As if there is a pocket of darkness there, darkness that I cannot penetrate. But the word from Gaffort is alarming: *something* came ashore between there and Relenda, it seems, and whatever it is, it is making its slow way northward, leaving a swath of destruction behind it. I was about to ask Sebastian Magister if he knew of any device of the Great Dark One that would do such a thing."

Sebastian shook his head. "I saw Jilhukrihain only through the mirrors," he said. "I know very little about his powers and his magic."

"But you did confer with him," Barach said.

"Yes, frequently. I had to, of course; he offered me

instruction and aid in creating my mirrors. But we never exchanged pleasantries."

Tremien sighed. "Well, we shall soon know more of this, for I have a trusted friend on hand in Narofrod. It may be—and I hope that it is—that the destruction has nothing to do with the Great Dark One. Yet I fear that they are bound together, for the marshy coastlands south of Gaffort are less than two days' sail north of the beach where you found the burning ship. What of your journey? Did you note aught amiss?"

"Found dragons and unicorns," Nul said. "Nice old lady and nice young girl. And this." He pointed at Sebastian.

Barach said, "Hush, Nul. That is not what he meant. No, Mage Tremien. We traveled to Savoyan Delar, where we boarded the *Arrow*, as you had arranged. From there we sailed directly to Gateway Cay." He proceeded to summarize their journey and its success as Tremien nodded his understanding.

When he had finished, Tremien said to Sebastian, "You go far in atoning for your earlier excesses in helping us." Nul snorted and even Jeremy smiled at the thought of Sebastian's aid being voluntary, but Tremien ignored them both. "I have two of the wizards here: Idoradas and Jondan. Both are members of the High Council, and it was plausible that I should seek their aid in ferreting out the Great Dark One's purpose. Celissa, who is not yet of mage standing, has returned to her home in the Saboy Forest, not far from Savoyan Delar. I had no pretext to keep her here, but I have woven certain spells that should warn me if she attempts any unusual magic. So far she has not. I think it would be wise now for Sebastian to clothe himself in something less, ah, conspicuous and for him to listen as Barach and I speak with Idoradas and Jondan. Perhaps he can see something that one of us would overlook."

"All right," Sebastian said. "I want to get this over as soon as possible."

"Then you may change your clothing in the private chamber there. Change it all, mind you; I'll have a complete outfit brought."

Whitehorn Keep was a commodious palace as well as a mountaintop fortress, and it had innumerable stores of practically every necessity, including clothing. From somewhere

Tremien's servants brought underclothes, shirt, hose, trousers, and robes for Sebastian, who retired with them to the adjoining room. He returned dressed in the Thaumian style, looking quite at home in the robes—they were the nondescript light creamy brown of a student of magic—and if one overlooked his perfectly styled hair, Sebastian could easily have been a studious journeyman. Nul commented on his funny-looking hair, earning an annoyed glance from Sebastian. But then, as Barach pointed out, the men of Harond were known to affect extremely long braided hair, the men of the Vendella Valley shaved a quarter of their heads (the exact quarter depending on their birthdates and marital status), and those of the Cresokati Islands anointed their hair with thick layers of gray mud.

"It doesn't matter what my hair looks like anyway," Sebastian grunted, his fingers fumbling with the laces that fastened the short outer robe at his left shoulder. "Jondan will know me from the trial. And if one of them is housing Jilhukrihain's essence, he will know me from our past association. In fact, I don't see why I have to change clothes at all."

Tremien said, "There is a very good reason. I do not believe the Great Dark One knows your exact fate. As far as he understands the matter, you were finally banished to the Between. I would not have him know that there is a passageway open to Jeremy's world, or that you came from that world. He has a strong talent for reading magic, and if you bore anything from Earth, he would infallibly detect it."

"Why shouldn't he know of Earth?" Jeremy asked, suddenly uneasy.

"For another very good reason. If we fail to defeat him in Thaumia, his hunger for conquest is such that he would surely attempt to overcome Earth after the fall of this world."

Sebastian tied the last knot. "There. If you'll have your people see that my suit is brushed and properly hung, I suppose I'm ready. What do we do now?"

Tremien stood at his desk, the light from the tall windows beyond making the nimbus of white hair around his bald pate shine as if self-illuminated. "Now we have a simple meal with our friends Idoradas and Jondan. I will not bother to introduce you, and I will ask you not to speak. But listen

well, Sebastian, and observe. If any tiniest hint of the Great
Dark One's presence is in either of the two, let me know."

"After the meal, you mean."

"I mean at once. And we will have to pray that *at once*
will not be too late."

Themogar paced back and forth at the western foot of the
Great Bridge of Narofrod. He had picked up a staff somewhere, an ashwood staff nearly as tall as he, and he tapped
it on the cobbles as if seeking a hollow sound. An east wind
had sprung up, but a sultry and fitful wind, not strong
enough to ruffle Themogar's short gray hair and too moist
to bring Sanklar any relief from the choking heat. "Here, I
think," Themogar said at last. "We will take our stand
here."

"We are inside the magic field," Sanklar pointed out.

"True."

"That may interfere with any spells we may need to cast."

"It may protect us." Themogar stood in the center of the
way, looking across the arch of the bridge. Three hundred
paces forward the stone gave way to the heavy wood of the
middle span; that ran for four hundred paces or so, and then
the stone took up again. The bridge was wide enough to
carry a double row of wains, and it looked sturdy enough to
bear any load with its arches of gray-speckled granite and its
center cantilevered span of iron-colored strongwood.

Sanklar stood just behind the teacher, struggling for breath.
It seemed to him that the air had grown worse, almost like
twice-breathed air: there was little in it to sustain the lungs.
The whole sky had gone a coppery brown, and something
was traveling slowly, though still faster than a man's pace,
northward on the road on the far side of the river. What it
was, Sanklar could not say, nor could Themogar, for they
could not truly see it. Their eyes could detect only a mirage-
like blank spot, a center of darkness as it were, with indistinct
edges. When it had first come into view, Themogar had
tried to use a reveal spell, to no avail. Now it was very close
to the far side of the bridge, still coming at that maddening,
implacable pace, and now they stood to meet it.

Behind them the streets had become deserted. True to
Themogar's observation, Narofrod was far from empty: hundreds of people remained there, perhaps as many as a

thousand, one-tenth of the normal population. But as the oppressive morning had lengthened into the sickly foreboding afternoon, they all seemed to have found shelter within doors. Faintly Sanklar could hear from somewhere far behind the shouts and discordant music of a drunken revel, but he ignored it, focusing all of his attention at the approach of something that looked like a dark mist.

Themogar chanted a soft magic of revelation and raised his staff. Nothing happened. "I seem to be wasting my spells today," the older man said with a grunt. "At least you spoke yours aright." Squinting, Sanklar looked up at the sky. The nearly invisible lines of force, the wards over the city, still quivered there, apparently strong. At least there was that; nothing evil, if his spell had gone rightly, could possibly come any closer than the nearer stone portion of the bridge.

Sanklar felt sweat pouring down his neck and trickling along his back like creeping insects. He noticed that Themogar's robe was darkly stained under the arms too. The afternoon temperature had climbed, but it was more than that. Something was smothering them both, something as thick and heavy as steam in one of the stone rooms of Firepeak, the volcanic mountain that had been tamed into a spa.

"It has stopped," Themogar said suddenly.

The day had gone that same weird copper color. Sanklar had seen nothing like it, save only a total eclipse of Sawel, the sun, years ago when he was a boy. He had been frightened, and his older sister had teased him that the moon was devouring Sawel. His father had reassured him, and Sanklar had a vivid recollection of how he had rested his cheek against his father's scratchy beard as the eclipse had progressed. The sun had been dimmed then, and the blue of the sky had bled away to a weak pewter color. But the sun shone overhead now; though its light seemed filtered through a dense layer of smoke or haze, no eclipse had caused this weakening of the day.

From where he stood Sanklar could not see the far side of the bridge, only the long stone incline up to the wooden portion. He could tell, however, that the darkness on the other side of the river radiated from a point nearly opposite them. "Do you think the spell has halted it?" he asked.

"I do not know. But it has certainly paused. Whatever it is, it stands on the other side of the bridge exactly as we stand here. It may be sensing us, feeling us."

"Through the barrier of the spell?"

"I know. It doesn't seem possible. Yet I have the odd feeling that some force is probing at the city and at the spell."

"I have the odd feeling that I'm drowning," Sanklar said. "What has happened to the air?"

Themogar shook his head. "I cannot say. It seems that the virtue is being sucked from it. Had I the leisure, I would try to summon an air elemental and question it; but I think we had best concentrate on what lies beyond the bridge and breathe the air as best we can."

"Perhaps I should cross the bridge and see what lies there," Sanklar told him.

"No. I think we both had better stay within the protection of your spell. I . . . Wait a moment. There is movement on the other side of the bridge now."

"It's coming to us," Sanklar said.

"It seems to be."

They fell silent. Sanklar's hair was matted to his head with perspiration, but he felt the nape of his neck quiver nonetheless. He stared at the bridge so hard that his eyes ached, watching for something, a sign, anything. "See that?" Themogar whispered.

But Sanklar saw nothing except the dimming of the light. It was exactly as if a floating mist of darkness were approaching across the wooden part of the bridge, as if the beams and planking were flickering out of view as the mist advanced. There was a sudden loud splash from the far side of the river, making Sanklar start; and then another, and another.

"The bridge is coming apart," Themogar said. "The arches on the far side are crumbling."

The air was worse than ever. Breathing it was like breathing thick steam. Sanklar's eyes bulged in his head; his throat seemed to swell. "Men," he croaked. "See, Themogar, in the dark—there are men!"

Themogar swore softly to himself. "I see them," he said. "One, two—five in all. But not men. Dim shapes, giants, bent forward. They seem to walk abreast."

The five figures were nearly across the wooden portion of the bridge. They seemed ghostly in their floating, eerily rapid movement, in the dimness of their outline, in the silence of their advance; but other tumult could have covered the sound of footfalls. Sanklar heard a rending sound, more splashes, and the high-pitched groan of wood bending, twisting, and splintering under unendurable stress. "What are they doing?"

Themogar shook his head. "I think . . . I think the binding spell that holds the bridge safe is weakening as they pass. The magic itself is failing."

Themogar's words made no sense, for spells bound into stone and wood were the strongest and the most lasting spells of them all. Yet the bridge was beyond doubt falling to ruin. With a crack that Sanklar felt through the soles of his boots, a portion of the center span gave way and collapsed. The five shadowy walkers set foot on stone again, not far from the edge of the protection spell.

With wide eyes Sanklar watched the end of the great bridge: the cantilevered strongwood folded on itself, bent down, fell slowly to the right, toward the river. The gap it left seemed wrong, insane, for the bridge had stood as long as memory. The stone arches on the far side, though out of sight, crumbled with the sound of an avalanche. Off to the right, Sanklar glimpsed a muddy froth streaming down the face of the river, huge beams of strongwood floating like sticks in a millpond.

"Who are you?" Themogar cried out in a loud and terrible voice. "In the name of the One, I demand it! You shall tell me, by the name—"

Sanklar gasped as Themogar cried the True Name aloud, the wizard's last and most desperate cantrip. For a reeling moment the world seemed to spin: the sky grew dark beneath his feet, while the ground overhead flashed as with lightning. In that fragment of time Sanklar saw them clearly: five towering figures, faceless, bending forward. He felt their natures, cruel, without mercy. Looking at the darkness of them was like staring into a bottomless open grave.

From somewhere, from everywhere, Sanklar heard a sighing wind that spoke aloud in a sigh of infinite weariness: *We are the Shadow Guard.*

The moment passed. Sanklar found his legs unsteady be-

neath him. He became aware that the five figures, mere
featureless shadows again, stood just on the far side of the
warding spell; and on this side, his back straight, his staff
lifted before him, Themogar confronted them.

Light began to flicker around the indistinct figures, a pale
purple light. Sanklar cringed within, bracing himself against
a blast of magic: but it never came. He tried to draw in
enough breath to speak, when ahead of him Themogar's
hoarse voice suddenly began to chant desperately, a song of
strengthening.

The dome of protection that Sanklar had wrought with so
much pain was dissolving.

He felt the power drain from around him, felt the dissolu-
tion of the lines of force that he had woven with his will and
his words. It was a terrible pain, not physical but spiritual,
but no less keen for all that. He felt as if he were being
flayed alive as part of his own *mana*, his own magic, was
ripped from him.

"I cannot hold them," Themogar panted, not turning.
"They snatch my spells away. Leave here, Sanklar! You
must travel to Whitehorn to warn Tremien. Now!"

Sanklar nodded, though Themogar could not possibly have
seen him. He spoke his private travel cantrip, trying hard to
envision in his mind his destination, the high valley that he
had never visited but had only read about. For an instant he
thought the spell had worked, for everything faded—

But then he was back on the verge of the bridge again. It
was as though the magic had been snatched from him, not
canceled or counterspelled but simply removed. The world
flared again, a heatless explosion of purple, and the five
shadows advanced through the place where the spell should
have stopped them.

Themogar turned slowly toward Sanklar, looking like a
feeble beggar imploring alms. Sanklar cried out.

Themogar had become a thousand years old.

The skin on his arms and face had cracked and shrunk,
his eyes had fallen in, his mouth gaped in a skull-toothed
grin. He collapsed, undoubtedly already dead, with a rattle
of bones.

Sanklar stood his ground. Already he felt the vibrations
around him as magic was pulled away from riverside buildings, as stones spelled to stones let go their hold and fell

under no command but gravity. The world darkened, sounds went away; even the pain he felt abated as his senses fled from him. Still he stood his ground, shouting the best spell he could think of, a spell to blast and bind these uncanny foes—

He felt himself dying.

His knees hit the stones with no pain; still he struggled to scream out the spell. It seemed to be torn from his throat, seemed to pull his spirit after it. His heart thudded and stopped.

For one moment of time his mind was very clear. For one instant he realized why he had failed, why Themogar had failed; he knew why the five shadows had triumphed.

Then the world was gone and Sanklar Aveskhan knew nothing more at all.

7

"**W**e have learned one thing for certain," young Idoradas said over the meal. "And that is, mundanity is increasing at an alarming rate."

The older Jondan nodded. "It is almost as if something were draining Thaumia of magic," he said. "Of course there is an enormous amount of *mana* immanent in the world. I cannot concede that the increased mundanity is 'alarming,' at least not yet. But it is disturbing. It hints at a want of balance." He glanced to his right, at Jeremy and Sebastian, who sat at the foot of the table, but did not speak more.

"The absence of magic," Tremien mused. "Yes, that might account for my difficulty in detecting events to the south. I am frankly worried; my representative in Narofrod should have been in touch with me by now. I can no longer feel his presence in Narofrod, nor indeed anywhere in Cronbrach; and yet he must be there."

"I will journey to Narofrod if you wish, Mage Tremien," Idoradas said. His blue eyes were level—Jeremy thought he had to struggle to keep fear out of them—and his chin was set, but his disheveled reddish-blond hair gave him the appearance of a timorous adolescent. "I could go anytime—"

Tremien waved a hand. "Thank you, Idoradas, but your work with Jondan is very likely more valuable than anything you could learn to the south. I have other eyes to send there. You will remain in Whitehorn for the time being."

"It could be some trick of the Great Dark One," Jondan said. "He may have found some means of masking—" He broke off as a ferocious rumble of thunder clattered the hanging chandelier and made the silver spoons dance on the table. "Unusual weather," he muttered with another glance

119

toward Sebastian. "However, I was saying that the Great Dark One may have found some way of masking his presence. I would advise you to send a party south to report at once."

"And so I shall," Tremien replied. "Well, well, evening comes on. I thank you, Idoradas, and you, Jondan. I would ask you to rest now, for more work will come with nightfall." Tremien stood from his place at the head of the table, gathered his white robe, and beckoned to Barach, Jeremy, and Sebastian. "Please let me speak with the three of you now; we really must try to learn of the situation in Narofrod."

They followed him back to his study, where Tremien crossed to the windows and stood staring out into the early twilight, deepened by storm clouds. "Well?" he asked without turning.

Sebastian cleared his throat. "I saw nothing to indicate Jilhukrihain's presence," he said.

Jeremy jumped as a fork of lightning flashed outside, turning the figure of Tremien for an instant into a photographic negative. Thunder rattled the leaded panes. When the sound had died down, Tremien said, "I thought not. Well, there is one left to visit. Will you set off at once?"

With a wry look on his face, Sebastian said, "Mage Tremien, I am doing as you ask. But may I, too, request a favor?"

"Speak it."

"I came to Thaumia—I will admit it—unwillingly. I came, too, most suddenly. Will you permit me to return to my own home for tonight if I promise to return tomorrow afternoon? I have left a wife behind, and she does not know where I am. I have responsibilities that must be addressed; tomorrow morning there are people to whom I must speak. Name the oath you will have me swear, and I will swear it; but let me go, I pray you."

Tremien, his hands locked behind him, turned and looked at Sebastian for a long time, his saddle-brown face grave, his beard and hair astonishingly white in the dimness of the room. "You have changed somewhat, Sebastian Magister," he said. "It is not just the loss of magic. You are a different person from the old days."

"I've grown up a little," Sebastian said. "I'll admit that I never wanted to return to Thaumia. But now that I have

returned, I see your need. If it is in my power to help, I will
help. But look at the cost—that storm is my fault, mine and
Jeremy's. And if I do not go back to Earth to offer some
token of explanation for my absence, I will face another
kind of storm there."

Tremien nodded. "Jeremy? What do you say?"

"I wouldn't trust him," Jeremy replied. "He's lied before."

Another searing bolt of lightning flashed outside the window, and again thunder shook the room. When it subsided,
Tremien said, "And you, old friend? What do you say?"

Barach, who had settled into one of the chairs, spread his
hands. "They tell a tale of a scorpion and a willowhawk.
The scorpion lived in a land of famine, and when he saw the
hawk flying over, he cried out, 'Save me! Please take me to
a place where there is food!' The hawk refused, saying,
'You would sting and kill me if I came close to you.' But the
scorpion insisted that he would not; and so the hawk picked
him up in its talons and flew over the sea. Before long the
hawk was astonished to feel the sting of the scorpion. 'What
have you done? Now both of us must die!' he cried out.
And the scorpion replied, 'Alas, I made my promise, but
my nature is not to keep it.' "

"And Sebastian is a scorpion?" Tremien asked with a hint
of a twinkle in his eyes.

Barach shrugged. "I have not felt his sting so far. Perhaps
we should trust him."

"I'll go with him and keep an eye on him," Jeremy said.

"Ah, but on Earth you may well be at his mercy," Barach
said. "You tell me that magic is frowned on there. If you
could not use your power, you might find yourself the
victim, not the guardian."

"I think not. I've been warned that if we spend three days
together in the same world, the unbalancing of forces—magic
in this world, energy in the other—will hurl us apart. But it
won't necessarily be choosy. I don't think Sebastian would
risk having me locked up if it meant that at the end of the
week he stood a fifty-fifty chance of being permanently
marooned back here in Thaumia. Right, Sebastian?"

"You don't need to come," Sebastian said. "Look, if I
don't show up again, you can pop through that Gate and
drag me back, even if I'm in a crowd."

Tremien nodded. "Do this for me," he said. "Use the

travel spell to return to the Gate; but stop first in the town of Narofrod and report to me from there. I am particularly concerned about my kinsman Themogar and the young adept Sanklar. Jeremy, I think you may trust Sebastian for this one night. And tomorrow, if he does not present himself alone for the journey back to Thaumia, you have my permission to, ah, drag him back as he says."

Their preparations were brief: Sebastian attired himself again in Earthly garb, and Nul had to be rounded up. They departed from the library itself, contrary to the usual practice (it was deemed safer to begin and end travel spells out-of-doors, but not during thunderstorms). Scarcely had the spell begun when Sebastian said, "Kelada has changed greatly. I hardly knew her."

"Yeah," Jeremy said. "Well, Cassie looked as if she's changed too. Must be marriage."

"I never thought of Kelada as attractive before," Sebastian continued. "Yet there is something about her—a glow almost. You two must be good for one another."

After a few moments of silence, Jeremy said, "I would never have guessed that Cassie Briggs would leave Taplan and Taplan. She was the youngest department head there three years ago. She must love you a lot."

"I . . . Yes. Well, we both love each other, I suppose." Sebastian shrugged and looked embarrassed. Nul, who doted on learning more about human emotions, stared at them both with his orange eyes, but for once did not say anything. Barach had closed his eyes and seemed almost asleep.

Sebastian cleared his throat. "The travel spell is a little different," he said after a space. "It used to take much longer."

"An improvement of Walther's," Jeremy said. "He introduced it a year and a half ago."

"Ah, I see. Speaking of Walther, what of his daughter? Is, uh, Melodia—"

When Sebastian did not finish the thought, Jeremy said, "Melodia is betrothed now."

"Oh." Sebastian had once been enamored of Melodia; his face held enough forlorn disappointment to give Jeremy a sneaking feeling of satisfaction. No more was said for the rest of the travel spell, and each of them seemed lost in private thought.

They popped into existence again on a grassy hillside. Here the sun was still barely above the horizon, and the sky was clear, although Jeremy suspected that the weather would swiftly change now that he and Sebastian were together there.

Barach opened his eyes very wide. "This is not Narofrod," he said. "Nothing like it. We've gone astray somehow."

Nul sniffed the air. "Funny smell," he said. "Sweet and sick."

Barach waded to the top of the hill through calf-high grass, his shadow long before him. "There is the Bronfal," he said, "a good five thousandpace away. What could have happened?"

The others joined him at the crest of the hill. The land fell away to the east to a wide, brown-faced river. "Look at other side," Nul said. "All dead there."

It was true, Jeremy saw now. A wide swath of yellowish gray bordered the far side of the river, a swath at least five hundred paces broad. Nothing, neither grass nor weed nor tree, seemed to be alive there. Sebastian, off to his left, cried out suddenly. "Look north. Could that be the great Narofrod Bridge?"

Jeremy shaded his eyes and stared. Between them and the river a bulk of buildings intervened. Beyond it, he saw only a couple of piles of rubble on either bank of the river, and between them a disturbed line across the face of the water, as if it flowed over an uneven surface and was disrupted in its passage.

"Let us see," Barach said, striding down the other side of the hill.

It was a good distance to the town, but Barach moved with surprising speed and the others had some trouble keeping up. Still it was dark enough to require wizard-light before they reached the first houses. These were deserted and empty, and as the path became a road and then a street, so were the other dwellings. Some had collapsed entirely into rubble; others stood still; but all were empty of life.

"I feel odd," Jeremy said.

"Yes, well, it's an odd business," Barach replied.

Jeremy sat down on a good-sized timber, part of a collapsed inn. "No. I feel *odd*," he said. "And the light's flickering. Notice?"

Barach blinked. It was true; the blue wizard-light had become uncertain, its illumination hesitant, like the light of a fluorescent tube on the verge of burning out. "Something has taken the magic from his place," he said. "You have only your own resources to draw upon here. Diminish the light."

Jeremy did, and felt somewhat restored. "I am sorry to burden you, Jeremy," Barach said. "But I think we must have a look at what is left of the bridge. It was a work of great sorcery, an ancient doing, and if it has fallen through some evil magic—" He did not complete the thought, but his broad face was grim enough.

"Let's go," Jeremy said, standing. "I'll be all right. It's just that I've gotten used to plugging into the local magic field; didn't realize I was providing my own battery now."

Barach led them on as straight a path as he could, though it required a few detours around fallen structures. In the center of town they saw the first horribly shriveled bodies; five men and two women lay facedown on the cobbles, as though killed from behind while fleeing. They saw more between there and the river: and on the ruin of the bridge they found the last two, one attired in the tan robe of an adept and one in the dark brown of a teacher. Jeremy took one look and turned his face.

Barach, however, knelt beside the mummified remains. "So," he said in a soft voice. "Themogar, Tremien's kinsman; and this, I suspect, must be Sanklar Aveskhan. Peace and long rest to them!"

"The bridge is ruined," Sebastian said. "I have heard that it was built by a student of the great Durelianus himself."

"A true-enough story," Barach said, grunting as he raised himself from beside the bodies. "Jeremy, we must leave this place at once."

They walked away from the river. "Listen," Nul said.

Jeremy felt dizzy. "I don't hear anything."

"Yah, yah. That what Nul mean. When in city you not hear anything? No cat, no dog, no horse. No bird or bug, even. All dead."

Sebastian spoke once more, his voice trembling: "If the Great Dark One did this—"

"You may be sure he did," Barach said.

"He has to be stopped," Sebastian finished.

They tried the communication spell on the outskirts of town, without success. They entered the fields beyond town—and at last they saw a sign of life, a cow bawling with a full udder. There Jeremy tried again, and this time they made contact with Tremien. When he had heard the news, his voice was deeply troubled: "then the evil has indeed come to us. And you say it has drained the magic in its passage?"

"Yes, Mage Tremien," Jeremy said. "Barach says it is as if the essence of magic, the *mana*, has been sucked away. The bridge has fallen, as have all buildings held together by spells; and nothing lives in the city."

"More stories have come in from along the North Road between Narofrod and the Bronfal marshes. They tell of much the same kind of devastation: villages ruined, the people dead. We must think of the living now; I will speak to the people of Broadpools and Downsdale of this, for it is certainly making its way north. I think you had better continue your journey tonight; visit Celissa tomorrow; and come here as soon as ever you may. Thaumia will have need of you."

"You really don't have to come with me," Sebastian said. Night had fallen, and they faced the Gate once more, its focus still anchored in Sebastian's office.

"I'll feel better about it," Jeremy said. "Let's go."

They stepped into the shimmer of the Gate and emerged in the darkened office. "It's almost night here too," Sebastian said. "The correspondences are even better than I once believed—"

"I think you'd better let your wife know you're back," Jeremy said.

Sebastian grunted, switched on a table lamp, and picked up the telephone. Jeremy wandered to the window and looked out across a dark expanse of pines to the busy Perimeter highway beyond. Behind him Sebastian said, "Hi. Thought I'd better check in." Pause. "No, just the usual rat race." Pause. "No, I'll eat in town. Sure, I remember. See you in about an hour. Love you, too."

When Sebastian hung up, Jeremy turned toward him. "Let's go."

But Sebastian shook his head. "Not with you dressed that

way." He sighed. "Check the closet. There should be something there."

Except for underwear, the closet held three complete outfits. Jeremy selected a simple one, a blue cotton shirt, tan slacks, and a navy-blue sport jacket. His own garb looked strange hanging on the rack, but with Sebastian's assurances that the cleaning people would not open the closet, he left it there. A pair of soft brown boating moccasins—there were no socks to go with them—completed the ensemble. "What are we going to tell Cassie?" Jeremy asked.

Sebastian shrugged. "Tell her you're my cousin. With your beard, we're not that much alike." He sighed again, a sound of resignation. "But we can't have you show up with no luggage at all." He checked his Rolex. "If we hurry we can hit one of the malls before closing time. We'll get you a suitcase and a few odds and ends of clothing, anyhow."

"Okay with me. But let me try to do something about this Gate first. It's spooky, following you around the way it does." Jeremy stood very close to the Gate, looking through it at the dim figure of Nul, who lay before a campfire on the other side. After a moment of thought, he spoke a spell designed to anchor it in place. He felt power flow from him, more flowing through from the Thaumian side. "Let's try it now. Cross the room." When Sebastian did, the Gate swayed slightly, but it stayed put. "Great. Now we've got a permanent portal—or we do for as long as the spell holds, anyhow."

"Let's go, then," Sebastian said.

They left the building—the security guard gave them a puzzled look, but Sebastian simply went past him with a careless wave—and went out into the parking lot. The heat was oppressive and muggy, though not as bad as the steamy junglelike climate of Dubruliond. As they crossed the asphalt, the parking lot lights buzzed to life overhead. "New car," Jeremy said as they approached the sporty black convertible.

"Porsche 944 S2," Sebastian acknowledged. "Greg tried to talk me into a VW Corrado, but—"

"Greg?"

"Hot new radio writer. Don't think you'd know him. He's a nut on VW's, but I prefer the Porsche because—"

"Never mind," Jeremy said with a grin. "I doubt that cars will ever mean very much to me again." Sebastian unlocked the car, and Jeremy got in, the new-car smell hitting him with a rush of memories of his old life on Earth.

They drove a few miles to a major mall, where they had just enough time for Jeremy to pick out a suitcase, a few pairs of trousers, four shirts, some underwear and socks, and some toilet items. It all went onto Sebastian's plastic—though from his double's nonchalance Jeremy guessed that his purchases were modest enough. Sebastian had Jeremy change clothes again, because Cassie would be sure to recognize the outfit from the office. Obligingly, Jeremy stopped in the mall rest room to change into a tan shirt, dark-brown trousers, and matching tie. He put Sebastian's clothes in one of the department-store bags.

"Better," Sebastian pronounced when Jeremy rejoined him.

Then they climbed back into the car and headed west. "You moved from my old apartment," Jeremy said.

"Of course. Cassie's apartment was too small for us, and yours—forgive me—was too dingy. We have a condo on the Chattahoochee now."

"Of course."

Sebastian sighed. "Look, don't make judgments about my life-style, all right?"

"I wasn't."

For a few moments Sebastian drove in silence through the gathering darkness. Then he said, "You know what your trouble is? You see things in black and white. Let me give you a news item, friend. There are no heroes."

Stung, Jeremy said, "I never claimed to be one."

"No?" Sebastian's voice took on a sardonic edge: "I'll bet you thought of yourself as one, though. And Tremien. Look, I said I'd help the old man, and I will. But you have to realize that he's as ruthless in his own way as Jilhukrihain is in his. Both of them are committed to a way of viewing the universe, and each of them thinks his way is best. And by God, neither one of them will stop at anything to get his way. You just ought to realize that, that's all."

Jeremy glanced out the passenger window. They were speeding west on I-285, threading their way through heavy traffic, passing everything on the busy superhighway. "I know this much: Tremien believes in letting other people alone, and the Great Dark One believes in subjugating others to his will. From where I stand, that makes Tremien's philosophy more attractive."

"Sure, I know. But you have to be realistic, all the same. Suppose we succeed in unmasking Jilhukrihain. And suppose he's beaten. I mean finally beaten, once and for all. I don't for a moment think that will happen, but let's say that it does. Then what happens?"

"You tell me," Jeremy said.

"All right. Then Tremien has to find another devil. He'd never step down as Chief Mage of the Council. There'd be something he had to do, some evil left to root out. He's had power too long, Jeremy. He'll never let go of it willingly."

"What are you saying, then? That I shouldn't support Tremien, even though his governance is better than the Great Dark One's, just because he's had power for so long?"

Sebastian twitched the Porsche into a middle lane, then into the left, just in front of an Allied Vans truck. "Suit yourself on philosophy," he said. "But see things realistically. That's what I'm saying. And make sure that no one, not even good old Tremien, uses you. Be your own man." He sighed. "Feel like seafood for dinner?"

"Whatever you say."

"Okay. Let's stop at the Loft. It's on the way, and it's halfway decent."

They stopped at the restaurant, perched on a steep bluff not far from the highway. Since the hour was so late—it was almost nine-thirty—they got a table right away. Jeremy glanced at the menu and said, "Some things haven't changed, anyway. The grilled sole still good?"

"I suppose so. I'm partial to swordfish myself."

"You would be. It's higher on the food chain." They ordered their meal.

"Look here," Sebastian said, "we'd better decide a few things about you before I introduce you to Cassie."

"Such as?"

"Who you are, for one thing." Sebastian had a point there. As they ate, they worked out a background for Jeremy. By ten-fifteen they had finished; they got in the car and in another five minutes reached the Chattahoochee River, where Sebastian maneuvered the Porsche off the Perimeter highway and through a wilderness of new buildings. Despite himself, Jeremy was impressed when they arrived at the condominium: it was a sleek, modern, handsome building in a sort of mock-thirties style, with enough glass to enclose a rain forest. A valet took charge of the Porsche, and Jeremy and Sebastian rode up to the nineteenth floor in a silent elevator. "One important thing left to decide. What's your name going to be?" Sebastian asked on the way up.

"Sebastian?"

"No good. That's my middle name."

"Okay. Say I'm Arthur, after my grandfather."

"Art. Sure."

Cassie opened the door for them, her eyes growing round at the sight of Jeremy. Sebastian kissed her and made the introductions: "Sweetheart, the damnedest thing happened. I stopped for dinner at the Green Loft, and there sat my cousin Art. Art Moon, this is my wife, Cassie."

"I see the resemblance," Cassie said, offering her hand.

The new hairdo suited her, emphasized her fine bones and her brilliant eyes. Jeremy smiled, his heart thumping a little as he squeezed her hand in his. "Everyone's always said we're practically twins," he said.

"Yes," Sebastian said. "Well, Art here is from Ohio now. He's passing through Atlanta, and when I saw him, I told him he had to stay with us. So he went to his hotel, picked up his bag, and here we are."

"Hope you don't mind," Jeremy said, releasing Cassie's hand.

"No, of course not. What business are you in, Art?"

"He's a writer," Sebastian said. "Technical stuff."

"Bore you silly," Jeremy agreed.

"Well, come and tell me about it anyway. Jeremy, will you make us some drinks?"

It was odd to hear Sebastian called by his own name, but Jeremy saw the deception through. The weather outside began to worsen, as he knew it would, and when the three of them called it a night at twelve-thirty, thunder was beginning to rumble outside. Jeremy slept in the extra bedroom, a room with a broad view of the Chattahoochee River—though at this time of night he could see it only in the flashes of lightning—and felt unreasonably lonesome, unreasonably jealous of Sebastian. Most of all, he felt a sick little sensation of insignificance. He had noticed the condominium's furnishing all through the evening. As far as he could tell, nothing, not one stick of furniture, not one photograph or painting on the wall, remained from his old life.

It was as if he had died when he traveled to Thaumia.

And it was obvious that in "death" he had not been missed in the least.

"I suppose," Sebastian said, "you want to go along with me on this little jaunt."

"Sure," Jeremy said, yawning and stretching. Morning light poured through the windows, light filtered by a heavy overcast and a thin rain. Sebastian sat on the foot of the bed, wrapped in a white terry-cloth bathrobe over rumpled pajamas. His hair, though, was as impeccable as always. "What's up?"

"A breakfast with potential donors," Sebastian said. "About a hundred or so businessmen. I have to say a few words."

"Let me get dressed."

"I think you might wear the gray slacks and the light gray shirt. I'll lend you a pair of shoes and a jacket."

Jeremy ruffled his own untidy mop of hair. "Okay. You'd think you were my mom. How is she, by the way?"

"Great. She and Bill visited earlier this summer. She's better than she has been in years, and he's just been named salesman of the year for that sporting-goods firm in Baltimore."

"Good."

"Hurry up, then. You've got half an hour."

Jeremy swung out of bed—they had not bought pajamas for him, so he was in his underwear—and stretched luxuriously. He padded into the guest bathroom, which bore a light but definite feminine scent, rose soap and the lingering memory of cosmetics. He took a quick shower, marveling at how much he'd missed that simple act; in Thaumia baths were the order of the day, and the only time that he and Kelada had ever showered was when they discovered a little waterfall in a stream below Whitehorn. Of course, the water there had been icy cold even in summertime, but still— Jeremy grinned to himself—the experience had not been unpleasant.

He dried himself with a towel almost immorally thick and

tried to adjust his hair into something like civilized shape. He had gone shaggy in the last couple of years, wearing his hair a good deal longer than he ever had, but he gathered that he did not look terribly unfashionable by current Earth standards, at least not for a technical writer from Ohio.

He dressed himself—true to his word, Sebastian had brought into the guest room a pale blue linen sports jacket—and found Sebastian pacing back and forth in the living room. "This okay?" Jeremy asked, spreading his arms.

"Yeah, fine," Sebastian said with hardly a glance at him. "Okay, let's go."

"What about Cassie?"

"No, she's sleeping in. She's put in a long week already and she's got a business trip ahead of her this week."

"Okay, I guess I'm ready."

They drove south through spats of hard rain and sudden gusts of wind. "I wonder if it gets worse," Sebastian said.

"What's that?"

"The weather. I mean, if we stayed together, would it just keep getting stormier and stormier until there was a full-scale hurricane? Or does it hit a plateau?"

"The prophecy I read in the book said something about stormy days, but not about their getting worse. Let's try not to find out."

"Fine with me."

They drove through a deserted downtown, with Sebastian pointing out recent construction. Jeremy was faintly amused and somewhat appalled at some of the information. "How much of Atlanta do the Japanese own, anyway?" he asked at one point.

"A good bit." Sebastian reeled off a list of properties.

Jeremy shook his head. "Seems odd."

"I like the Japanese," Sebastian said. "They're good businessmen, and they honor friendships."

"I didn't say it was bad. Just odd."

It was almost nine by the time they reached their destination. They left the Porsche with a valet and walked through an enclosed pedestrian bridge to the hotel. The lobby was almost empty, but a pudgy man in a gray suit rose from a chair beneath a potted fern when he saw them come in. "The liaison man," Sebastian said in an undertone as they approached him. To the man Sebastian said, "Phil. They ready for me in there?"

Phil shook hands with Sebastian. "Ready and waiting."

"Phil Brock, this is my cousin Art Moon from Ohio. Art, this is Phil, my conscience and my link to Atlanta's business community."

Brock had a florid face beneath dark brown hair too perfect to be anything but a toupee. From a distance Jeremy had put his age at thirty-five or so, but now he saw the man was at least fifty. His handshake was firm but perfunctory. "Yeah, well, we got a ways to go yet before we put your cousin in the state house," he said to Jeremy. "You guys ready?"

"Let's go."

Brock led them into a banquet room where breakfast was already being served by white-jacketed hotel employees. A lectern stood at one end; Sebastian strode to that. The clatter of dishes stilled as he stepped behind the microphone and smiled out at the crowd. "Don't stop eating," he said, his voice warm and suddenly more Southern-accented than before. "Y'all know me: Jeremy Moon. And in a little bit I'm going to hit you up for some money. But right now I'm hungry too, so I'll let you be for a few minutes."

Applause rippled through the room. Brock had shown Jeremy to a table off to the right of the lectern. Sebastian joined them there. "Representative Costikan, Mrs. Costikan," Sebastian murmured to the other two people at the table, a silver-haired man and his much younger blond wife. "Glad you could join us."

Jeremy nodded to more introductions, sat down, and was happy to give his attention to breakfast. He was silent as Sebastian carried on a running conversation with Brock and the Costikans, though he could hardly suppress a smile at Sebastian's earnest attention to the older couple. At one point Sebastian did say to Jeremy, "Charles is my political mentor, Art. The man who showed me the ropes in this town."

"Great," Jeremy said. Costikan beamed.

At length Costikan rose from the table, went to the lectern, and said in a buttery voice, "Everybody about filled up now? If you want another cup of coffee, you tell these fellas. They're here to see you get what you want. And so am I."

As if on cue, a man across the room said, "You serving coffee now, Charlie?"

Costikan grinned. "I'm serving whatever you folks want served up," he said. The room applauded. Costikan waited for the noise to crest, then held up his hand. "But this morning it's my privilege and honor to serve up to you a young man who's ready to go to the state senate and represent your interests. He's a young fella who's worked his way up rapidly and really made a place for himself in the Atlanta business scene. He's a native of the state, so he knows our special needs and quirks. And he just told me not five minutes ago that this was the best breakfast he's had since he left his granddaddy's farm up in Dawson County." That wasn't true, but Sebastian nodded and grinned all the same. "Ladies and gentlemen, I present to you, Mr. Jeremy Moon."

Sebastian strode to the lectern through an enthusiastic sea of applause. He shook hands again with Costikan. "Thank you, Charlie," he said into the microphone. "You know, this breakfast would've been perfect if they had served some of my granny's cream gravy along with the biscuits."

Jeremy sighed and settled lower in his chair. Sebastian began to speak in general terms of the legislature, of the business scene in Georgia, and of himself. The oblique sell, Jeremy decided: there was nothing to pin down in the talk. "And I can only say," Sebastian told the crowd, "that your values are my values; that your interests are my interests; and that if you make me your senator, you can be sure of having a friend in the state house. Of having someone who understands you and your needs. Of having an advocate for your side of the story."

Lord spare me, Jeremy thought.

Sebastian drew a folded piece of paper from his inside pocket. "But you know campaigning doesn't come cheaply, friends. I have here a breakdown of our expenses just for the past month. From the looks of it, the chest is getting mighty low. Fact is, we'll be lucky to keep the lights on in our headquarters building for another month at this rate. That is, unless you help."

Despite himself, Jeremy had to admit that the appeal was a good one, direct, unadorned, and simple—everything that the TV ads had not been. And it seemed to work; as Sebastian finished his speech, a group of pretty young girls rose from where they sat near the back of the room and went from table to table with beribboned baskets, collecting an impressive pile of checks. Sebastian came back to the table smiling.

Brock patted him on the arm. "Way to go," he said. "You keep that up and you're home free, kid."

Jeremy hovered in the background while Sebastian spoke to several of the individual donors. At last they broke away from the group and headed back for the car. "What do you stand for?" Jeremy asked on the way.

Sebastian shrugged. "What does it matter?"

"And you accuse me of not being my own man."

They were in a covered walkway now, with rain drumming on the windows and roof. "I could make out a good case," Sebastian said, "for my being the ideal representative of these people. I don't have any real convictions of my own; so what? That means that I can wholeheartedly represent what my constituents want."

"So what about your advice to me? Seems to me you're serving a few hundred thousand masters, not just one."

Sebastian's smile was quick and white. "Doesn't mean I don't have my own agenda, friend."

The weather had worsened. Thunder vibrated the windows as they drove back north to Taplan and Taplan. "I've arranged to be away tonight," Sebastian said over the tumult of rain and wind. "And I'll leave a note for my secretary tomorrow so she won't open the office door. I hope we can get this thing over with by tomorrow afternoon."

"We'll try," Jeremy said.

They reached Sebastian's office without incident—if being soaked on the run from the parking lot to the building did not count as an incident—and after Jeremy changed clothes, they passed back through the Gate. Barach and Nul waited for them.

"Changed the spell," Nul said as soon as they were through. "Gate stay in office-place, not follow Sebastian."

"I thought it was better to give him a little bit of privacy," Jeremy said. He did not add that he had considered Cassie's privacy as well. "Any news from Tremien?"

"Ya, ya, I talk to him little bit this morning. He emptying

villages and towns along the Bronfal River, far north as Arkhedden. Still not know exactly what happening there. Say for us to examine Celissa as soon as possible."

"Then let's go." As soon as Barach had gathered up their belongings, Jeremy pronounced the activating cantrip for the travel spell, directing it according to Barach's prescription. This time they did not have to go so far, for the forest of Saboy was on the Dubruliond Peninsula, but the spell was a bit tricky if the magician had never been to his destination, and Jeremy had to compensate for his own failure to have visited the forest by tapping into Barach's nonmagical knowledge of the place.

They emerged in the dim green shade of a subtropical wood, tall trees forming a canopy scores of feet overhead. The air beneath them was stifling and breathless, the spongy ground covered with springy layers of old fronds but almost bare of undergrowth. "We seem to have arrived," Barach observed. "Now the trick is to find Celissa's home. I would suggest the communication spell."

Jeremy spoke to the sorceress briefly. "We're not far from her home," he said to the others. "If we go straight ahead, we should come to a stream. Then we turn right, and before long we should see it."

But the trip was easier said than done. Near the stream the canopy of trees thinned, allowing enough sunlight to the surface to encourage a wild growth of spiking bayonet-leaf and trailing lianas. The four travelers kept to the eaves of the forest as they followed the course of the stream. Jeremy peered ahead for any sign of a house, but he saw nothing.

"There it is," Barach said at last, slapping at a stinging fly on his neck. "And none too soon. I know how Bricklebane felt when the ants ate him alive."

"I don't see anything," Jeremy said, peering through the tall boles of the trees.

"I don't either," Sebastian agreed.

"Do not look on the ground for the nest of the paradise bird," Barach returned. "Up, you striplings. Up."

Jeremy blinked. "That platform? That's a house?"

"A home," Barach returned. "There is a difference."

There surely was. Celissa's "house" proved to be a tree house, fifty feet above the forest floor. It was reached by a kind of rope ladder woven of living vine. At first Nul declined to try it, but Jeremy coaxed him into the effort, and at last the little pika hauled himself up hand over hand, grumbling all the way. Jeremy followed, keeping his eye on Nul's scrambling figure and not trusting himself to look down. Sebastian was behind him, and Barach brought up the rear, huffing and puffing but uttering no word of complaint.

Celissa met them at the top of the climb. She wore a dress of thin lawnlike material, a pale green; it matched her eyes and set off her raven-dark hair in a striking way. "My home is not terribly easy to reach, I fear." She smiled. "I usually use the travel spell myself, but it wastes time when one is so close to the ladder."

Jeremy rubbed his hands together and looked around. The tree house had no walls at all, except for some flimsy-looking movable panels. It was essentially two platforms, one a floor and one a thatched roof, open to the treetops. At least there was a refreshing breeze here, and at least his and Sebastian's presence had not yet summoned up storm and rain—though that would come, he was sure.

Nul stretched his arms. "Long way up," he said in an unhappy tone. "Almost as bad as Gray Stair."

"I do not know the Gray Stair," Celissa said.

"It in a cold place, way up north." Nul shuddered extravagantly. "Tall cliff. You go up on rope."

Barach put his hand on the pika's shoulder. "Nul is quite a traveler," he said. "But we did not come to tell of our adventures. What have you learned, Celissa, of the devastation?"

Celissa shook her head. "Not much. I have traveled to Gaffort and have looked at the course of the great North Road. All I can tell for certain is that something has taken the life from everything along the way. I cannot even guess what has done it."

Sebastian had been watching her sharply. Jeremy raised an eyebrow at him in silent question; Sebastian gave a noncommittal shrug. "Tell us about what you found," Barach said.

"I will, but come first and eat with me. It is nearly noon, and you must be hungry after your journey."

"Ya, ya," Nul agreed happily. "Hungry."

Nul's appetite was the strongest of the lot, as usual.

Celissa gave them a tray of strange, exotic fruits: green-gold plumlike things with a stinging sweet taste, brilliant scarlet "pears" that proved to have the consistency if not the taste of bananas, and others. Nul tucked in with great contentment; the others ate politely but sparingly as Celissa went into more detail.

Not that the detail helped much, for the story was painfully simple. Jeremy gathered from her words that a vast strip of land, beginning in the swamps near the coast and then reaching northward along the great road, was just the same as the devastation they had witnessed in Narofrod. Celissa was plainly troubled about the swath of death, for part of her magic, it appeared, was the care of growing things.

"I was apprenticed to Mumana of Vertova when I was a girl," she explained. "Mumana is Keeper of the Heartlands, with a strong interest in spells to protect and encourage crops and growing things. My talents are not the same as hers and not as strong, but from her I learned to give a certain amount of reverence to the world of plants. And whatever passed that way stole the very life essence from everything that grew."

"To what purpose?" Barach asked.

"Who can say? But the tale is that the Great Dark One reduced the land of Relas to a barren desert ages ago. Perhaps it is the same type of magic."

Barach nodded, smoothing his beard. "Yes. Little is known of that time, for few survived it; but the story is that the Great Dark One first conquered the peoples of Relas, the great land far to the south and east. This was in ancient times, when the study of magic was still unsystematic and haphazard. Still, the greatest wizards of Finarr and of Cronbrach leagued against him and, if the story be true, sealed him away in his realm of Relas for a thousand years. At last the confinement spell weakened—or he removed it, according to some—and when it lifted, Relas was only a wasteland."

Celissa nodded. "I have heard the story. It is said that the Great Dark One grew mad in his captivity, for he yearned to master the entire world. It is said that he drew demons into the land, and that they killed it."

"As to that," Barach said, "no one knows for certain,

save only the Great Dark One himself, and he has not spoken. But it is true that the few who have seen Relas and lived say the entire continent, half again as large as Cronbrach-en-Hof, is a dead place now."

Jeremy, his eyes intent on the black-haired woman, said, "How do you feel about that, Celissa?"

Her green eyes took on a faraway look. "Saddened," she said. "All life is precious; to destroy it is an act of madness and anguish. I think the Great Dark One must be most miserable inside."

During the meal and the talk, the clouds had begun to gather again. Sebastian rose from his place and walked a good distance away, to the very edge of the platform. After a moment Jeremy followed him. "Well?"

Sebastian shook his head. "I don't think so."

"But you can't be sure?"

"Sorry." For a few moments they both stood in silence, staring away across an unbroken plain of treetops tossing in the fitful breeze. Then Sebastian sighed. "When Jilhukrihain seizes a new host, he becomes that person. And then, over a course of days or even years, that person becomes Jilhukrihain. I believe Celissa was right about one thing: he is mad. Or at least he is mad as an outsider would know madness. Think of it: each incarnation knows that he or she is fated to die, individually, personally; but before that happens, each one infects a new host with all the memories, all the desires of Jilhukrihain. And during the transition process there are two personalities, not one, in the new host. It's classic schizophrenia."

"I don't know about that. I'd better speak to Tremien."

Jeremy summoned the old mage by means of the communication spell. "I feared as much," he said. "Well, there is nothing to be done there now. Celissa must come to Whitehorn with you; since we cannot detect the Great Dark One, I fear we must try to destroy him. Give Sebastian our thanks and send him home."

Sebastian had been unable to hear the colloquy, since he no longer had usable magic. When Jeremy explained what had been said, he looked troubled. "He's going to kill them all, isn't he?" he asked.

"I don't know."

Sebastian snorted. "This is your great white magician. Ready to kill two, maybe three, innocent people."

"What do you care? You're out of it now."

Sebastian looked away and shook his head. "There must be something. Look, I . . . I'll stay for one more day. Maybe we can come up with something. Somehow I don't feel right about letting Tremien just kill Celissa and the others. And it's my fault."

"How do you figure that?"

Sebastian shrugged. "You asked me to identify Jilhukrihain. If I could've done that, then the other two wouldn't face execution. I don't know—somehow it makes me feel responsible."

Jeremy took a deep breath. "There may be hope for you yet," he said.

8

Jeremy, Barach, Sebastian, and Nul waited in the library of Whitehorn until a frail and pained-looking Tremien returned from his conference with the three suspects. "They know," the old wizard said as soon as he sat in his chair behind the cluttered desk. "I am sure they know."

Barach's broad, ruddy face showed concern. "Then if you are correct in your first surmise, Mage Tremien, it must follow that the Great Dark One also knows."

"Unquestionably. Though of course he would expect suspicion; that is his nature." Tremien's deep-set eyes focused on Sebastian. "Think very hard," he said. "Are you absolutely certain that nothing any of them said, nothing that they did, betrayed the presence of the Great Dark One?"

Sebastian spoke with a hint of anger: "If there were even as much as a hint, I'd tell you. But there isn't. As far as I can see, Idoradas is Idoradas, Jondan is Jondan, Celissa is Celissa. But of course I never witnessed a transference of Jilhukrihain's essence before."

"No one has." Tremien leaned wearily back in his chair. "No one living, at any rate. And, Sebastian, you have decided to postpone your return to Earth? May I ask why?"

"It is for no love I bear Whitehorn, I assure you. Perhaps it is just that I don't like leaving a task undone," Sebastian said shortly.

Tremien spread his fine-boned old hands wide. "But I see nothing more that you can do."

"There must be something." Sebastian paced to the fireplace, turned, and glared at them all with something very much like defiance. "I find that at the last I object to this: your readiness to kill all three of them, for nothing more

140

than suspicion. Even your considering it lessens my opinion of you. To murder innocents is not like you, Tremien of Whitehorn."

The old brown eyes were level and steady, never faltering as they returned Sebastian's challenging gaze. "Can you find that so strange? You yourself served the Great Dark One by making his magic mirrors for him—and had his plan succeeded three years ago, then many more than Idoradas, Jondan, and Celissa would have died."

"But I never claimed to be the protector of Cronbrach," Sebastian returned. "I was only Sebastian Magister, disdained by the greatest mages of Cronbrach for my impetuosity. If I turned to the Great Dark One as a teacher, it was only because no one else of power would stoop to instruct me. And I never killed anyone, least of all someone held hostage and impotent, as you propose to do."

"The Great Dark One is far from impotent." Tremien sighed. "As to the execution of the others, yes, it is an evil," he acknowledged. "But it may prevent a greater evil still."

"And it may not!" Even Jeremy was surprised at the intensity in Sebastian's voice: "Has it occurred to you that perhaps you're quite wrong? Maybe—just maybe—these magi are exactly what they seem. Perhaps the Great Dark One comes in that wave of death I keep hearing about; perhaps he has taken some other host altogether."

"I am aware of that possibility," Tremien said. "But I feel it unlikely. I confess that I do not know what the power sweeping north toward us is; but whatever it may be, I do not think the Great Dark One is in its midst."

Sebastian balled his fist and rapped impatiently at the mantel. "Then perhaps he has seized some lowly person. Even now he may be safe in Ranfora or Shoringal or some other city, waiting for the triumph of this spell."

Tremien shook his head. "No, I think not. Remember, we know that it takes weeks or perhaps months before the Great Dark One fully manifests all his force, his own magical power, in a new host. Until that time, he must rely on the *mana* inherent in the host. From every indication I have seen, the power sweeping north is mighty indeed, and it would take a strong magician to exercise control over it. Of all those who might have been vulnerable to the Great Dark

One, only Idoradas, Jondan, and just possibly Celissa would offer enough inherent power to tempt him into taking them."

Jeremy said, "You're assuming, then, that the destructive force is some kind of spell and can be controlled by magic?"

Tremien settled back in his chair, looking very weary as his knotted old hands gripped the armrests. "We must assume so. I know of nothing else that could cause such destruction."

Barach cleared his throat. "It is unquestionably so, Jeremy. What is happening is beyond the force of anything except possibly an elemental. But it is certainly not elemental magic. It must, therefore, be either an unknown spell or the inherent magic of some unknown being under the Great Dark One's control. And, spell or being, it is assuredly controlled, for not even the Great Dark One is insane enough to unleash a force that he cannot direct. But the nature of the force and the nature of the magic required to influence it—those are riddles still."

Sebastian shook his head. "Riddles that you have precious little time to solve, it seems to me."

"Perhaps the destruction of Narofrod is merely a diversion," Jeremy said. "It may have no bearing at all on the Great Dark One's main plan."

Barach laced his fingers across his stomach. "That is a possibility. I would put nothing past that one, not even the cruelty of destroying a city to distract his enemies. The Great Dark One is quite capable of murdering hundreds of people just to hide his true intentions," he said.

"Hundreds have been destroyed, certainly," Tremien returned. "The force seems intermittent. It passes by lightly populated areas, possibly by some sort of travel spell, and then ravages settled places. It has moved hundreds of leagues in just one day and has wrought great ruin. Half a dozen villages south of Narofrod. Narofrod itself, as you witnessed. But I cannot believe that the attack is incidental. I feel in my bones that it is woven into the Great Dark One's major purpose, and that it has as its end the subjugation and destruction of the north."

"Cronbrach is big," Jeremy objected. "Why, even if the Great Dark One seized control of everything from Dubruliond to Whitehorn, there are still Triesland in the west, and Akrador, Markelan, Vertova—"

Barach shook his head. "No, Jeremy. The main protection of Cronbrach rests here, in Whitehorn. Should it fall, the rest would fall in time. And as you have observed, the Great Dark One has much time at his disposal."

Sebastian grunted in frustration. "Time and whatever this mysterious force is. Can he have found a way to negate all magic?"

Barach's voice assumed its lecturer's tone: "Magic can neither be created nor destroyed, according to the principles of thaumadynamics. I do not know what is happening to the magic drained from the passage of the force, but it must still exist in some form."

Tremien held up a hand, cutting the lecture short. "It does not matter at the moment. Whatever the force is, it will reach Downsdale this evening; but I have seen to it that Downsdale is truly empty." He sighed. "I am sending Master Radusilf there to try to deal with the destruction."

Barach sat upright in his chair, his whole demeanor changed. "Radusilf! You are joking."

Tremien shook his head. "It is far too serious a matter for jests."

Jeremy said, "Excuse me—who is Radusilf? I've never heard of him."

Tremien ran a hand over his bald pate. "With reason," he said, "for Radusilf has been in retirement these fifty years, ever since the first onset of the Wizards' War. He was Chief Mage of Cronbrach before me; his power is very deep and very strong still. He and I do not always agree, for he has ever used his magic for defensive purposes only, while as Chief Mage I used mine aggressively during the Wizards' War to destroy the armies the Great Dark One landed here in the north. Still, Radusilf's powers are at least as great as mine, and he recognizes the grave dangers we face. I have persuaded him to come out of retirement and assist us."

Barach settled back into his chair, his expression troubled. "But if he fails," he said, "then that is a sign that you, too, would fail. As you say, his *mana* is easily a match for yours, Tremien. Do you think it wise to take such a risk?"

"We must," Tremien said. "Already I have evacuated Broadpools and the villages northward; already the force has swept through them, leaching all residual magic from its path. Mumana herself has looked at the trail of destruction farther to the south, along the great North Road; she says the lines of magical force are beginning to heal and reknit themselves, but slowly."

"At least recovery is possible," Jeremy said.

Tremien said, "But it is a slow recovery. If only we could fathom the nature of this thing! It is as if a sponge were soaking up all the *mana* along the path, leaving not even enough to sustain life. That is what is headed northward along the Bronfal; and if it passes through Downsdale, then it will be beneath the southeastern eaves of Arkhedden itself. If it does not turn aside, say northwest along the Dinsfaer Road, then it will be at our doorstep in three days. Before that happens we must make every attempt we can to destroy the director of that force—however unpleasant the attempt may be."

"But what if Sebastian Magister is right?" Barach asked. "What if the Great Dark One is in the midst of the force?"

"As I say, I do not perceive him there; more, I do not think it possible. To this hour the force has shown no discrimination in the *mana* it has absorbed. It has taken everything: the natural life force of plants, animals, people; the *mana* of spell-casters, too, like the unfortunate young Sanklar and my cousin Themogar. I do not understand how the Great Dark One could insulate himself from its magic-draining effects."

"But you do believe," Barach continued, "that the Great Dark One is directing the force?"

"I do. I must believe that; the coming of the force and of the Great Dark One are too suggestive to be mere coincidence."

"Then that, too, is an argument against executing our three suspects," Barach said.

"Forgive me," Tremien returned with obvious asperity. "I do not see that. Surely if he is directing the force from here, the best way to remove both him and the spell is to kill him."

"Mage Tremien, I mean no insult, but you might be wrong. What if you should destroy Idoradas, Jondan, and Celissa, and what if one of them should indeed be the new Great Dark One? And what if removing him should then remove all control over this magic-destroying force—but not the force itself?"

Tremien bowed his head. "Oh. I understand you now. If the Great Dark One controls the force, and if it persists after his death and we cannot contain it, then Cronbrach may be doomed."

Jeremy felt a chill along his spine. "You mean that it might just continue, soaking up all the magic until there's none left? It could . . . could"—he swallowed—"eat up the whole world?"

"Exactly," Barach said. "Until Cronbrach is left as mundane as Twilight Valley. Worse, until it is as lifeless as dead Relas of the south."

Despite himself, Jeremy shuddered, recalling all too well the eerie, empty countryside of Relas, a flat and dead wasteland under a gray sky like a flat lid. "God forbid," he muttered.

Barach tugged at his beard. "Mage Tremien, I suppose you have tried to combat the force with nonmagical means?"

"Unfortunately, I have. Two detachments of soldiers between Narofrod and Broadpools. We lost almost two score men; the survivors report nothing to combat, nothing tangible. Indeed, they saw nothing at all except a sort of wave of darkness."

Barach puffed out his breath, ruffling his mustache. "Do this for me, Tremien. Delay the execution until Radusilf tries his luck; and in the meantime, let me consult my books of lore. It seems to me that somewhere I have read something about a dark force that drinks magic; but it was long ago, and I cannot recall where I read it. I need some time to study."

Tremien smiled, his eyes weary. "I had not intended to strike so soon, for as Sebastian observed, it is not my nature to deal death readily," he said. "You have time to consult your books, Loremaster."

"Tremien?" Jeremy asked. "May I travel to Downsdale?"

Tremien frowned, but before he could speak, Sebastian added, "I would go with him, if you please."

"Why?" the master of Whitehorn asked.

Jeremy glanced at Sebastian. "Well, I'd like to have a look at this force, for one thing. My magic has always been a little odd. It's possible it could have some effect on the force even if yours or Radusilf's could not."

"And I might be able to detect Jilhukrihain's presence,"

Sebastian added. "After all, even you cannot be absolutely certain that you have him safely locked away in Whitehorn. Despite what you feel in your bones, there is still at least the possibility that he could be in the middle of that wave of darkness."

Tremien drummed his fingers on the desk. "You offer good arguments, both of you. But it would be foolhardy of me to send you into unknown danger."

Barach spoke up: "I beg your pardon, Mage Tremien, but both Jeremy and Sebastian have said that they will undertake the journey willingly. Since they both know the risks, and since they may do some good, I would send them, were I Tremien."

The older mage nodded at last. "I do not wholly like the notion, but you may indeed do more good there than anyone else I could send. Very well; I shall arrange matters. But Radusilf will not confront the force directly; he will stand well away from its passage. The two of you must do the same."

"Thank you, Mage Tremien," Jeremy said.

The old man smiled again. "Good heavens, boy, don't thank me yet. Wait until you see what we are dealing with; and then you may wish to curse me for sending you."

Not long afterward, Jeremy and Sebastian arrived at a hillside overlooking a broad blue lake, so wide that its eastern shore was completely lost in the mist of distance. Jeremy took a deep breath of warm afternoon air, scented with pine balsam and the sweet smell of sedge grass, and looked around. To their left, at the northern edge of the lake, a town clustered, a town of stone and wood buildings at least as large as Narofrod; to their right the broad, unpaved, but firmly packed road led southward along the shore of the lake and off into the lightly wooded distance. The sky overhead was filmy blue with a haze of cirrus; the sun, already beginning to decline in the western sky, filtered its heat and light through the high cloud layer.

"Lake Doras," Sebastian said, nodding toward the sparkling blue water, its surface rippled by light breezes, the far shore just a dim blue-green pencil line nearly lost in mist. "And the town is Downsdale, the major inland market for Arkhedden, Estowolt, and the eastern dales. I once bought a remarkably good horse there. I wonder what has become of him."

Jeremy nodded toward the next hill. "And I suppose that is Radusilf," he said.

A stone crowned the hill, and motionless on the stone sat a thin old man. He was clothed in dark gray robes and sat so still that he might have been overlooked or misinterpreted as an odd spired boulder of dark-colored granite somehow set upon a broader, rounder one. But he was plainly aware of them, for his eyes were turned in their direction. "Let's see what he has to say," Sebastian muttered.

As Sebastian and he walked closer through swishing tall grass, Jeremy amended his original impression: the person seated on the stone was a *very* old man, almost completely bald, with a sparse white beard only half-concealing the pinkness of his pointed chin.

Despite the warmth of the summer afternoon, he huddled deep inside his garment, the collar almost covering his ears. With his seamed face, the skin stretched tight across the skull, and the brown liver spots spattered across the dome of his head, he looked at least a hundred years old. In the case of a wizard, appearances probably meant that he was two hundred and fifty or even more; certainly he seemed considerably more aged then Tremien, who had turned two hundred and thirty-seven on his last birthday.

"Jeremy Moon and Sebastian Magister," the old man said in a cracked voice like the sound of the last cricket of autumn. "Tremien said you would be joining me. And his soldiers are supposed to arrive soon as well."

Sebastian spoke, his voice holding a trace of awe and a great deal of deference: "Mage Radusilf; from my earliest recollection I have heard many stories of you. It is an honor to meet you."

The old voice was sharp: "And I have heard of you, young Sebastian. You had a great deal of talent once; it is a pity you wasted it in the service of our enemy."

"With deference, sir, I did not see it that way."

From behind, Jeremy heard the soft *vap!* of more travel-spell arrivals. He glanced over his shoulder. Gareth and a detachment of several dozen soldiers had materialized on the hilltop they had just left. Gareth waved, said something to his men, and strode toward them through the lush green calf-high sedge.

Radusilf turned brooding eyes back to the city below. "Times have changed," he said in his quavering voice. "Once the magi of Cronbrach sought only to heal, to build; now we must deal destruction instead. It is a perversion of magic to use it for such ends. I do not like it."

"We face a great enemy," Gareth said, having come close enough to hear the remarks. "If we do not defeat him, then all of Cronbrach must fall."

"And so we must become like him ourselves?" Radusilf sniffed. "It seems to me that if we remake ourselves in his image, then it does not matter whether the Great Dark One lives or dies; he has in the end conquered us."

"I see it," Sebastian said suddenly. He stared southward, shading his eyes. "It is advancing along the road."

Jeremy gazed in that direction too; and he could see a darkening of the world, a draining of color and intensity, focusing on the road beside the Bronfal. He spoke a spell designed to enhance his vision, but that was of no help. Even viewed as it might have been through a good pair of binoculars, the disturbance was little more than a darkening of the air, a dimness, a transparent gloomy fog. He canceled the spell.

"Your magic is odd," Radusilf said from behind him. The old man had risen, leaning heavily on a staff nearly as tall as himself, a staff intricately carved from some reddish-brown wood. "I have felt nothing exactly like it."

"I come from Earth," Jeremy said. "I think my *mana* is different from any you have encountered."

"Ah, of course. Yes, I have heard of you. I recall the story now—you and Sebastian are dimension twins." Radusilf turned his head sideways, like an inquisitive bird, and glanced up at the sky. "And surely enough, I see the clouds are forming already," he said. Indeed a scattering of small gray-white cumulus had begun to appear directly overhead, like popcorn suddenly bursting from nothing. "That is your fault, of course; the two of you, I mean."

Sebastian shrugged. "It's a by-effect, part of the nature of magic. It cannot be controlled," he said, "Nothing we intend, I assure you."

Gareth broke in: "Mage Radusilf, my men are at your disposal. What shall we do?"

The old, old man smiled without humor. "Do? Keep out from underfoot and try not to die, of course. How far away would you estimate the foe is now?"

Gareth took hardly a glance to the south. "Four thousands, no more. And it moves rapidly, faster than a man could run."

"Then we have little time."

Jeremy and Sebastian had moved a little aside. "Tremien was right to worry," Sebastian said. "I've never seen anything move quite like that. It's as fast as a cantering horse, and an untiring horse at that." He pointed away to the north, toward a smudge of dark green on the far horizon. "See the forest there? That's the southernmost point of Arkhedden. The river and the road curve off to the northeast there. On the left side of the river is Arkhedden, on the right Estowolt, the East Forest. Except for villages like Drover's Ford, there's nothing between Downsdale and Whitehorn to slow whatever this is."

Jeremy was thinking of something he had seen not long after coming to Thaumia. "Do you remember," he said, "the invisible riders of the Hag?"

Sebastian nodded. "I met one or two of them when the two of us were negotiating. But they're different from this thing. They were only men under an illusion enchantment, wrapped in a cloak of invisibility. This doesn't look the same to me."

"No. But Nul used a spell when we encountered one of the riders that revealed him, that tore away the invisibility illusion. I wonder if I could work up something like that?"

"You could try. God, that's coming on fast."

The soldiers had come closer at a gesture from Gareth. Radusilf, standing beside his stone, addressed them: "You are here to observe," he warned. "None of you leave this hillside unless I give you permission. I have a spell of some considerable power ready; it may or may not destroy our enemy. It will affect everything in sight except for our stronghold here on the hillside. If you venture away, I do not think you would survive its effects." He took a deep breath and leaned on his staff. "Well, Jeremy Moon, if you have a spell to prepare, get it ready. And stay out of my way, for I mean to do some magic here."

Jeremy withdrew a little from the others, his back to the city and the lake. He took deep breaths, as Barach had taught him; he began the magical processes of formulation and visualization. These were steps in tapping into his own *mana*, into the potential magic that he had brought with him from Earth and had developed on Thaumia; and, too, they allowed him to tap and to channel the local lines of force, for all of Thaumia was composed of magic, as all of his own universe was composed of energy. Once the first two stages of the spell were complete, all that would remain would be realization, the speaking of the magic spell that would release the pent latent magic summoned and shaped by the first two stages.

It was difficult. The task required a great deal of concentration and absolute clarity of mind. Though magic could exist on Thaumia without spells—elemental magic, for example, or such naturally occurring magic as that which animated the stone gargoyles over the gate of Whitehorn—men found spoken magic the most effective for their purposes.

Different magicians used different formulas in releasing their spells. Some used intricate poetry; some simple rhymes. Some spoke in prose, some in allegory. The important thing was that the spoken spells had to have shape and direction; unless they were carefully crafted, they slipped out of control, performed too strongly or too weakly to be of use. With part of his mind Jeremy heard the chant that Radusilf had begun: it was an archaic poetic form, something roughly analogous to an Italian sonnet in modern English terms—though it was much more intricate, running to a hundred and forty lines or so.

The air began to crackle with the building magic of Radusilf's spell. Jeremy shut it out and concentrated on his own, couched as always in the form of advertising copy. He felt silly enough at times, but he had spent six years of his life back on Earth developing his skills at copywriting, and that practice seemed to come to his assistance here. He shut his eyes, feeling a moist and gusty wind on his face as the weather continued to worsen, and completed preparations for his spell.

But when he opened them he saw the others standing in

positions of watchfulness and anticipation. Old Radusilf, his arms extended over his head, his dark gray robe whipping about his frail figure, was crying out the last of his spell. Beyond him the disturbance had almost reached the outskirts of the city; along the road to the south, extending outward for many paces, a zone of death had sprung up, vegetation wilted as though blasted by heat.

Radusilf brought his staff down, holding it with both hands, extending it, directing the force of his spell; and when he spoke the last word, Jeremy felt a breathless rush of power pouring out from the hill, almost saw it leap toward the darkness, where—

Nothing happened.

Radusilf tottered, a sob clicking in his throat. Gareth sprang to his side, helped him down to the stone, where he sat collapsed, shuddering. "Did it help?" he gasped.

Sebastian, who had been standing beside Gareth, caught Jeremy's eye and shook his head. Jeremy walked over, looking down the hill. As far as he could see, nothing had changed. A tall building on the edge of the town suddenly collapsed into ruin; the force of darkness was now in Downsdale itself.

Gareth had been speaking to Radusilf. The old man seemed too exhausted even to lift his head, but he nodded listlessly. "Then the young man from Earth must try now," he said. "I will prepare a spell to return us to Whitehorn."

"Look!" one of the soldiers shouted.

Jeremy turned and felt his muscles freeze. He had been wrong; something *had* happened, after all.

Between the hillside and the city lay two miles of grassy open land. And cutting through the grass, making directly for them, was a twenty-yard-wide swath of death.

Part of the force had broken off and was coming straight for them.

"How you find anything?" Nul grumbled to Barach.

"I have my ways," Barach said. "I know the inside of my books as well as you know the tunnels of Zarad-zellikol, and perhaps better."

"Hope so," Nul grunted. "Last time there, I got lost."

Barach ignored the pika. "Kelada, see if you can find a large green leather-bound book stamped in silver. The language will be unknown to you, but the top edge of the pages is stained red, I believe."

Kelada began to regret volunteering to help Barach. She cast a despairing glance at the walls of books, the stacks of books in Barach's rooms: shelves ran from floors to ceilings, and more books piled on the floor, on chairs, on mantels, on every level surface. "What's the title?" she asked. "I can read, you know."

"You couldn't read this, my dear. It is a translation into Ulfish from ancient Suderain, and the alphabet is unlike anything you would have seen. Look for letters that resemble fish scales."

Kelada pulled a chair to the shelves housing the tallest books, the oversize folios. "That's a great help."

Barach, standing at a chest-high table, was stooped over an open volume of lore. "I regret putting you through this, my dear. Had I any magic left, it would be a simple task; alas, though I keep intending to give more order to my books, I have not gotten around to that since losing my magic."

"This the one you asked for earlier?" Nul asked, extending a fat brown volume in his three-fingered hands.

Barach took it from him and scowled at the stamped title. "*Unseen Sorceries.* Yes, thank you, Nul. I do not believe it will be helpful, but one never knows." He closed the huge volume before him carefully. "Well, it does not seem to fit any ordinary enchantment. It is certainly not Hakanav's Mana Drain, nor is it a negation spell. So I shall see if it is allied with spells of invisibility." He opened the smaller book that Nul had given him and began to leaf through it, pausing now and again to scan a page.

"Too bad we not have Gatekeeper's book," Nul said.

"I almost wish we had," Barach agreed. "Unfortunately, we have not. Or perhaps fortunately so, if what she says of the book is true."

Kelada had clambered up onto the chair and stood there on her tiptoes. "There are ten or eleven green books up here," she called. "You would have to put them on the tallest shelf."

Barach glanced around. "Yes, I think you're right. It should be one of them. It will be the only one stamped in a strange language."

Kelada ran her finger across the spines of the books: *On the Transmutation of Flesh; The Problem of Great Spells; Elemental Magic; Tales of Lust and Magicians*—"Really, Barach!" she muttered under her breath—and, yes, a huge tome whose spine bore silver letters in an intricate crisscross pattern of scallops. "Found it," she said. She tugged, but the books were jammed in tight. It took some patient working back and forth before the heavy book finally slid out, bringing with it a cloud of dust that made her sneeze. She got down from the chair and lugged the book to Barach's table. "Here it is."

"Yes, that's it," Barach said, looking up. "Well, let's give it a try. I don't see anything too promising in the treatise on invisibility." He put the smaller volume aside and opened the one Kelada had brought. It was very tall and broad, though thin, and the pages were black, imprinted with the bizarre silver lettering. Barach leafed through it, occasionally pausing to run his finger up a column—"Ulfish," he explained, "is read from bottom to top, right to left"—and reading aloud in a muttering undertone. At last he stopped speaking and stood silent, rubbing his nose as he read.

"Anything?" Nul asked.

Barach nodded. "Something. This is a translation of a very ancient text, supposedly an eyewitness account of the fall of Relas to the Great Dark One. A great deal of legendary rubbish has accumulated around the original story, unfortunately, but this may be our best chance at understanding the nature of this spell or force or whatever it is. Now, if I can find the proper account . . ." He leafed through the book, his brown eyes intent on the pages, his bird's-nest eyebrows knit in concentration.

Kelada moved a stack of books from a chair to the floor and sat with her chin on her hand watching him. "I hope Jeremy is all right," she said.

Nul grinned at her. "He fine. Jeremy very smart. He stay out of way of trouble."

"I hope so." She sighed. "Tremien is talking about making us leave Whitehorn. Emily and me, I mean."

"Nah, nah," Nul said with a scowl. "Too soon to think about leaving."

"Here it is," Barach said in an odd voice. "The passage I remembered."

Kelada watched him. "Well?"

He looked up from the book, his face troubled. "The story is that the Great Dark One summoned up five demons—that is what the Ulfish word means, at any rate—to help him win dominion of Relas. He controls them and he alone can return them to their own place, which is not of our world. They remove power from others, according to the tale, and they increase his power. But I will need some time to read the full account."

Kelada settled down in a chair, drawing her feet in under her, and waited in silence. Nul, who grew bored as easily as little Emily, wandered off, muttering to himself about men who were not content to spin stories out of their mouths but who must trap them in letters and put them in books.

Kelada was unusually good at silence. The knack had served her well in the old days, when she was an orphaned waif in the teeming city of Ranfora Harbor. She was still in her teens when a thief named Niklas File took her in and taught her the rudiments of her trade. She was a good pupil; and her gift of silence, coupled with the odd magical talent of never being lost, made her an excellent thief before she was twenty—and a few years after that, her abilities contributed to her being exiled from Thaumia to the Between, where she first met Jeremy.

Well, her days of robbery were behind now. She was too much in love with Jeremy and with her daughter ever to feel the urge to go thieving, making her way cat-quick across the roofs of Gundol, that odd city where all the men were deathly afraid of house cats. But if she had abandoned her old calling, her skills had not abandoned her. Kelada sat silent as a stone as Barach read, so still that she was sure Barach was not even aware of her eyes on him.

His face registered a passing array of emotion: intense interest, surprise—denoted by an abrupt upward movement of his shaggy gray eyebrows—concern, and—the pupils of his eyes widened and his forehead creased—even a little fear. He looked up at last and started at seeing her. "I'd quite forgotten you were there," he said.

"What have you learned?"

Barach took a deep breath. "Enough to make me uneasy. If the story may be believed, the force on its way toward Whitehorn is no force at all, but rather five beings. The book calls them the Shadow Guard. What they are is not at all clear to me; beings from some other world, I imagine."

"Like Jeremy?"

"No. Not like him at all. And certainly not from Earth. They come from some magic-using place, but their magic is different from ours. The Great Dark One summoned them and somehow enslaved them to his will. He is loath to use them, for they strain against him, trying to break free of his control. But as long as he can hold them, he holds great power, too, for they absorb the *mana*, the very essence, of our world. Somehow he can compel them to pass a portion of it to him, when he is in their presence."

"And so he grows more powerful."

Barach stroked his beard. "Yes. But so do they; and at some point their power will overmatch his spell on them. What will happen then, God knows. Perhaps our whole world will be swallowed by them as they strive to gain enough *mana* to return to whatever dimension he called them from. Or perhaps the Great Dark One's death, his true and final death, would be enough to break the spell and release them."

"Tremien had better know."

Barach pushed himself up and tucked the heavy book under his arm. "I will go to him at once."

Kelada rose too, and put a hand on Barach's arm. "Tell me this. Do you think Jeremy is in danger?"

The mage patted her hand kindly. "Now, now. Your husband has a very keen mind and, if I may say so, an exceptionally good teacher. I'm sure he will be fine." But Barach's troubled eyes betrayed a doubt that did not exist in his reassuring words.

For a moment Jeremy was too surprised to move or speak. It was as if some enormous invisible ball were rolling his way, crushing the grass as it came. And the flattened grass immediately withered, went ash-gray, and crumbled.

"I have failed," Radusilf said in a calm voice. "I will move us."

But before he could speak a travel cantrip, Jeremy recovered. He shouted out his own spell, one couched, as most of his were, in advertising terms and in English: "No more mystery! A wave of your hands strips all the power from invisible forces and makes them easy to control—and now it's your very own!" Simultaneously he swept his hands forward, toward the onrushing desolation.

Something happened.

For a breathless moment Jeremy felt himself suffocating, as if the air had been sucked out of his lungs; the whole sky went unbearably bright, then dark. The earth shuddered beneath his feet, making him take four or five crazy steps to keep from falling. A wind from nowhere howled around his ears.

And the dark force halted.

The air shimmered for a heartbeat, like waves of heat rising off asphalt made molten by a hot summer sun. Then the shimmering patterns collapsed, coalesced into something out of a nightmare landscape by Bosch.

Jeremy was vaguely conscious of the soldiers crying out around him, of Radusilf's groan of despair. Then he shouted his own travel cantrip—

Silence crashed around him, the silence of the travel spell.

Sebastian, who alone had been focused into Jeremy's cantrip, shared the dreamlike whirl of travel with him. He broke the silence: "What in God's name was that?"

Jeremy found that he could not stop shaking. "Don't know," he said. His memory flashed back to the scene: the broad lake, the town off to the left, the field of grass—and a few hundred yards away a standing, looming horror, a thing almost three times man-size. It was red and rugose, like a flayed animal carcass, and the limbs that protruded from it had no symmetry. He could not say where the head was, for he had seen nothing that might be ears, eyes, or nose: but on the front of the thing was a maw, perfectly round, surrounding a ring of jagged teeth.

As for the rest, he could not recall enough to place the creature accurately. It had arms of a sort and legs of a sort, to be sure; possibly five or six appendages in all. But whether they were tentacles or legs or—something else—Jeremy could not say. He shivered again. "Didn't you recognize it?" he asked Sebastian.

"Hell, no. By the way, that was an idiotic spell."

"Worked, didn't it?"

Sebastian shook his head, disgust evident on his face. "That's not the point. It worked because it's in English and because you patterned it. But as advertising copy, it stank."

Jeremy's heart had subsided to something like a normal rate. "Next time I'll try the oblique sell," he growled.

"It couldn't hurt. We're going to the Gate now, I take it?"

"Right. I hope the others got away."

Sebastian shrugged. "I think they'll be okay. Radusilf was working his travel spell for them, and he's not exactly an amateur at spell-casting. The thing looked baffled to me. Did you see how it just stopped?"

"I didn't notice it stopping."

"It did, though. And if your travel spell worked, then Radusilf's will too."

Jeremy stood facing Sebastian—actually, he maintained the posture of standing, since there was nothing to stand on in the interspace of the travel spell. Experimentation had shown Jeremy that one could assume a sitting posture or a lying one, but the results were not always happy, for height was difficult to judge. Materializing three feet off the ground while lying down was good for a breath-snatching jolt. "You really don't know what that thing was?" he asked Sebastian.

"Not a clue."

"But it must be something the Great Dark One called up."

"I guess it is, but he never said anything about such a horror to me." Sebastian paused. "I just thought of something. That thing split off from the main trail of destruction."

Jeremy nodded. "There were others."

"One's enough." Sebastian was silent for a moment. Then he said, "Jesus, I hope Tremien can deal with these things."

"What do you care?"

"I do, though," Sebastian said. "Damn it, despite everything, I do care. Look, I have an important engagement tomorrow morning, a debate with Tidburn before the League of Women Voters—"

"Tidburn? Harlon Tidburn?"

"Yeah. My opponent. You know him?"

"He used to be the second-crookedest politician in the state," Jeremy said. "I guess I didn't realize you were against him."

"He's changed his standing lately. I'd call him number one in the state now. Anyhow, I have to spend two hours

with him tomorrow morning in the Civic Center. Cassie will
be out of town for the rest of the week—she's got a free-
lance assignment in Boston—so tomorrow noon I'll be free
for a reasonable period, say a couple of days. I'll come back
if you need me."

"What can you do that Tremien can't? And besides, it
isn't your world anymore."

Sebastian thought that over for a long time. Finally he
nodded. "You're right. Still . . . damn it, Jeremy, I do miss
it at times."

Jeremy thought of Cassie, of his old place at the advertising agency. "I know you do," he said at last, and for the
rest of the journey they were silent.

They materialized before the vine-flanked Gate. "So then
I guess you won't be coming back," Jeremy said.

"I guess not. But try to look out for Idoradas, Jondan,
and Celissa for me. There has to be another way."

"I'll do my best. Well, thanks for trying, anyway."

Sebastian waved away the thanks. "I didn't do anything.
And I was shanghaied, after all."

"Still, you could have made it more difficult. I—" Jeremy
grinned suddenly. "We're speaking English. It's been a long
time. Anyhow, thanks. I'll take you through now."

"Let's go."

Jeremy put his hand on Sebastian's elbow and they stepped
together into the Gate—but this time Jeremy felt an odd-
ness that he had not noticed before, a backward tug, a
slippage—

And he stood alone in Sebastian's office.

"Sebastian? Where the hell—"

His heart thudded back into his throat.

The Gate had completely disappeared.

Jeremy Moon was stranded back on Earth.

9

"**G**one?" Kelada screamed so loudly that little Emily, held in the crook of her left arm, jumped and began to cry. "What do you mean, he's *gone*?"

They were in the study before Tremien again: Barach, Kelada, Nul, and Sebastian. And Sebastian was having some ado keeping Barach between himself and the enraged Kelada. "He can't be gone forever," Sebastian pleaded. "It was an accident. We were both about to go through the Gate when Tremien snatched us back—or tried to."

"I acted too hastily," Tremien acknowledged. "But I acted out of concern for our friends. I felt the terrible upheaval in the magical pattern of Cronbrach and immediately called back to Whitehorn all of our people. I succeeded with Radusilf and the soldiers, but it seems that Jeremy had activated his own travel spell before I worked mine. My spell of recalling did not find or affect him until he was actually on Gateway Cay."

Sebastian nodded. "And even then Tremien's spell wasn't wholly successful. He got me, but Jeremy must have passed through the Gate to Earth an instant before Tremien could focus on him. All we have to do is return to the Cay and let him come back through the Gate—"

"Oh, dear," Barach murmured. "It may be not as simple as that. Jeremy tied the spell he put on the Gate to your presence as well as his. I do not know how thoroughly he anchored the Gate to Earth. It may be that the Gate has lost its focus now that you two are on the wrong sides, so to speak."

Kelada was trying to shush Emily, who bawled more

lustily at the encouragement. "All I can say is there had better be a way to bring my husband back—"

Tremien rose and came to her. He reached out his hands for the crying baby. Emily came to him, cuddled her head into his long white beard, and immediately fell silent except for a few recriminating sniffles. "There, there," Tremien said. "Kelada, be assured that we will do everything possible to bring Jeremy back. But there is more to be thought of: Radusilf has described the creatures to me, and Barach's research bears out the description. Beyond a doubt these things are what the old ones called the Shadow Guard, and they are surely making for Whitehorn. What the Great Dark One plans is hidden from me, but it surely bodes us ill, and for reasons of my own I greatly desire Jeremy's safe return and his aid. I will send Barach and Sebastian—"

"Nul too," said Nul.

"—yes, and Nul, back to Gateway Cay as soon as may be. But the whole magic field between here and Gateway has been disrupted by the presence of the Shadow Guard in between. I cannot use Jeremy's own travel spell, for I do not know the cantrip he devised; and I cannot risk trying to send them directly to the Gate, since the path lies over seawater. But I will send them all to Savoyan Delar, and there they can find passage to the Cay."

Nul said, "Nul know Jeremy's word for travel magic."

"And I dare not allow you to use it," Tremien said. "For you lack Jeremy's directing *mana*, and if the upheaval at Downsdale has affected the magic fields, the spell may no longer suffice to transport you directly to the Cay. My way is the best, for it is the safest."

"But I try travel word. When we get safe to island, then I will try it, Mage Tremien."

"I'll go too," Kelada said.

Barach broke in: "Kelada, if I may say so, Jeremy would not want you to undertake the journey. I think you would be better off here; and if the Shadow Guard do indeed approach, then Tremien can send you to a place of safety."

"Where?" she demanded. "To my old home in Ranfora? To the haunts where I was caught in Gundol? I'm no thief, not anymore. My place is with Jeremy."

"No," Tremien corrected in his gentle voice. "Your place is with your daughter."

Kelada's head drooped. She began to shake with sobs. Before she realized it, Sebastian was there, holding her. She cried on his shoulder, marveling even in her grief at how like Jeremy he was. And because he was like Jeremy and he was close, she clung to him until she could weep no more. He stroked her hair and held her, not speaking. At last she pushed away, wiped her eyes, and took Emily from Tremien. In a voice still hitching with sobs, she said, "What of the spell?"

Barach frowned. "I have one or two ideas about that. We placed a good enchantment on the Gate; I think it will probably hold for some time to come. However, without the presence of both Jeremy and Sebastian, the Gate may have gone blank, so to speak; that is, without Sebastian's being within the magic field on this side, the Gate may not show at all on Jeremy's side. If that is so, Jeremy may not be able to find his way back to Thaumia. However, if Sebastian places himself back within the field—well, the Gate may well open again."

"May?" Kelada demanded, her face red.

"Probably will," Barach amended with some haste. "And if not, why, I believe Adelaide will come to our aid. She has very strange powers, you know, quite similar to Jeremy's. And there is one very remarkable book that will surely show us the way to bring Jeremy back. It may take a little time, but I believe we can remedy matters."

Sebastian directed a challenging look toward Tremien. "And the executions?"

Tremien turned away and paced to the window. The day outside was ebbing, the sky already violet. "They are out of the question now. I am seeking answers about the Shadow Guard; specifically, I am trying to learn what effect on them the death of the Great Dark One might have. We cannot risk unleashing such power in Thaumia by killing the only person who exercises control over it."

"Fortunately," Barach said, "we have certain allies who will be able to help us. The scholars at Vanislach are working on the problem now; I'm sure that in time they will be able to tell us how to send these creatures back to their own plane of existence."

"In time," Tremien said. "As Jeremy put it in his play, there's the rub, of course—time is the very thing we lack.

Barach, there is really nothing else for it: you must bring
Jeremy back as soon as possible. If you cannot succeed
immediately, then I am afraid you shall have to consult that
book of Adelaide's."

"Jeremy's levitated book, you mean? That's supposed to
be dangerous," Kelada said.

Tremien bowed his head. "It is dangerous, certainly. But
if it comes to that, I am sure Barach and Nul are anxious
enough to bring Jeremy home to risk the danger. Well,
Kelada, there it is. Our friends will try their best to bring
Jeremy back to you. Will you remain here with us in
Whitehorn and care for the safety of your and Jeremy's
child?"

Kelada looked miserable and defeated. "All right. I'll
stay because I have to. But bring my husband back. That's
all I can say: you'd damn well better bring my husband back
to me."

In Sebastian's office, Jeremy passed through four distinct
phases of panic: first he had a powerful urge to run screaming in circles. When that passed, he thought he would faint.
When it became clear that he was going to remain conscious, he thought fleetingly of leaping out the third-story
window. When suicide did not seem like a viable alternative, he next needed to talk to someone, to anyone. He
picked up the telephone and called Cassie, only to get a
"disconnected-number" recording. Somehow that at last
calmed him down and gave him the ability to think again.

Of course. Cassie was now Mrs. Jeremy Moon; she would
have a different number. Jeremy dialed his old number and
got the same recording. Again, of course; Sebastian, who
was now Jeremy Moon in this world, had moved from his
old apartment, had moved to a different community and
county. The telephone number would have changed.

But the information operator told him that his own number was unlisted.

At least by now Jeremy was thinking. He checked the
office wall clock: it was six-forty-three in the afternoon. A
Sunday afternoon, he recalled. It seemed longer to him, but
Sebastian's sojourn in Thaumia had been that brief. Well, of
all the people on Earth, the one most likely to offer aid was

Cassandra, and Sebastian had said something about Cassie's going away on some kind of business trip—

Inspiration struck. Jeremy went into the adjoining secretary's office and flipped through the Rolodex on the desk. There he found Sebastian's new number. He tried that, and Cassie answered on the third ring, breathless: "Hello?"

"Uh, hi—" Jeremy began.

"Oh, sweetheart, I'm glad you called. I was just about to leave for the airport. Sam left a message for you—wait a minute. Here: 'Don't hit Tidburn too hard on the industrial-development question.' Make sense?"

"Ah, yes, but—"

"Your cousin getting his business done?"

"Yes, he—"

"You know, it's creepy how much alike you two look. Art could almost be your twin, not your cousin. Is he older?"

Jeremy swallowed. "About the same age, actually."

"I wondered. His beard has that little streak of gray in it. He seems really sweet. Oh, God, look at the time, I have to run—you'll be all right for dinner, won't you?"

"Sure. Uh, Art and I will work out something."

"Fine. Did he give you an idea of how long he'll be staying with us?"

After a moment Jeremy said, "He'll be gone by the time you get back home." One way or the other.

"I'll call you from Boston tonight. 'Bye, hon. Love you."

"Love you too."

Cassie hung up. Same old Cassie—always on the run. But not much help under the circumstances.

Jeremy leaned back in Sebastian's chair and glanced around the office, looking for the least disturbance, the slightest suggestion of mist in the air. There was nothing, not even a hint of the Gate's presence. He thought for a long time, then tried a spell. He felt the merest tingle of magical power, but the Gate did not materialize.

"Damn," he muttered. He was trying to think up a new, stronger spell when he heard the outer door open. He got up silently and went to the closet. He stepped inside and pulled the door closed just as he heard the office door open. It closed again after a moment, and when he heard a key turn in the lock of the outer door too, Jeremy left the closet. The security guard, of course, making his rounds. Jeremy had thought of sleeping on the notorious sofa, but with a guard touring the building three times in the course of the night, that clearly was out of the question.

Jeremy sighed. He took off the robe, boots, shirt, and trousers he wore, hung them in the closet, and put on one of Sebastian's outfits. If he were going to be arrested as a burglar, at least he would look like a normal human being and not like a refugee from a road-show production of *Camelot*.

And now that he was at least partly rational, Jeremy went into Sebastian's private rest room. Under the glare of fluorescent light, he studied his face in the mirror. Cassie was right, of course. He and Sebastian were very much alike. The face Jeremy saw in the mirror now was, detail for detail, the same as Sebastian's had been three years ago when he had first seen it: then Sebastian had worn the short brown beard and Jeremy had been the clean-shaven one. The gray streak that Cassie had mentioned was new. He had been cut by glass when the magic mirrors of the Great Dark One had all shattered, and although he bore only a faint scar on his right cheek, the whiskers beneath it had all grown in white.

A safety razor and shaving cream were in the medicine chest behind the mirror, along with a prescription vial of Tagamet. Despite himself, Jeremy smiled; it was in a grim kind of way amusing to think of the sorcerer Sebastian developing an ulcer in the rat race of American business and politics. He went back to the secretary's desk for a pair of scissors, and with them and the razor he removed the beard.

After half an hour he patted his face dry and cast a critical eye at the mirror again. It was a shock: now he truly looked just like Sebastian—all except for his hair, which was longer and more unkempt. And his forehead and cheeks were tanned, while his chin was pale in contrast. There was the scar, of course, though without the white patch of beard to mark it, it was difficult to detect from a few paces away. Taken all in all, Jeremy decided, he might be able to pass.

Back to Sebastian's desk. Jeremy rummaged through the drawers, finding nothing of use. But the bottom-right drawer was locked. After a wrestle with his conscience that consumed all of twelve seconds, Jeremy used a paper knife to pry the drawer open.

Eureka. Inside he found a rectangular gray metal box, itself unlocked; and that contained a set of keys, both auto and door, and an envelope with twenty-five new twenty-dollar bills and ten fifties in it. A thousand dollars of petty cash; walking-around money. Jeremy lifted one of the fifties to his nose and sniffed. He had not realized how strong American money smelled, sharp and astringent. Thaumian money—gold, silver, copper, and bronze coins—had an entirely different aroma.

There was more in the box: a passport in his name (Jeremy fleetingly wondered if his fingerprints exactly matched Sebastian's), a pocket notebook with a list of credit-card numbers, a second envelope with various receipts stuffed inside. A brown envelope held a copy of a current contract between Taplan, Taplan, and Moon and Jeremy Moon; reading it, Jeremy involuntarily whistled at the size of the salary. The drawer and box held nothing else that looked remotely useful.

Well, there was enough for a start. Jeremy went through the keys until he found a small one that slipped right into the drawer lock and closed the drawer, relocking it. He took with him only the money and the key ring.

He lacked the magnetic key card that unlocked the main door of Taplan and Taplan, but he didn't need that to get out. Assuming the security man held to the same schedule the ones he had known had used, he would be down on the second floor by now. The rear stairs were handy, and Jeremy clattered down them undetected. Sure enough, the lobby was deserted, and he slipped out without being detected. He found the Porsche where he and Sebastian had parked it, climbed in, and had another moment of panic. What if he wrecked the damn thing, or what if a cop stopped him? He had no license.

But then, he had never been stopped for speeding. Indeed, except for parking tickets he had never been cited at all.

He started the engine and drove, hoping that after three years his skills were still good enough to contend with Atlanta traffic.

It was full evening by the time he reached Sebastian's condominium. The parking valet greeted him by name and wheeled the car away. He got to the apartment, locked the door behind him, and collapsed in a chair, trying to control the jitters.

All right. He was stuck here, temporarily at best, permanently at worst. How to make it temporary?

Well, he'd have to go back to the office tomorrow and try another spell, and if that one didn't work, then another and another—and it would be hard, because this universe, the universe of energy and matter, had precious little free magic to draw upon. But he would have to—

Jeremy was hungry. While he thought, he went to the kitchen and checked the refrigerator. He built himself a sandwich of lettuce, tomato, and salami and opened a frosty bottle of Coors Extra Gold. After the hearty ales he had become accustomed to in Thaumia, the beer was little more than soda pop, but the sandwich was good.

All right. He would have to isolate himself in the office. He would go there early in the morning—no, he'd be spotted. He'd have to have a haircut first. He'd call in and tell them that he would be in late. Then he'd go to that place on Peachtree, the salon that opened at nine, and have his hair styled in a simulation of Sebastian's. And then—

Jeremy almost choked on the sandwich.

How could he have forgotten?

And then, damn it all, there was a political debate before the League of Women Voters.

Jeremy Moon against the state's number-one crooked politician.

The unicorns had been killing chickens again.

Regina sighed at the sight of a ripped and bloody bundle of brown-and-white feathers, draggled and dark with morning dew and half-hidden in a tall hummock of sweetgrass near the fence. She grimaced with distaste, picked up the body by one scaly foot, and threw it as far over the fence as she could. With a soft plop like a pillow tumbled from a bed it fell under the eaves of the wood, where the unicorns would find and eat it later.

Regina looked for other bodies but found none; then she inspected the wooden fence for breaks, but it seemed whole. The sole victim had been just a fool hen clucking and scratching too near the fence, near enough for a 'corn to swipe its head through the fence bars and catch the brainless bird with a sideways toss of its horn—but the unicorn had not been quite dexterous enough to toss the body out where it could get at the meal.

Regina scrubbed her hands on some of the soft, tall, dewy grass, though she had been careful not to get blood on her fingers. She was naturally fastidious—too fastidious, her mother had thought, to be sent to Gateway Cay and its simple farm life—and needed to wipe away the feel of death.

In the one-acre chicken lot the other hens were awake and active, scratching and buck-bucking, leading their little flocks of fuzzy yellow chicks. One of the roosters flapped its wings and crowed at her. "Hush," Regina scolded, though in a soft voice. She smiled to herself when the rooster fell silent and began to strut around her. But she smiled not so much at the rooster as at the memory of their visitor Jeremy Moon. He was handsome, he was gifted—she still had the leaf he had given her, and she still used it to sail down from high places like a wind-ball seed—and he was from the mysterious world beyond the island. Regina was pretty sure she was in love.

None of the birds that clucked at her feet seemed to mourn the fallen, and certainly when Regina opened the feed shed and came out with a half-full sack nestled in her elbow, the survivors had nothing but food on their minds. Regina scattered arcs of golden grain with graceful sweeps of her arm and hand, and the chickens moiled around her, frantically pursuing each kernel. The oldest red rooster came flapping down from his post in a tremble-leaf tree and chased part of his harem away from some especially choice bits.

"Bully," Regina told him. "I shouldn't even give you anything." But she did, for she admired the scarlet crown of his comb, the majestic glitter of his black eye. Oh, he was battered from years of ruling the yard, missing patches of feathers on his breast; his comb was scarred and his strut had become arthritic. Still, with his fearless walk and his clarion voice he seemed every inch a monarch. And besides, there was more than enough food in the bag to go around.

Regina finally shook out the last few grains and then went egg-gathering in the nests the hens had built in the roost shelter. It was a good morning: she counted forty-seven eggs into her basket and had to use both hands to lug the burden through the chicken yard. She set it down, opened the gate, moved the basket through, and closed and locked the gate again, feeling its magic tingle. The spell was an old and strong one, protecting the chickens from foxes, which would kill and carry them away, and from the unicorns, which would devour them on the spot.

The magic was wholly necessary. No wooden fence alone could hold a hen inside or a fox out, of course, but one of Regina's uncles had put a good spell on the fence years and years ago, and the magical wards seemed to do the job well enough—until some foolish bird grew familiar enough with the feel of magic to wander too near the rails.

Regina grunted a little as she picked the basket up again. Perspiring from the effort of hauling her basket of eggs down the path to the house, Regina yawned. The sun was climbing rapidly, as it did in high summer, and the air was already steamy. On the rocky shoulders of the mountains farther inland, the dragons would be out by now, their wings fully opened on a day like this. And after a night of prowling for grubs and worms, the little hissing basilisks would be creeping into cool beds of moist leaves beneath stones in the woods, and the fairies would be dipping into the cold mountain rills and shaking the water off their translucent wings. They would sit in loose groups on shady tree branches and pant, their eyes squeezed tight, their pink mouths open, their tiny chests fluttering as they breathed. It was going to be a broiling hot day.

Regina's path took her beneath the grape arbor, the vines already heavy with swelling green clusters of grapes. Bees droned there, and her nose twitched at the itchy, prickly smell of the grapevines. The path to the cottage wound through the arbor, maze-fashion, seeming longer than it actually was. Almost before she knew it, Regina was at the back door of the house. She rested the basket on her knee until she got the door open, and then she was inside the cool pantry.

It was always cool in the pantry. That was Great-Grampa's spell, she had been told: the whole house was always comfortable, and every room was just the temperature it should be: bedrooms cool and drowsy, bathrooms toasty-warm, pantries almost chilly even in the summertime. And the virtue of the spell preserved foods too. With a sigh Regina added today's eggs to the rest, wrote "47" on the pad near the egg bin, and added that to the existing figure. As of today, she and Grammy had exactly 1,229 eggs, filling every rack in the bin. "I hope the traders come soon," Regina murmured.

Grammy was bustling in the kitchen, singing something without words to the tune of her whistling teakettle as she made breakfast ready. "Good morning," she said, her shriveled-apple face bright beneath her blue bonnet and her shining white hair. "You are very efficient, Regina. But you will grow up, just like all the rest of them. You are going to cause me a great deal of trouble someday, my dear."

Regina gave her a peck on her wrinkled cheek. "I hope not, Grammy." She paused and bit her lip. "The unicorns have been at the hens again."

Grammy clucked. "Oh, dear. Those wretched things. I suppose the spell over their valley must need more mending than I first thought. Those nasty creatures simply will not mind their manners, will they? We used to think them so pretty, too; such enchanting beasts. If I had known what trouble they could be—"

"I could find them and chase them back to their grounds," Regina said.

"No, that simply will not do. The magic must have weakened too much to hold them. I suppose we'll have to move the herd all the way to the other side of the island for a bit; we'll attend to that next week. I simply haven't the time at present to attend to creating a whole new spell to keep them in their valley. Will you have tea, my dear?"

"Yes, please."

Grammy poured the strong amber tea and added two spoons of honey—the beehive was in the center of the grape arbor, tended by friendly bees who never stung—and a generous dollop of fresh cream. They kept only one cow, Bessie, a good milker and a gentle creature, though Grammy had never allowed Regina to attempt to milk her.

Regina waited until Grammy had served herself, had removed her apron and bonnet, and had vaguely prodded her white hair back into shape. The preliminaries attended to, Grammy bowed her head and asked a blessing. Then Regina sipped her tea and said carefully, "I think that Mr. Jeremy was quite a proper man, Grammy."

Grammy patted her hand. "Bless you, child, I know. But you are very young and have a great deal to learn about the world. Pray don't be too hasty to grow up."

When they had finished their meal, Regina helped with the dishes. Grammy, who was washing, handed her a plate to dry and said suddenly, "Regina, my dear, you know why your mother sent you to me, I suppose."

"Because I have no magic," Regina answered.

Grammy inspected a teacup critically before rinsing it and passing it to Regina. "Not quite, child. It is because you have manifested no magic; there is a difference. Our family, you see, is quite special. My talents are, well, odd. So odd that I found it far better to stay at Gate Cay all these years rather than to mingle with the rest of the world. Do you think that a hard fate?"

"I suppose it would be hard only if you felt it to be hard, Grammy."

"And do you find it hard to be forced to stay here with me? The others have told you how silly I am, have they not?"

Regina, stacking the dried plates, felt her face grow hot. But she knew her Grammy better than to evade a direct question. "Well—Aunt Gloriana says you're a little touched. Aunt Victoria says you're harsh and cruel. But I haven't found you so."

"You are a wise child not to listen to foolish opinions. And you are telling me nothing I don't already know. None of your aunts or your great-aunts amounted to much, I fear; we found their magic, all right, but they're far too silly to have made decent use of it. You may be different. You may be the one fated to take my place." The dishes done, Grammy sighed. "Don't bother with the wretched unicorns today, child. I feel we are to have visitors soon."

"Mr. Jeremy?" Regina asked.

Grammy smiled. "I don't know, child. I think not, however; certainly I cannot feel his approach. But perhaps his companions will be along. The little creature, Nul, and that attractive Mr. Barach, I think." Grammy didn't bother to explain how she knew a ship was on the way, but she didn't have to—Regina knew that, somehow, Grammy simply *knew*, that was all. It was one part of her magic. "I believe they are on the pathway to the cottage right this moment, in fact. Perhaps you had better go meet them."

Regina went, blinking at first in the hot sunshine. A noise from one of the oak trees attracted her attention; she squinted up and clucked her tongue in disgust. "Bad cat," she said. Alice, the flying cat, was perched on a limb of the tree nibbling at the remains of a little brown bat. She was a good batter, but Regina could not help feeling sorry for the little flying mice. She hoped the victim was not the same wounded bat Grammy had healed just a few days ago. Looking away from the tree, Regina cast one glance toward the west, toward the sea, invisible behind the rolling hills but not too far away: its sun-glinting surface lightened the sky in that direction to a pale blue, almost to white. And, sure enough, she saw figures making their way uphill along the path that led down to the anchorage. She waited at the cottage door as the men approached. There were three sailors, two older men whom she recognized from previous visits, and a boy about her own age. Behind them came three others, the limping pika, Nul, the heavy Barach, and . . . Jeremy? No, the other one, the one without the attractive beard.

The elder sailor, a man named Balbacar, took his red cap off a shiny bald dome as he neared. "A good past-dawn to 'ee, young lass," he said with a kind of polite gravity. "Is Herself about, now?"

"Yes, sir," Regina said. "Won't you come in?"

"Aye, we will, mum, and thanks to 'ee. This here's my spell-mate, Laralen Fadred"—Balbacar indicated the other man Regina knew, a tanned, red-bearded sorcerer—"and this here's my nevvy, who's after learning the trade, his name's Mak. T'others reckons as how ye know 'em already." Regina smiled at Mak, the boy, whose face went crimson with embarrassment beneath his mop of springy-looking brown curls. He suddenly seemed to find something of absorbing interest at the end of his bare toes, for he turned an intense gaze there.

"Come in, sirs," Regina repeated, opening the door for them. The three shuffled inside. Regina saw them into the parlor, then went to bring Grammy.

Regina found the old woman lying fully clothed on her

bed, her eyes closed. "Grammy," the girl said softly, "the men are here."

The china-blue eyes opened. "Thank you, child. Did the others come as well?"

"Yes, Grammy."

"Good girl. Then you may make them some tea and bring a bit for the men to nibble on while we talk. Then you may rest for a time." Grammy had risen while she talked, had smoothed her dress, had prodded her white hair. She went into the parlor for the ritual haggling that always preceded any dealings with traders; Regina went to the kitchen and busied herself with preparing the tea.

For the men she made up a tray with teacups, teapot, little squares of sweet dark bread, and a small bowl full of creamy white butter. Regina carried the tray to the parlor, where Balbacar was protesting his utter poverty and calling on the elements to witness the great favor he would be doing Grammy by taking her eggs, cheese, and goat's milk for a pittance. Grammy was smiling at his performance and calmly waiting her turn. Mak, the curly-headed boy, was shuffling his feet as he stood behind his uncle's chair. "Thank you, child," Grammy said.

"I brought enough for the others too," Regina replied.

Grammy took the tray. "They were in a great hurry to get to the Gate and couldn't stay. My dear, young Mak looks quite hungry. Take him into the kitchen and find him something a little more filling than this, please."

It was Regina's turn to blush. "Yes, Grammy," she said. To Mak she said in a voice so soft it was almost a whisper, "Come with me."

Mak followed her meekly enough. He sat at the table in the kitchen. "Would you like some milk?" Regina asked.

He nodded and shrugged at the same time.

"Would you rather have some ale?"

Mak repeated his gesture.

Regina couldn't help smiling. "Well . . . what would you like?" she asked, feeling quite grown-up and ladylike.

"Whatever you please, mum," the boy mumbled.

"Oh, don't call me that," Regina said. " 'Mum' makes me feel as old as Grammy. My name's Regina. Call me that instead."

The boy nodded mutely.

Regina sighed and prepared a plate with beef, bread, butter, and an apple for him. She poured him a mug of frothy white milk. He sat frozen in an attitude of apprehension as she put the food before him, and once he began, he ate without manners and without silverware, tearing pieces of beef with his fingers, breaking the bread into chunks, spreading no butter on it but instead using two pieces of bread to sandwich a fragment of beef. When he drank, he slurped noisily, and the milk left him with a white mustache.

He was halfway through the meal before he noticed Regina's amused look. With a red flare of mortification in his face, he picked up fork and knife and used them awkwardly. "Never have much call for these on a ship," he said with a weak smile.

"Have you traveled much?" Regina asked him.

"Oh, aye. M'father, he owns the *Storm* out o' Savoyan, and he's had me aboard his vessel, oh, since I could first walk. But it's hard, you see, for him to teach me the craft, on account of he's that tender-like for me in his heart. And so he's gone and 'prenticed me to my uncle, who takes me in hand, so to speak." Mak had grown so animated as he spoke that he knocked his mug over with a broad gesture, and he looked on with an appalled expression as milk spilled across the table.

Regina jumped up and came back with a towel. She righted the mug—it had been almost empty, and the spill was a small one—and mopped up the milk. "No harm done," she said, feeling absurdly motherly at the stricken expression on Mak's face. "Here, I'll pour you some more."

"Sorry, mum—Regina. It's just I'm a clumsy bull-calf in polite company. Should've stayed on the ship."

"It was just a little milk." Regina put the refilled cup in front of him.

"Thank'ee." He drank deeply and then asked, "You got magic?"

"Not really."

"I got some magic of my own," he said. "I can witch ropes. Oh, I ain't good at it yet, but I'm getting better. One day it'll stand me good use as a sailor, I reckon."

Mak had finished eating. Regina cleared away the dishes, and with one long swallow Mak drained the last of his milk. From the parlor Grammy called once for Regina. The two young people went back to the room, where the older ones were now standing, business concluded. "Regina, is there anything you would particularly like?" Grammy asked.

"Well, I could use some new shoes," she said.

Balbacar, who was really a very generous man at heart once the ritual of bargaining was over and done with, beamed. "Bless you, little lass, I've some slippers aboard that will set your toes a-dancing—"

Regina laughed. "Thank you, sir, but if it's the same, I'd rather have good sturdy walking shoes. I don't dance with the chickens and the goats, you know."

"So it shall be," Balbacar said. "Laralen, see to it, if you please."

The exchange of goods was done magically, by use of a modified travel spell, and before another half-hour had passed the egg bin was empty, the larder restocked, and Mak and his fellow sailors on their way back to the ship on foot.

The rest of the day passed in the usual round of chores until early afternoon. Regina was just sweeping the hallway when she heard a faint popping sound outside, and a moment later someone knocked on the door. She opened it to see Barach, who looked vexed, Sebastian, and Nul. "We must see your great-great-grandmother, Regina," the old wizard said.

"Where is Jeremy?" Regina asked.

"Ah. That is what we must speak to Adelaide about."

"I'll tell her you are back."

But Grammy knew already; she had been lying down for a bit of a rest, and when Regina tapped on her door, she called back, "I will see them in the parlor, dear. Thank you."

Regina escorted the three visitors to the same room they had occupied before, and they found seats. Nul seemed rather anxious about animals, but since Redfellow had crawled away into the woods the previous afternoon, there were none to speak of still in the cottage. After a few moments Grammy came into the room. "I understand. You are having difficulty with the Gate, are you not?"

Barach stood and heaved a great sigh. "Alas, we are. The spell is still holding, after a fashion; at least the Gate is not flashing from world to world. But neither is it showing us a picture of Earth."

"No. I understand from Regina that Mr. Moon tied the spell to a particular spot on Earth."

"Yes, that is correct," Barach said.

"And the Gate no longer shows that spot?"

Nul, who had been fidgeting and swinging his legs, said, "Nah, nah. Show nothing. Just blank white fog in Gate now."

Sebastian, who had also stood when Adelaide entered the room, said, "And I cannot pass through it myself. I tried; but instead of going through the Gate into my own world, I simply passed into a little hollow in the cliff behind the Gate."

Adelaide sniffed. "It is perfectly plain. To make the Gate active once more, you and Jeremy must be on opposite sides of it, simultaneously. That will fulfill the original requirements of his spell, though in reverse—you will be in Thaumia and he on Earth. Once the two of you are in proximity, the safeguards will relax and you will once again be able to use the Gate as a passageway to Earth." She seated herself in a chair. "Oh, pray sit down."

Barach, sinking into a chair, said, "There is the problem, madam. We have no way of knowing if Jeremy is capable of presenting himself on his side of the Gate; we have no means of communicating with him at all. And I cannot think of a way to effect either transportation or communication on my own. As you know, I no longer possess magic."

Adelaide looked at him with her keen eyes. "Are you asking me to work a spell for you?"

"Exactly," Barach replied. "You see, you have not only a great store of *mana* but also at least a remnant of Earthly magic. I would be happy to help you formulate a spell—"

"No," Adelaide said. "Quite impossible."

Nul almost leapt from his chair in his agitation. "Impossible? Must get Jeremy back!"

Adelaide's smile was sympathetic but aloof. "I understand your anxiety for your friend. But I am afraid of the Gate."

"Afraid?" Sebastian asked.

"With reason. Do not forget that I am some one hundred and twenty years old. If some accident should occur—if perchance the Gate transported me to Earth—imagine what would happen to me. There were tales of people from Earth wandering in Faerie who came home apparently hale, only to shrivel into hideous old age and death—" Adelaide broke off and gave a delicate shudder. "Besides, my magic is not the sort you need. It is far too narrow and restricted to attempt such a feat. I am sorry, gentlemen, but I cannot help."

And then, as if he could contain himself no longer, Barach said, "Madam, I am afraid there is no alternative now; we must have a look at the book."

Grammy sighed. "I know," she said. "I felt it. Regina, would you please fetch it?"

Regina knew without asking which book was wanted. She went to get it, feeling her stomach turn over with something very much like fear.

In three different rooms of Whitehorn Keep Tremien's voice boomed simultaneously from thin air: "Idoradas. Jondan. Celissa."

Three different heads turned in anticipation; three different voices answered Tremien.

"One of you knows certainly why I have detained you," Tremien continued. "The other two no doubt have their suspicions. I have had news from the south which troubles me and shows me that we have not much time; therefore I must speak to all of you now.

"One of you is the Great Dark One."

In his room in the north keep, Idoradas said, "So that is it. Mage Tremien, I swear to you that I am Idoradas and only he; I have never seen the Great Dark One, and he certainly has wrought no spell upon me."

At the same moment, in a room two stories away, Jondan, who could not hear Idoradas at all, said, "Of course. We have known for many years the Great Dark One's trick of possessing a new host from time to time. But, Tremien, you have my word that I am not a host to that foul spirit."

And also at that moment, from her place in the northwest tower, Celissa said, "I understand. Tell me what trial you will make of me and I will submit to it, Mage Tremien. You will see that the enemy has not seized upon me."

"You all deny yourselves possessed," Tremien said. "But the Great Dark One is an old liar; so would he deny it. And we do not clearly know how the spell operates. It could even be possible that the affected one has no memory of his or her possession, that the host does not yet know of the infection."

The three were silent to that, each no doubt wrapped in private fears or plots. After a pause, Tremien continued: "Yet I think it is not the case. I think the Great Dark One corrupts first the voluntary will, then the powers, of each host. If my supposition is correct, then the one of you whom he has taken must know of his presence. The other two must be innocent. I have woven a strong spell, the strongest of which I am capable, about Whitehorn. If you hear me, Great Dark One, know this: in my own place of power even you cannot prevail. If you are indeed within Idoradas, or Jondan, or Celissa, there you must stay, so long as you remain in my castle; no spell of yours, however strong, could overcome the wards I have wrought. You cannot now possess another."

"Then," Idoradas said, "you have him, Mage Tremien."

Celissa said, "If that is true, then why keep us prisoner in these rooms? If the Great Dark One has no power, why confine him bodily? I could do more good if I were able to confer with you, at least."

Jondan was silent.

Tremien responded: "One of you thinks that I am right; one wishes to be set free of your imprisonment. Let me tell you all this: if I thought it possible to destroy the Great Dark One and all his works at a blow, I would not hesitate to execute the three of you. But there is a complicating problem."

Jondan spoke then, his voice full of knowledge: "The spell that is disrupting magic to the south. It must be something beyond your expectations."

"One has spoken what all must divine: we cannot be sure that destroying the Great Dark One would destroy the spell that works to the south of us now. The death of the Great Dark One might even make its effects worse. Therefore I need your help. Two of you are innocent, and I am sure you know who you are; one of you has become the new incarnation of the enemy, and I believe you know that as well.

"Very well, then; here is my proposition. Let the two who are innocent rack their brains for a way to prove themselves innocent, or to prove the third one guilty. When we know for certain which of you has been taken, we may plan a course of action; and the sooner you devise a plan, the sooner you will be set free."

The voice fell silent then, and three minds began to work on the problem at once. But away in his rooms, Tremien turned to his old master, Radusilf, who sat slumped in a great chair. "You do not approve," Tremien said.

Radusilf shook his head, making his sparse white beard swing back and forth. "I do not."

Tremien studied him for a long time. "What would you have done differently?"

The ancient mage sniffed. His moist, liver-colored lips quivered as he thought through what he was about to say. "I was turned out as Chief Mage more than fifty years ago." His voice held a peevish edge to it, an old man's irritability. "You had no need of me then; I could be of no assistance, you said, in the combat with our great enemy. Why, then, do you presume to ask me for help now?"

Tremien smiled. He spoke in a soft and kindly voice: "You are wrong, Mage Radusilf. You were never turned out; you stepped aside of your own will. And besides, fifty years ago I, and all of Cronbrach, had great need of you; and if memory serves, you rendered aid to us then. We have not lost the need."

A diamond-patterned glass carafe of pale yellow wine was on the table at Radusilf's elbow. He picked it up with a shaking hand and poured himself a glass, the neck of the bottle chattering on the rim of the crystal. "I thought it would come to this," he muttered, setting the carafe down. He picked up the glass carefully, holding one hand under it to catch any spilled drops, and lifted it to his lips. He drank the wine noisily, with smacks and gulps, finishing it with a gasp of satisfaction. "Yes, I helped you, unwillingly. You did not take my advice; you did not even listen. I told you, Tremien, and I told the rest of the Council as well, that it would come to this in the end. We should have made Cronbrach impregnable, as I wished. In those days we could have done it if we all acted together. It is too late now."

"I well remember what you said. Yes, and your plan, too, Mage Radusilf." Tremien had been standing, his back to a tapestry that showed Whitehorn Peak as it had looked five hundred years ago, before the castle had been built to crown its crest. He sat now in a chair opposite Radusilf's. "Perhaps we could have done as you wished; we could have made Cronbrach safe against the Great Dark One. What then? Should we have let the Great Dark One take the rest of the world without a fight? Finarr is a land of fifty governments and many people. Hadoriben, to our south, is a continent already half under the sway of the enemy; the monarchs of that land, they say, already pay tribute to the Great Dark One. And Relas was lost long ago. Could Cronbrach be the only continent to stand if all the rest should fall?"

"We must know the limits of our power, Tremien," Radusilf returned. "One land is enough for me."

"We disagreed with you then, Master. I find that I still must do so."

Radusilf had got hold of an idea, and he shook it as a dog might shake a rat: "The limits of our power. We must find the limits and know them, and we must not try to exceed them, or we are lost."

"Perhaps," Tremien suggested, "our powers are greater than you imagine."

The ancient mage shook his head, his face screwed up in fear. "No, we are no match for them. The things I saw at Downsdale—you could not stand against them, nor all the Council together. But now they are here, among us; if we had set up a wall of wizardry fifty years ago, they would never have been able to burst into our lands."

"Perhaps not," Tremien said. "But then, if we had not fought the war the way we did fifty years ago, then possibly all of Hadoriben would be ruled by the master of Relas; and perhaps all the splendid palaces of Finarr would be empty husks, their people dead in the battle. We defeated the Great Dark One then because we united with the others; and now I believe this is the way we must defeat him once more."

Radusilf's reply was to pour himself another glass of the straw-colored wine. When he had drunk half of it, he said, "You cannot know how uncanny the creatures are. I tried a banishing spell. It was the strongest I knew. It should have sent the dark force back to its origin. Instead, I felt my own power being pulled out of me, the *mana* simply disappearing."

"Yes," Tremien said. "We know now that the Shadow Guard is capable of doing just that."

Radusilf drank again and without any self-consciousness smacked his lips and wiped his mouth with the sleeve of his robe. "But the young Moon's magic—that affected them. The world seemed to be turned upside-down for an instant. You would have thought the sky had fallen. I have never known such a feeling of powerful magic at work." Radusilf's face twitched. He stared at Tremien with wide, bleary eyes. "He is your hope, Tremien. That boy is your only hope."

Tremien nodded, his own eyes grave.

Suddenly Radusilf leaned forward, reaching to grasp the sleeve of Tremien's robe in his wasted, bony fingers. He tugged at the sleeve with terrible urgency. "You did not listen to me then, Tremien." The old voice was thin, rapid, cracked. "Listen now. Send him against them. Send Moon. You must do that. You have no idea what these things are—" He broke off, shivering as if from an ague.

Tremien put his hands on the older man's shoulders, steadying him. "I will listen this time, Radusilf," he promised. "Of course you are right."

For a few moments Radusilf merely trembled and panted for breath, the wind wheezing and whistling in his nostrils and his open mouth. At last he said, "I will try again if you wish. I disagree with your methods, but something must be done. Send me again if you wish. I will try once more." But the rheumy old eyes were shiny with fear.

"No," Tremien said carefully. "This time I have listened carefully, Master, and I think your advice is right. We must allow Jeremy Moon to act."

The other wizard groped for his glass, nearly knocking it off the little table at his elbow. "That is best," Radusilf said. "This is very good wine. May I—?"

"Certainly, Mage Radusilf." Taking the goblet from the knotted hand, Tremien poured another glass and then knelt ceremonially before the older wizard, offering the wine to him. With a vague smile Radusilf accepted the glass.

"You used to serve me so when you were an apprentice," he said. "Years and years ago. How plain it all seems yet. Well, well. So the Council still needs the assistance of an old fossil like me. I *will* try again, you know; if you wish, I will try again."

Tremien rose from his kneeling position with some difficulty, his knees cracking as he straightened them. "I know, Master Radusilf," he said. He watched the old, old man drink. He did not give the least indication that he knew what Radusilf did not know: the ancient mage's power was spent. He was not completely drained, not as empty of magic as poor Barach, who could not do so much as activate a travel spell on his own; but Radusilf would never again work a Great Spell. He was right this time: now they had to depend on the magic of Jeremy Moon.

If, that is, they could recover him.

10

Gareth Gremarkin was a good soldier.

For a frantic night and a weary day he and his men had
flanked the moving line of blight that marked the passage of
the five creatures called the Shadow Guard, and in all that
time he had lost not one of his men, nor had he fallen
behind the progress of the Guard. The five weird creatures
had been made fully visible by Jeremy's spell; looking like
nightmares even in the light of day, they moved much more
rapidly than men could run, and they did not ever seem to
tire; or at least they did not rest. Unless, Gareth thought,
they snatched some kind of sleep when they occasionally
used a travel spell to leap ahead fifty or sixty leagues. On
foot, the soldiers could not hope to keep pace with them.

So Gareth resorted to using his own travel spell, adjusting
it so that he always kept the Guard in view. He and his men
took dozens of short hops with the spell, moving a few
thousand steps ahead of the rolling tide of destruction,
trying whatever they or Tremien could devise to turn aside
the Guard, watching the foe sweep forward unregardful of
their efforts, and then leaping ahead once again.

Back on the hillside west of Downsdale, his men had been
struck with horror at their first sight of the things—not that
Gareth could blame them, for he had felt unreasoning fear
himself. But the more they saw of the creatures, the less the
men were afraid of their ungodly appearance; if familiarity
did not in this case breed contempt, it at least gave birth to
a certain ability to tolerate the frightful.

And frightful the creatures of the Guard were. To Gareth
the . . . beasts, the beings, whatever they might be, looked
like nothing so much as dragons turned inside out and

crossed with sea creatures, jellyfish perhaps, or perhaps red crabs. Rearing high above the pathway, they glistened in the sun, looking moist and decayed; like an open wound, as one of Gareth's sergeants put it. And yet their surface could not be as raw and bloody as it appeared, for the billowed dust of their passing did not cling to them. They scuttled, supported on three improbable appendages that resembled the legs of no creature Gareth had ever seen, jointed peculiarly and arranged in an asymmetrical spread.

The legs were not the only oddity about the creatures. If they had organs of sense, Gareth could see no trace of them; they towered on those three scuttling legs in a forward-bending crescent shape somewhat resembling a cow's horn, if a cow's horn were made of corrugated, glistening flesh and were five paces high. The concave side, the "face" side, showed nothing but a round black mouth, gaping and ringed by thorn-sharp "teeth."

But although all five creatures shared roughly the same body build, somehow no two of the things looked precisely alike: in addition to the peculiar legs, each had other appendages, but one had three, another five, another two, and two had only one apiece. More, the "arms" were different. Some were jointed and ended in wicked-looking claws, some were loose, boneless, and tentaclelike, writhing like snakes, snapping through the air like whips. The creatures made no use of them that Gareth could see; they did not physically tear down obstacles in their path.

They did not need to.

Their passage itself pulled down all obstacles. As they absorbed magic, living things crumbled to pasty gray ash; things built with magic lost their shape, their substance, and crashed down. The Guard had no need to pound stone or wood. Only the minority of structures put up by mundane means stood in their way. All the rest were reduced to piles of jumbled rubble, plumes of dust strewn from them by the wind, ignored by the implacably advancing creatures.

And they seemed impervious to harm. Gareth's best archers had sent volley after volley into one of the things. The arrows glanced off the curved back, or sank head-deep into the raw flesh. But those that found purchase never held it. They dropped out after a few simi, oozed from the wound as if the wound itself had gone soft and rotten. The recov-

ered arrows were useless, the steel heads pitted and holed as
if from acid, the wood of the shafts as limber as green reeds
on a riverbank.

Yet the creature hit with no fewer than fifty arrows gave
no sign of injury, seemed not even to notice the wounds.
When Gareth tried more desperate measures, these, too,
were ineffective: an avalanche of boulders toppled from a
bluff onto the things buried one completely. But before
Gareth could have tallied a thousand, the thing had heaved
itself free of the rubble and had continued on its apparently
mindless way, to all appearances unharmed. It made somewhat more haste than it had, and within two hona it had
overtaken and mingled with the other four.

A ditch, cut by the magic of two sorcerers working together, opened athwart their passage, too broad to leap and
so deep that a fall would be fatal. But the Guard toppled
over the edge unheeding, and before they had fallen a
finger's breadth the magic had been pulled from the ravine
and the ground had healed itself. The Guard rolled on
inexorably.

Fire had no effect on them either, not even the hottest
fire that Smokharin the salamander could engender. Smokharin, who was a fire elemental with an unusual fondness
for Melodia, Gareth's intended bride, had set an imposing
barricade of freshly felled trees and the very road beneath it
aflame, so that the sand ran and bubbled. The fire leapt
higher than the tops of the forest trees, and even from a
distance of nearly a thousand paces, Gareth could feel its
heat on his face. The barrier of flame seemed altogether
impenetrable, and for a few moments the soldiers had hope.

But when the Shadow Guard reached it, the beings did
not turn aside, but scuttled on through the heart of the fire,
scattering burning logs, sending flights of orange sparks
skyward. Smokharin reported that they would not burn;
that they were not of the world of the elements and therefore could not be harmed by elemental magic. The blight
and the Guard continued northward.

And as the creatures went on their way, Gareth and his
soldiers saw the great and ancient trees of Arkhedden wither
and crumble; the road, which ordinarily followed the western shore of the Bronfal River and which was overarched by
the old trees, became a broad avenue of brittle gray ash as

trees fifty paces from the Guard's passage succumbed. The affected wood sometimes dissolved of itself; sometimes a slight breeze would fell an enormous old tremble-leaf, the trunk exploding into a cloud of dust as it struck the ground.

Ahead of the Guard lay a dozen villages on the edges of the forest and on the Westforest Downs; already they were being evacuated. As their tracking of the Guard went into the afternoon of the first day, Gareth felt himself growing more and more apprehensive.

Nothing he could do seemed to stop the Guard.

Nothing Radusilf had done had stopped them.

And all Jeremy had done was to render them visible.

What, Gareth wondered, would happen to Whitehorn?

Jeremy Moon's secretary was an efficient lady named Felicity Eberhart. Jeremy faintly remembered her from the old days: a thin gray-haired woman somewhere between forty and sixty with sharp blue eyes behind black-rimmed bifocals. She had been Escher's secretary for a while, before Bob had found a younger and blonder replacement. Now that Jeremy knew he was Sebastian's secretary, he no longer wondered so much about Cassie's complacency in allowing the younger Taplan's sofa to remain in the office. It was impossible to picture Mrs. Eberhart horizontal, much less undressed.

"Check your schedule?" Mrs. Eberhart asked now, her thin voice buzzing over the phone lines. "Certainly I can do that, Mr. Moon, but I didn't think you were even coming in today."

"I may be in later," Jeremy said. "After this debate thing. Didn't I give you a schedule or—"

"You've forgotten your pocket reminder again," Mrs. Eberhart said in an accusing voice.

Jeremy, who was at a pay telephone in the lobby of a Peachtree hotel, agreed at once: "You're right, Mrs. Eberhart. I should have known I couldn't fool you. I left it in the office, I guess."

"Honestly, it does you no good if you forget it every day. Just a moment." Jeremy fidgeted while he waited for her to get back on the line. He felt oddly naked: his beard was gone, his hair was cut to half its accustomed length. Even the warm air of mid-July felt cool on his bare cheeks, and his chin still burned from the memory of the razor. But dressed in Sebastian's suit and manicured into an approximation of Sebastian's style, Jeremy hoped he could pass. He checked his watch—not the Rolex, but a black digital Casio that he remembered from the old days, its battery still holding out. Jeremy wondered how long it had been winking off the minutes in Sebastian's top dresser drawer. Now it told him that the time was nine-twenty-seven A.M.

"Mr. Moon?"

"Yes, Mrs. Eberhart?"

"My datebook shows that you are to meet Mr. Norris at campaign headquarters at ten. The debate is at the Civic Center from eleven to twelve-thirty. You are open for lunch. Tomorrow morning at nine you have a meeting with the Secura people on the new account, and at two there will be the usual staffing." After a moment's pause she added somewhat archly, "I presume you *will* be at work tomorrow."

"Yes, that's right," Jeremy said. "Uh, and I probably will be in later this afternoon. I have some odds and ends to finish up. And, uh, one last thing." He gulped. "Where would I find the campaign headquarters?"

For ten seconds the line was dead. Then with evident astonishment Mrs. Eberhart asked, "Why, has it moved?"

"No, but . . . I've forgotten the address, that's all."

"You have forgotten the address of your own campaign headquarters."

"I've had a lot on my mind."

"Honestly. One moment." After an exasperated pause she came back with exaggerated courtesy: "Do you by any chance want to write this down?"

"Just a second." Jeremy fished a gunmetal-gray Cross pen from his shirt pocket and tore a page corner from the back of the hanging Yellow Pages. "Okay, shoot."

"Are you quite certain you're ready? It's 1220 South Hampstead." She read off the telephone number too, and Jeremy copied that down as well. "Will that be all?" she asked him.

"Yes, thanks. You're wonderful, Mrs. Eberhart."

For the first time her frosty composure thawed a degree or two. In a slightly flustered tone she said, "Why, thank you, Mr. Moon. Not at all. I . . . That's very kind of you."

"Remind me to see about arranging a raise for you,"

Jeremy said on impulse. He hung up the receiver and stood for a moment staring at the corner of paper in his hand. Then he got another coin from his pocket and fed it to the phone. This time he called the campaign headquarters. A woman answered on the second ring; he asked for Mr. Norris.

"Just a moment," the woman said. He heard her say, "It's for you, Sam."

A few seconds later a man's voice, hoarse and flat, came on the line: "Sam Norris here."

Jeremy cleared his throat. "Good morning, Sam."

"Hey, how's the boy? Ready to go get him, buddy? You get my message?"

"Cassie gave it to me—"

"Sorry about the timing. We just haven't got all the numbers together yet, so you want to stick to the better issues. Hope you got through the briefing books."

"Uh, yeah. Look, Sam, is there any way we could . . . could postpone this thing?"

There was a long and ominous silence. "I laugh now? You're joking, right?" the hoarse voice asked at last. "Postpone it? You know how hard it was to pin the bastard down to a public appearance at all? And you know Tidburn—if you backed out, he'd make that a big deal. If you pull out now, you might as well give him the election on a plate."

Jeremy sighed. "I'm just not ready for this."

Norris asked, "What's wrong? You sick?"

"I'm not feeling very well," Jeremy acknowledged.

"What's the matter?"

"Nothing definite."

After another pause Norris said, "Is it Cassie?"

"No, she's fine."

"I mean, you two haven't fought or anything, have you? She hasn't been all that keen on your running for office. I know that. I could sense that."

Jeremy was surprised. The previous evening Cassie, as she had promised, had telephoned him just before eleven, and she had been all solicitude then, encouraging and supportive. *Sebastian doesn't deserve her*, he thought. But to Norris he said, "You're pretty sharp, Sam. No, it's not that. I . . . well, I'm afraid I can't explain it all—"

"Stage fright, isn't it? Butterflies?"

"Well—"

"Look, are you gonna be here?"

"I was on my way."

"Well, hustle. We'll talk it over in the office. Gotta run. See you in a few minutes." The line clicked and went dead.

"Right," Jeremy said as he hung up. He checked his watch again: nine-thirty-eight. And South Hampstead was a few miles east of Peachtree. He'd have to hustle to make it.

He threaded Sebastian's Porsche in and out of traffic, heading east out of town on Ponce de Leon. It was a gorgeous day, unusually clear for a summer morning. Jeremy reflected that the hoodoo on the weather operated only when he and Sebastian were together, either here or on Thaumia; neither universe seemed to care when they were separate, but when the two were in the same cosmos at the same time, nature spat rain at them, lashed them with lightning, complained in a voice of thunder. This universe ain't big enough for the both of you, kid. But alone, you're beautiful, I love ya, baby.

He turned south on Hampstead not far from the tony campus of Agnes Scott, then crept along at twenty-five miles per hour until he spotted 1220, a discreet brick building set among a stand of white oaks and fronted by a deep green barrier of waist-high boxwoods, well-tended and neatly kept. No sign identified the building as headquarters of anything, but it had to be the place.

Jeremy found a parking place in the cramped asphalt lot behind the building—it looked like the sort of place a dentist might choose to locate a sedate and remunerative practice, he thought—and then he walked around front, gravel crunching under the soles of Sebastian's Gucci oxfords. The door was unlocked and led into a reception area where a pretty auburn-haired girl in a yellow dress was on the telephone. She smiled up at him. "Yes, that's right," she said into the phone. "I'm sure that could be arranged. Very good. Thank you." She hung up and said, "Good morning, Mr. Moon. Mr. Norris is waiting for you." She picked up the phone again, punched a button, and said, "Mr. Norris? He's here."

A tall man, his black hair showing a pronounced widow's peak, emerged from a door to the left of the receptionist. "Here's the boy," the man said in the hoarse voice Jeremy remembered from the telephone. "He's gonna kill Tidburn, right, Patty?"

"Sure he is," the girl said. "Go get him, tiger."

Norris, who was taller than Jeremy by a good six inches, took Jeremy's arm and ushered him back into a cubbyhole office well-papered with election posters and bumper stickers. In various shades of red, white, and blue Jeremy saw his own name blazoned over and over again, together with a slogan that was anything but oblique sell: *It's Time for a Senator Who Works for You!* "Have a seat," Norris said, waving toward a chair. "What's the matter, son? Is it a bad case of stage fright?"

"It isn't that exactly—"

Norris tilted his head, his eyes critical. "It's nothing to be ashamed of, kid. Tidburn can be plenty tough, we've talked about that. You're pale, you know that?"

Jeremy shrugged. "I told you I didn't feel well."

"Drink?"

"Too early for me."

"Wouldn't be a good idea, anyway. Coffee, then." Norris left him alone for a minute. Jeremy looked around the office in wonder, seeing his own face—well, actually Sebastian's face, but it *looked* like his own—displayed in at least half a dozen different color and black-and-white photos. There was a sincere poster, a tough poster, a spiritual poster, a determined poster, and an all-American poster. A large blue loose-leaf notebook lay on the desk. Jeremy opened it and realized that it was the briefing book Norris had spoken of. It seemed at least a hundred pages long.

He flipped through it in despair, noting the contents: Tidburn's position on the state lottery question, on industrial development, on crime. Newspaper clippings detailing the hundred and one instances of Tidburn's corner-cutting, of his close brushes with ethics committees and oversight groups. It merely added three years of information to what Jeremy recalled from the old days: Tidburn was basically a genial con man, a crook.

"Cramming a little?" Norris asked. He handed Jeremy a mug of coffee. Garfield the cat was cartooned in shades of orange on the mug, sleepy-eyed and grumpy-mouthed, above the line "I'm just not human before my first cup of coffee." Jeremy absently sipped it.

"Light, no sugar. Right?" Norris asked.

"The coffee's fine," Jeremy said. "Look, go over the format with me one more time."

Norris settled into his own chair at the desk and leaned back, his hands interlaced behind his head. "Tidburn goes first. He has twenty minutes for a position statement. Then you get your twenty. Then you get to put a question to him; he has five minutes to respond. He asks you one; you get your five minutes. And so on for a total of six questions each. Then you each get a five-minute wrap-up. Remember, the wrap-up is the important part for you—the news bites are gonna come from that."

Jeremy closed his eyes. All he wanted was to get back to Sebastian's office and look for the telltale shimmer of the Gate. But first he had to go through this.

"Remind me again," he said, not opening his eyes, "of the type of questions we thought it would be good to ask Tidburn."

"Well," Barach said, "I suppose it is time for a question."

The three of them, Barach, Sebastian, and Nul, stood alone in Adelaide's parlor, the closed book on the table before them. Sebastian swallowed hard and began, "Do you want me to—"

"I think I had better ask the question," Barach said. "If evil consequences are to come from this, it is better they are tied to Thaumia than sent with you to Earth. Let me think for a moment."

Nul was behind the table facing the other two, so from his perspective the book was upside-down. "Maybe Nul should ask," he said. "Not matter so much to pika-people if answer bad for him."

"No," Barach said with some firmness. "Pikas do not use the same kind of magic that made this book; and I have. I think the choice is mine. I have it: here is my question." He cleared his throat and then addressed the closed book: "We know that there is a way to bring Jeremy back to Thaumia. We know that the way will not cause harm to him or mischief to our cause. We know that none of Jeremy's friends will suffer from our undertaking. Our question, Book, then, is—how may we safely return Jeremy?"

For a few moments nothing happened. Then the book opened, not gradually but with a snap, and pages ruffled, turning themselves. When the last one had whispered open, Sebastian said, "Shall I read it?"

"My eyes are like those of the beshrike in the story," Barach said. "Not yet so bad that night and day are the same." He bent forward and then read aloud: *The mirror maker must see his reflection when the time is between shadows. A worker of magic must then say the word and allow one traveler to pass, though he go two different ways. A time of terror rises, when those from without must surrender their power to him who is within. There shall be giants and horns upon the mountainside before a final journey. He who loves Earth must pass to Earth at last; and if his journey is too soon, a world must die. If it is late, the traveler must die.* Barach looked up, his face haggard. "That is all."

"A riddle," Sebastian said.

"Fate," Barach corrected. "Fate is ever a riddle."

"What means *between shadows*?" Nul demanded.

"We must determine that," Barach said.

"Guess, you mean?" asked Nul.

"That is right."

Nul exploded in shrill indignation: "Always the way with human talk! Nothing what it seem. Talk, talk, talk, all smoke and shadows! Everything mean something else. All riddle, riddle, riddle. Should have asked in pika tongue; no foolishness about it then, just what we must do."

"Maybe we should ask the book to solve the riddle," Sebastian offered.

Barach shook his head. "That would not be wise; I tried to hem the question in with assurances of safety, and look at the hazards we see: the death of a world. Our world or Earth? Or some other? The death of a traveler, perhaps of you, Sebastian; when is *too late* and when is *too early*? We have our answer, but it is sown with quite enough danger to suit me. I do not think another question would help us, and it could very well make matters worse."

"We go to Gate," Nul said. "We wait there. Try to find answer close by it. Only way."

"You're right," Sebastian said.

Nul blinked. "Am?"

"You have been right before," Barach pointed out. "Perhaps not often, but once or twice."

"Just surprised you admit it, that all," Nul said.

"Nevertheless." Barach closed the book and stood for a moment with his hand on the cover. "Well, let us go outside and then Nul can work the travel spell. Thank heaven it's functioning properly again! I'd hate to make that long walk twice in one day."

Adelaide, who seemed to know their business with the book was finished, bade them farewell in the hallway. They went outside, under the shade of one of the oaks, and Nul carefully pronounced the English word that activated Jeremy's variant of the travel spell. It took them to the Gate, after the normal period of subjective time had passed; and on the way they debated meanings and tried to unravel riddles.

Afternoon was advancing when they entered the Gate glade again. The cavern opening of the Gate was different now, full of dark gray formless fog, like an opening to haunted midnight. Just looking at it made Nul feel cold, reminded him of chill damp nights spent out-of-doors, when the mists rose and beaded in his fur, changing his color from dark gray to shining silver—but soaking him and making him shiver.

They continued to wait, continued to wonder what the book had meant when it said a word must be spoken. The travel word, Nul thought; no, Barach said, some other word, some single word of magic, but one that had to be obvious. A word, Sebastian suggested, that had to do with mirrors. The two men instantly disagreed and began to argue in heated tones; Nul held his head in his three-fingered hands and moaned in frustration.

The sun declined. An errant dragon blundered by through the trees not fifty paces away, saw them, and belched in basso alarm before turning and crashing away through the undergrowth. Still they seemed no closer to solving the mystery.

Nul's head began to spin with suggestions, with riddles, with answers—or were they in fact answers? The more the other two debated, the less sure he felt. Finally, as Sebastian and Barach entered another thicket of words, words, words, Nul grew despondent and wandered some distance off. He sat on a fallen log, his head in his hands. Humans, he thought with disgust. If only each one of their words had one meaning, like pika-speech; then fate would be clear and not a puzzle. Idly he picked up a stick and began to scratch patterns in the gray volcanic sand at his feet. He wore no shoes, for they pinched his odd-shaped little feet, and he clenched and unclenched his six toes in the sand. The cool, gritty feel of it reminded him of the clean sand flooring of Zarad-zellikol, the underground kingdom that he had given up to serve Tremien and to be friends with Jeremy, whose stories—unlike the wearisome fables of Barach—transported him to a world of imagination and excitement.

Finally Nul stuck the twig in the center of a circle he had drawn. Looking at it, he thought of the sundial in the forecourt of Whitehorn Keep. Something else that men did and pikas did not: slicing a day into bits, into simi and hona, into little pieces of time. To a pika, *day* began with waking and ended with sleeping; underground creatures cared little for the passage of the sun across the sky, and a pika's day could be long with enjoyment or short, just as the pika pleased. But humans had to make things different, and so they split the day into fragments, beginning with sunrise and ending just before dawn. They had to mark—

Nul sat up very straight, staring at the stick and the circle.

Of course.

How obvious.

He got up and ran toward the clearing, and then slowed, chuckling to himself. There was time. He changed his gait to a casual stroll.

Sebastian and Barach had gone through most of the words in the lexicon, it seemed, and they still had not settled on one; and the debate was growing ever more heated.

"Is the word to be a magical one or a mundane one?" Barach said, his voice thick with irritation. "That is my only question."

"But that isn't your only question," Sebastian said. "You've asked me a hundred others, and I don't know the answer to any of them."

"Even if we divine the word, what then? Do we speak it here, or does Jeremy speak it on Earth? And the time—"

Nul coughed.

"But the business about music and giants on the mountainside," Sebastian put in. "That can only mean Whitehorn. What does it mean, giants? There aren't any real—"

"Got it," Nul said.

"Well, the book did not say human giants," Barach objected. "The Shadow Guard, perhaps—they are certainly large enough to be considered—"

Nul kicked him, not too hard, in the shins. "Got it."

Both of the others stared at him. "Nul know answer," he said. "Got the riddle." And he told them.

Tremien leaned back in his chair with a heavy sigh. The two women and one man in the room—motherly Mumana, tall and imperious Wyonne, and the bald, gnomelike Altazar—held their silence. Tremien met their eyes and saw there the unasked question. "Nothing has worked," he said. "The Shadow Guard are still coming."

Mumana clucked. Wyonne said in her slow and elegant voice, "Then what are we to do?"

"What we must," Altazar said. He had his long-stemmed black pipe in his mouth, unlit. It muffled his words: "Tell the lot of them they must be executed. And we must do it now, before the Guard are on Tremien's very doorstep."

"We could move the three to my country," Mumana said. "That is farther to the west and will give us more time."

Tremien smiled, though it was a wan smile. "Thank you, Keeper of the Heartlands. But Whitehorn is a place of much power. I do not boast, but speak only the truth in saying it is our strongest bastion against the Great Dark One; they shall remain here." He added kindly, "I know what anxiety you must feel for Celissa, your former apprentice."

Wyonne inclined her head in agreement. "I cannot find it in my heart to believe that she is evil. But like you, I cannot be certain of her innocence. What you say is true, Mage Tremien. And time grows short."

"I know that all too well." Tremien slumped a little in his chair. 'With Barach away and Jondan and Idoradas under suspicion, we are all that is left of the High Council. I have a plan to propose; it seems a good one to me, but I would not put it into practice without your counsel and advice."

Altazar took the pipe from his mouth and frowned at it as if he had never seen it before. "We know what you will propose, Tremien. We have discussed it. We are in agreement."

"It is a drastic step," Mumana said in a small voice.

Wyonne tossed her hair. "Yet it must be taken. We cannot allow the Great Dark One the least chance of overwhelming Whitehorn."

Mumana's eyes flashed, but her voice remained gentle: "You have never felt the Great Dark One's wrath, Wyonne. You live in Triesland, far to the west. The soldiers of the Great Dark One, the hobs and the Hadors, did not despoil your land as they did Tremien's, Altazar's, and mine."

Wyonne's reply was cold: "No; nor do I intend that his foul Guard shall now do what his men and monsters could not. It is true that three ranges of mountains, the great Lofar gulf, and the northern arm of Arkhedden are between the Shadow Guard and my homeland. But even that offers no surety, no safety."

"Where the Great Dark One is concerned," Altazar said sententiously, "there is neither surety nor safety."

Wyonne scarcely acknowledged the interruption. "Therefore, I would have him stopped here, now, before Whitehorn itself is threatened."

Mumana bit her lower lip. "I do not question the necessity of stopping him," she said. "Merely the wisdom of making the attempt here. Should we risk unleashing these creatures of darkness by destroying their only control? Will the Guard not prove worse than their master if no trammel is upon them?"

Tremien said, "We have discussed and discussed. Time grows very short now; none remains for more talk." He looked around the table, his brown eyes clear and full of gratitude. "You have been good friends, and you have ever cared for Whitehorn almost as much as have I. I thank you for your consent in my decision, and whatever comes of it, know that your friendship has made my lot easier."

"Tush," Altazar said, toying with his pipe. "We are all in this together, live or die."

Tremien nodded. "You are correct, I fear. Gareth says that the Guard will surely be upon us by tomorrow night at the latest, and perhaps even before that, for their speed has increased. I have strengthened all my spells of warding around Whitehorn. Not even the Great Dark One himself could break them, were he to exert all his power; yet the Guard may overcome them, taking the *mana* from their working and rendering the spells as impotent as those of my old master Radusilf."

"We will all lend you power," Mumana said.

"Thank you, Keeper of the Heartlands. But I think what power is here shall have to suffice. I hope that Jeremy will return tonight or tomorrow; but whether he does or no, here is what I must do. I will let each of the prisoners know of our sentence; I will tell each of them to prepare, for tomorrow morning at sunrise, in the forecourt of Whitehorn, the three of them shall be beheaded."

Altazar said in a troubled and low voice, "We know the enormity of this, Tremien. The stones of Whitehorn have never tasted innocent blood."

"Nor," Tremien said heavily, "has it ever dripped from my fingers before."

Jeremy sat on the stage of the auditorium, a smile frozen on his face, and listened to Harlon Tidburn's skillful crucifixion of Sebastian's political ambitions.

Thank God, Jeremy thought, that the audience is so small. Maybe a hundred and fifty people sat in the auditorium, their number reduced to insignificance by the size of the hall. The news cameras were there, though, from five different organizations, the three network affiliates, and two UHF stations. And no doubt the *Journal-Constitution* reporters were there as well, listening to the unctuous ceremony of human sacrifice, with words substituting for knives and with Tidburn acting as the unofficial witch doctor.

"All I'm saying," Tidburn said in a voice as sweet and thick as sorghum syrup, "is that the people deserve strong representation. Far be it from me to disparage young Mr. Moon. I could say, who do you think you are, young fellow? And I doubt he could give me a very good answer. He ain't even got his full growth in yet. But y'all have to remember, bein' young ain't his fault. Now, it's fine to be a young man. Times come when I wish I was a young man myself. But when you send somebody to the state house, my friends, you want somebody with a little experience under his belt. I got that—"

That's not all you have under your belt, Jeremy thought. Tidburn stood five-feet-eight and weighed at least a hundred and ninety, with a gut that gave him a pear shape despite

the careful tailoring of his pearl-gray suit. His hair, daz-
zlingly white in the stage lights, was carefully styled, so that
it looked almost brittle; his broad pink face radiated good-
will and easy humor. His plantation accent, no doubt carefully practiced, was redolent of magnolias and moonlight.

And the man was as crooked as a snake on a ten-day
drunk.

Jeremy crossed his legs, attempted to stitch a studious
expression on his face, and tried to ignore the stricken
countenance worn by Sam Norris, over in the wings. In
making the initial position statement, Jeremy had gone second as challenger, and he thought that things had gone
relatively well. For about half a minute.

That was when he ran out of generalities. Unfortunately,
generalities were all he had—what did he know of Sebastian's politics and policies?—and so he fell back on plati-
tudes, on promises of better government, lower taxes, happier
times for all. It did not, unfortunately, differ in any material
way from what Tidburn had just told the same audience.
Jeremy had become an echo, not a voice.

And Tidburn was eating him alive. Every word the old
rascal spoke was another nail in the coffin. Every smiling
implication that youth was youth, but experience would tell,
was just another turn of the knife in the wound.

Jeremy sighed. At least it was almost over. They had
batted questions back and forth like shuttlecocks, Tidburn
effortlessly diverting his offerings. Except for the cynicism
of it, Tidburn's performance was a marvel of choreography:
he danced around everything, skirted every issue, did a *pas
de deux* with the truth in which he never touched his partner. In turn, his "questions" were no questions at all, only
more snide implications of callowness and inexperience. Jeremy floundered with them, making any weak point he could
and—as Norris had advised—staying away from personal
attack.

It had not worked well. Now Jeremy had one final opportunity for a wrap-up, and then he would be free.

And Sebastian would come back to a campaign in tatters.
If he could come back at all.

Jeremy drifted. What if he couldn't get back to Thaumia?
What if he were again stuck on Earth as himself—but as the
version of himself that Sebastian had built in the last three

years, as husband of Cassie, as the hotshot who had come up with oblique advertising, as aspiring politician—

He shuddered at the thought. And back home—for Thaumia was his home now—what about Kelada, Emily, what about his friends—

"All I'm sayin'," Tidburn said with an expansive gesture, "is what my ole daddy always knew. It's what you folks know, 'cause you're good sensible folks. When you got a good hoss broke to plow, why, you don't swap him for a mule colt just 'cause the jackass is young."

And they laughed.

Oh, the laughter was scattered and unaccompanied by applause, but it was jeering laughter all the same. It was the kind of nervous laughter a loser gets for his efforts. It was maddening laughter. Jeremy, roused from his reverie, felt his face burn. The old hypocrite! What Tidburn knew was not public service; he served a constituency of one. Jeremy knew of Tidburn's past, all right, and so did—

"Mr. Moon," the moderator, a woman in a black dress and blue hair, said into the microphone, "will now conclude." And she gave him a smile of simpering pity.

Something snapped.

Jeremy got up and strode to the lectern. He gripped the edges hard and glared out at the sparse audience, most of them not even looking directly at him now. He looked at the red lights of the cameras, all five of them, ready for their news bites.

What the hell, he thought.

"I'd like to thank Senator Tidburn for the lesson in animal husbandry," he said.

"But you know as well as I do that Senator Tidburn's old daddy was no farmer.

"If memory serves, he was a politician.

"If I recall correctly, he bled this state of about seven million dollars over his long and crooked career."

"Wait a minute!" Tidburn said in a sharp undertone off to Jeremy's right.

"My turn, Mr. Tidburn," Jeremy said, more loudly. "You know and I know that Estes Tidburn never drove a plow through one inch of soil. He never had an acre of corn or cotton that he could call a real farm. He never owned a farm; he owned a tax dodge, ladies and gentlemen. And it's time for his little boy to stop dodging."

He leaned toward the microphone; people were paying attention now. "I'm new to this, yes. I don't deny that. But if you want to check me out, check me out. My history is open. I was born on a farm not fifty miles north of here. I grew up in a town not forty miles from the spot where I stand; I went to school over in Athens. I entered the business world in Atlanta. I worked hard. I've made something of myself because I worked for myself. And now I want to work for you.

"Want to hire me? Look at my record. Then look at Tidburn's. You've sent him into government over and over again, but have you ever taken a good look at what he's done? Ever looked at all the great things he's accomplished? It's time to take that look.

"Sure, he's done you favors. But haven't you paid for them? Paid for them in the graft you know he takes? Paid for them in the humiliation of knowing you voted for this man whose main interest in politics ends inside his wallet pocket?

"My time is almost up. You know where I stand. If you don't know, just watch me. A minute ago, Mr. Tidburn asked me who do I think I am." Jeremy leaned very close to the mike now, his voice level and even. "I'm someone who works hard. I'm a businessman who knows what it means to struggle. I'm one of you." His voice rose: "I am Jeremy Moon, your next state senator, that's who I am. The question, Mr. Tidburn," he said, and paused until the whole auditorium was quiet. "The question is: who the hell are *you*?"

Recognition dawned in the face of one of the newswomen directly in front of the stage. She giggled.

And then the laughter spread. The audience began to applaud. Some of them stood up. The applause grew; it filled the hall in the way that the small audience did not.

And Tidburn's florid face had gone purple, livid, when Jeremy grinned at him and strode off the stage.

Later, after Jeremy had struggled to find enough vague responses to satisfy the reporters, after the last straggling well-wishers had shaken his hand, after Tidburn and his entourage had swept off in indignant silence, Sam Norris slapped Jeremy hard on the back. "You had me worried," he said. "I'll admit that. But I swear to God, I really think you might have pulled it off. Of course, now things are really gonna heat up. You know what we said about Tidburn's tactics. The gloves are coming off now."

"I can take whatever he dishes out," Jeremy said. "It's time to get down to issues anyhow. Let's make this a real campaign. Give people something to think about."

Norris shook his head. "It isn't what we planned. Tidburn's done a lot of favors for a lot of people over the past twenty years, so he can drift by on grins and good-ole-boy stories. If you get pinned down to a specific program, you'll lose some important blocs of votes—" He stopped, thought a second, and shrugged. "What the hell. If we lose them, we lose them. Who knows, we may even pick up enough to offset our losses. I'm with you. This time let's let them know that if Tidburn is reelected, by God, they deserve him."

"Not a bad slogan," Jeremy said.

They stood in the parking decks. Norris laughed. "Well, it isn't the way I would've played it, but if it works, what do I know, right? Don't forget the breakfast Thursday. And I'll be in touch about the interviews and the press releases." They shook hands, Norris climbed into his BMW, and then Jeremy got into the Porsche. He thought hard all the way back to Taplan and Taplan—he could not get used to the firm's new name—but he couldn't think of any way to reopen the Gate.

Mrs. Eberhart expressed surprise at seeing him when he came into the office at two-fifteen. He said with a shrug that he wanted to get *some* work done and that he might even stay late. "You might bring me the files," he finished, knowing that there were always files.

"Very well."

She brought him a sheaf of papers, and as long as she was in the office Jeremy studiously leafed through them, seeing outlines of campaigns for soft drinks, for airlines, for footwear. But the moment she had left him alone, he tossed everything onto Sebastian's desk.

Despite himself, he felt ashamed of what he had done to Tidburn. For the truth was that Sebastian had nothing on the old war-horse; Sebastian, if elected to the senate, would surely pursue Sebastian's interests alone, and to hell with any other constituency. And if Sebastian did not return from Thaumia to be elected—

Jeremy rested his chin on his hands and stared at empty air so hard that his eyes began to water.

The Gate had not returned.

Not yet, anyway.

God help me if I have to go through with the election, he thought. I could lose.

Worse.

I *could* be elected.

11

"**S**hadow there," Nul explained, pointing to the elongated silhouette of himself cast by the declining sun. "Sun go down in ocean, then no shadow. But moon come later at night; moon very bright now. Then moonshadow. Time between shadows is time between sunset and moonrise."

Barach stared at the pika, his thick gray eyebrows climbing high in honest astonishment. "I believe you've hit it," he said. "The time between sunshadow and moonshadow: of course." His face clouded. "Unless it is the other way around."

Nul grinned, showing a crescent of sharp white teeth. "Cannot be. Think: moon past full now, waning each night. Sets after sun is already up. So between shadows has to be in evening, not in morning; in morning moonshadow and sunshadow pass into each other."

"But that isn't the whole riddle," Sebastian protested. "What about the word someone must speak to bring Jeremy back from Earth?"

"We wait," Nul said with his ferocious grin growing even wider. "You see." He glanced toward toward the Gate, which still was overcast with the gray featureless fog. No movement, no shape, was apparent in its depths now. "Any change there?"

"None," Barach said. "It has been just as you see it. But at least it has not slipped back into its old way of changing from view to view and from world to world. It is inactive now, but not uncontrolled."

"If it isn't dead altogether," Sebastian said.

Barach's voice had lost the edge of irritation the debate had put in it and had become as genial as always. "If it were, then we should see nothing at all in the opening; nothing but perhaps the stone at the back of the cavern. No, this is some token of waiting. The magic of the spell is still present, showing itself as this dormant fog. If Nul has indeed solved the puzzle, then the Gate can surely be reactivated."

"Only hope Jeremy is where he should be," Nul said. "We know what to do; Jeremy has not had book to help him."

"I think we're safe enough there," Barach told him. "Jeremy can be exasperating sometimes, but he was always a good student, and he has a head on his shoulders—"

"Neck, you mean," Nul said. "Only people with head on shoulders are—"

Barach threw up his hands. "Never mind, Nul. Have it your way. What I meant to say was that Jeremy will surely attempt to return to Thaumia; therefore he will be as close to his side of the Gate as he can manage. I think we need have no fear on that score." Turning to Sebastian, the old mage continued: "A graver concern is your position. If the book indeed decrees fate, it has given you a painful choice— when to return to Earth. What will you do?"

Sebastian looked rueful. "As yet we have had no giants on any mountainside that I know of, and no music. I suppose I'd better wait for that to happen before returning. I only hope it's soon."

"Then when Jeremy comes through—"

"If Jeremy comes through," Sebastian corrected.

Nul stamped his feet in the sand. "Will come, Nul tells you. You see."

"All right, all right, Nul," Barach said, his tone soothing. "When we are all together again, we must return at once to Whitehorn. Tremien will have need of us there if Gareth has not managed to stop the Shadow Guard."

By this time the sun had sunk below the dark-green canopy of trees to the west. Day shadows had not died, for the three of them stood in the long shade of the forest, but shadows were certainly fading. The trumpet-shaped orange flowers on the vines flanking the Gate had folded themselves closed for the evening. Already the sky overhead had taken on the dusty cast of sunset, and over the trees to the west the deep blue shaded into a ruddy pink. The three settled in to wait. "Have question," Nul said as he sank onto the gray sand and sat with his disproportionately long legs crossed. "Barach think it all right if Nul pass through Gate to Earth?"

"Certainly not," Barach said shortly. He grunted as he bent and sat on a boulder close to the cliffside. "The spell Jeremy and I set up was quite specific; it takes into consideration only the dimension twins Jeremy and Sebastian. Your passage might completely disrupt the magic, and then where would we be?"

Nul drew up his knees and wrapped his long spidery arms around them. He shrugged. "Too bad. Like to see cars. Like to see Earth."

"It's just as well," Sebastian told him. "Believe me, you'd be out of place on Earth. People wouldn't know what to do about you—unless they locked you in a cage and tried to teach you sign language."

Nul's facial fur bristled, a sure sign of pika indignation. "Put Nul in cage? What that mean?"

Sebastian sounded a bit surprised at the pika's belligerence. "Calm down. I meant no insult to you—Earth people are strange about creatures that resemble animals. It means you're better off here."

Nul sighed, his fur relaxing. "That too bad. Earth look so different. Want to see what it like. But suppose you're right. One world enough for Nul."

"I commend your decision. You are wiser than you know," Barach said. "There is an old story of a fish who wanted to travel—"

"Should have known better than to bring it up," Nul groaned. "Everything remind you of story."

Barach, quite undeterred, continued his story about the fish, the turtle, the crane, and the dragonfly. It was a particularly long one, and while he told it the shadows faded away completely in the deepening twilight of dusk.

And at the same time, far to the north of Gateway Cay, Gareth watched from a great distance as the Shadow Guard passed along the North Road just west of the town of Drover's Ford. "Is there nothing, then, we can do?" he asked the woman standing beside him on the side of a hill, not far from the eastern edge of Arkhedden.

"I did not say that," she responded, her voice light and thin, seeming older than her appearance. "Merely that we can do nothing at this moment."

Gareth looked at her. She was tall, almost as tall as he, and she seemed to be in her mid-thirties, slender, fair-haired and pale of skin, aristocratic of mien; but Beriol was far older than that, for she had been one of the leading minds of the wizard schools at Vanislach for fifty years at least. Gareth had heard only a little of her and of the vanity that led her to cast an illusion spell of youth about herself, but what he had heard convinced him that she spoke with certainty only when she was truly certain. He asked her, "When, then, can we act, and what may we then do?"

Beriol wore a sky-blue mantle and carried a staff as tall as herself, a staff of silver crowned by an intricately wrought orb set with rubies and sapphires. She leaned on the staff as she spoke: "All of our researches show us there is but one moment of vulnerability for the Guard, one fleeting instant when they may be touched by Thaumian magic. And that is when they surrender their power to the Great Dark One. Seven hundred years ago they were nearly defeated down on Fila Island when we of the north came closest to entrapping the Great Dark One; then the aged Druvidion cast a spell that rendered the Guard immobile and helpless. But all of his resources were focused on them; the Great Dark One, whom he had believed disabled, had received new *mana* from the Guard, and his counterspell killed Druvidion and won the battle for the island."

"I have heard of that battle," Gareth said. "But as a legend only, not as history. I wonder that you can be so sure of things lost in the mists of time."

Beriol's lips twitched into a smile. "Legend it is," she admitted. "But we of Vanislach do not wholly discount legends; we find in them what truth we may."

"Then we must wait until they are vulnerable. At that time, what must we do?"

"Alas, you jump too far ahead. We must indeed wait," Beriol said. "But I fear that is not what Tremien has decided. My colleagues are closeted with him even now; they are trying to change his mind from a plan of action that must surely fail. He is set upon executing the three possible incarnations of the Great Dark One, and if he does that, then we lose all power over the Guard."

The Guard had by now passed their hillside and had gone far to the north. In the growing darkness Gareth could no longer clearly see them, although he could glimpse hints of movement along the road very far away. "And if your colleagues succeed in persuading Tremien, what then?"

"At the moment of the transfer, and only at that one moment, the Guard belongs fully to this world, for just an instant of time. You see, they are not properly here at all, for they do not belong to Thaumia, and their essences lie elsewhere. They are projections; they are captured bits of an alien world with more appearance than reality. But when they surrender the *mana* they have absorbed, they must be a part of the magical matrix of Thaumia. Then a well-wrought spell of banishment, given a sufficient amount of power, will send them forever back to their own world, freeing them from the domination of the Great Dark One. They will be eternally beyond his power to recall them then, and we shall be safe from their terrible presence in our world."

Gareth turned a troubled face toward her. "But if that is so, then they will have already given their power to our enemy. The Great Dark One will be stronger than ever."

"True; however, he will lose the Guard, and with them much of his power to destroy. Some of us at Vanislach believe that his long life may be attributed to the *mana* the Shadow Guard have absorbed over the centuries. A great deal of that magic must have gone to maintaining his existence far past the normal life span of even the greatest wizards."

"But it doesn't matter if the Guard are gone. The Great Dark One, if he's strong enough to overcome Tremien, won't need them anymore. Is there a way of destroying the Great Dark One and the Guard at the same time?"

"That is not the problem we were set," Beriol said. "But I would suppose it possible. Very difficult, though; for if only a tenth of a tenth of the *mana* the Guard have absorbed is passed to the Great Dark One, he will be most frighteningly strong indeed. More powerful than all of the magi of Cronbrach-en-Hof put together, I should think."

The wind was from the east, and on it rode an acrid and bitter odor, stinging the nostrils like hot ash. It was the smell of ruin, the scent of the collapse of life. Gareth had almost become accustomed to it in the time he had dogged the Shadow Guard's progress northward; it proceeded from the swath of destruction the Guard left behind. Not sickening, like the stench of rot, and not overwhelming, the odor was merely ashy, pungent, more like regret than anything else Gareth could name.

"Then what is there to do?" he asked.

Beriol's voice came from the growing darkness. "I believe the most important thing is to persuade Tremien to spare the lives of the three. For if we can banish the Shadow Guard, we have at least a chance of dealing with the Great Dark One; but if we destroy the Great Dark One, the Guard will be forever beyond our reach, and they will not be able to leave our world until all the magic has been drained from it."

"So the end of Thaumia is certain if the Shadow Guard remain; it is only very likely if the Great Dark One does," Gareth said.

A form struggled up the hillside toward them; it was Hanth, one of the soldiers detailed to observing the passage of the Guard. "They are out of sight," he reported to Gareth.

"Is their speed still the same?"

"Seems to be." Hanth's voice, normally a cheerful baritone, was stretched and tired. "What next? A jump ahead?"

"Yes. Assemble the men. This time I think we will go east of the road; we will travel to the western shore of White Lake."

"The Guard will be there before midnight," Hanth said. "Unless they turn or slow. Or unless they use the travel spell again."

"They never turn or slow, and they have not used the travel spell since before dawn, so I think we can rely on them to do neither," Gareth told him. When Hanth had gone back to the main group of soldiers, Gareth said to Beriol, "White Lake by midnight. The East Pass sometime late tomorrow. And Whitehorn itself tomorrow night. We have little time."

"I shall not travel with you," Beriol said. "I go to Whitehorn to help press our case to Tremien."

"I wish I could wish you luck," Gareth said.

Perhaps Beriol smiled in the dark. "And I wish I could send you good fortune in your combat; but we are both realists at heart. Let us part, then, with at least the hope that neither of us finds more ill fortune than is bearable."

It was a gloomy enough parting; but it suited the night and the occasion.

Nul was almost visibly swollen with self-importance. "Stand there," he directed Sebastian, indicating a spot close to the Gate.

Sebastian gave Barach an amused look of inquiry.

"Perhaps you had better do as Nul says," Barach told him. "For I have nothing to offer myself."

With one shake of his head Sebastian went to the spot. "All right. Now what happens?"

"Have to wait," Nul said. "Jeremy will look at you; then Gate be like mirror."

"And then?"

"Then Nul speak and make magic. Wait and watch."

Darkness was drawing on. They had not built a campfire, and the riot of noise closed in, the night noise made by the nocturnal insects, by the belching, booming dragons, even by the distant unicorns. Overhead the sky had gone a rich violet, and already a few stars twinkled there. Before long the moon would rise, heavy and gibbous, and then—if Nul was correct in his surmise—the time for the spell would be past.

The three of them spoke little as the night closed in. Nul, standing slightly behind Sebastian, peered forward with some anxiety, but the surface of the Gate remained smooth and clouded, almost invisible in the dark. Sebastian shifted his weight from foot to foot with evident impatience. "Wait, wait," Nul breathed. "Time will come."

But when it did, it was almost trivial. Barach was first to notice. "Have I stared too long, or is the Gate *glowing*?" he asked from behind Nul.

Nul blinked. His huge eyes, well-suited for dim surroundings, told him that Barach was right. The Gate did have a glow about it, but not the glow of the travel spell, not the shine of magic. This was a warm, dim, yellow light, a bit like firelight but not really. It was such a light as Nul had never seen—

"My desk lamp," said Sebastian suddenly. "He's just turned on my desk lamp."

Peering for all he was worth, Nul began to make out shapes: a blocky one, surely the desk, and on it a fuzzy glowing center to the light—the lamp that Sebastian had mentioned, surely. But where was Jeremy?

"I don't see him," Barach said, and Nul realized that he had spoken his question aloud.

"He must be in the office. If he'd just move," Sebastian said. "What's happening? Why can we see through the Gate now?"

"I think I know," Barach said slowly. "It's because we are in the dark and there's light on the other side. The spell is not dead, but it is dormant, very low in power at the moment. It's like looking through a thick mist; if you have a torch in your hand, all you see is the mist. If someone else is approaching with a torch, then you see the person approaching. On the far side, the Gate must be so dim that it cannot be seen at all."

"We make it stronger," said Nul. "But where Jeremy?"

They waited. the night insects grew louder, more abandoned; more stars sprinkled the dark sky overhead. Barach began to cast anxious glances toward the east. "The moon will rise before long," he said. "If that marks our last hope—"

"Something's moving," Sebastian said.

Something had momentarily blocked the light. But was it Jeremy? Nul strained to see. Yes, there was a moving form, a shape—

It paused in exact mimicry of Sebastian's pose. Mirror images.

And Nul immediately shouted—

"The word!"

Sebastian whipped his head around. "You must be jok—"

"There he is!" Barach shouted.

Jeremy gaped at them, then grinned, then ran to a door. He dragged a bundle of clothing and a pair of boots out, and came barreling toward them. Nul stepped back as Jeremy catapulted through the Gate and out into the clearing—

"Look at that," Barach said, pointing. Nul, following his gesture, saw the silver edge of the moon just showing above the treetops.

"Thank God," Jeremy said, hurriedly shucking his jacket. "What happened?"

Sebastian stared at him. "You shaved your beard—"

"Yeah, I'll tell you about that." Jeremy kicked off his shoes and pulled his trousers off. He began to don his Thaumian garb. "But what happened?"

"I wish," Barach said in plaintive Presolatan, "that you would speak some language I know."

"Sorry," Jeremy said, making the change. "I sort of got used to English again. I was asking Sebastian what went wrong with the Gate."

"A confluence of magic disrupted it," Barach said.

Jeremy, shrugging into his robe, glanced over. "Seems all right now." And surely enough, the Gate once again showed Sebastian's office back on Earth, as clearly and realistically as it ever had.

Nul was almost strutting. "Nul fix," he said. "Book told us how, but hard to figure. Nul figure. You tell, Barach."

"Yes, yes," Barach said. "Nul is quite right. The book set us a conundrum, and only he was sharp enough to see through it. But we have no time to lose; we must return to Whitehorn at once."

"What about the Great Dark One?"

"Still not accounted for," Barach said. "And the Shadow Guard closes on Whitehorn."

"The Shadow Guard?"

"Those things you made visible," Sebastian said. "Don't tell me you were passing for me back there."

"Afraid so. And you did really well in the debate, but I'll have to tell you about that later. Want these?" Jeremy offered the suit and shoes he had worn, rolled into a bundle.

"Where would I put them?"

After a moment, Jeremy stuck the bundle into the tangle of vines just to the left of the Gate. "They should be all right here. Is Kelada well?"

"She fine," Nul said. "Sebastian kiss-kiss her."

"And Emily, is she . . . ? What?"

"It was nothing," Sebastian said. "She was just upset, and—"

"You bastard," Jeremy said. "You mean to tell me—"

"Jeremy." Barach's voice was gentle but pained. "We have matters of most great urgency. If you are quite ready, we should return to Whitehorn immediately."

"All right. But I want to hear more about this. Who's going?"

"We all are," Sebastian said.

"I thought you were in a hurry to get home."

"Things have changed. And there's a danger we didn't know about earlier. Let's get started and I'll explain."

"You'll explain more than that," Jeremy said. "All right, get close together." He activated the travel spell.

During their passage, Jeremy listened to Barach's explanation of the Gate's malfunction, but he listened with an abstracted air. He seemed far more interested in questioning Sebastian about Kelada; and Sebastian for his part grew hotter and more evasive. "It seems to me I ought to ask you some questions," he said. "You come back looking exactly like me, wearing my suit—"

"But your wife is safe in Boston," Jeremy returned.

"But you took it on yourself to ruin my career—"

"Best thing that's happened to your campaign so far. When you get back, ask Sam Norris—"

"Gentlemen," Barach said. "Please. I do not wish to sound melodramatic, but the fact is that we have a great problem before us, and if we cannot solve it, then the question of Sebastian's return may be completely academic."

"Sorry," Jeremy growled.

Nul spoke up: "All this trouble over mates. Same as in your plays, Jeremy. Hard for pika to understand."

"I know it is," Jeremy said. "And I haven't thanked you, Nul, as I should. You did a wonderful thing when you guessed the riddle. I'm grateful to you."

"Answer obvious," Nul said, though he felt his eyes going pale with pleasure. "That why Nul get it. Barach say Nul is always literal; that what this riddle need. That all."

"I am afraid," Barach said, "that we shall have an insufferable pika as our companion from now on."

"Then you are committed to this course of action?" Ogion asked.

"He is," Radusilf said. "You may try to argue him out of it if you please, Master Ogion; but if I could not do it, I doubt whether even the magic masters of Vanislach may."

Tremien, sitting at the head of a polished table, smiled gently. Radusilf was very drunk, and in his cups the old man sounded merry, an autumn cricket singing for all he was worth. But Tremien's expression sobered soon enough, for the topic at hand was a serious one.

He paused a long while, considering his answer and meeting the stares of the three delegates from Vanislach: Ogion, the Master Enchanter himself, as old as Tremien and even more steeped in works of lore than Barach; next to him the diminutive Fenwolt, thin of face and intense of gaze, one of the chief theorists of magic in Cronbrach; and on the other side of the table, next to the intoxicated Radusilf, Mistress Terese, a solidly built woman of middle age renowed for her work on the vocal element of magic.

Each face, except for Radusilf's red and befuddled one, bore a look of tolerant hostility. Tremien sighed. "You do not understand," he said at last. "None of you fully understands; and I am afraid I cannot fully explain."

Ogion's brows, dark in contrast to his silver hair, drew together. "We have labored hard to do what you asked, Tremien. We believe that at the proper moment we can banish the Shadow Guard to their own place and seal the breach forever. But all of our calculations have been aimed at the moment of transfer; and it is far too late to try to recast the spell now, for it is the most intricate one any of us has ever attempted. If you kill the Great Dark One now, you unleash his creatures on Cronbrach."

"But the creator is more dangerous than his creations, is he not?" Tremien asked with some heat. "If you have any test, any way of telling me who houses that evil spirit, then tell me now and the headsmen will not swing their axes tomorrow at dawn. But I have exhausted my ingenuity on the problem. Celissa, Jondan, or Idoradas—one of them is now the incarnation of the Great Dark One. But each is still his or her proper self as well, with all the memories and all the seeming of the original. Can you tell me a way to make that dark spirit show forth? If so, I will try it, and gladly. But none of my tricks, none of my queries, have served."

"Listen to him," cackled Radusilf. "I remember when Tremien was a lad. Troublesome he was, always wanting to know what was under every stone, behind every tree. Well, here is a nut too tough for even him to crack." The old, old man laughed until the laughs turned to gasps. His chin dropped on his breast and he subsided into sleep and silence.

"I hardly think he helps matters," Fenwolt said in a soft voice, little more than a whisper.

"He is your elder and mine," Tremien said. "I fear he may have outlived his wits. But Radusilf made a valiant attempt to stop the Shadow Guard, and for that I will honor him and will allow him to sit at Council whenever he desires."

"Yes, but that is hardly the issue," Ogion resumed. "You say the creator is to be feared more than his creations. But consider, Tremien: the Guard are not really the Great Dark One's creatures. They spring from another reality, one so bizarre that we can only guess at its natural laws and its constraints; it is, to our view, a universe of negative magic, of *mana* in reverse polarity to our own. No sorcerous attack on them may avail us now, for the magic of these creatures is a sink that swallows up all other magic; at the same time, no physical force avails, for they either have their own protective magics or else the Great Dark One has somehow cloaked them in a spell of his own."

"You think it is neither," Tremien observed.

"You are right there. My opinion is that the Guard simply are not in our world enough for us to harm them; they do not, rightly speaking, exist in Thaumia at all. We cannot destroy these creatures. The most we can hope to do is simply to exile them from our universe. And even that hope may fail without the Great Dark One."

"And if the Great Dark One is allowed to live," Tremien returned, "he shall absorb power from the Guard. No one knows what that may mean; it may be that he cannot use the power immediately, and he may be vulnerable for some time. Or he may not; he may at once become the most formidable force for evil the universe has ever seen, as far advanced above us all in magical powers as you, Ogion, are to a two-days' child. It is a bad bargain if we exchange the Shadow Guard for that. But again, I must remind you that you do not fully understand my means or my motives. Will you trust me?"

Ogion looked at the other two. Fenwolt shrugged, though his expression still showed how disgruntled and dissatisfied he was. The face of Terese, square-jawed, blunt-featured, homely, was much harder to read. But she made some small signal, for Ogion sighed and with reluctance inclined his head. "You are Chief Mage," he said. "That counts for much. But should Cronbrach be faced with the Guard unleashed and uncontrolled, you shall not be Chief Mage for long."

Tremien leaned back in his chair, both of his hands spread palm-down on the table before him. "My friend, that is the least of my worries." He seemed on the verge of saying more, checked himself, and merely repeated softly, "The least of my worries."

The travel spell wasn't supposed to go wrong.

Mage Walther had invested much of his time and power in devising it; it was a stunningly complex Great Spell, one that should endure for a generation of travel by millions of inhabitants of Cronbrach-en-Hof. The success of the spell had brought Walther deserved fame and rich rewards, and people assumed that it was infallible.

But for some reason Walther's Fast Travel dumped Jeremy, Sebastian, Nul, and Barach in cold, fast water.

It was a terrible shock for Jeremy: one moment he was listening to Barach recounting the events of the past day and night, and the next he was tumbling heels over head over smooth stones, his lungs frozen to breathlessness by the sudden cold. He heard Nul's dismayed bawl, and then his head was underwater and he heard only the roaring of the stream.

Jeremy fetched up hard against a stone, rolled away from it, and found himself in calmer water, where he was able to stand. It was still waist-deep, and in the darkness—for full night was now on them—he could see little other than the spuming white fountains of a rushing mountain stream. Something clutched at his back, and he grasped out to find Nul's spidery arm, thin as a child's. Jeremy dragged the pika's head above the water.

Nul came up coughing, snorting, choking. "What happen?" he asked in a rusty voice not like his usual guttural tone.

"Are you there?" came Barach's voice from their left. Jeremy made his way toward it, fighting the reduced current. "Barach! Are you safe?"

"Except for wet feet, yes. Where is Sebastian?"

"Here!" came a voice from downstream. "Coming."

His teeth chattering, Jeremy pronounced a light spell and

was rewarded by a blue glow that showed him a stretch of rushing water, white over black, and near the bank the bulky form of Barach just wading ashore. Jeremy was about eight yards away, and he had to breast a strong sluice before joining the teacher. A moment later Sebastian, bedraggled in his Earth suit, squished along the riverbank to join them.

Nul collapsed, wheezing and gasping, as soon as they were on land again. "Water in lungs," he said. "Where are we?"

Barach shaded his eyes, though the wizard-light really was more like strong moonlight than the glare of the sun. "Short of our destination," he said. "This is the Bronfal, certainly. I think we are in the valley a few thousand paces north of Drover's Ford; we are north of Milk Falls, at any rate."

Sebastian's teeth were chattering audibly. "Something went wrong," he said.

"It may be the proximity of the Shadow Guard," Barach mused. "I rather think it is. They absorb magical energies; they probably also disrupt magical fields. The spell simply ran out of magic before we were quite far enough along."

Nul had risen and tramped uphill from the stream, disappearing into undergrowth that was waist-high to Jeremy and chest-high to a pika. "God, it's cold," Sebastian said miserably. "Even in summer."

"The sources of the river are springs fed by the snows of the Wizard's Mountains," Barach said. "No wonder it's cold."

"You don't seem very wet," Sebastian said, wiping his hair back from his forehead so that it bristled up. "What happened to you?"

"I found myself in the shallows, fortunately," Barach said. "My boots are full, but I did not fall in." He sat on a stone and laboriously pulled off his boots, pouring a stream of water from each. "You, Nul, and Jeremy were not so lucky. You were more in the current, and it swept you off your feet and downstream before you could recover."

Sebastian was hugging himself and shivering. He gave Jeremy an annoyed glare. "You don't seem to be too cold."

Jeremy shrugged. "Barach's had me exercising bare-chested in all weathers," he said. "I guess I'm more accustomed to hardship than you." He did not add that he was wearing an enchanted garment, a robe that Tremien had given him some time before. It kept the wearer comfortable in any temperature, and now Jeremy felt wet but not cold.

The undergrowth rustled and Nul came back, his sleek fur black from the wetting he had received. He bore in his arms a good-sized bundle of deadfall wood. "Make fire," he said. "Dry off."

"Practical as always," Barach said. In a matter of moments they had scraped together stone to make a rough enclosure for a campfire and Barach's tinderbox—fortunately not wet—summoned a spark. Some fire elemental inherent in dry wood accepted the offering and a good yellow blaze sprang up at once. Nul stripped off his wet tunic and trousers and huddled close to the fire, shivering and rubbing himself. Jeremy noticed that the pika was so cold that his short tail was clamped tight against his buttocks. Struck by conscience—of the four of them, he probably was the most comfortable because of the robe—he made a second trip for more wood, brought back a bundle three times the size of Nul's original one, and they soon had a good bonfire roaring.

Sebastian stripped to his underwear and spread his clothes on a smooth rock close to the fire to dry. "Suit's probably ruined," he moaned. "My wallet's soaked."

"But you're alive," Jeremy said. "Be grateful for that." He, too, had removed trousers, stockings, and shirt, and had them drying on a branch close to the fire.

Sebastian snorted. "I don't see how you can stand to wear that thing," he said, meaning the silvery-gray robe. "Isn't it soaked?"

"Good wool sheds water," Jeremy said. And magical wool sheds it faster than the ordinary kind. He turned to Barach. "What are we to do now?"

"Well, I should not advise trying the travel spell again," Barach said, holding his hands out to the warmth of the fire. The blaze made his gray hair and beard seem almost blond. "The alternative is to walk up the valley, but that will take all night. Of course, there are farms all the way up, and most of the farmers know me. Possibly we can borrow horses."

"Not horses," groaned Nul, who did not much care for the beasts.

"If you have a better idea, let me know," Barach said.

Nul merely grumbled, tested his trousers, and found them dry enough to pull back on. He stood with his back to the fire, steam coming from the fabric over his seat. "Better start quick," he said.

Jeremy felt his own trousers, but they were still very damp. "I can make do with the robe," he said, rolling up trousers and shirt into a bundle. "How are you getting on?"

"It'll do, I guess," Sebastian said.

Barach stirred himself. "My boots are confoundedly damp, but what cannot be transmuted must be endured, as the saying goes. We've probably been here for an ona already. We should start for Whitehorn at once."

Jeremy took a deep breath, the heat and the aroma of the fire strong in his nostrils. "All right," he said. "Let's go."

They doused the fire—allowing the water elemental overseeing the river to banish the fire elemental housed in the blaze, according to the exotic physics of Thaumia—and trudged their way upstream. They had materialized on the western shore of the river, but there were many fording places to the north, so that was of little concern. As Barach pointed out, their main worry was time.

"The Shadow Guard move very fast, at a good pace even for a horse," he said. "We have no way of knowing whether they are behind us or ahead of us. If they are ahead, we may arrive to find Whitehorn besieged. If they are behind us—and far enough behind—then we may hope to arrive before they do, but only if we do not rest."

Nul gave a nervous glance over his shoulder at the darkness. "You think they coming up behind?"

"Not directly behind, not unless they have left the North Road. We're going overland, some thousands of paces east of the road. I shouldn't think they will directly overtake us."

Nul breathed a sigh of relief. "Good. Rather face horses than Shadow Guard."

As luck would have it, they soon spied the warm glow of lamplight ahead. It proved to come from the windows of a rambling but snugly built farmhouse made of black river stones and half-timbered stucco. Barach grunted as they came close. "Well, we are not too badly off. We are actually much closer to Whitehorn than I thought at first. That is surely the farmhouse of the Gale family, and we are hardly a three-hona ride from Whitehorn."

Henkar Gale, a knotty farmer of sixty, opened the door to them and expressed his astonishment at seeing the great

Barach in his humble home. Six or eight of his children, ranging in age from a muscular fellow of thirty to a toddler who couldn't be much older than Emily, crept in to see them as they stood in front of a rousing fire built by Henkar in honor of his guests. Henkar's wife, who must have been at least his second, for she was no older than the eldest son, brought them good nutty ale to drink as Barach explained what they needed.

"Oh, aye, ye're welcome to borry horses off me," Henkar said at once. "Let's see, there's three of ye and the pika there. Can't do much for him, 'less he rides ahint one of ye; but there's my mare Softfoot, the gelding Golden Boy, and old Jak, and they'll ride the three of ye up to Wizard's Mount right enough. Grinnel, run and saddle the three of 'em for the gentlemen."

"Take time," Nul said, his mouth flecked with foam from his second glass of ale. "Need warming."

Barach and Gale haggled about recompense for the horses (Barach wanted to pay; Henkar stubbornly insisted that the lending of horses was merely something a friend did for friendship's sake), and when they had reached an agreement, the eldest boy came in. "Got 'em ready," he said in a shy voice.

"They do say that there's been a sight o' trouble off to the south," Gale remarked as he accompanied the four out to the horses. "Hearn as to how folks've had to leave their homes all up and down the gret road. You men a-workin' again' that now?"

"We are," Barach said. "And thank you for helping us."

" 'Tis only the neighborly thing to do. Wizard's made this valley a good place t' live and raise a fambly. Couldn'ta said that when I was a lad; dark things they was in the valley sometimes then, and my old dad wouldn't stir after sunset. But wizard chased 'em all away, even from down here where he didn't have to. So I'm proud to do some little part to help him now. You, Master Barach, better take the mare. The young fellow in the robe looks right to handle the gelding, and old Jak will give the outlander a gentle ride. Master Nul can go with which he will."

Nul rode on a blanket behind Jeremy, his arms hooked around Jeremy's waist. The moon gave unsteady light, showing through the gathering clouds that dogged the passage of

Jeremy and Sebastian, and to aid it, Jeremy recast the traveling spell of wizard-light. Still, they could drive the horses only to a good fast walk, for the roads between farms in the valley were at best casual, meandering and unsurveyed and occasionally slippery when they passed over outcrops of stone.

Soon Jeremy began to recognize landmarks. He and Kelada frequently rode in the valley, even taking Emily with them earlier in the summer, and they had enjoyed picnics along the banks of the river here south of Whitehorn. The farmers called it the White River, though Jeremy knew that this tumbling, rushing mountain flow eventually became the broad, brown, placid-faced Bronfal River he had seen far to the south, near ruined Downsdale.

They made steady, if not good, time, and Jeremy, warm in the robe, found himself lulled nearly to sleep by the reassuring clop-clop of the horses' hooves. "There," Barach said suddenly, reining in.

Jeremy looked ahead. Sure enough, the lights of Whitehorn shone ahead and above them. The mountain was somewhat isolated, and it was the tallest in this part of the range. The castle crowned it, and tonight watch fires blazed on its battlements, adding to the glow of wizard-light shining through the windows of its towers and spires.

Barach started the mare forward again. "We'll join the road at Easy Ford," he said. "The horses are exhausted, and I'm not much better; we'll need the enchantment of the road to make it comfortably to the gates."

Years ago Tremien had placed a kindly enchantment on the ways of the valley around Whitehorn. It was a powerful act of magic, to impress power into inanimate objects; second only to the power required to shape living flesh, in fact. The effect of Tremien's spell was to speed the kindly disposed traveler along his way, so that, without seeming to move rapidly at all and with no feeling of tiredness, even someone on foot could make the speed of a trotting horse along the pathways.

Jeremy found himself feeling anxious now. He was worried about Kelada and Emily; he had tried to keep them out of his mind back on Earth, but of course that was impossible. And now that the Shadow Guard were close, they were in peril. His fear for them partly accounted, he supposed, for the anger he felt toward Sebastian.

But part of that was jealousy, too.

They splashed across Easy Ford, a rapid but broad and very shallow place in the river, and then started up the winding road to Whitehorn itself. The horses perked up noticeably under the benevolent influence of the spell. Almost before Jeremy knew it, a grating voice cried out from ahead of and above them: "Visitors to Whitehorn! Mage Barach, Jeremy Moon, Nul the Pika, and Sebastian Magister return!" It was, of course, the voice of Busby, the gargoyle. In a less public way, the stone guardian added, "Hurry inside. Tremien is very anxious about you."

They realized as they reached the main gate that it was manned, not a normal state of affairs. Gruff Captain Fallon, who had instructed Jeremy personally in the art of crossbow archery, was in charge of the watch. He grunted them inside, barked at a hapless young soldier to take charge of the three horses, and escorted them as far as the main door of the castle. "Have t' keep an eye skinned tonight," he said there in farewell. "All sorts o' mischief comin', if the tales be true. Well, well, we can face 'em, hey, lad?"

"We'll fill them full of arrows," Jeremy returned. Fallon rewarded him with a painful but hearty slap between the shoulder blades.

"It's nearly midnight," Barach said. "But everyone seems to be awake."

Kelada met them in the great hall, for word traveled fast in Whitehorn, and she ran toward them. But she pulled up short not far from them and gaped from Jeremy to Sebastian and back again. "Which is which?" she wailed.

Jeremy threw his arms open, and she was in them in a moment. "Your beautiful beard," she said, but she kissed his cheeks and mouth as ardently as ever. Only after a sufficient number of kisses did she greet the others. Barach returned her greeting in his usual unflustered manner; Sebastian seemed a little short; and Nul grinned lasciviously, as he always did on witnessing human smooching. "But what happened to your beard?" Kelada asked again.

"Had to shave it," he said. "I'll grow it back, don't worry. Is Emily all right?"

"Asleep hona ago. She missed her da, too. What happened?"

"Wait until we see Tremien, and I'll only have to tell it once," Jeremy said.

"I don't know how soon that will be." Kelada put her arm around his waist and they walked together like that, behind Sebastian and Barach but ahead of Nul. "There are some great wizards from the magic schools with him now. They've been talking all night. Is it really as bad as they say?"

"It's bad," Jeremy acknowledged. "Tomorrow early you're leaving, you and Emily. We'll send you up the valley, and then you can use the travel spell—"

"We're not leaving," Kelada said.

"Oh, yes you are."

"We're not leaving."

"Kelada," Jeremy began in the voice of a man who already had lost an argument.

Sleep that night was a thing grabbed in fits and snatches. Although Emily had been particularly wakeful all during her first eleven months of life, she was perhaps the only one in Whitehorn Keep to sleep soundly that night.

Tremien greeted the returned party warmly and expressed gratitude that Jeremy had managed to return, but apart from that one brief meeting they saw little of the old mage, for he was fully occupied in arranging the defense of his castle. Barach closeted himself for some time with Ogion, whom he had known well years ago in the schools of wizardry at Vanislach, and came away from that conference wearing a very long face.

Barach found Jeremy and Sebastian on the wall walk in the cool hours of early morning. Sebastian had changed from his still-damp Earth clothing to a pair of Jeremy's trousers, a shirt, and a short jacket. Now the identical young men stood staring out at the dark valley with occasional murmurs of concern. "I see the wind is up again," Barach said when he encountered them

"Rain before dawn, if the pattern holds," Jeremy acknowledged. "This is the third day Sebastian and I have been together. We must be coming up on the limit of tolerance for Sebastian's stay here."

Barach grunted. "I have news," he said, and he told them of the planned executions.

"That's the worst I've heard yet," Sebastian commented when Barach had finished his summary. "Tremien is really desperate."

"Can you blame him?" Jeremy asked with some heat. "He's spent his whole life fighting the Great Dark One—"

"You don't have to defend him to me," Sebastian retorted. "But whenever you think of the great and good wizard from now on, remember what he's prepared to do."

"He wouldn't be planning it if you'd managed to spot the Great Dark One."

Now Sebastian sounded angry too, in a voice eerily identical to Jeremy's: "It wasn't my idea too try to ferret out Jilhukrihain. You—"

"Peace," Barach said loudly. "Two hunters once tracked and killed a female fang-cat. They fell to arguing over whose arrow had struck the mortal wound. They came to blows at last; and while they were wrestling on the ground, the fang-cat's mate came and killed both of them." The wind sang against the pinnacles of the castle spires. "We have enough enemies there," Barach said, nodding into the darkness. "We need no more within our own walls."

And because he was right, the two ceased their argument, though for his part Jeremy kept his resentment bottled and fresh inside him.

The night wore on, and when day came it was lost in scuds of low, gray, ragged clouds, whipped on their way by a northeast wind that was chilly for the time of year. Spats of intermittent rain fell, slapping against the castle walls and windows with loud cracks, hitting bare flesh hard enough to sting. Jeremy, who had spent half the night trying to persuade Kelada to take Emily to some place of relative safety and the other half apprehensively watching for signs of the Shadow Guard's baleful approach, joined a crowd of onlookers, mainly soldiers, in the forecourt just at sunup. His eyes felt as if the lids had been sandpapered, and a great weight of weariness hung in his head; but for all that, he was not really sleepy.

Fallon was in the courtyard too, with six or eight of his men around him, all conversing in nervous low voices. "Been to bed?" Jeremy asked the grizzled old soldier as he neared.

The captain gave a curt nod. "Four hona o' sleep. All I'll need for the day's work."

"I guess it's about time," Jeremy said.

"Yah," Fallon grunted. "Don't know who the headsmen are. Funny. I seen lots o' men cut down in battle, seen blood enough in my time. But this kind o' killing sort of strikes me wrong. Never thought the day would come when old Tremien would lop someone's head off this way, in cold blood, and not in the heat of a fight."

Jeremy was peering around. He saw none of his friends in the crowd, and he began to wonder where everyone was. He did not have to wonder for long, however; the large tower door opened up on the east wall walk and a file of men and women came out, walking slowly along until the whole top of the wall was lined with them, their robes and hair and beards tugged and tossed by the fitful wind. Barach was there, most solemn in a black robe; and Wyonne, Mumana, Altazar, and several other magicians. Their faces were closed, grim, as they took their places. All seemed reluctant even to glance down at the courtyard.

The main castle door opened and Nul came out, wearing an elaborately brocaded tunic of gray velvet and trousers of a darker shade of gray; that, he had told Jeremy once upon a time, was the pika color of mourning. Nul glanced around, saw Jeremy, and made his way through the crowd to stand by his side. "They come now," the pika whispered, shivering a little.

Major Gareth led the way, his face as gray as the morning, drawn and tense in the filtered light. Behind him were three soldiers, each one carrying a wicked-looking ax over his shoulder; and behind the soldiers came the three wizards Celissa, Jondan, and Idoradas. Celissa looked around rather wildly; the other two kept their eyes downcast. Jondan's face was thunderously angry. Idoradas, younger, seemed pale and frightened. Not one of the three looked toward the place where Jeremy stood. More soldiers came behind the prisoners; and at last Tremien himself came out, leaning on a staff.

Jeremy half-expected some kind of ceremony, but there was little of that. Brother Thomas, the Keep's chaplain, stood up on the wall walk with the other wizards, looking ill. Gareth led the execution detail to the center of the courtyard, where the stones had been raked clean earlier that morning. He said something to the headsmen and then spoke to each of the three condemned wizards. Jeremy saw Jondan shake his head in an angry gesture. The other two merely listened quietly. When Gareth had finished, he nodded to Tremien.

The master of Whitehorn raised his voice, and some spell made it boom louder than it normally would: "Friends of Whitehorn! Know that I approach this moment with regret and with anguish. But the decision is mine; and the responsibility lies with me. Whatever happens, I take all blame upon myself freely. I absolve you of any blood-guilt in what must be done." He paused, head slightly bowed. The nimbus of white hair around the bald crown of his pate trembled in the wind, and his beard whipped back and forth in the gusts. When he spoke again, his voice was somewhat softer: "Celissa. Jondan. Idoradas. One of you only bears guilt; but you all must die. I beg the innocent among you to forgive those who strike the blow. Direct your bitterness at this evil decision to me alone." Tremien nodded once.

Gareth put his hand on Idoradas' shoulder and the young mage fell to his knees, head bowed forward. Five paces away, Jondan followed suit. Celissa knelt slowly, and as Jeremy watched her he could not help thinking of her forest home, of the stark contrast between this bare, windswept courtyard and the lush treetops of her native woods.

Nul, elbow to elbow with Jeremy, shuddered a little. Jeremy put one hand on the pika's trembling shoulder. "Not her," Nul said in a low troubled voice.

"I don't know," Jeremy said. "It could be any one of them."

"Or none," said a voice behind Jeremy and to his left. Sebastian had come out to join them.

"I can't believe that Tremien could be wrong about that," Jeremy said.

Sebastian did not respond.

The three headsmen stepped into place. Jeremy could see that Idoradas was shaking hard from fear. Jondan held himself absolutely rigid, as if locked in rage. Celissa merely knelt with head bowed, in the attitude of prayer.

Gareth had stepped to a position in the center of the courtyard, just a few paces ahead of Jondan. The three headsmen went to their places and held their weapons poised.

Gareth looked at each of them, hesitated for moment,

and then raised his hand. He brought it down in a swift chop.

Instantly the three headsmen followed suit. Three blades hissed through the air, heard even above the sound of the wind, and they passed through the necks of Idoradas, Jondan, and the fair Celissa.

12

To the south and west of Whitehorn, the soldiers detached by Gareth to follow the progress of the Shadow Guard saw the five weird creatures suddenly pause in their forward motion. "Now, what the darkness is going on?" growled Hadrel Cabraksas, the blond-bearded young captain leading the detail in Gareth's absence. He peered through the dawn-gray distance at the great horn-shaped beasts, still now, wreathed in drifting mist or in billowing dust. "What are they doing now?"

"Nothing, far's I can see," a sergeant returned. "Just standing there. If you call it standing."

The soldiers were well off to the west of the North Road. Behind them, a league or more away, was the dark line of Arkhedden, its shadows deep and mysterious: before them was the road and beyond that were the rising green hills and the more distant gray-purple mountains of the Wizard range, none of them tall enough to be capped with snow at this season. On the road itself were the five creatures that made up the Shadow Guard, still but not inactive.

As the dust or mist dissipated, Hadrel stared hard at them, their rugose bodies made paler in the gray light of a heavily overcast dawn. The mouths—at least Hadrel thought of the round, toothed openings as mouths, though he had never seen the things eat—opened and closed, silently as far as he could tell from this distance. The upper appendages, some jointed, some tentaclelike, waved and writhed with no apparent purpose, though perhaps the seemingly aimless commotion signified some sort of communication.

"Least there's not much for 'em to kill here," the sergeant said, rubbing his nose.

It was true; except for three or four inns and a like number of isolated hamlets—anywhere from a dozen to twenty houses in each—the Guard had passed no site of human occupation since Hendry Rapids, a few leagues south of Drover's Ford. The soldiers had seen to the evacuation of each place. So far, no more lives had been lost, and since most of the houses had been built by human hands and not by magic—the people of this land were very careful about not squandering *mana* when hammer and nails would do—destruction was light.

Even the forest suffered less, for here the margin of Arkhedden fell far away from the road, with only secondary growth disintegrating from the blight brought by the Guard. Indeed, at this point of their passage only the grass showed the signs of the Guard's draining power. The sedge was withered and gray in a path fifty paces broad on either side of the road. When you stepped on such grass, it powdered to fine ash and blew up around your boots in great acid-smelling billows.

"Moving again now," the sergeant observed.

"Faster," Hadrel said. "A good deal faster."

The Guard was going forward now at half again their former pace, the conical, crescent bodies leaning forward like triangular sails before a stiff breeze. Faintly across the distance came the scrabbling, scratching sound of the chitinous feet against the hard-packed road. "Look at that," the sergeant said. "Grass isn't dying back as bad."

The difference was striking. The Guard still left a wake of gray death behind them; but it was much narrower than it had been. There was a broad circle of desiccation where they had stood, but then the line north narrowed to only eight or ten paces wide, not a hundred. "Must be going too fast to suck out all the life," Hadrel hazarded. "Better call Whitehorn."

He tried the communication spell. Nothing happened. "It's them ahead of us," the sergeant said. "Been getting worse and worse. At first the major could talk to Whitehorn right along; then he had to pull away a thousand paces; then a league or more. And the travel spell ain't reliable now either."

"Let's try it anyway," the captain said. "Assemble the men."

The detachment—there were only twelve of them now, since there seemed nothing any number of soldiers could do to affect the Shadow Guard—fell in at once, and Hadrel activated the travel spell. There was some nervous joking during the simi that the spell endured; cracks about the similarity of the foremost of the Guard to the sweetheart of one or the other soldiers, an odd kind of boasting contest in which several men vied to outdo the others in describing the amount of fear each one felt.

When the spell concluded, Hadrel cursed most whole-heartedly. They came into reality again, not close to the road, which had been his goal, but under the heavy, gloomy shadows of trees. Enormous boles were on all sides of them, their ancient trunks mossy in the dimness. The soldiers were somewhere in Arkhedden, springy aeons of leaf mold beneath their feet, the odors of growth and decay strong in their nostrils. "I'll try the communication spell again anyhow," Hadrel said. "Then we'll see about making our way back to the road."

But though Hadrel managed to speak to Gareth this time, he was not destined to lead his men back to the road at all. "Come on in," Gareth ordered. "It looks like we'll need every man here on the mountain."

"March, you mean?"

"No. You must be north of the Guard now; the travel spell should get you into the valley safe enough. Wait a bit."

The soldiers shifted uneasily until Gareth spoke again: "I was right. Tremien says you're about twenty leagues west of where you intended to be, probably near the old forest road to Jalot. Aim for the valley floor, not the mountain; that way, if you miss, the worst you'll get is a soaking in the river, not a fall from a cliff."

"Yes, sir. But must we come in? There may still be folk along the road," Hadrel protested.

"They'll have to take their chances," Gareth said. "We need you here. Whitehorn is in for a siege. And God help us, it's such a siege as we've never known."

Chrespul Vitters had heard nothing of the Guard.

He was a farmer, was Chrespul; and he farmed on the green hills west of the Wizard's Mountains. He was not quite thirty, and it was his boast that his old dad had fought side by side with the great Tremien in the Wizards' War ages before he himself was born. Tremien himself had granted Chrespul's dad the farm, and there the old man still lived, though in his age he was half-blind and these days more apt to be found in the Crooked Arm drinking ale and reliving the battles he had fought than mucking out a stable or planting sheaf.

Chrespul and his young wife, who was a Mackelberry from Broadmeadow before the wedding, did the work now and were raising a family of their own, three sturdy boys and a young girl who was her dad's darling. A good growing family like that kept a man stepping. Today, for example, Chrespul was driving three yearling heifers down to Lake Market to sell. Ordinarily he would have taken the route through the valley, for Tremien's thoughtful magic made the journey an easy one, but for some reason he had decided to take the road instead, and cut east through Saddle Pass to the lake and the small market town.

It was a good day's amble there, and Chres planned to put up in Market Inn for the night. Tomorrow he would look for something specially nice for the missus, maybe some good pretty cloth for a dress, and he counted on finding some well-disposed fellow heading north in a wagon for his return journey. He had left before daylight—by sunrise he had almost decided to turn again, for the sky was ugly and gray with racing low clouds, and a hard wet wind came from the northeast.

But he decided to go on, for two reasons. One was the buxom barmaid at Market Inn, who had laughed so winningly at his little jokes the last time he was in town. The other was the need Chres felt to assure himself that his marriage was a good one and that he was man enough to withstand the charms of the barmaid. He was almost certain he could do it. At least he was eager to try.

And that perhaps was the real reason for his taking the long way round: Chres had much to think over and could use the extra time. His wife was a good woman, no argument on that score. She was a lot like the barmaid, in fact. Jolly, rather stout but not actually fat, bright-faced, eventempered. Older, of course. Thirty already. A good deal older.

A good deal.

The barmaid couldn't be twenty yet.

Musing on this and similar thoughts, Chres kept the unwilling heifers, a roan and two brown spotted ones, plodding south, their progress encouraged by occasional judicious touches of a long, limber withe on haunches and flanks. The cows grumbled a bit in their bovine way, but all kept moving at the same slow plod. Every once in a while one would pause to crop some of the wayside grass, and when he was preoccupied or puzzled over his own feelings, Chres would allow the grazing. Other times, when he was being very determined to prove his husbandly virtue, he had no patience and would touch up the offending cow with the withe, making her bawl her disappointment.

For whatever reason, his care for his cows or his wandering thoughts, Chres did not notice anything especially odd until daylight was well advanced. Then it occurred to him that he had seen no traffic, not a rider, not a wain, not a cart, on the road all this time, and that was unusual. The farm folk hereabouts used the great North Road for most of their business with the Arkhedden foresters or with the market towns to the south and east. It was uncommon to travel on the road for more than half an ona without spying at least one other traveler.

Chres chewed on that problem for a while. But then, just as he was getting past the first stage of tiredness and into his second wind, he saw movement ahead of him and brightened up. Looked like a whole parcel of folk coming toward him, to judge from the great cloud of dust they raised. Someone to tip a good-day to, anyway, someone with whom to exchange rueful comments on fickle weather.

But they were coming almighty fast, it seemed to Chres.

He tried to make out what they were. Not jacks or horses, surely, too big for that. Some kind of outlandish wagons, perhaps? Maybe some sort of traveling show? His dad had taken him to one long ago—at Winter Festival that had been—where they had big shaggy sapads from the far deserts of Akrador, a caged fang-cat, even a small red dragon, though its poison sac had been removed to prevent it spitting in folks' eyes.

But these things were bigger than the splay-footed sapads. And the wrong color, like. Sort of red-like, remindful of a fresh-skinned hare—

The back of Chrespul's neck prickled in fear. Not wagons or animals, but living things, god-awful-looking—these red, glistening, demon-plagued things were *alive*!

And bearing down on him incredibly fast.

For a heartbeat Chres thought only of saving the cows, which seemed in a fair danger of being trampled. Then his concern was all for himself, for he was as much in the way of these things as his heifers were.

He left the cows to their own devices and ran as hard as his long legs would carry him. Fortunately for Chres, he ran away from the road and not along it, for he had not gone far before he heard an anguished bawling from behind him. Invisible fingers seemed to pluck at him, and he felt the strength of his legs falter. Suddenly limp as a wet rag, Chres pitched helplessly forward, impelled by his running speed. He went sprawling and spilling into the deep grass, his outthrust hands skidding over the dew-damp sedge.

His chest heaving for breath, Chres pressed his face close to the ground, smelling the sweet scent of hay and vowing in his heart eternal fidelity to his wife.

After a while, he risked looking up.

The things had gone. Two humped shapes lay close by the road. Chres pushed himself up with trembling arms and walked back, his legs quaking under him; he felt as weak as he had back when he was ten and just recovering from a bad bout of the crimson ague.

He took in a sharp breath when he saw the cows. Mummies of cows, more like: lying on their sides, legs already rigid, hide gone crumpled and ashy-colored, like the gray paper of a wasp nest, stretched drumhead-tight over the bones. No hair left at all on either of them. The eye sockets yawned, a clutter of some webby stuff barely visible in their shadowed depths. As he came close, the tail of one simply dropped off, stiff as a stick.

He knelt by the other one—he could not recognize which cow she was—and touched its side. His hand sank into the gray surface, which had an awful crumbly texture. It flaked away under his fingers, nasty and greasy but dry at the same time. Frantic, Chres shook his hand, scrambled back into the good grass, scrubbed his palm clean against the green stalks. Looking back, he could see the print of his hand impressed deep in the heifer's belly. Chres retched a stream of hot, sour bile.

A plaintive lowing made him look across the road. The last cow, the roan, had possessed at least as much sense as he. She had run in the opposite direction, but she seemed all right. "Well, young Bellflower," Chres said. His voice squeaked strangely, gone back to the treble of adolescence with the fright he had felt. "Tell you what's come into mind. Think we should get ourselves back to home, soon's may be. What do you think of that, now?"

"Moo," said Bellflower.

Chrespul Vitters took that as a yes. He kept a wary eye out all the way for those hellish things again, but they were far out of sight by now, not even their dust visible. He turned the cow off from the road at the lane—the grass on the edge of the road was a grotesque sight, as dead and powdery as Bell's poor sisters—and when he saw the stone farmhouse snug and right, his gangling, rawboned sons at work with hoes in the field beyond, he could have cried out in relief.

His pace quickened as he neared the house, and so did the cow's. Fleetingly it occurred to him that when the time came and he was a doddering grandsire, he would have his own tale to spin over a good glass of ale in the pub. And then his sons might laugh indulgently at old dad's adventures along the road and his daring escape from the thing that killed the cows.

For the first time since he had seen the approach of the deadly creatures, the farmer smiled. The scene he had conjured up in his head seemed somehow right, fitting, just the proper sort of old age for him to have, now that it looked like he might indeed have one.

He touched Bellflower's rump with the withe, to no real purpose, for she too seemed relieved at the sight of home and picked up her gait into a lumbering cow-trot. One of the boys leaned on his hoe and waved. With a broad grin, Chres waved back and shouted his love.

And not once during the whole trip home had Chres so much as thought of the barmaid's alluring smile, her shining teeth, her intriguing bosom.

*   *   *

"I thought surely it would work," Tremien said, sounding both tired and resigned.

"You convinced *me*," Sebastian said. "I thought they were all dead."

Barach nodded. "I could say the same. However, I think you might at least have confided in an old friend," he said in mild rebuke. "The idea of using an illusion spell to make us all think the soldiers had real axes was a particularly nasty one. I felt very ill when the stroke was given."

"That's nothing to what Celissa, Jondan, and Idoradas must have felt," Sebastian returned.

"I counted on that," Tremien acknowledged. "I thought surely the Great Dark One, he who fears death so much, would reveal his presence by attempting a spell."

"Which of course you had already countered," Sebastian pointed out. "As Julhukrihain certainly would have guessed you would do."

"Maybe you were wrong to begin with," Jeremy said. "Maybe the Great Dark One is somewhere else."

"Impossible," Tremien said. "Else the Shadow Guard would not be coming here; and they would not have increased their speed at the very moment of my mock execution. No, Sebastian is certainly right. Jilhukrihain understood me better than I understood him. He knew, somehow he *knew*, that the beheadings were a trick of mine. And he is intelligent enough to understand, too, that here in Whitehorn my magic can overpower his own." Tremien shook his head, his beard swaying with the movement. "What iron nerve the adversary has! I took great care with that spell. No one, I thought, could penetrate it to see that the axes were in fact bladeless. But either the Great Dark One did, or else he divined that it was all bluff."

"Celissa was terrified, at any rate," Jeremy said. "She fainted clean away, and when she came to again she was in hysterics."

Barach nodded. "And Idoradas could not cease weeping, while Jondan was pale but composed. True to their natures in every instance. I saw no sign of the Great Dark One in any of their reactions."

"I am ashamed of myself," Tremien said. "Whatever the hoped-for result, I frightened two good souls beyond all reason. Surely they will never forgive me."

"Yet it might have worked," Sebastian said, sounding rather grudging in the admission. "It's funny; you came up with just such a trick as Jilhukrihain might himself have used. Except, of course, he would have used real axes, probably. But if what the soldiers said about the Shadow Guard speeding up is correct, then you at least scared Jilhukrihain. I don't know everything about it, but he is somehow or other in touch with the Guard, and they must have felt his terror."

Tremien's hands were clenched, his brows drawn together in anger. "And they will be in my valley this afternoon, and on my doorstep tonight."

"What do we do now?" Jeremy asked.

Tremien shrugged and made a visible effort to relax. "Ogion has a spell that should avail against the Guard. Unfortunately, it will not work until the moment of transfer occurs. That means the Great Dark One will have more power than I. More than all of us put together. If we cannot circumvent the transfer somehow, then we stand no chance at all."

"Then let's work on that."

Tremien smiled, very faintly. "The thought had occurred to me, Jeremy. I have an idea or two; whether they will work, only God knows." He gave Jeremy a kind look. "I think it might be best for you to take your family from this place. You might yet travel north or west in safety. Nul's people would be more than pleased to shelter you, and you do have a wife and child to consider."

Jeremy's laugh was hollow. "I couldn't keep Kelada in Whitehorn when she was pregnant and I was going into danger up at Twilight Valley. Now I can't get her to budge out of the place, though I've tried hard enough. I'll stay, anyhow. You've been more than good to me, and I owe you whatever help I can give you."

"Thank you for that. Now I must meet Ogion and the others to plan for the coming of the Guard, since nothing seems to hold them back. Get what rest you can, and be ready for battle on a moment's notice."

They left Tremien's apartments in silence and gloom. Barach and Sebastian went to the outer courtyard, where scores of men kept anxious watch on the valley. Jeremy started for the tower where his apartment was, but he was

only halfway there when Winyard, the chief mummer, rolled
out of a cross-hall and accosted him.

"My boy! My soul!" Winyard exclaimed, his sentiments
rolling out heavily scented with wine and in a voice as fruity
as a good deep port. "Arms and alarms! The hour of valor
approaches, eh? Let me ask you, now, frankly, as one man
to another—do you think I should play Capulet with a beard
or without?"

Jeremy stopped in his tracks and stared at the man in
shocked incredulity. Winyard was a handsome (though increasingly stout) man of middle age, one of those humans in
Thaumia who possessed only minimal magic and so used
other talents instead. He had a strong-featured face, square
of chin and noble of brow. And he could be at times a
complete idiot.

"You want my advice about the play? Now? Winyard, I
don't know if you realize what's going on," Jeremy said.

Winyard took Jeremy's arm in his and strolled along
beside him. "Alarums and excursions! Swordplay on the
battlements! Thrilling scenes of bravery, piteous moments
of grief. High tragedy! Blood and thunder!"

"This," Jeremy said, disengaging his arm, "is a bit different. It's real, Winyard. Not playacting."

"Ah, but as you so nobly put it, 'All the world's a stage,
and the men and women merely mummers—' "

"Don't quote my own stuff to me," Jeremy protested. He
still felt the occasional stab of guilt at his plundering of
Shakespeare and other writers for the plots of the majority
of his plays.

"Ah, of course not; why paint the gilly, eh, lad?" Winyard's
chuckle was deep, the elbow he dug into Jeremy's side
uncomfortably sharp.

"A beard," Jeremy said. "Definitely play it in a beard."

Winyard nodded. He ran his hand over his medium-
length hair, which had become iron-gray in the past year.
"Excellent idea, my genius. Yes, a beard. And a wig, I
think. I have a wonderful beard, chestnut brown, much like
your own used to be, and it goes with a cunning wig that
was made especially for me by one of the finest hair-weavers
of Faskol—"

"Yes, well, that sounds wonderful," Jeremy said.

Winyard came to a halt, his head lowered. He raised

troubled eyes to meet Jeremy's gaze. "But, lad, are you sure? My view is that Capulet is a mature man. Perhaps the wig and beard will youthen me overmuch. Capulet, I think, should be no more than forty; a mature forty; a forty that has seen ships and sailors, a forty that has known the day of crying 'Ho! To arms!' A forty that has loved tender women and has fought bitter duels with hard men; a forty that knows the world—"

"Then don't play it in a beard," Jeremy almost wailed.

"Good, good. You say wisely, lad." They began to move again, Winyard stroking his shaved chin. "Let the playgoers see my open countenance, yes, give them the full range of expressiveness, very wise. Yet think: there is something in a beard that gives an attitude of gravity, is there not? Something that says to the world, 'Lo, I have settled down at last. No more for me the rolling decks of pirate ships wet with blood; no more the captain's call. I play the part now of a gentleman, his hot blood harnessed like prancing coursers, his force turned to peace and—' "

"Winyard," Jeremy said with rising desperation.

"Yes, lad?" Winyard composed his features into an expression of intent alertness. "Speak on; I am nothing but attention."

"What do *you* think?"

Winyard stopped walking again and for a few moments tapped his lips with his forefinger. "A good question, that. It cuts to the heart of the matter, after all. I think a beard, perhaps." He brightened at some new idea and added, "But I shall not have it fully trimmed. The idea, you see, is that Capulet is now a gentleman of trade, but lurking beneath is the high-blooded old campaigner, ready to spring to action—"

Jeremy put both hands on the man's shoulders and gave him the gentlest of shakes. "You are truly the most brilliant mummer I have ever known," he said with what he hoped was deep sincerity. "An untrimmed beard for Capulet. What a marvelous idea. Wonderful, simply wonderful."

Winyard beamed. "It is rather good, if I say so myself. And it simply came to me out of the air." He ruffled his fingers through the atmosphere, as if playing an invisible harp.

Jeremy patted his shoulders. "Marvelous. And you know what? After the battle, all the soldiers and wizards would welcome some entertainment. If I were you, I'd get the troupe together and do a good thorough rehearsal in the beard. Then you can give a performance for everyone at Whitehorn, and when they go back home—"

"That's right," Winyard said, his eyes lighting up like twin gold coins reflecting a ruddy light. "They come from all over the continent, those people. They could spread my—I mean our fame across the swelling bosom of Cronbrach—"

"Brilliant," Jeremy said again. "You are an absolutely brilliant mummer."

Winyard waved him away. "I cannot speak further now, Jeremy, my lad. I must away to the rehearsal hall. Tell them all to expect the play of their lives, and Winyard shall not disappoint." He placed his hand over his heart and made a stately bow. Then he turned, struck an attitude, and stalked off down the hall, muttering, "Is this your house or mine? You'll set basilisk-a-hoop! Go to, I say, go to!"

Jeremy rolled his eyes heavenward, shook his head, and went on to his rooms.

Kelada was there, sitting next to the window, her chin resting on her hand as she looked out at the slopes of the mountain and at the valley below. Nul was there too, sitting on the floor and rolling a ball to the giggling Emily, who tried her best to roll it back to Nul. "You don't seem especially concerned," Jeremy said, stepping around the pika.

Nul grinned, showing the alarming mouthful of white teeth that had been Jeremy's first startled impression of him. "Not time to worry. If battle go bad, that when worrying begins. Till then just be ready." He pushed the ball back across the floor to Emily, who gurgled.

Jeremy went to sit next to Kelada. She took his hand in hers and squeezed. "I'm glad I didn't watch the execution," she said.

"So am I." Jeremy shivered a little at the memory. "In fact, I'm sorry I saw it. Look, Tremien thinks it might be best if you leave Whitehorn for—"

"No." Kelada shifted her position slightly but did not look at him. "We've been through this."

Jeremy caught his breath. "Look, you could take Emily to Zarad-zellikol—"

Nul perked up at once. He leapt to his feet, enormously

excited. "Yes! Sisters love Emily. My mate Grall too. It a good idea, Kelada. You stay, we keep you safe under mountains. Then—"

"Thank you, Nul," Kelada said. "No."

"It's going to be dangerous here," Jeremy said. "Not even Tremien knows what's going to happen. If the Shadow Guard breaks through, and there's nothing to halt them, the Great Dark One is going to be unstoppable. And you know he has no love for me."

"I know that."

Jeremy tried one more time. "If not for yourself, go for Emily."

"No. I think it's a good idea for Emily to go, though. I think Nul should take Emily to the caverns himself, just for the night. But I'm staying here with you."

The argument stretched out, but to no avail. Just past noon Nul took Emily, her nurse—a cheerful, bustling little woman who had been nanny to dozens of children in the untidy extended family of Whitehorn—and an impressive assortment of clothing to the caverns. He was gone for only a few simi, from Jeremy's point of view, before he returned via the travel spell. "All well," he reported. "Got right into main cavern, just as planned. No trouble at all. Guard not disturbing magic between here and Bone Mountains yet."

"Was she good for you?" Kelada asked, her voice sounding a little teary, a little wistful. She missed her daughter already, even though to her and Jeremy, Emily had been away for only a moment or two.

"Ya, ya. Laugh and make baby noises whole time. Talk little bit. Call me 'Nulnul.' And all pikas fall in love with her, I think." Nul chuckled. "Should have seen. Put Emily on clean sandy floor. She pick up handful of sand, try to eat it."

Kelada's expression grew murderous.

"All babies do that," Jeremy said hastily.

"Ya, ya," agreed Nul. "Pika babies too. She make funny face, nurse get sand out of mouth. Everyone come around to see, everyone say how pretty she is for human."

With a nervous glance at Kelada's increasingly threatening eyes, Jeremy said, "Well, that's just . . . uh, Nul, let's go out to the walls and see what news there is. It's getting late."

The storm outside was fierce, but somehow he preferred it to the one that threatened to break in the apartment.

As it passed noon, the weather grew progressively worse. Gray curtains of rain swept through the valley now, and the ragged clouds snagged on the spires of the castle itself. Even in his robe Jeremy was uncomfortable, for the whipping wind was wet and chilly for the time of year. The wall walk was well-built, the stone gritty and hard underfoot, so his step was not threatened by the lashes of rain. But the wind tried hard to shove him over the parapet.

Jeremy spoke to several of the soldiers, finding them all nervous but in good enough spirits. He listened to Hadrel Cabraksas' account of what had happened that morning, then passed on to the front wall, to the thrusting niche between the two stone gargoyles. "Anything in the valley?" he asked them.

Busby, the elder of the two, spoke from his right: "Nothing yet." A sudden flash of lightning flooded the mountainside with intense light, and immediately thunder vibrated the very stones of the castle. When the sound died away, Busby added, "Nothing except this terrible cyclone, anyway."

"Yes, I'm sorry about that," Jeremy said, his ears still ringing from the concussion. "It's my fault, or at least mine and Sebastian's."

"No worry," Fred said from his left. He turned his hawkish head to give Jeremy a jaunty look. "Stone doesn't mind a little rain and thunder, you know."

"Flesh isn't so lucky," Jeremy said, his hair streaming and cold water running into his eyes.

"You removed your face hairs," Fred said, giving Jeremy rather more intense scrutiny.

"I had to so that I could pass for Sebastian. It's too long a story to go into now."

Busby laughed in his stony way. "Humans! Your notions of what is a long time are so amusing. Wait until you've lain under a glacier for a few thousand years waiting for the end of an ice age, then see how long you think a mere story is."

"I'll pass," Jeremy said. The wind howled again, and he had to turn his back on a pelting spray of rain. It passed, and the shower became merely soaking rather than outright painful. Jeremy straightened again and saw that both gargoyles had resumed their accustomed stance, staring down at the approach to the Keep with their forbidding raptorlike glares. He felt an unreasonable affection for these monolithic behemoths. "Look, you two, you might consider leaving this part of the Keep. The Shadow Guard soaks up magic, all magic. And that's what keeps you both alive."

"Abandon our posts?" Busby demanded, and if stone could bristle, he did. "Never. No matter what the danger."

"Besides," Fred said in sly tones, "if Tremien is right, the Guard won't be absorbing magic by the time they near the castle; they'll be sending it forth. That, I think, we should be able to endure."

"Still, do be careful. I'd hate for anything to happen to you two," Jeremy said.

Busby was indulgent: "Never worry about us, Jeremy. Your skin, if I may say it, is far softer than ours." The grating voice became gentle. "Promise us in turn that you will watch out for your own safety."

"I always try to," Jeremy said. "I always try."

At last, in the ona past noon, Barach and Tremien were alone. Barach poured one almost abstemiously small glass of wine—the same straw-colored wine of which old Radusilf was so fond—and gave it to his friend. Tremien smiled his thanks, smoothed his thick mustache out of the way, and took a thoughtful sip.

"They are contentious," Barach observed.

"The magi from Vanislach? Yes, they are; but I suppose that comes of a life of scholarly debate and little experience with the demands of magic in the real world." The wind howled in the chimney as if protesting Tremien's pronouncement.

Barach had to raise his voice a little over the tumult of the weather: "You met their objections, though."

Tremien drained the glass and set it on the corner of his desk. "Old friend, we have always been honest with each other; pray do not keep your thoughts from me. Do you believe I am in the wrong?"

Barach settled into one of the comfortable armchairs. "They do tell a story of two fish in the sea. It seems they argued about which could leap the highest. One tried and sailed so high that he caught a dragonfly, which he brought back as proof of his flight. The other tried even harder and leapt even higher. Unfortunately, he could not bring back the proof of his feat, for it was a pebble which he snatched up from the dry land over ten paces from the water that sustained him. Before he was quite dead, though, he made a fine meal for a passing crane."

"So that in my concern to have my own way I may be obstinate enough to perish in the end?"

"The thought has crossed my mind." Barach reached for the carafe and poured himself a glass of wine. Looking at it, he said, "Surely you must know that even should you succeed, you will fatally weaken your position as Chief Mage."

"That is no concern," Tremien said. He picked up his glass by the stem and twirled it between his fingers, staring at the flashes of reflected light playing off it. "Should I fail, I will certainly die in the attempt. Or worse. Should I succeed, well, with the Great Dark One no longer our adversary, Cronbrach will have no need of Tremien as Chief Mage."

"With respect, I differ."

"That is your right. Yet you speak more in friendship than in truth, and while I am grateful for your opinion, I cannot agree with it." He put the glass down again. "And somehow neither of our opinions seems of much account to me at present."

"You have little hope," Barach observed.

Tremien frowned. "Not true. I have considerable hope, my friend, for the Great Dark One is so tortured in his thinking that he is frequent to tangle himself in his own toils. I fear the Guard, yes, for they are most uncanny. Yet I cannot help believing that our friends the professors are wrong; that the Great Dark One is our primary foe. Well, they have a means of dealing with the Guard, in theory. It remains for us to devise some way of handling their master."

Barach lifted his glass in salute. "May we find it soon, then, for time is growing most uncomfortably short." He drained the glass at one go, cast a longing gaze at the carafe, but forbore from pouring himself a second drink. A rattle of hail clattered against the tall arched windows. Barach raised his eyebrows. "And our time, yours and mine, is not all that seems short. I think Sebastian's stay with us must be brief now. The storm is frightful."

"Yes. I asked one or two sorcerers with special abilities at weather conjuration to do what they could; but that is not very much, not in the face of a dimensional disturbance of this magnitude. How long has Sebastian been in Thaumia this time? A few days? Three, is it? It seems much longer."

"The presence of the Guard complicates matters, I expect," Barach said. "I can no longer feel them, but the lines of force must be seriously imbalanced. I would not tell Jeremy this, for it would only add to his worry, but it wouldn't surprise me if something gave way. Sebastian could be catapulted back to Earth at any moment, and perhaps with no warning."

"Or Jeremy," Tremien said. "Remember, he is the one born on Earth, not Sebastian. And the two are identical as far as the forces of our universe are concerned."

"I haven't forgotten."

The two old friends sat for a time in silence, save for the wind and the thunder. The mages ignored the sounds of weather as they sat, companionable and calm, even in the face of the approaching threat, even with the tumult of the terrible storm heavy in their ears. Each was lost in his own thoughts; both blinked in some surprise when the door flew open and banged against the stone wall.

"Jeremy?" Barach said as the robe-clad figure strode into the room.

"Sebastian," the newcomer snapped. He came to a stop at the edge of Tremien's desk. "I've been thinking."

Barach smiled. "Forgive me for my mistake. Now that Jeremy is bare-faced, you two are so difficult to tell apart—"

"Listen," Sebastian said. "It's beginning to look as if I won't get home again until all this business with the Guard and Jilhukrihain is over. I've been thinking about it, and I may be onto something. Jeremy says Jilhukrihain was fascinated with his combination of powers, with his blending of Thaumian magic and Earth energies. He looked on Jeremy as a prime candidate for hosting his spirit. Is that the way you understand it?"

"That is true," Barach said. "Jeremy had a terrible moment or two away down in Relas, while the Great Dark One told him how he planned to take him over. It seems that the enemy gained a taste for Earthly magic through the mirror you created for him. Perhaps he sees Earth as yet another world to conquer."

"That's it," Sebastian said. "He probably does. And he needs Jeremy to attempt anything like that. That's what you have to sell."

"I beg your pardon," Tremien said, sounding confused. "I do not understand."

"Jeremy's the bait," Sebastian said. "He's what the Great Dark One wants. What he'd give anything to have. We have to work with that. See, it doesn't matter who's the host for Jilhukrihain now—doesn't matter if it's Jondan or Idoradas or Celissa. None of them is as good for his purpose as Jeremy would be. And certainly none of them would offer him the hope of conquering Earth after he completes his conquest of Thaumia."

Barach frowned. "I see what you mean, but what good does it do us?"

Sebastian leaned on the desk, midway between Tremien and Barach, his palms spread flat on the wood, his arms straight and braced. He had the look of a man absolutely intent on an idea. "It doesn't do us a bit of good, not as things stand right now. But we can change that, with the right kind of campaign." Thunder vibrated the windowpanes as if in punctuation to Sebastian's words.

"Your words are most strange," Tremien said. "Perhaps you had better tell us exactly what you mean."

Sebastian straightened. With a fierce smile he said, "Gentlemen, it's simple. Jilhukrihain wants Jeremy. All we have to do is give Jeremy to him."

And again the thunder boomed, sounding for all the world like war drums summoning men to blood and death.

13

The wind was worse than ever, blasting so hard it fairly snatched one's breath away, and the rain it flung was mixed with pellets of hail that exploded with brittle *cracks!* against the stone walls of Whitehorn Keep. On the northern wall walk, Gareth had sought the shelter of a parapet and stood with his head turned away from the wind, his back pressed against the stone. It kept off the worst of the weather, but the furious gusts whipped around the stone bulwark and swirled in mad little cyclones, soaking Gareth and Jeremy as they shouted their conversation over the din.

"So nothing worked?" Jeremy yelled.

Gareth bowed his head lower as a sudden blow sprayed them both with icy rain. "Nothing," he boomed back, his voice almost lost in the roar. "Mundane weapons have no effect on the Shadow Guard. Magical ones are spoiled by contact. Ordinary magic they absorb completely. Elemental magic they ignore. Two of the professors from Vanislach even tried to erect a mundanity barrier—"

"What?"

"A barrier of mundanity." Gareth evidently saw Jeremy's confusion, for he added, "I mean they used their own spells to pull the lines of magical force away from a stretch of the road. Made it as nearly mundane as they could, like a swath of forest cut clean to the ground to stop a wildfire. Didn't do any good at all—the Guard just went right past. The only thing different was that the mages killed the grass along the barrier, not the Guard."

Jeremy straightened his back and chanced raising his eyes above the parapet. He got a faceful of cold rain and could barely manage to squint down the mountainside toward the

244

valley. The gently undulating landscape and the sinuous course of the river were almost lost in the gray rain, but at least he could not see the Guard there. He ducked down again and looked at the sky, packed with ragged flying clouds so low that it seemed he could stretch up an arm and brush the trailing black tatters with his outstretched fingers.

A blinding streak of blue-white lightning hit the Keep's tall east tower, and thunder pummeled him. He blinked away the dark afterimage and to his relief saw that the tower remained whole. At least the protective spells woven into the fabric of the castle still held, thanks to Tremien's care in devising them over the long years, to his skill in joining words with stone and glass and wood to make a kind of enduring spell, not a spoken one, in the works of Whitehorn.

It was impossible to judge time accurately in that weather, with the sun not seen all day, but Jeremy guessed it was late afternoon. He had almost forgotten the Earth way of gauging time from midnight to midnight, but in those terms it would be four or five o'clock, he supposed. "How long do we have before they get here?" he shouted into Gareth's ear.

"Who knows? They will come sometime tonight, most likely. I estimate midnight, but that is only a guess. It does not matter, really; they will come when they come."

"Maybe Sebastian and I should leave, head west or north. The bad weather will follow us. At least then you could see what you have to fight."

"Right now I would be glad to bid farewell to this moil. Might be as much a help as a hindrance, though," Gareth returned. "If it makes it hard for us to see the Guard, it will make it at least as hard for the Guard to see us. If they see at all in our sense of the word."

The rain stopped unnaturally, all at once, as if cut off at the source, though the wind yammered even more loudly than before. It took on a wild, keening note as it rushed over the parapet, creating a breathless suction in the shelter of the wall. Both men rose up cautiously. The shower had passed, as the squalls had done all day. Now the thick cloud darkened the landscape, but without the pouring rain, the valley below was at least visible. A few warm yellow windows showed here and there in the distance, marking the cottages of farmers and foresters on the other side of Easy Ford. "They didn't leave?" Jeremy asked, pointing.

"They are leaving. Going up the valley, those that aren't coming to the castle. But they hang on as late as they can, as folk always do. Animals to see to, tasks to work at. Always busy, these valley people are. They'll be doing their chores right up to first arrow of the battle."

Jeremy supposed it was true. Things had to be done, Shadow Guard or no. Cows had swollen udders that demanded to be milked, and there were eggs to be collected, horses to be fed, tools to be taken care of. And if the farmers held on too late, if they were caught by the battle that was sure to come, if they died on its fringe simply because they were trying to continue their lives—well, there might even be a kind of heroism in that, Jeremy thought. The valor of the ordinary in the face of the incredible.

Gareth said something, but the wind snatched his voice away. Jeremy leaned closer to him, feeling his wet hair being yanked by the fingers of the gale. "What was that?"

"Said that Tremien wants all the walls fully manned. We have outposts along the Valley Road to warn us of the Guard's approach, one or two strong points along the path up the mountain to try what they can do against the Guard. He's even had us drag out those things." He nodded down into the courtyard, where three catapults waited, already cocked and loaded with great round stones. "Not that they'd do any good. I suppose a direct hit might tumble a Guard off the trail and down the mountain a little way, but from what I saw, you can't kill the damned things. They'll just get up and come again."

"I imagine they have spells to help them."

"The catapults, you mean? Yes. Spells of seeking, as it were, to make them accurate. Oh, they'll hit their targets, all right. The problem is that even a direct hit won't do what has to be done."

"Still, Tremien has to try."

Gareth nodded. "We all do."

Another bolt of lightning flashed overhead without hitting anything, but it turned the gloom to a weird kind of noonday. In the momentary light Jeremy was struck by the forlorn look on Gareth's face, sad and infinitely lonely.

Gareth looked the way Jeremy felt, and possibly for the same reason. Jeremy asked him, "Where is Melodia?"

For the first time Gareth smiled. He was much in love with the beautiful, gentle healer. "Safe enough in Arendolas. We built her a cottage there while she was working with the vilorgs. She's back in that, well out of harm's way, for the moment at least."

"Arendolas. I haven't been back there since the fall of the Hag," Jeremy said.

"When this is over, you ought to visit it. You wouldn't recognize the Hag's Vale now. Illsmere Castle's all gone, of course, tumbled into the bog and sunk without a trace. Not even a stone of that remaining. But things are growing again, and all the swamps are gone. The deeper meres are rich in life, fish of all kinds, wading birds, thick green reeds at their edges. The shallow ones have drained out. Lots of good black land there now, ripe for the plow; but as you might guess, the vilorgs are not much on farming."

The wind, which had slacked for a short while, built up and buffeted them again, and Jeremy shivered a little. He remembered the vilorgs as horrible parodies of human forms, amphibian creatures twisted to a semblance of humanity by the Hag's evil magic. When the Hag had died, the creatures lost their malignity and became helpless and rather pathetic, lost without the direction of a controlling mind. Melodia had taken upon herself the task of helping them learn to make their way without the protection of the Hag. "How do they live?" Jeremy asked.

"They farm the meres, I suppose you'd have to say. Have villages on the banks, low domelike houses made of mud and reeds. The vilorgs dive right in the meres for fish and water plants." Again Gareth smiled. "I think they almost worship Melodia. And no wonder, for the Hag was all cruelty toward them; Melodia's kindness is like a blessed sip of water to a man thirst-crazed in Akrador. But you ought to see them now."

Jeremy, haunted by his memories of the vilorgs, could not agree. The slimy gray-green bodies, the huge heads with lidless staring eyes and great slashes of mouths, were far too clear in Jeremy's recollection. "I don't think I'd care to look at them again."

"Ah, you recall the way they were. You'd find them

changed. Not at all warlike, not really. They fought because the Hag made them; but their great numbers were their only real advantage when they were playing soldier. They look different out of the mists and fogs of the Hag, not threatening at all. In the sunshine now they're just fat frogs squatting on the lake banks."

Jeremy remembered the struggle for the Haggenkom, the Hag's Vale, and how he had been forced to kill some of the creatures. He still did not like the nasty feeling of triumph that had run through him when he brought down his first victim with a crossbow bolt. It still showed him a side of himself that he preferred to keep in shadows. Oh, he was capable of killing, all right. He thought he could probably strangle the Great Dark One if it came to that, and have no regrets afterward.

But the vilorgs were different, somehow. Killing one of them, even an armed one, was somehow more like striking down a dumb animal than a formidable adversary. "They weren't very good as soldiers," he said.

"Well, they don't hold together, not as a people," Gareth said. "Melodia still hasn't been able to teach them that. I suppose the trait was planned from the first. The Hag did not care to have cabals and intrigues among her servants. The only unifying force among them was her evil will; without it, they have no interest in being a tribe, no organization past that of the mother vilorg and her brood. They're not intelligent enough to do much on their own past the simple life in the water they seem to enjoy. But their lack of organization makes the task of civilizing them harder, and it made them very poor troops, as you say."

Jeremy stood with the wind in his face and looked down into the valley one last time. Still he could detect no sign of those crescent-shaped beings, those monstrosities. "I'm going in for a bite," Jeremy yelled over the voices of the wind. "Looks like a long evening."

"Better eat while you've leisure for it. And don't worry about missing anything. You'll know soon enough if we sight them," Gareth shouted back.

Jeremy made his way back into the keep, pushed along by the wind at his back. It slammed the door behind him with a percussion like a small cannon going off. Kelada had at least consented to stay in the Dowager's Tower, named for

Tremien's long-dead mother. There she would be with the women and children of the Keep, though Jeremy expected she would be armed and would play the part of a soldier rather than that of a patient wife.

So Jeremy did not go back to his tower rooms, for they seemed forlorn and empty without Kelada and Emily there. Instead he wandered to the kitchens, where he talked one of the cooks into making him a thick sandwich, cold slabs of roast beef on a pleasantly bitter brown bread made from arret flour, something like Earthly rye but milder and a bit sweeter. The cook scolded him, but good-naturedly, for such simple dishes demanded none of her skill or her considerable culinary magic.

Her scolding was all nerves and having nothing to do, though, and she was not really upset, for sandwiches were relatively staple fare in Whitehorn now—an innovation Jeremy had brought from Earth, along with his books of Shakespeare, his strange approach to magic, and other interesting tidbits. When other members of the Whitehorn household had sampled his concoctions and had found them good, he had for a time toyed with the notion of calling them "jeremies," but in the end he said farewell to vanity and imported the English word for them. Of all his friends, only Nul showed much interest in actually learning Jeremy's native tongue, but now any soldier, any serving boy could ask for a sandwich in perfectly clear American-accented English.

He drank half a pint of pale ale with his meal, then set out to see what everyone else was about. Jeremy blundered into Winyard and his company in one of the larger rooms—he had forgotten the player's resolve to rehearse, or he would have avoided that particular hall—and discovered the troupe deep in Act IV, scene v, of *Romeo and Juliet*. Winyard, playing Capulet in the untrimmed brown beard as he had promised, stood over the beautiful reclining form of Selura Colt, the young actress who essayed the role of Juliet. Winyard threw his head back, his cheeks glistening from copious tears; in the play, Capulet had just found his daughter "dead," actually catatonic from Friar Laurence's mysterious potion.

"Alas!" Winyard cried in a lament broken with grief. "She's cold, her blood is settled, and her joints are stiff." A sob caught his voice, and it dropped to a thrilling lower register: "Life and these lips have long since been parted. Death lies on her like an untimely frost upon the sweetest flower of all the field." He trailed off into weeping, but noticed Jeremy and gave him a broad wink and a cheerful wave as he did so.

Jeremy waved back. As tiresome as he found the mummer's presence, he was always amazed at the acting ability Winyard revealed. He threw himself into a characterization, losing all the pomposity, all the falseness, of his own personality. Jeremy supposed it might be a relief for Winyard himself to become someone else, if only during the time he was onstage.

Glad that the windy player was otherwise occupied, Jeremy roamed on. He found Nul in the pika's own quarters, perched on the edge of his specially constructed small bed and industriously touching up the edge of his short sword with a black honing stone, playing a thin music of steel against the bass growl of the wind outside. "Time getting short," Nul observed, testing the bite of his sword gingerly with a thumb.

"That won't help," Jeremy said.

Nul stood and swished the weapon experimentally. "Sword, you mean? Maybe not. We see. You never know; might be a use for this." Satisfied, he slipped the blade into its scabbard and repacked his tools, giving Jeremy a peculiar, almost shy sidelong glance. "You scared?" he asked.

Jeremy considered. "Yes. In a way."

Nul frowned. "Me too. But not so much for self, somehow. Scared for world. Scared for my people. What happen to pikas if Great Dark One win? We small and scattered folk now. Just at beginning of summer Brother Tol find pikas of Wolmas Mountains again. They still angry with my tribe for words of Nul's father years ago. Take long time to be friends again. But one day we want to make trade, travel possible between pikas of Bone Mountains and those of Wolmas. If war come, maybe that never happen. Not right. All pikas need to be one people again."

"And the Great Dark One believes in no unity, except that of death," Jeremy said. "I know what you fear. It's something of the same with me, I guess. Tremien's given me a home here; Barach's been like a father to me. If the Great Dark One overthrows all this, we'll all be lost, on our own

against him. And I think it's the loneliness I fear more than
death itself."

"Ya, ya. That right. Tremien believe all beings of world
must be one family. Pikas, humans, all. And Great Dark
One hate that; he not belong, cannot belong, so he want no
one to belong. Want all dead."

Jeremy smiled. "I don't know if your sword will stop him,
but your spirit might," he said. The wind sobbed and yowled
outside the window, setting up enough of a draft to make
the candles that Nul used in preference to wizard-light flicker
and falter.

In the shaky light Nul grinned, his expression not a happy
one. Despite his knowledge of Nul's essential harmlessness,
Jeremy felt a prickle at the sight. That huge mouth was a bit
too reminiscent of a shark's mouth (though turned upside-
down) to make the furry Nul seem even remotely cuddly.

Tremien's disembodied voice suddenly spoke out from
the disturbed air: "Jeremy. I have need of you. Could you
join us in my study, please?"

Jeremy raised his eyebrows. "At once, Mage Tremien.
And Nul?"

"Certainly. He is welcome to come, if he wishes. Time is
getting away from us, and we have much to discuss."

The tumultuous afternoon raged into a tempestuous evening. The rain held off, except in fitful battering squalls,
quickly come and quickly passed, but the lightning grew
more intense, the thunder more vibrato. The men on the
walls, ever more nervous, kept their eyes on the dark valley,
and in every flash of lightning some sentinel thought he saw
the approach of the Shadow Guard; but the next flash
would show him wrong, would reveal the figures that he had
mistaken for the otherworldly creatures to be merely trees
bowed before the wind or the red chimneys of one of the
cottages on the far side of the ford. The advance posts were
silent and invisible, using neither magic nor their fallback
plan of signal fires to warn the castle. Except for the screaming winds, the scene was quiet.

Gareth neared a sergeant—Belisto, he saw through the
driving rain that had begun to fall again—and came up
beside him. "How are your men?" he shouted into the other
man's ear.

Belisto cupped his hand beside his mouth. "Jumpy, they are. And me along with 'em."

The rain eased off again, ending as suddenly as it had come. "Everyone's nerves are bad," Gareth shouted.

"You're right there. Can't say's I blame 'em. I don't like this one bit," Belisto bellowed back at him. "Stuck up here with the wind tryin' to snatch us off the walls and them Guard things comin' at us through the dark."

"I've seen them close," Gareth told him. "Be glad we have the high ground. It's some advantage, anyway."

The sergeant seemed to consider that for a moment, but still he grumbled: "It's not seein' 'em as gets me, though. It's the dark. I feel like we're blind to 'em. Like they was some kind of blasted moles, tunneling toward us through the ground, like, and us on top not able to see 'em coming."

Gareth put a hand on the older man's shoulder. "Don't worry yourself overmuch. We'll see them when they're close enough."

"Yah, when they're on the path to the front gate, yonder." Sergeant Belisto, his stubbled face visible in the flickering light of a wind-whipped wall torch, turned his eyes back toward the valley in a baleful stare. "See 'em when they get close enough, all right, no argument. But will that be too close?"

Gareth had no answer for that. He passed on, his thoughts hardly less bleak than the sergeant's parting words. He tried to cheer himself with the fact that the Keep had held its own through more than one battle.

For Whitehorn had been besieged before, most recently in the Hag's Uprising, when an army of walking dead had assaulted it, only to be held off by blasts of magic rolling down the slopes at them, and only to lose in the end when the Hag died and her will deserted the mindless puppets of bone and decayed sinew.

Gareth, away in the Hag's Vale with Jeremy, had missed that battle as he had the Battle of the Valley during the Wizards' War some forty years before. He had not even been born for that one. But his father had fought in it, and he had often told Gareth of the bleak day when five thousand men, swarthy southerners whose tongues gave flight to strange words, had poured into the valley from the east. Held by counterspells from loosing any incantations that would have physically injured the invaders, a younger Tremien had worked a mighty magic to confuse their speech and disorganize their cadres.

Even so, it had been a very near thing, for the invaders had great magic on their side too, magic ultimately derived from the Great Dark One. But in the end Tremien's army of fewer than a thousand had cut them down along the river, had edged grudgingly up the hill under the pressure of sheer numbers, and at the end had found shelter behind the walls of Whitehorn as the last of the confused enemy wave broke, turned, faltered, and fled.

This time, though, the foe was different, not hobs or human soldiers at all. Tremien said that the wizards and the professors would deal with the Guard. Well, if they could, so much the better! But Gareth had his doubts. He did not know how much magic was tied into the stones of Whitehorn. A great deal, he supposed, for Tremien had lived in the Keep for years and years and had devoted much of his magic to the castle and to the valley below it. If the Shadow Guard chose to absorb that power, to pull it out of the structure—

In his mind's eye Gareth saw again the collapse of a stone inn the Guard had passed. Put up by magic, the structure could not endure the close passage. First the mortar had run out like sand, pouring from between the stones; and then the stones themselves moved, first one or two falling from their place, and then all cascading down as the roof fell in and a cloud of gray dust exploded into the air. And when the Guard was well past and the dust had settled, there was naught but a man-tall pile of rubble where the inn had stood.

Gareth imagined the stones of Whitehorn cut loose from their places and rolling down the shoulders of the mountain to the river below.

But he kept up his outward determination, speaking to his men, giving them an encouragement that he himself could not feel.

Night deepened.

The three prisoners stood in Tremien's study. Idoradas had gone pale at the execution that morning and had not recovered a jot of his color or his bearing. The young

sorcerer trembled visibly, and since that morning his cheeks
had gone hollow; he seemed to have aged ten years. Next to
him Jondan stood, his own face white above his short, curly
black beard. Jondan's cheeks were gaunt too, but his eyes
were level and angry and not frightened. Celissa did not
show her eyes, for she kept them downcast, but she, too,
stood in silence.

"I know it will make no difference to one of you," Tremien
said from where he stood before the tall arched windows,
"but I am truly sorry for the trick I played on you today. I
can only offer as an excuse the fact that we are desperate
and that no one, not even the two of you who must be
innocent, have been able to suggest ways of discovering the
identity of the Great Dark One."

Tremien paused, looking from face to face. A guard of
three soldiers stood behind them, weapons ready. On
Tremien's side of the room Sebastian, Nul, and Barach
stood, Sebastian dressed in his dry but rumpled Earth garb,
Nul clad in white shirt and blue breeches, and Barach still
wearing his somber black robe.

When none of the prisoners gave any sign of wanting to
speak, Tremien continued: "I speak to Jilhukrihain alone
now. Sebastian Magister, who has spent part of his life in
another world, had an interesting word for you, Great Dark
One: a mole. Like a burrowing creature, you have crept
into a belowground home that is hidden from all eyes. And
there you have remained, quiet and wary, while we on the
surface ran this way and that trying to find a way of spading
you up.

"I know well why you have been so very quiet. You have
been my enemy for a long, long time; and careful adversary
that you are, you have made yourself fully aware of my gifts
and my powers. You know all too well that, though you
inhabit the body of a friend, your disguise is perfect so long
as you use that friend's seeming and that friend's own benevolent powers. But if you should draw on your own
mana, then the least operation of magic from you would
reveal your hiding place to me. You may disguise your
being and your face, but you cannot change the temper of
your own proper magic. That is a sign that I, Tremien of
Whitehorn, can surely read, for the knowledge of magic and
the knowledge of my land have always been my special cares."

Tremien paced as if he expected at least one of the three to speak, but the sorcerers kept their silence. Idoradas shifted from foot to foot; the other two remained immobile. Stepping closer to them, Tremien continued: "This will be no news to you, Jilhukrihain: even now a most formidable force is making its way into the valley, heading for my keep. We are preparing our defenses to meet the challenge, desperate though the battle promises to be." He stopped a few paces away from Jondan, who kept his eyes steady on Tremien. Sparks of anger burned in them, and two hectic spots of color began to show in the Sea Mage's lean, pale cheeks.

"I will not hide from you," Tremien continued, "the fact that we have dissent among us. You always count on that, I think: the disagreement of minds still free to think for themselves. At any rate, the magi of Vanislach, learned ones whose knowledge I respect and whose word I trust, were opposed to my ordering your execution—for, no more than you, did they know that the executions were a sham. The professors of magic fear that if you are dead the Shadow Guard will prove immeasurably too strong for us; and I know that if the Shadow Guard comes close enough, the one of you who is now the Great Dark One will himself gain almost infinite magical power.

"Such, I must admit, was one of the considerations that led me to stay my hand, to pretend to sentence you to death. But you, Jilhukrihain, were too clever for me again. You knew that I would not willingly strike down the innocent along with the guilty. I must admit that I admire your nerve, for it took courage to submit to the swing of a headsman's ax, even though in your heart you must have suspected you would come to no real harm. I expected you to use your magic and reveal yourself, and by refraining from doing so, you won the day. You knew that I would not kill you, though I think you must admit that I frightened you."

Again Tremien paused. "Nothing to say? Gloating over your cleverness, are you? Do not be too quick to call yourself the final winner, Jilhukrihain, for now we have another alternative; one that will spare your life and the lives of the two who are innocent." Tremien turned and nodded to

Barach. The stout gray-bearded mage nodded in return, went to the side door, and opened it.

"Jeremy Moon of Earth," Tremien said, his voice raised, his tone somewhere between a summons and an announcement.

Jeremy came in, his hair and beard still damp from the weather, but his magical silvery-gray robe already dry and neat. Jeremy came to Tremien's elbow and waited quietly there, his intense hazel gaze on the three wizards before him. Of the three, only Jondan met his eyes, and his gaze was haughty, scornful.

Tremien spoke again: "You have all met Jeremy; you all know of his past and of how he came to Thaumia from distant Earth." A jarring peal of thunder interrupted the old mage for a moment. When it had grumbled away, he said, "But you may not know of the peculiar nature of Jeremy's *mana*. I have never seen its like; nor has anyone in Thaumia, I suspect, for long ages past. It partakes of two worlds, and in its strangeness it will challenge even the ingenuity of such an old fox as Jilhukrihain himself.

"And Jeremy is the one who will solve the problem we now face with you, Jilhukrihain, whoever you may be. In a way, your own creatures have given us the clue we needed. The Shadow Guard are a threat to all of Thaumia because they drain magical power. But what they do by nature can be imitated by magic; their function can be duplicated by a suitable spell. Jeremy?"

Jeremy cleared his throat. He spoke softly but with obvious assurance: "Mage Tremien asked if I could formulate a Great Spell to imitate the power of the Shadow Guard—but in a focused way. With Barach's aid, I have done that now. None of you will be harmed by it, at least not physically. But when I have spoken it, you will all be taken from this keep and will be put in safe places in distant corners of Cronbrach. You will then be harmless. And if the Shadow Guard begins to make its way toward one of you with the aim of replenishing your *mana*, your identity will be revealed; then the guilty one, and that one only, will be put to death."

"What is this boy preparing to do to us?" Jondan demanded, so loudly that Idoradas actually jumped at the sound of the sorcerer's angry voice.

"It is plain enough. He will drain your *mana*," Barach

said. "Jeremy told you exactly what he is about. He will make each of you utterly and permanently mundane. Such a thing is possible." He spread his arms and his untidy mustache lifted in a sardonic smile. "As you all know, I myself lost my magic in the Hag's Uprising. Behold! I am proof that one may live without magic."

"No!" It was Celissa, her brimming eyes raised now, her sweet voice anguished. "Mage Tremien, do not do this thing. Better that I be dead than powerless. Think not of me, but of my people! Without my enchantments, the forest of Saboy will fall again to jungle; the thousands of lives that depend on me will be at greatest peril."

"You would rob us of our talents?" Jondan demanded, fury hot in his words. "You would disregard all the good we have done for the people of Cronbrach—for you yourself, Tremien—on mere suspicion?"

"We have no alternative," Tremien said in a voice that was not unkind, though it was unyielding. "None, at least, other than the one you know I will not choose. If you have a different and better way, then tell me. But you must tell me now."

Idoradas raised a timid hand, like a schoolboy before a harsh master. He seemed to realize the childishness of the gesture and dropped his hand, blushing. When he spoke, his voice was tremulous and marred by an unaccustomed stammer: "I . . . I have a suggestion. Could . . . could you not merely send us to different places, as we are? And . . . and then if the Shadow Guard changes course and . . . and tries to make for one of us, then . . ." He left the thought unfinished.

"No," Barach said. "That would not do. For one thing, the Great Dark One has some control over the creatures that we do not understand. If Celissa, say, were the Great Dark One and ordered the Guard to travel toward you, Idoradas, they would do so. We would be misled, you would die, and the enemy still would escape us."

"And there is another concern," Tremien put in. "Although I have not been aware of any testing of my wards, Jilhukrihain knows how carefully I have wrapped Whitehorn in spells. So long as he is within my walls, the worst of his evil magic is contained, its edge blunted. But I could not protect one other place so well, let alone three; and if he were out of my influence and power, the Great Dark One would be far too dangerous."

Another flash of lightning, so close that the crackle was audible a half-heartbeat before the stone-shivering thunder. "Jeremy," Tremien said, "it is almost midnight. Pray commence your spell."

Jeremy raised his hands, fingers spread—gestures were not strictly necessary for verbal spells, but they sometimes aided concentration—and in English he said, "Now commences a spell of sapping. Now I call on the forces at my command to absorb the *mana* of these before me—of Jondan, Idoradas, Celissa—"

Sebastian, seeming fascinated, mouthed some whispered words along with Jeremy, as if in sympathy with him. The room seemed to grow dimmer: and all within it felt the prickling feeling of magic at work, a tingling as if thousands of ants were running over their skin.

Another, more terrible blast of lightning and immediate thunder drowned out the English words of the spell, but Jeremy never faltered, and the maddening itch of magic grew ever stronger.

And then one of the three cried out, not in protest but in spelling. The air crackled with magic, spell fighting spell. Jeremy reeled backward, began to fall.

But before he had fallen, the Great Dark One, revealed by his magic, leapt forward to grasp the front of his robe, to haul him upright on tottering knees.

Tremien took a half-step forward.

The door slammed open; Gareth stood there, his eyes wide at the scene in the room. "They are here!" he shouted hoarsely. "It was a travel spell—they materialized in the valley. The Shadow Guard are on the mountain!"

14.

"**T**remien!" screamed the Great Dark One in a voice not at all like the one they had heard from the same throat only moments before. "You must not stay me. The Shadow Guard will destroy you, Whitehorn, and all your world if you keep me from them."

The soldiers had closed, but Tremien waved them off. "So," he said, his voice so low that it was almost lost against the sound of the raging storm outside. "Idoradas."

"I took him," the voice snarled. "He is lost now. I am Jilhukrihain, the master of Relas."

"Then you must die."

"No!" Idoradas shook the stunned Jeremy. "No. For if I die, then you, and all of Cronbrach, and finally all of Thaumia, must die too. Fool! The Shadow Guard are beyond any control but mine. And in a year's time they could swallow the whole of the world's magic."

Barach stepped closer, but the Great Dark One lifted Jeremy so that the toes of his boots dangled free of the floor—a feat of strength that seemed impossible for the thin arms of Idoradas. "No closer, Loremaster, or your pupil dies!"

"What would you have of us?" Barach said in a surprisingly even voice. "What do you offer?"

The Great Dark One licked his lips. "I want escape," he said. "Tremien, you are an old spider; indeed you are. But I am far older than you. You took me by surprise, I must admit, when you found the burning ship with my old husk aboard. And you guessed almost right. Yes, I was coming for you—but in my own time. When the summons to the Council meeting came, I stepped forth and took over the mind of your young Idoradas; and I called forth the Shadow Guard, who until that time were safely contained. It would have happened sooner or later, though I had hoped to have a year, two years, to grow strong here in Cronbrach. Now you catch me with my plans unready, my life endangered. I offer you this: let me meet the Shadow Guard, and I will contain them again. Give me leave to operate my own travel spell away from your cursed wards, and I will leave Cronbrach for Relas."

"To come again," Tremien said.

The Great Dark One grinned. "To come again. And again, and again, until your stars are right, until your precious land falls to me, yes. But take comfort in knowing that it is not this time, O spider. In knowing that you have thwarted me for this once."

"And Jeremy?" Barach asked. "What of him?"

"He is mine," the Great Dark One said.

Tremien shook his head. "No. I cannot allow that. I will risk our fortunes with the Shadow Guard. You cannot take Jeremy from Whitehorn."

"Then I will leave the whelp with you," the Great Dark One said. "But not until I have met the Guard, and not until I am away from Whitehorn Keep and your confining spells."

Barach stared at him for a long moment, then turned to Tremien. "Alas, we must trust him."

"Let him go," Tremien said to the soldiers behind the Great Dark One. "But know this, Jilhukrihain: if you do not set Jeremy free, I am coming to Relas for you."

The Great Dark One set Jeremy on his feet. The young mage stood, though he seemed weak and dazed, his eyes nearly empty. "Have them clear the way for me."

"Do as he says," Tremien ordered. "Gareth, to the walls; the defenders will have need of you."

The soldiers withdrew. Then, his arm around Jeremy almost in the posture of a lover's embrace, the Great Dark One backed from the room and turned down the hall.

"Go," Tremien said. Barach, Nul, and Sebastian hurried out the side door. To Jondan and Celissa, Tremien said, "I cannot apologize to you enough. But we are very busy now; stay here or come to the battlements as you will." And the old mage vanished.

Jondan cursed bitterly. "Well?" he asked Celissa. "What do we do now?"

"We help Tremien. of course," Celissa said, her voice raw. "What else can we do?"

The lightning showed them toiling up the hill, as did flashes of magical energies: the five alien, bizarre creatures that made up the Shadow Guard. The catapults struck them, knocking them back, physically hindering them; but they came on regardless.

They flickered now.

Each wore an aura of purplish-blue light, each was now transparent, now seemingly solid. All came on together. When one was toppled by a catapult stone, the others waited for it to right itself and make its way back up the slope.

Barach, Sebastian, and Nul ran onto the wall walk of the main gate and saw the creatures already halfway to Whitehorn Keep. Ogion of Vanislach was there at the parapet, and beside him the other professor-mages. Ogion, seeing Barach, cried out, "Lo! My theory was correct. They are becoming solid. They no longer drain magic; but they are shielded from it, and their own *mana* is building. They will be ripe for banishment at the moment they transmit that power to the Great Dark One."

"Where is he?" Nul shouted, scanning the courtyard. "Should be here now!"

Tremien appeared, flashing into existence on the walk of the inner wall, alone, a white-clad figure against the gloom of night. He beckoned.

Barach shouted, "He wants me. I must go to him." He made his way down the tower stair, across the courtyard, and past the soldiers busy with the catapults. He climbed the inner stair and joined Tremien. "Yes, Mage?" he puffed at last.

"I will need your strength," Tremien said. "Stand with me, friend."

"I am here."

And for long moments the world seemed suspended in storm and darkness.

The Great Dark One strolled beside a somnambulistic Jeremy. He crooned as he walked, his arm around the other's waist.

His voice took on a different quality and timbre. It was

soothing, oily. It was a singsong, almost a lullaby. It spoke an ancient language no longer heard on Thaumia, a tongue from old Relas that was no more, words not heard since those far-gone days when the dead continent was living and green.

He spoke a spell.

It was indeed a Great Spell, for it had endured over two thousand years.

It was a spell of transference.

One that he had spoken only a few days previously.

One that he had crooned to doomed Idoradas.

Jilhukrihain walked slowly, for it took some time to enunciate this complex spell, this enduring cantrip. And he dared not speak its three completing words within the walls of Whitehorn, for Tremien's power could yet thwart the spell's operation.

But in the courtyard, that was another matter.

He would have power enough in the open, just as soon as the Shadow Guard were within a thousand paces of him. Power such as he had felt hundreds of years ago, power that he had absorbed after the fall of Relas, would be his again.

And this time the world would be his as well.

Beside him the young man walked on the loose legs of a somnambulist.

The Great Dark One crooned lovingly to him and paced slowly onward.

"They are coming," Gareth cried.

It took the catapult operators time to reload and respell their machines—not much time, but enough to allow the Guard to make some progress after every salvo, always a little closer. Across the court Tremien stood, his staff upraised in his right hand, his left arm thrown around the shoulders of Barach, who stood sturdy as a pillar in the maddening wind.

Ogion shook his head. "Hopeless! They are not fully material yet. If they reach the gate, they may be able to drain all of Whitehorn's magic. They must be kept away a little longer."

"We can't do it!"

Nul looked up at Sebastian. "Was something in book," he said. "Something about heroes."

But a shout on the walk drew all attention away. The great door had opened, and from it came a gray-robed figure and another one, that of Idoradas. Only now—

Barach shouted something. "What?" Gareth said, cupping his hand behind his ear.

"Open gate, he said," Nul screeched. "Open main gate, let Great Dark One out."

Gareth looked at Ogion. The academic nodded. "It is best. We can work our spell from here." And he and the others from Vanislach began to chant.

The wind caught the syllables of their spell and muffled them. They came at short intervals, like the snapping of a flag in a gale.

The catapult operators below had drawn to the far wall, leaving the courtyard clear.

Gareth gave the order to the two guardians, the gargoyles. Operated by their will and its own magic, the ponderous gate swung open, smoothly even against the blasts of the unholy wind. Down the slopes, not more than two thousand paces away, the Guard toiled upward, illuminated by the lightning and by their own flickering halos of magic building to a climax.

The Great Dark One and Jeremy passed from the sight of those on the wall, then emerged outside Whitehorn Keep, on the short stretch of level roadway that followed a shoulder of the mountain before it began to wind downward.

The discharge of magic around the coming Guard brightened.

The Great Dark One took his stand there, waited until the Guard had come a little nearer.

Those on the wall saw him grasp Jeremy's shoulders, spin the young man to face him.

And then—

Something happened.

The moment had come. Jilhukrihain turned his captive, so that he could look into the eyes. It always had to be thus, just at the moment of possession; he had to see the eyes.

He pronounced the last three words of his spell: "Jeremy Sebastian Moon."

The name.

That was the cantrip that activated the whole, the spade that planted the seed in the victim. The true name made the next host irrevocably and forever the Great Dark One's own.

The eyes blinked.

The face smiled.

Jeremy reached up and—

"No!" Jilhukrihain screamed.

—peeled away the false beard.

"Sebastian," said the young man in his grasp. And now he spoke in English, a tongue that Jilhukrihain could not possibly understand. "Sebastian Magister, you son of a bitch."

Jilhukrihain struck him across the face, so hard that Sebastian tumbled down the slope at the road's edge. The Great Dark One looked wildly downward. They were coming, not quite close enough, just a few paces short—

He cried out another spell, this one screamed in desperation.

"Now!" Nul shouted. "Do it now, Jeremy!"

And Jeremy, wearing Sebastian's clothes, did the only thing he could think of. He cried out in English, in the powerful language of magic, "They come from the past! The heroes who shaped my life—and they fight against darkness and evil!"

His breath was snatched from him. He had a dizzy moment of semiconsciousness and came to himself on hands and knees. Already hands were on him, pulling him up. He gasped, trying to make his lungs work. Magic had poured from him, in a rush the like of which he had never before felt. And though he did not know what it was, something had happened.

"What that?" Nul yelled.

He heard them then, the horns, playing music, real music, on the air of the storm. The tune was a stirring gallop played in a pounding rhythm—

"My God," Gareth said, pointing.

He stood on a parapet of the wall, alone, a lean man dressed all in green, illuminated by some inner light of his own. The storm howled around him in madness, but not even the jaunty feather in his cap was disturbed. He reached behind him, took an arrow from his quiver, nocked it, drew, and released.

The bolt sprang from his longbow in a streak of flame. It sang through the air even louder than the storm, true and straight and fine. It pierced the leader of the Shadow Guard—

And the leader halted, frozen, immobile, the crackling of magic around it dimmed.

The archer was gone.

"There," said someone to Jeremy's left.

He came up behind them, a rider on a white horse, a rider dressed in silvery gray and masked. Without slowing, he drew and fired his weapon. The second of the Guard stopped, held by a stronger magic than any it had absorbed, pinned to its place by something Thaumia had never known. By a bullet.

And only Jeremy knew it was made of silver.

And then there was a man clothed like a king, wearing a golden crown, right before the next of the Guard. When the creature was close enough, the figure raised a great shining sword, drew it back, and took one slashing blow.

Excalibur stopped the third Guard.

A girl in gingham, an animated scarecrow, and a man made out of tin threw a bucket of water on the fourth. It sagged in its tracks as though melting.

And that left only the last of them, still doggedly coming on through the tempest. The man who appeared in front of it was ridiculously small by comparison, and he was the most oddly dressed of any of the specters yet seen, wearing blue tights and a billowing red cape.

He simply punched the last of the Guard.

It fell over.

Then they were gone, all of them, the heroes Jeremy had somehow summoned from childhood memory, from nostalgic dreams. He blinked, his face wet with rain and with something more. The book had been right, after all: there had been giants on the mountain.

It had happened in a heartbeat, all of it. Jeremy, still shaky, saw the Great Dark One spin toward him, felt those malevolent eyes on his own, saw the hands clutch into impotent, threatening claws. Then the Great Dark One ran down toward the Guard, his voice screaming, faint over the wind, speaking in an unknown tongue. The light of magic began to swirl around the inert Guard again.

A great billow of light flashed from the figures, a silent explosion of power.

Ogion cried out and pointed his staff. The air sizzled, and

down the slope the Guard shimmered, glowed, and then vanished.

Jeremy heard another voice, that of Tremien. And he saw the figure of the Great Dark One crumple in the roadway. The light from the Guard had resolved itself into a spinning galaxy. It dipped toward Jilhukrihain, hesitated, and lifted again, above his wailing form. It swept over the front wall of the castle, its passage as hot and as disturbing as a near-miss lightning bolt.

"We have to kill him," Gareth said. "Archers!"

The roadway had gone dark with the passage of that spinning galaxy of magic. Lightning illuminated it again, showing them Jilhukrihain rising to his hands and knees. Bows sang. Most of the arrows went badly, snatched by the wind. Four of them struck true.

Jeremy turned away, unable to watch.

"Again!" Gareth shouted. One of the Vanislach wizards conjured wizard-light. Jeremy heard the bowstrings twang once more.

"Not working," Nul said. "Not killing him."

Jeremy looked back. Jilhukrihain stood with no fewer than seven arrows in him, five through his chest and two in his left thigh. His face was wrenched into a mask of hatred, and his mouth moved as he spat out some new spell.

Jondan was suddenly on the walk beside Jeremy. "Let me," he said, and he shouted out a spell of his own.

The clouds answered.

Jeremy would see it again and again in his sleep: the lightning bolt, nearly straight from sky to ground, that enveloped the form on the road below. It was instantaneous, less than an eyeblink—but in Jeremy's memory the blackened figure of Jilhukrihain, surrounded by that white-hot purifying light, was stamped for the rest of his life.

They all stumbled downstairs and through the open gate then. The rain began to fall, unregarded by anyone. They stood in a loose circle around the blackened corpse.

Sebastian Magister came clawing up the hillside. The wind whipped Jeremy's silver-gray robe around him. Jeremy went and extended his arm, helping him up. "That was something," Sebastian said. He clutched in his left hand a sodden thing, like the pelt of a small and mangy animal: Winyard's prized false beard.

"You're a mess. I thought he'd knocked your head off."

Sebastian rubbed his cheek. Already his eye was puffed and swelling. "So did I. You should have seen his face, though, when he realized he'd wasted his spell."

"You sold him," Jeremy said.

"Well . . . we did. Both of us together."

They went to the fringe of the circle and looked again at the fallen form. The wind was insane now, and they stood against it only with difficulty. Sebastian put his mouth close to Jeremy's ear. "I don't have much time left," he said. "Just until dawn, if the book was right. Better get me out of this. Send me back to Gateway, and then come as soon as you can."

"I don't know if I have any magic left. But I'll try." The two of them stepped away from the rest and Jeremy pronounced his travel cantrip. Sebastian vanished—and the wind seemed to die down too, just a bit.

Nul tugged at Jeremy's arm. "Come," he said.

Jeremy, still half-numb, followed the pika. Barach and Tremien were still atop the inner wall of Whitehorn Keep, Tremien slumped against the parapet, Barach supporting him. The master of Whitehorn gave Jeremy an uncertain smile. "We have done it at last," he said in words Jeremy almost had to read on his lips. "I have reached out and sought him, and I find him nowhere. The Great Dark One is dead at last, truly dead."

And then Tremien said an odd thing.

"Peace to his spirit," he whispered. "And long rest."

Then Tremien fell.

15

Jeremy leapt forward, and with Barach he caught Tremien. At the same instant, the clouds that had been building over Whitehorn broke suddenly in lashing waves of sustained rain that thundered on walls and roofs.

"We'd better get him inside," Barach bellowed above the din. Somehow, holding on to Tremien and each other, they staggered through the tower doorway, down the stair, and into the Keep.

Jeremy, drenched, began to shiver. The room was dark and deserted, its accustomed wizard-light extinguished. "It's awfully quiet," he said through chattering teeth. "Do you suppose Tremien is—?"

"I think," Barach said, "that we should take him to his rooms."

They got him there somehow or other, and the healer Tintaniel was waiting for them. She had them put Tremien on the bed, and then shooed them away. Barach stayed just outside the door, but Jeremy went to his own apartment, where he found Kelada already waiting for him.

After a time they drew apart. Kelada smiled and wiped her eyes. "I'd better get to Zarad-zellikol now," she said. "No telling what the pikas have been feeding my baby." She promised to return in the morning, as soon as Emily was awake. Jeremy sent her on her way with some regret, for he felt hollow and lonely. Sitting in a chair, cold and wet, Jeremy did not sleep exactly, but he fell into a sort of doze.

He woke with a start, shying away from some dark grasping thing—

"Oh," he said. "It's you."

Nul nodded, his orange eyes wide in the dimness. "Need

you. You come," he said. "You have to talk to Mage Tremien, tell him not time to die."

Jeremy followed the pika through the oddly dark, hushed castle. The door to Tremien's bedroom was open. The room was crowded, packed: Barach, of course, and Gareth; old Radusilf; Jondan and Celissa; Ogion and his entourage from Vanislach. And dozens of others, it seemed. And stretched out on his bed, quite still, was the pale form of Tremien, silent as a tombstone effigy.

Jeremy felt his throat tighten. Others parted for him as he came to the bedside, as he reached to take the old mage's hand. Tremien's eyelids fluttered and opened, and the brown eyes looked piercingly at Jeremy. "It is over at last," the old man murmured.

Tears stung Jeremy's eyes. "No, Mage Tremien. You have much left to do. There is a world to heal."

Tremien's chest began to spasm. The old lips parted. The mustache fluttered.

And the Master of Whitehorn laughed.

"Of course there is," he said in a voice his own, though still very weak and faint. "My word, did you imagine that I lay here ready to give up the ghost simply because that troublesome Jilhukrihain has finally been laid to rest? I am tired, my boy, not dying."

He sighed, and the sigh seemed to pass through everyone in the room: a relaxation of tension, an easing of anxiety. "But my days as Chief Mage are over," he said. "I have done hurt to those I would protect. More practically, I could not bear to work any more wonders like the last. We shall have to attend to the election of a new Chief Mage soon."

The healer, Tintaniel, put her hand on Tremien's forehead. "Be that as it may, you must rest now. Plans and plottings later! Sleep and recovery for tonight, what little remains of it."

She shooed them out, but not before Tremien's remonstration: "There are things to do. I suspect that young Sebastian direly needs to return to Earth; and I, for one, would be glad to see an improvement in the weather—" The doors closed on the last of his remark. Jeremy heard his name called from somewhere ahead through the crowd. He pushed his way through, and in a moment he found himself embracing Kelada.

"Emily woke up?" he asked in surprise.

"I woke her, stupid." And she was kissing him hard, holding him tight. Jeremy did not even mind that Nul, standing close by, gave the operation his full attention.

The dispossessed crowd of Tremien's retainers and friends adjourned to the Great Hall, which Jeremy made cheerful with wizard-light. "I suppose Tremien was right," Jeremy said to Barach. "It's time to get Sebastian back to Earth. If I don't do it before daylight, I may find myself banished from Thaumia instead. Are you going?"

"I think not," Barach said. "Why not take Kelada, though? She has not seen the Gate, and it occurs to me that you will have much to tell each other on the way."

"A wonderful suggestion," Kelada said, nibbling Jeremy's ear.

Good Lord, he thought. Can you do *that* in a travel spell?

"Jeremy," Barach said, "I think you had better go now."

"You're sure you don't want to come with us?" Jeremy said, hoping his insincerity did not show.

Barach, who was still bedraggled from the downpour, shook his head. "Not while my old friend is ill. But you had best make some speed; all the magic loose here may influence your spell on the Gate."

"I don't want any more mix-ups," Jeremy said. "Come on, Kelada, and I'll show you the Gate."

"Wait!" came a querulous little voice. "Nul go too."

"Certainly," Kelada said.

"You've been already," Jeremy protested to the pika.

Nul gave them his startling ear-to-ear grin. "Ya, ya, but like to go again. We talk English while we on the way?"

Jeremy sighed. "Sure," he said. "I don't want to make you mad."

"Mad," Nul said. "Mad as a hatter."

"Close, but not quite right," Jeremy said in Presolatan. "All right, if you have to go, come with us to the courtyard and I'll work on your English as we travel."

"Is the weather bad all over Thaumia?" Jeremy asked.

He, Nul, and Kelada had materialized before the Gate, in the presence of his double. The wind troubled the tops of the palmlike trees, and thunder already growled in the clouds. Sebastian, who had been sitting next to a fitful campfire,

stood at their appearance. "I think it probably is," he said.
"And if I don't get back, it's going to be worse."

"Are you ready to go?"

Sebastian touched his face. He had a black eye well along
in bloom. "I should get this attended to by magic first. I
can't think of any way to explain it to Cassie."

"I'm no healer, but let me give it a try." Jeremy considered and then spoke a beefsteak spell in English, couched in
the terms of an ad for a supermarket sale of the century.
Sebastian rolled his good eye at it, but the swelling subsided
and the bruise began to lighten. Within a few seconds he
was gingerly probing his cheek and eye socket with his
fingers.

"That seems to have done it," he said. "Maybe you're a
better wizard than I thought."

"And you're a better advertising man. You really used
the oblique sell on the Great Dark One."

Sebastian nodded. "You could call it that, I guess. But it's
hard to believe he's finally dead."

In English, Jeremy said with a grin, "He's not only merely
dead, he's really most sincerely dead."

Nul perked up at once. "Say again," he demanded, and
when Jeremy did, Nul repeated the words over and over in
his strange accent.

"Nul told me you were teaching him English," Sebastian
said. "But he didn't say how well he could speak it."

"Yes, well, he's got a lot of surprises up his sleeve,"
Jeremy said dryly. "We'd better change clothes and get you
back through the Gate."

Kelada obligingly stepped a few paces away as the men
undressed and passed clothing back and forth, but Nul saw
no reason to stray and stood there watching. "How is
Tremien?" Sebastian asked as he pulled his trousers on.

"Weak. Weaker than I've ever seen him. I hope he will
be able to recover—"

"Talk English," Nul said.

"Okay, okay." Shrugging the familiar robe into place,
Jeremy repeated his hope in English.

Sebastian nodded. "I think he will be. Tremien is a resil-
ient old ba . . . old fellow, with a lot of reserves to draw on.
Did you see him working his spell at the end? I wonder
what it was for. Powerful, that's for sure; it raised my hair

on end when Jilhukrihain dragged me out under where Tremien stood. But he's right about losing the position of Chief Mage; he won't have it in him anymore."

"I wonder who will be next," Jeremy said. Then with a blush, he added, "By the way, good luck on your campaign back in Atlanta. I'd better tell you all about the great debate."

Sebastian listened, at first with a scowl, then with growing amusement, and finally with laughter. "I'll be damned," he said at last. "So you used my catchphrase?"

"It worked," Jeremy said with some defensiveness.

"It would. That spot's sold more Kiwis than anything the company ever tried before. Of course, I can't agree with all your policies, but it doesn't sound as if you gave me too much of a problem. Maybe you even gave me a whole new slant on the campaign."

Nul tugged Jeremy's sleeve. "Who the hell are *you*?" he asked in a parrotlike squawk. Jeremy swatted at him, not seriously, and Sebastian laughed harder than ever.

As they finished dressing, they talked briefly of half a dozen other things: of the phantom warriors Jeremy had conjured from his memory of childhood heroes, of the *William Tell* overture played by ghostly horns, of the power of belief, of the Great Dark One's foolish complacency. "I was positive we could do it," Sebastian said. "And that was a good idea you had, borrowing the false beard from Winyard."

"He'll be angry because you trimmed it," Jeremy said. "Lucky that the Great Dark One fell for the trick."

Sebastian zipped his fly, to the absorbed interest of Nul, to whom zippers were a baffling kind of Earth magic. "Well, it was a safe-enough risk. I knew Jilhukrihain wouldn't have noticed us in that mob at the execution—hell, if your head was about to be chopped off, would you study the faces in the crowd? And of course he didn't know that you had shaved. We really put him on the spot. By the way, that was a nice touch that you added, supplying the feeling of magic at work as I spoke the fake draining spell. Anyway, once we shook Jilhukrihain up, he simply never had time to remember that we're so identical that even he couldn't distinguish between us. Hiding in another's skin. It's his own trick, really—and that's why he had no defense against it."

With a quizzical smile Jeremy said, "I seem to recall your

accusing me of wanting to be a hero. Seems to me I'm not the one who did the heroic act."

Sebastian shook his head. "No idea what you mean."

"Well, I was in the Great Dark One's clutches once before. There's nothing—literally nothing—that would make me get as close to him again as you did. That took courage, Sebastian. And I appreciate it."

"But you and Tremien did the magic."

"But you had the guts to go through with the impersonation."

Sebastian looked away. "Maybe I was wrong about you earlier."

"The feeling," Jeremy said, "is mutual."

"What the hell. Maybe your world needs heroes every once in a long while. Somebody to shake things up. Somebody to be so idiotically good that everyone else sees the measure of what people can be."

Jeremy looked at the man, so much like him, for a long time. "Maybe both of our worlds need heroes from time to time," he said at last.

After that no one spoke for a while. Finally Sebastian broke the silence: "Well, back in Atlanta I've been missing for a whole day now. I'll have some explaining to do back home about my whereabouts."

"You'll think of something," Jeremy said. There was an awkward pause as the two faced each other, strange mirror images.

Sebastian's eyes crinkled. "Sure, I'll dream up a story." The old grin was back. "Hey, I'll even make it into an asset. I've gone into the wilderness and now I've seen the light. That sort of crap. Electorate'll eat it up." After a moment of silence, he chuckled. "If I can beat the Great Dark One, I can beat a two-bit politician like Tidburn. I'll never forget the look in Jilhukrihain's eyes when he first realized the switch we pulled. He was so damned astonished that he could be fooled. You could see, in that last second, that he knew he'd been had."

"It was such an obvious trick. Such a little thing to trip up on," Jeremy agreed. He looked down, for Nul was again pulling at his sleeve. "What is it?"

Hopefully, the little pika said, "Had as a matter?"

* * *

At length they stood before the Gate. "This is it," Jeremy said, looking through into Sebastian's darkened office. Kelada, who had returned, stood behind him and with almost frightening interest peered through into Earth.

Jeremy put an arm around her and continued to speak to Sebastian: "Once you go through alone, my spell is broken. Then the Gate goes back to random activity. I guess we won't see each other after this."

Sebastian, very rumpled in the suit Jeremy had given him, had retrieved the other bundle of his clothing from the vines where Jeremy had concealed it and had tucked it under his arm. "Well, I'll think about you from time to time. Just because the Great Dark One's gone at last, don't think you'll have it easy. There's a whole world out there, and there's still an ornery character or two in it to tame."

"Hey," Jeremy said, "you just worry about the lobbyists and the opposition party. Leave my troubles to me. Ready to go?"

"One moment," Sebastian said. He stepped to Kelada, drew her apart from the others, and kissed her on the cheek, quite chastely. Jeremy, though, could not keep a frown off his face as Sebastian whispered something to her. Then they both came back. "Well—" Sebastian put out his hand. Jeremy relaxed his features into a smile that felt strained, and then he shook hands. "So long, brother."

"Yeah," Jeremy said. He put his free hand on the other's back and gave him a gentle push.

Sebastian stepped through the Gate—

And turned just inside for a final smile and a curiously regretful wave. Then the Gate shimmered and his image was gone, swept away by a roil of colors. "Will miss him," Nul said. "Not friend like you, but"—the pika tongue struggled for a moment with an English word—"interesting."

"He is all of that," Jeremy said.

"Listen," Kelada said. "Listen to the silence."

And indeed for a moment all the world was quiet, the rushing winds finally hushed, the pattering raindrops stilled, the growls of thunder stifled before they burst from the clouds. But the silence did not endure, for almost at once it was replaced by the sounds of a tropic night. All around them rose the discord of insects, the distant booming, mooing cries of dragons, the thin and even more distant shrilling of unicorns, all the sounds of a magical night in a magical world. Jeremy took a deep breath. "Well, let's get home," he said.

The morning of their second day back at Whitehorn found Tremien much improved. Jeremy and Kelada saw him after breakfast, the old man propped up in bed on half a dozen down pillows, his pallor replaced by his customary saddle-brown complexion. "Well," he said in a deep voice much more like his own than his earlier husking whisper, "the sky has cleared, so I imagine your twin is back in his place on Earth."

"That's where I left him," Jeremy said.

Tremien cocked his head. "You look much younger without your beard, you know."

Jeremy scraped a hand over his stubbly cheek. "I know. That's why I'm letting it grow in again."

"Meanwhile," Kelada said with a scratchy nuzzle, "I suffer."

"Well, well, things are in order again. Ogion tells me the Shadow Guard are gone forever, sealed back in their own strange universe. More, I have felt recovered enough this morning to probe a bit wider than I did after the battle: and the Great Dark One has truly vanished for good. At last he has achieved his old dream. He has beaten death, by the simple expedient of dying." Tremien sniffed. "I must admit that for a short while I thought of going the same way, but a clear morning brings a clear head, Barach says, and now I'm quite reconciled to living a bit longer. I've all manner of reading to do, and it's been ages since I did anything just for the fun of it. I mean to have a bit of fun now." The brown eyes were sharp and bright. "I expect there will still be enough to keep you younger mages busy."

"Don't number me among the mages," Jeremy said. "It's a courtesy title with me."

"Nonsense," Kelada said. "You're as good as any of them."

"Your wife is right, Jeremy. You are, you know. Your remarkable spells have proved that." For a moment Tremien was silent, though he seemed on the verge of saying something else. At last he came out with it: "You are truly a mage now, Jeremy, and no longer a student. Your apprenticeship is ended."

"But Barach is my teacher," Jeremy said. "If my studies are over, he should tell me that—"

"No," Tremien said gently. "Barach will have other duties soon. He will be Chief Mage of Cronbrach-en-Hof, serving in my stead. The Council gave him their voice this morning. He has already agreed, and I am glad of it, for he is a man with a heart wise in the ways of kindness."

A lump had somehow formed in Jeremy's throat. He tried to swallow it. "Barach, Chief Mage? But I thought—"

Tremien lifted a thin hand. "He has already agreed," he repeated. "Of course, he will stay here in Whitehorn with me. And I hope that you and Kelada will agree to remain as well. Oh, I'm sure you'll have your journeys and your quests to undertake from time to time—Barach tells me he'd like to set about reclaiming the lost continent of Relas as soon as may be, and all that—but I would be glad of your company."

Jeremy looked at Kelada, then back at Tremien. "Of course," he said. "Where else could we go?"

Tremien laughed. "Where else, indeed? Kelada, you really must try to tell this husband of yours what a celebrity he's getting to be. Maker of plays, teller of tales, and now full mage. My boy, you could go anywhere! But pray don't; not for a while, at least. It will give a retired old man joy to have a substitute granddaughter about to spoil."

Kelada stepped forward and kissed Tremien on the forehead; the wizard actually blushed. "We wouldn't think of leaving Whitehorn," she said.

Later that morning Jeremy and Kelada strolled out into the broad forecourt, where Barach and Nul stood looking down over the valley. Gareth and his men had been busy. Nothing remained of the weird battle, not even a stray arrow. Kelada carried Emily, who squirmed with her wish to get down and do some serious crawling. From over the main gate Fred, the younger of the guardian gargoyles, cried out: "A splendid day, *Mage* Jeremy!"

Hearing the special emphasis on the title, Jeremy darted a mock-irritated glance up at the sandstone figure. "News travels fast in Whitehorn Keep," he growled.

Busby, the older and more sedate of the two, responded

imperturbably, "The walls have ears." His eaglelike beak seemed to carry the hint of a smirk.

Barach, who had taken Emily from Kelada, laughed. "In the case of those two scamps, that is literally true," he said. "Do you know, the world seems curiously altered today. I am reminded of the story of Adelart the Storm King, the mage who specialized in weather. Challenged once to display his powers, Adelart stood on the pinnacle of a mountain and spoke a spell; instantly the sky darkened, a hurricane of wind howled, lightning shivered the stones around him, hailstones as big as my fist pelted the onlookers—and then the sky was clear and he wore a rainbow around his shoulders. When someone cried out in admiration, Adelart looked down at him with a frown. 'At least,' Adelart said, 'have the courtesy to wait until I get *started*.' "

"Something starting?" Nul asked.

Barach heaved a great sigh. "Jeremy, your child is more susceptible to instruction than this overgrown mole."

Emily had thrust two fingers in her mouth and had grown calm, her eyes intent on Barach's bushy eyebrows. She seemed to recognize the reference to her and smiled around her fingers.

"Oh, Nul has his points," Jeremy said. He looked out over the valley. The river far below rushed white over stones, made its way through sheltering coppices of great trees, watered the lush green fields of the farms—all was summer-green and growing, except for the ugly gray scar off to the west that marked the passage of the Shadow Guard. "That will need healing," Jeremy said.

"Yes, there is much to do," Barach agreed. "Celissa and Jondan are back to the south, doing what they can to reknit the lines of magical force. And others from Vanislach will join them soon. We have our own troubles here to see to. Tremien's spells faltered a bit last night and need mending. The road, too, will have lost its beneficent enchantment; I must see about remedying that soon."

Jeremy turned to his old teacher. "You? Forgive me, Barach, but I thought the Chief Mage had to . . . well, had to have his own magic."

Barach lifted an inquiring eyebrow. "Well?"

"Well, you haven't. You lost your—" Jeremy broke off. "What don't I know?"

Barach smiled and whispered something softly, the way he had pronounced his minor spells in the old days. Jeremy felt an odd tug, cried out in surprise—

And found himself floating in air twenty-five feet above the courtyard, almost level with the leering faces of the gargoyles atop their gate. He bobbed like a toy balloon at the end of its string. "You fraud!" he bawled out. "What happened?"

Barach's eyes twinkled up at him from below. "It was Tremien's doing," he called. "He realized that the Guard's major function was not destruction; their real purpose was to channel *mana* to the Great Dark One; and in that last magnificent spell he wrought, Tremien simply redirected the flow. I have been, so to speak, recharged. Levitation spells, as I believe I remarked to you some time ago, are really quite simple."

Jeremy made swimming motions, which resulted in his going into a lazy spin. "Get me down!"

But before Barach could speak again, Kelada tugged at his arm and said something too softly for Jeremy to catch. Jeremy saw the old man nod, then saw his lips move—and then, with a girlish laugh, Kelada floated up to him. He reached for her, took her hands in his, and pulled her close. Their spin increased a bit, something like a stately midair waltz. Jeremy said to Kelada, "I suppose he *will* let us down?"

"Oh, eventually," she said, her elfin face wrinkled in a smile of pure mischief. She threw her head back, her blond hair gleaming in the sun, and looked all about her with wide and delighted eyes. "What a lovely view!"

"Yes," he said, looking at her. "Kelada, I've been wondering about something. You have to tell me—what was it that Sebastian whispered to you just before he left?"

She kissed the tip of his nose. "Oh, you're jealous. I'm so glad."

"It's not that I'm jealous—but I am. Come on, what was it?"

"Well, perhaps I should keep it secret. You might be more interesting jealous. But that would be cruel, I suppose. He told me to take care of you. He said behind every hero there's a good woman. And he said you'd say that's sentimentality and nonsense."

"I think not," Jeremy said.

From far below them on the ground their daughter laughed in glee, and they heard Nul's strange urfing chuckle. But for the moment they paid no attention, lost in each other as they embraced, as they kissed, as they slowly revolved together in the delirious and beautiful air of morning.

AUTHOR'S NOTE:
The Naming of Names

A few readers who have been interested enough to follow Jeremy Moon's adventures in the magical universe of Thaumia have asked about the unusual mixture of names evident in the stories. Some names, they point out, are odd and even grotesque; the Great Dark One's true name of Jilhukrihain, for example. Other names are understandable, like Melodia or Whitehorn. Why the disparity?

Well, to begin with, Jeremy, Tremien, and almost all of their friends are not really speaking "English"; they are speaking the common language of the continents of Finarr and Cronbrach-en-Hof, a tongue called Standard Presolatan. No one today would believe that the humble island of Versolt, the rocky home of a seafaring race, was once the center of a proud empire, but so it was, ages and ages ago, back in the days when the human occupation of Thaumia was still tentative at best; back in the time before the birth of the Great Dark One himself.

In that long-forgotten era the island was called Presolat, and according to legend, its people were the first humans to make the heady discovery that magic could be shaped and bent by spoken spells. One must temper belief, however, with the fact that the Presolatans were the ones who eventually wrote the histories. At any rate, they did know of the power of magic and, turning the knowledge to aggressive use, they rapidly conquered two sparsely populated continents. In the years that followed, as their island became the wealthy center of empire, so their tongue became the common speech of both northern lands.

But times change, and so do languages. Revolts occurred, the empire declined, and eventually Versolt emerged as the sleepy backwater it is today. Over the centuries the language changed too—for the worse, according to the grammarians, and for the better, according to those who see the modern tongue as simple and direct and the ancient one as tedious and complex. The Presolatan of today is quite different in grammar, intonation, and vocabulary from ancient Presolatan.

However, to this day many place names are in the old, or High, variety of the language; even though to the modern speaker such names are quite meaningless except as names. Vaskflod and Bronfal, two of the rivers mentioned, may serve as examples. In High Presolatan, "Vaskflod" means "Wide Water," with the connotation of fresh, not salt, water. "Bronfal" can be rendered as "Dry-leaf Stream" and probably refers to the muddy brown color the river assumes in the coastal plain. Indeed, north of its junction with the Black River, the Bronfal loses its original designation and is called the Apfol by the local inhabitants of the Westforest Downs. "Apfol" is a Modern Presolatan name that translates as "White River"; it refers to the appearance of the stream as it spills out from the Wizard's Mountains in a series of whitewater rapids, in strong contrast to the dark color of the Piksfol, the Black River, a tributary stream that flows southwest from the Five Fens over a bed of ancient black stone.

In Modern Presolatan, however, many terms like Bronfal and Vaskflod are archaic and without meaning, save as names, and so I have presented them "as is." Had the place names kept pace with the language, "Bronfal" would today be rendered as something like "Beronlafol" and "Vaskflod" as "Vestfol"; but such modernization has not happened in Presolatan, and so I have left the older names alone.

As an analogy, we see the same kind of thing in English. When we say "New York," few of us pause to recall the Duke of York for whom the city and state were named; when we say "Pennsylvania," we do not think of "Penn's forestland"; when we see the name "Strickland," we have no reason to remember that it means, or once meant, "cow pasture." Even though we could, with a little effort, decipher the meanings behind these names, for the most part we content ourselves by using them merely as names.

However, some proper names are good current English.

No one need be told what the name of Bad Axe, Michigan, literally means, for example. The same holds true for Horse Thief, Arizona; Plain Dealing, Louisiana; and Wounded Knee, South Dakota. Similarly, some names in the series are good Modern Presolatan. Melodia's "real" name, "Lelinivel," can be translated into English as "harmonious" or, better, as "melodic." "Melodia" seems to be a good rendering. Similarly, the Modern Presolatan "Weskabola" can be exactly transcribed into English as "Broadpools." Since these names would make descriptive sense to anyone speaking the same language as Jeremy, Tremien, et al., I have rendered them as English.

Still other names are semirecognizable. The word "Thaumia," for example, is commonly used to mean "the world"; but "Druskenton," the original High Presolatan word from which it came, had other connotations as well, one of which was "magic." Further, as it has to come to be used by speakers of Presolatan, the name can be extended to encompass all of creation, not just the planet. We have no exactly correspondent word in English; some coinage like "Magic-Cosmos" or "Enchantment-Creation" would perhaps come closest. But that is reaching, and it still lacks the full sense of the Presolatan name. I have settled for "Thaumia," since it sounds like a place name, comes from "thaumaturgy," an old word for human-wrought (as opposed to natural) magic, and has a faintly archaic ring to it. Such compromises are sometimes necessary.

In addition to traces of Old High Presolatan, there are fossil remnants of other languages here and there in the books, for before the time of the Presolatan Conquest each city-state or minor kingdom had its own dialect or even language; and the Presolatan Empire never extended to the two southern continents, where, of course, unknown tongues were spoken. For that matter, the Great Dark One's real name is in one of these ancient tongues, a southern speech now dead; the same language gave Relas, the southeastern continent, its name. By the way, no one, not even that indefatigable scholar Barach, is certain what "Relas" once meant, though he guesses that it was something like "The Land." Most individuals, he observes, are firmly convinced that their land and people are the only true land and people.

Even in the lands of the north, occasionally words in

these ancient dead languages have survived. The word *gisrel*, "inherent or potential magic," is an example; it was adopted by the Versolt Islanders from the tongue of another island people, the Askalandri, and has not changed its form in generations. To represent it in English, I chose a similar exotic locution: the Maori "mana," which has much the same meaning and a similarly unusual ring to it, at least to my ear.

But the most common survivals of other languages in Presolatan come in the form of place names. Arkhedden Forest, for example, is a slightly worn-down version of a much older name, "Arakihet-tan," a name which in the speech of the ancient Vonns meant "Greatest Forest." The speakers of Presolatan merely append their word for "forest," "wolt," to "Arkhedden" and produce "Arkhedden Wolt" as the modern name for the remnant of a woodland that once covered almost all the eastern part of the continent from the Bone Mountains south to the fall line.

There are other linguistic oddities here. Strictly speaking, the portion of the forest east of the Bronfal River is simply another part of Arkhedden, but it has acquired its own name, Estowolt, the East Forest. The fact that the valley of the Black River lies west of the East Forest allows that area to be called Westforest Downs, though it is east of a larger forest, the Arkhedden. There is little logic apparent here, but such is often the case with the vagaries of language.

Of course, if one does insist on strict logic, "Arkhedden Forest" means "Greatest Forest Forest," but as the present population has quite forgotten the original language, that troubles no one. Similar fossils from long-dead languages are Akrador, the name of a great gravel desert in the south and west of Cronbrach; Ranfora, a harbor town of great antiquity and still a thriving deep-water seaport; and the Kothora River, a principal waterway flowing from north to south through Vertova and Markelan. Each has a long-forgotten meaning, but today each is simply a particular place name and nothing more. To use another example from English, when using the word "Chicago" today, no one stops to remember that in a long-vanished American Indian tongue the name meant "wild onions." To us it is a city, and that's that.

Finally, some people have asked why a few characters

"talk funny" in the books, if everyone is speaking the same language. That is not my fault, but the fault of geography. Presolatan, just like most languages, is prone to the development of dialects, and there are a great many of these. The differences may be extreme. It is very difficult, for example, for a native of Akrador, that desert region in the southwest quarter of Cronbrach, to understand a speaker from mountainous northern Finarr and vice versa. It is in fact at least as difficult for them as for a speaker with a broad Scots dialect to communicate with someone who speaks the street talk of Los Angeles. If the trend continues, in another few hundred years Finarrian Presolatan will be effectively a whole different language from that spoken in Cronbrach.

And even within Cronbrach there are strong regional differences. Tremien comes from the northeastern part of the continent, where winters are cold, consonants crisp, and vowels nasal. The southlands tend to a broadening of vowels and a slurring of certain consonants; sailors have their own talk (generally perceived by landlubbers as rapid, flat, and startlingly profane), and so on. Although the dialects of Cronbrach are for the most part mutually understandable, they are noticeably different from one another, to the extent that speakers of each major dialect are firmly convinced that speakers of other dialects talk funny; and so I have tried to indicate the differences in the books, though I have also tried to resist the temptation of eye-baffling phonetic spelling and overly bizarre locutions.

For those who find such matters tedious, I apologize; for those who have expressed an interest, I hope this discourse has been sufficient.

—Brad Strickland

August 1989

ABOUT THE AUTHOR

Brad Strickland has been writing science fiction, fantasy, and horror since 1982. In addition to *Wizard's Mole*, he has written the adventure fantasies *Moon Dreams* and *Nul's Quest*, published by Signet, and the horror novels *ShadowShow* and *Children of the Knife*. In everyday life, Brad is an assistant professor at Gainesville College. He lives with his wife, Barbara, and his children, Amy and Jonathan, in Oakwood, Georgia.

FUN AND FANTASY

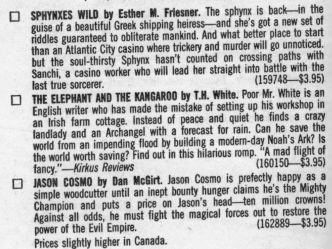

☐ **SPHYNXES WILD by Esther M. Friesner.** The sphynx is back—in the guise of a beautiful Greek shipping heiress—and she's got a new set of riddles guaranteed to obliterate mankind. And what better place to start than an Atlantic City casino where trickery and murder will go unnoticed, but the soul-thirsty Sphynx hasn't counted on crossing paths with Sanchi, a casino worker who will lead her straight into battle with the last true sorcerer. (159748—$3.95)

☐ **THE ELEPHANT AND THE KANGAROO by T.H. White.** Poor Mr. White is an English writer who has made the mistake of setting up his workshop in an Irish farm cottage. Instead of peace and quiet he finds a crazy landlady and an Archangel with a forecast for rain. Can he save the world from an impending flood by building a modern-day Noah's Ark? Is the world worth saving? Find out in this hilarious romp. "A mad flight of fancy."—*Kirkus Reviews* (160150—$3.95)

☐ **JASON COSMO by Dan McGirt.** Jason Cosmo is prefectly happy as a simple woodcutter until an inept bounty hunger claims he's the Mighty Champion and puts a price on Jason's head—ten million crowns! Against all odds, he must fight the magical forces out to restore the power of the Evil Empire. (162889—$3.95)

Prices slightly higher in Canada.

Buy them at your local

bookstore or use coupon

on next page for ordering.

WORLDS OF WONDER

☐ **BARROW A Fantasy Novel by John Deakins.** In a town hidden on the planes of Elsewhen, where mortals are either reborn or driven mad, no one wants to be a pawn of the Gods. (450043—$3.95)

☐ **CAT HOUSE by Michael Peak.** The felines were protected by their humans, but ancient enemies still stalked their trails to destroy them in a warring animal underworld, where fierce battles crossed the species border. (163036—$3.95)

☐ **THE GOD BOX by Barry B. Longyear.** From the moment Korvas accepted the gift of the god box and the obligation to fulfill its previous owner's final mission, he'd been plunged into more peril than a poor dishonest rug merchant deserved. Now it looks like Korvas will either lead the world to its destruction—or its salvation.... (159241—$3.50)

☐ **MERMAID'S SONG A Fantasy Novel by Alida Van Gores.** In the world under the sea, the Balance hangs in jeopardy. Only Elan, a beautiful, young mermaid can save it. But first she must overcome the evil Ghrismod's and be chosen as the new Between, tender of the great seadragons. If not, the Balance will be destroyed—and darkness will triumph for all eternity. (161131—$4.50)

☐ **ANCIENT LIGHT—A Fantasy Novel by Mary Gentle.** Lynne de Lisle Christie is back on Orthe, caught in a battle to obtain high-technology artifacts from a bygone civilization, while struggling to protect the people of Orthe from its destructive powers. But who will protect *her* from the perils of discovering alien secrets no human was ever meant to have? (450132—$5.95)

Prices slightly higher in Canada.
